What the critics are saying...

4 ½ stars "A fast-moving action-packed romance. The sex scenes are hot…The sense of place is so real…it gives you a you-are-there feeling…" ~ *Romantic Times*

5 Cups "On Danger's Edge is an action packed romance that grabs the reader and holds on till the last page. This is absolutely a keeper…" ~ *Coffee Time Romance*

"On Danger's Edge is loaded with romance, danger and intriguing secondary characters…Throw in action…and a run through the jungle and On Danger's Edge is an entertaining read for any romance fan…I'll be waiting for the next addition to what looks to be a must-read series." ~ *Joyfully Reviewed*

"I found myself unable to stop reading this book!" ~ *Romance Junkies*

4 ½ stars "Rorie and Tom are such realistic individuals with depth of character, and their current and past situations ring true-to-life. My heartstrings were tugged for both of them." ~ *ECata Romance*

ON *Danger's* EDGE

Lise FULLER

CERRIDWEN PRESS

A Cerridwen Press Publication

www.cerridwenpress.com

On Danger's Edge

ISBN 9781419955587
ALL RIGHTS RESERVED.
On Danger's Edge Copyright© 2005 Lise Fuller
Edited by Sue-Ellen Gower
Cover art by Willo

Electronic book Publication December 2005
Trade paperback Publication March 2007

Excerpt from *Intimate Deceptions* Copyright ©Lise Fuller 2006

Cerridwen Press is an imprint of Ellora's Cave Publishing, Inc.®

Also by Lise Fuller

ଊଠ

Cutting Loose
Intimate Deceptions *(Sequal to On Danger's Edge)*

About the Author

ଊଠ

This award winning author, after writing and producing a neighborhood play at the tender age of six (earning all of twenty cents), took a sabbatical of many years before she found the love of creative writing again. Now, having earned her MBA and CPA, raised four children (three as a single parent), Lise brings her adventurous spirit and extensive experience to her captivating stories. Lise has traveled to several countries, studying the culture and enjoying the native way of life, and has explored our world from the watery depths of the Caribbean to the heights of the Rocky Mountains. Having married her hero, an ex-82nd Airborne paratrooper, she devotes her time to writing, raising the couple's teenager, and her own personal accomplishment—body sculpting. Some comments of her work include:

It's the BEST I've read...in a very long time!

The emotion! Fast paced and sexy.

You just know it's going "to be Hot."

Great hooks! Drew me in right away.

You have a great voice. Love your characters!

Lise welcomes comments from readers. You can find her website and email address on her author bio page at www.cerridwenpress.com.

Acknowledgements

ઍ

God bless my critique group, the Dreamweavers
and my family for their love and support.
But most of all, I thank my real hero,
my husband and his 82nd Army Airborne outlook on life.
Thanks for believing in me. As you said, I'm a success
waiting to happen.
Well, I'm here, babe. Love you.

ON DANGER'S EDGE

Dedication

❧

In memory of Sergeant Len Dragnet.
And to the families of our military who serve in harm's
way. We will always remember the sacrifice.

A portion of the proceeds from the sale of this novel will go
*to **The Home Front Cares**,*

a nonprofit organization supporting families of troops
deployed in harm's way.

Trademarks Acknowledgement

❧

The author acknowledges the trademarked status and trademark owners of the following wordmarks mentioned in this work of fiction:

Armani: GA Modefine S.A.

Band-Aid: Johnson & Johnson

Beretta: Fabrica D'Armi P. Beretta, S.P.A

C-17: McDonnell Douglas Corporation

Chinook: Department of the Army State Agency

Harley: Harley-Davidson Motor Co. Inc.

Kotex: Kimberly-Clark Corporation

M-4: New Colt Holding Corp.

National Geographic: National Geographic Society

Chapter One

∞

Classy.

That's what Tom MacCallum thought of the woman staring back at him. From his small nook in the dim, smoky bar, the woman's eyes seemed luminous, huge. And in them, he could read her desire, the same wanting that stirred him when he first set eyes on the long brown-haired beauty.

She'd strolled in with her girlfriends wearing a skintight black dress. "Manizers" the younger guys in his Special Forces team had called the group of girls. Women on the prowl for a good time with no attachments. Exactly what he needed on a night like this. Tom wondered if the lady in black would be game.

The woman looked away and fiddled with the straw in her frozen drink.

Well, maybe not. Not tonight anyway. Still, he'd like to sink the weight of his trouble into her depths, and wondered if she needed something like that, too. Perhaps he could approach her some other time—if he came with these goons again. His buddies seemed to think her friends frequented the place.

He fingered his empty shot glass, thinking he could use one more. *To dull the pain.*

Swallowing, he reminisced over the day's events. Brodie Crawford, his weapons sergeant, had gone with him to the rocky crag in the Smoky Mountains of North Carolina. There Tom released a fellow soldier's ashes to the wind, letting each charred piece of his best friend go as if he'd been a poor man holding grains of gold. A guy he'd gone through Basic with, Charlie Hartman had covered Tom's back through the wars until his buddy got his own team. Tom stared at the glass. It'd been six months now, six months to the day that Charlie left this world—dead from a gunshot wound from some third-world bastard he'd been tracking, trying to help the faithful terrorist see the face of Allah.

Charlie hadn't failed. His friend shot the man clean through the heart—but not before the son of a bitch got a round off. In return, Charlie's death had been slow. Tom brooded over how much pain Charlie must have felt.

"Hey, Chief." Brodie strolled to the table with one of the brunette's girlfriends in tow. "You gonna be all right?"

After gazing over the grasp the sergeant had on the girl's backside, Tom lifted a brow and looked at Brodie. "I'm fine. You heading out?"

Brodie nodded. "If you don't mind. The others are waiting outside."

Tom looked around and realized the brunette and his troubles had made him stupid. He hadn't realized the guys had gone. "I don't mind." He reached for his wallet to leave a few bills for the waitress and overheard the blonde giggle. She whispered something to Brodie about wanting Tom to meet her friend. Tom glanced at the woman who'd held his attention all evening. They'd both just sat there, watching each other, neither of them getting up to dance or mingle.

Brodie jerked his chin toward Tom's mystery woman. "You want to meet Sally's girlfriend?"

Tom studied the attractive woman across the way. Her breasts pushed against the low-cut fabric of her slinky dress, exposing her generous cleavage. A redheaded woman talked to her while Rick Hansen, the team's intelligence man, lifted the redhead's hair and planted a kiss on her neck. Tom could see the woman "oooh" from where he sat, effectively ending the redhead's conversation with his brunette.

His brunette? Get real, MacCallum.

Tom had decided long ago a job in a Special Forces team left no room for a woman, at least, not a steady one, one a guy could think of having a family with. He'd seen too many of his buddies' relationships fail from infidelity or neglect.

Tom didn't like to fail. Charlie had felt the same, which was why his Army friend, a guy Tom had called brother, died alone with only Tom and a few of Charlie's team members in attendance at the funeral. They had left instructions for each other for what to do in case of death.

Unfortunately, Charlie had met the fate first, leaving Tom to sulk in this damn tavern on the outskirts of Fort Bragg.

A frown crossed the brunette's face. She mouthed the word "no" to her friend then rose and grabbed her purse. Tom figured she was leaving.

Time to go, he thought. Nothing for him here. "Have fun." He dismissed Brodie and dropped the bills on the table. Brodie hightailed it outside and Tom watched the brunette saunter into the ladies' room.

Letting the thought of any pursuit of her go, he went to get some fresh air, the smoke sticking to him like a whore's perfume. Three of his teammates were still outside. He wished them a goodnight before they took off.

Tom inhaled a deep breath as the last of his buddies left the half-filled lot. Reaching in his pocket for the keys to his Harley, he looked for the stars, seeing only the glare of the streetlights. "Sleep tight, bro," he muttered, utter loneliness gripping him. "Maybe I'll see you soon."

Flipping the keys in his hand, he walked along the sidewalk to the far end of the postage stamp-sized parking area. The lamplight poured over the chrome on his bike, making it sparkle in the dark. The door to the bar opened. Noise from inside spilled into the quieter night. Instinct made him look to see who exited. His mystery woman walked out, her head down and a hand in her purse. She strolled toward him through the dimmest part of the lot.

Smirking, he watched her. Tom liked the way the woman walked. He imagined the lady didn't realize the effect her swaying hips had on a guy. Tom leaned against the bike's seat to enjoy the view.

From the corner of his eye, he caught a dark image flash across the lot and hover between two parked cars near her. His nerves on end, Tom jumped to the sidewalk. Shoving his keys back, he fingered the knife in his rear pocket, hoping he wouldn't need to use the blade.

The brunette stopped and stared at him, licking her lips. Desire flared in her dark eyes—until the unknown assailant left the shadows. She froze, staring between Tom and her would-be attacker.

The man turned to look behind him. For the first time, the jerk saw Tom.

No one moved for the space of a breath. Then the guy in black took off like a rocket. Tom decided the creep didn't want to mess with someone bigger than him. *Good choice.*

Tom relaxed his stance and glanced at the woman. Her hand shook as she pulled out a set of keys. In a few steps, he stood next to her. "Always have those in hand when you leave a place, especially a dive like this."

The lady looked at him, the fear in her cinnamon-colored eyes mixing with some other emotion. She swallowed—hard. "Good advice," she rasped.

If Tom's lust hadn't peaked before, it did now. Her soft, ragged voice sounded like sex. He cleared his throat. "You should never be alone in a place like this either."

She bowed her head. Tom listened to her soft grunt. "Yeah. I didn't think a few minutes would matter." She looked up and her eyes riveted into his. "I…" She licked her lips again.

Damn. He wanted her. "Don't park in the dark anymore. You need to stay in the light." He thought he stuttered, and felt like a kid asking his best girl for his first piece of heaven. He turned to leave.

"Wait."

He didn't need any prompting. He faced her, recognizing the indecision crossing her face. This woman didn't buy completely into her friends' loose sex mores, he was sure of that, otherwise her activities during the night would have been more aggressive. But what did she want?

"Could I offer you some coffee?" She straightened, seeming more confident, less afraid. "I owe you. It's the least I could do."

His turn to swallow. The woman didn't seem like the type for nights on end of one-time sex, but what did he know? Maybe she was new to sexual exploration and wanted to try it? In that case, he'd be her first. Hell, sex with her would probably be safe enough. "You sure you want to?" He thought his voice sounded hoarse.

She nodded.

He stepped closer, enough so his body burned as he touched hers. "You act like your friends?" he whispered.

Her eyes glittered. "What do you mean?"

He put his hands on her shoulders and pulled her closer, letting his palms play down her back to her lower exterior. She leaned into him. "You only after a guy for sex?"

Her breathing deepened as her mouth parted. "I... They want me to try it."

Backing up, he dropped his hands and reached in his front pocket for his keys. "Maybe you ought to figure out what you want first."

Tom turned to leave and heard her steps on the sidewalk coming after him.

"Wait." She ran into his back when he stopped. He felt her hard breathing through his T-shirt.

Tom faced her.

"It's just coffee."

She'd shrugged at the comment, but Tom thought the need for a naked man called in her look. He pulled her into his arms and this time let his mouth hover over hers. "Only if it's at my

13

place." When he kissed her, she responded, and he poured all the anguish and need he'd felt throughout the day into his embrace.

Omigod. Rorie Lindsay's nerve endings fired on all thrusters. Stares from the tanned man holding her had put her on edge all night, and now she stood in his arms. She'd never experienced a kiss like this, one that scorched every fiber in her. Her body burned and when he started to back away, she pulled him closer. Rorie ran her hands through his thick, black hair, allowing him to penetrate her mouth with his tongue.

When common sense finally crept into her head, she released him—slowly—a primal need for him urging her on. What was she thinking? That she'd make love to him here in the middle of the parking lot? The one margarita she'd had told her yes.

But Rorie's strict upbringing and the uncertainty she thought lurked in his deep, green eyes gave her a definite no. Still, his hard, fit body spurred her needy libido. The man wanted her. A man who looked like him wanted her. Wow. A first—at least in a long time. She'd gained a lot of weight during her abusive six-year marriage to Stephen "Dickhead" Brockhurst. It'd been two years since they'd separated. Rorie's efforts to tighten and tone her plump body had taken over a year. Yet, the therapy to regain her self-esteem had taken much longer.

She let her hands roam over his broad shoulders and down his beefy arms. Strands of hair at her temple brushed his chin as Rorie studied him. Sally Shepard had been right about the men who came here. They were hot. But the only one who had caught her eye now held her in his arms, looking at her like he could devour her.

Rorie had to admit, she liked the way he studied her. It did funny things in the pit of her gut. Thing was, she didn't do casual relationships. To be more honest, she didn't do relationships at all. It had been over a year since her last sexual encounter—a brief affair with another photographer, a relationship Rorie could only describe as dispassionate. They didn't even have real sex, just touched one another, although she'd about died for the act of coupling, as needy as her body had been at the time.

"Coffee?"

The deep tones in his rich voice stroked her, sending delicious chills tingling through her. Sally had said to loosen up, take a risk and meet some guy. Not all men were like Stephen. "Who knows?" Rorie remembered her best friend from college saying. "Maybe you'll meet the man of your dreams."

She held her breath and looked at this man, her breasts pushed against his hard chest, the heady touch of his arms around her. Rorie had never dreamt of any man as good as him.

"Sure," she finally said, butterflies dancing in her stomach at the crazy thought of being with him.

"What's your name?" he asked and nipped her bottom lip.

She stifled a moan. "Aurora." She used her given name. It sounded more feminine than Rorie, the name all her friends used.

"Aurora." The stranger looked at her. A dimple in his right cheek appeared with the quirk of his lips. "As in, a heavenly body."

"Something like that." Her voice sounded flat. She'd never liked the name her mother had picked for her, and figured the drugs they'd used on Vivian Lakehurst Lindsay at Rorie's birth were to blame for the anomaly. Her nickname described her far better, especially her thirst for adventure. The name was all she'd ever used—until now. Tonight "Rorie" didn't seem to fit into the sensual tension between them.

He chuckled. Rorie liked the timbre of his voice. It softened him, made him seem less harsh than the somber man she'd been attracted to all night. She smiled as two dimples deepened in his cheeks.

"Follow me." He stepped back, and eyed her up and down. "I'll ride slow, but if you change your mind, I'll understand."

Rorie didn't tell him she'd already changed her mind a billion times—and still came back to the fact she needed to know what a taste of this tempting, brooding man would be like.

* * * * *

Tom pulled his Harley into the two-car garage. Dismounting, he smacked the hood of his Chevy pickup as he walked toward the driveway. He'd bought the house in the bedroom community near Fayetteville a year ago. The home was an investment, he'd told himself, yet the house reminded him of family. At least it was a place where he could be alone when he wanted.

He watched the brunette pull into the driveway and questioned what the hell he was doing. He usually talked to a girl for a while before they'd mutually agree to share a bed. Even then, he'd never bring them to his place. He'd hardly said two words to this woman, yet here she had parked behind him. She seemed an innocent, but her behavior could be an act. What woman in her right mind would go by the name Aurora? The tag sounded like some stripper in the more seedy areas off-post.

The lady stepped out of her car, an old Fix-Or-Repair-Daily, and Tom wondered what she did for a living. Her actions and the way she spoke exuded a pampered upbringing. That probably said something about her background. Had she come from money and somehow lost it? Or was the car a ruse to throw off a prospective lover, making it harder to track her down if she didn't want to be found? Tom derided himself. He hadn't asked for her last name, although for one night of consensual sex, would it matter?

She hesitated next to her sedan, staring at him, her fidgeting telling him she shared the same concerns. It was crazy, the two of them, just like that. But here they were. Keeping his thoughts to himself, Tom walked to her and put his hand at the small of her back, leading her to the front door. For some reason, taking her through the cluttered garage seemed demeaning to what he intended for them tonight. Tom shook off the odd sensation, knowing he wanted more than a quick lay. He wanted to make love.

Her hair gleamed in the moonlight. The urge to run his hands through her strands gripped him. Still, she looked like a frightened cat and he didn't want to scare her off. The warmth of her body would be comforting. Tom let himself feel at least that much. And this way he wouldn't be alone with his memories. "You ever go home with a strange guy before?" He stopped at the door, wondering—maybe even hoping—she hadn't, yet knowing her inexperience would blow his evening. He didn't want to take advantage of her.

She blessed him with a weak smile. "I didn't think you were strange. After all, you saved me tonight from someone much weirder."

"Oh, so coming home with me is in gratitude?"

She winced. "Well, not really." She licked her lips once more. The movement sent his testosterone through the roof. "You were looking at me a lot tonight."

He bit off a laugh. "Yeah. And you looked back."

"Yeah." She smiled, an honest one this time. "To answer your question, no, I've never gone to bed with a strange man. I'm still not sure I'm going to. For now it's just coffee, right?"

He grimaced. "Right. You can leave any time. But I warn you, I want more than a shot of caffeine." He stepped toward her and took her in his arms. Aurora's body was warm, soft in all the right places. Her cleavage peaked enough to give a guy ideas. He'd had plenty of them all night. "I knew I wanted you when you first came into the bar." He leaned over and nipped her bare neck.

She moaned. "Why? Why me?"

He straightened, their lips a breath apart. "I don't know. I just knew you were the one. The lady I needed tonight." Tom ran his thumb down her lightly tanned neck and along her

17

collarbone until he hit the edge of her dress. He fingered the bra strap he found underneath. "It's been a long day."

"Tell me about it." The woman sucked in a breath and stared at him, the cinnamon color in her eyes lightening to a unique shade of amber.

"What are you thinking?" he said, hoping she wouldn't change her mind.

The soft tips of her fingers stroked his face. "I wondered if I should ask who you are. What to call you." She leaned against him and lifted her chin. "I know this isn't real, us being together like old lovers. You and I don't even know each other. You might think this sounds stupid, but right now, I want to feel special, like a heroine in a fairy tale. And I need a prince to make love to me and chase the demons away."

Somehow, he knew what she meant. He bent his head and kissed her, his lips lingering on hers until he spoke. "Then call me Prince." Tom opened the door and flicked the switch for the small table light near the foyer. Whisking her into his arms, he carried her over the threshold. For some reason, being her protector, her prince, was what he wanted, too.

Rorie knew she'd gone absolutely insane the moment those words left her mouth. After he lowered her on his sofa, he removed her heels and joined her there, his body pure heat. She wanted to go slow. He must have sensed that, although she could feel the tension within him.

He cradled her in his embrace as they lay there, placing soft kisses against her temple and neck. When the stranger moved to her earlobe, he nipped it gently between his teeth. "You're beautiful," he murmured, "what demons could ever possess you?"

Rorie wanted to tell him plenty. Instead, she listened to his ragged breathing.

The man pulled back, studying her as he eased his hands through her long hair. "Talk to me," he said. "Tell me what you're running from."

The crux of her problem suddenly became crystal clear. "From myself mostly." And that was the truth, but she didn't want to ruin the moment with details. Tonight she lived a fantasy. She would take these moments with this one dream man into her future—as soon as she figured out what her future would be. Rorie readied herself, wanting to be forthcoming about at least some aspect of herself. "I should warn you. Unlike my friends, I...I haven't been with that many men." She watched for an expression of regret on the stranger's face.

His eyes narrowed and a smiled tugged at his lips, urging her to finish her thought.

"But a guy like you, one that looks like you, for once I wanted to know what it's like. How it feels to be desired."

Tom always knew he attracted women. If it wasn't his looks, it was the job. The macho stuff worked like a magnet. But that was after they found out. This woman didn't know him a lick. "So you want me for my body?" For some reason, the thought disappointed him.

She sighed. "Not exactly. You were willing to risk yourself to protect me." Her gaze took a turn to the serious. "The last lover I had, I needed to be protected against."

Something within Tom snapped. What kind of bastard would hurt a woman, especially one as soft as this? "Who was he?" His voice came out harsher than he'd intended.

She cleared her throat, the water in her eyes glittering like crystals. "It's over. I'd rather not talk about it. In fact, I don't know why I brought it up."

Aurora pushed against him, wanting to get up.

He didn't let her. "I won't hurt you," he said. "And I'd kill any bastard who would." Tom had probably added the last bit for himself. Thing was, he meant it.

She stopped and looked at him. "That won't be necessary."

Tom took a deep breath and sat on the edge of the couch. "Sorry. I didn't mean to upset you."

Aurora rested her upper body on an elbow and rubbed his back. "It's okay. My fault. I should never have brought the subject up. It's just, my divorce dragged on a few years. The trial finally ended today." She shrugged. "On my birthday. I gave him everything I had just to get rid of him." She leaned against the armrest and hugged her knees to her chest, revealing the long shapely legs underneath and the lace panties that met the tops of her thigh-high hose.

Why had Tom thought it a good idea to talk and get to know her? Then he looked at the vee between her legs and knew why. His day hadn't been so great, either. He wanted more than a night of sex. "So, birthday girl, how old are you?"

"Twenty-nine." She smiled. "Really twenty-nine. And you?"

He chuckled. "Thirty-two. But sometimes I feel like sixty."

She laughed. "I don't believe you," she said. "You don't look a day over fifty-nine."

For the first time in a long while, Tom enjoyed a woman's humor. "Believe it, sweetheart." He moved her hands and leaned the side of his waist against her legs, running his fingers along her hose and stopping halfway up her thigh. Inside, he gripped himself, holding himself from going further. What she'd told him hooked something inside. He grew uncertain if Aurora was emotionally ready for what he needed, or for what he really wanted from her. "You still want coffee?" Tom asked.

"No." She paused. The irises around her pupils turned golden and pierced him. She placed one of his hands on her shoulder and drew him into her. "I want you to show me how a man's supposed to make love to a woman."

His hands froze on her skin.

Rorie prayed he wouldn't take them away.

"Are you sure that's what you want?" the stranger asked.

She took a deep breath. It had taken all of her resolve to state that last desire, but something about him, about lying in his arms tonight, seemed right. "Positive." She bit her lip, hoping he wouldn't refuse.

"Okay." He nodded and eased her legs down, leaning over at the same time to kiss her. "On one condition," he whispered against her lips.

"Name it." She swallowed.

His dimples showed again. "You make love to me back."

She smiled and reached for him, brushing her thumbs over the indents in his cheeks. "I'll try my best."

"That's all I ask." Then the stranger picked her up. Cradling her to his chest, he walked with her into the bedroom.

Chapter Two

෨

The iridescent glow of the moon shone through the large window, deepening the shadows of the room. Rorie held her breath as she eyed the massive oak bed highlighted by the white lunar beams. Her protector lowered her into the rumpled folds of the bedding and a tinge of panic hit her. Just how did one go about making love to a man? Her marriage certainly hadn't prepared her for that. Sex with Stephen Brockhurst had been like following an old tried-and-true casserole recipe. *After thoroughly scrubbing your vegetables, take off your clothes...*

Her fantasy man settled himself next to her and ran his hands through her hair. He'd already excited her more than Stephen ever could and she hadn't even undressed.

He slid his palms to the side of her face. After capturing her lips with his, he trailed kisses down her neck. Rorie moaned from the exhilarating tension pooling inside her, and wondered what she should do next. She tried to remember some real turn-ons for men she'd read in *Cosmo*. Nothing came to mind. She grew a little nervous. "Prince?"

"Yeah." His head came up and he stared at her as if she'd interrupted him.

Rorie rubbed her palms against his back, fingering the nuances the sinew made in the hard planes of his body. "I might not be very good at this."

He gave her a lopsided grin. "You already warned me."

"I did?"

A low chuckle escaped the stranger's lips. He lingered a kiss against her neck before he lifted his head to look at her again. "You told me you hadn't been with that many men." His dimples faded and his gaze deepened. "Should I ask how many?"

She licked her lips, a bad habit her mother had always tried to break her of, but one Rorie used when she grew antsy and didn't know what to say. She would never see him again. Should she give him an answer?

She drew a finger around the corner of his lips. "One."

Her fantasy man grunted and dropped his forehead against her breast before he looked at her again, his eyes studying the contours of her face. "How long were you married?"

"Six years."

"Children?"

"No. Thank God."

"You don't want a family?"

His husky voice, the compelling look on his face seemed to hang over her, waiting, as if he needed to hear her reply.

"Someday. Just not with him."

"Six years." He stroked her temple with his thumb. An inquisitive brow peaked on his strong face. "And all that time you never made love?"

"We had the obligatory sex," Rorie said matter-of-factly. "I don't think you could confuse the process with making love."

He slid his hands around her and into an embrace. His tender fingers brushed lower against her back to her hips, tingling sensations sparking from his touch. "You ever come?"

The needy ache in her body sharpened with the question. She bit her lip again and this time only shook her head no, feeling more exposed, more vulnerable than if she'd been completely naked.

The stranger stared at her a moment, studying her again, his eyes assessing, penetrating. Rorie wondered what he thought.

"You will tonight," he promised. "If you don't, it won't be because I didn't try."

The thought of him pleasing her made her breath catch, her pulse race faster. The idea he cared if she enjoyed the act, got something out of this, too, became heady. A warm feeling grew inside her that had nothing to do with her libido. "What...what do you want me to do? What do you like?" She didn't usually ask such direct questions, at least not in this arena, but the fact Rorie wouldn't see him again emboldened her.

"I tell you what—" He nipped lightly on her lips and plunged his tongue to meet hers. A sound escaped her as his fingers reached lower, caressing her derrière, traveling upward along her side and stomach. In the wake of his touch, heated passion vibrated on her skin, causing tremors to ripple below the surface.

She listened to her own panting as his hands reached her shoulders and eased her on her back. Settling his weight between her legs, he raised himself on the elbows he'd placed on either side of her. His fingertips stroked the side of her neck and tracked along her chin. "Forget about everything in your life except tonight. Pretend I'm the lover, the mate you've always wanted. Then let your instincts take over."

Oh, God, yes. Great idea. "Okay," she said, her voice breathy, quiet.

His green eyes darkened, grew more turbulent with her response. Her prince dipped his head, his sensual mouth inches from hers, waiting. His eyes peered into hers as if he'd just revealed the depth of his soul.

His labored breaths deepened, causing his chest to push rhythmically against hers, making the tips of her breasts reach to meet him. Her lover must have felt her nipples peak, because he smiled, lust and longing in his gaze. Groaning, his mouth touched her lips, tasting her. His hunger stirred, reached into her to stroke some part of her she had long forgotten.

Moving his hands lower, he played with the edge of her bodice where her breasts swelled. Releasing her mouth, he placed beguiling, tortuous pecks along her chin to her neck, the sensations causing her skin to fire, her body to burn. When he reached the exposed part of her cleavage, he took a small nip of skin between his teeth and licked it with his tongue, repeating the act as he inched farther down. His gentle fingers slid from the edge of the fabric over one of her breasts. She arched her body, hoping he would stroke the nipple jutting into the cloth.

She wasn't disappointed. Her lover ran a finger around the top. The movement about drove her insane. Delving his chin into her loose bodice, his lips moved closer to the erect tip, the binding cloth preventing him full access. He tugged the budding of her breast with his fingers and brushed another kiss against her skin. The release of his heated breath caused her to quiver.

Her protector removed his hand from her mound, replacing it with his mouth. His teeth nipped at her bud through the fabric. She gripped his muscled shoulders and ran her hands along his powerful biceps. Reaching for the edge of the dress and her bra strap, her protector eased them downward along her arm. Soon, he released the other side and his fingers tugged the bodice of her dress, this time able to free the breast he'd teased. He placed soft kisses against her sensitized skin until his mouth reached her peak. Running the edge of his teeth against her bud, he drew her nipple into his mouth and suckled.

"Oh, God," she moaned and reminded herself to trust her instincts. She ran her hands through his short hair. His arms encircled her as he rolled with her slightly, raising her side in the process. She felt him tug on the zipper behind her. When he'd opened the fastener completely, he splayed his hands along her back, his calloused palms resting against her skin.

Leaving her breast, his mouth moved up her neck again. Her hands dropped lower against his body. When her fingers settled over the muscles in his rump, he contracted them, pushing his hardened need against her. Lifting her hips, she rubbed that part of him, her desire flaring from knowing this man wanted her.

She pulled the back of his T-shirt, wanting to see what the stranger looked like before they joined. Sliding her hands underneath, she inched the thin material upward, reveling in the warm smoothness of his skin, the hard muscle below. When she lifted the T-shirt higher, he pulled away to study her, his eyes dark pools of desire. The rhythm of his ragged pants matched hers. A corner of his mouth twitched as he raised himself on his knees and quickly removed the shirt.

"Oh my." The moonlight accented his ripped muscle and the smattering of dark hair across his chest. Never had she seen a man so beautiful.

The stranger released a low chuckle. Rorie smiled at his enjoyment. Licking her lips, she reached for his belt, fumbling with the clasp. His warm, large hands covered hers. Grasping her palms, he lifted them to place a gentle kiss on each one then returned to encase his jean-clad member. She held him as best she could through the cloth, the throbbing of his staff causing Rorie's pulse to beat harder.

The man groaned and clasped her forearms, the signs of pleasure apparent in the creases of his face. He slid her hands to his solid abdomen. She fingered the hills and valleys of muscle she found there as he undid the buckle and the metal button behind it. Bending forward, he lifted her shoulders from the bed and eased her dress down the remaining length of her arms.

Rorie tried to rise to remove her black garment, but the stranger stopped her. "No," he said. "Let me do this." He bent down and kissed her again. When she circled her arms around his neck, he held her bare waist and pulled her to her knees. The dress slipped easily away from her body and pooled on the bed. "God," he murmured as he stared at her, his gaze roaming over her skin, looking like he could devour her.

His roughened fingers caressed her waist. Rorie closed her eyes, thinking she would melt from the heady sensation. "You don't know how good you make me feel," she found herself saying, her fingers spread against his chest.

His throaty chuckle came again and he pulled her into him. "No better than how you make me, I imagine."

Did she really make him feel that wonderful? She pressed her hips into him. Even through the jeans, his hardened member lay stiff against her abdomen. His touch told her of his desire, the first from a man in a long time. The night seemed too good to be true. But it was only this one night, Rorie reminded herself. A night she'd always remember.

Her protector groaned against her neck. Running his hands along her cheeks and into her hair, he grasped her head, pulling her mouth to meet his. Then he lowered one hand to her back, easing his palm downward and slipping his fingers underneath her black lace panties.

She sighed against him and followed his lead, kissing his strong jaw, allowing her mouth to slip along his collarbone, coming to the crook between his ear and shoulder. She gentled his skin between her teeth, tasting his salty flesh, inhaling the natural, musky scent of him.

His other hand made its way to her upper back and he held her flush against his chest. She loved the taste, the smell of him and tried the same trail of kisses higher on his neck until she reached his earlobe, having read somewhere that stroking the spot stimulated men. She ran the edges of her teeth over the soft skin and laved the lobe with her tongue.

"God, woman," he whispered in her ear and pulled away, staring at her face a minute with his penetrating gaze. She dropped her hands as he stroked the front of her shoulders and slid his palms over her breasts, squeezing them. "I don't know who your husband was, except that he was an idiot." He fingered the clasp at the front of her bra and paused, looking at her as if asking permission. She ran her hands over his and slid her fingers across his forearms, urging him on.

The catch opened. His fingers caressed the skin below. Slipping his hands to her breasts, he massaged her tips. She rubbed her palms along his iron thighs as, slowly, he moved his hands to her arms where the remaining straps lay. He slid the cloth off her, the lace bra lying with her dress around her knees. Bending, he teased each nipple with his tongue.

She grasped his head, her fingers slipping through his strands with the heightening sensation, her body nearing the edge of her control. "I...I need you." Her voice grew hoarse.

"I know," he answered, capturing her lips with his. "But I'm on a mission right now," he said between breaths, "and I always complete my missions."

She wasn't sure what he meant, except if completing his mission felt anything like what she'd experienced so far, the result would be breathtaking—if it didn't kill her first. Could one die from such intense ardor?

His hands shifted to her last remaining vestige of decency. Slipping his fingers under the waistband of her high-cut undergarment, he rubbed his hands downward along her hips to her thighs, pushing the panties, along with her hose, off her. He moved his hand below her buttocks. Putting his other arm around her shoulders, he lifted her and laid her back on the bed, sliding the clinging hose off the remainder of her legs. In short order, he picked up her lingerie and the rest of her clothes and tossed them to the floor. Standing at the edge of the bed, he watched her bask in the moonlight.

She bit her lip, wondering what he thought now that he'd seen all of her.

"You're beautiful," he said.

"You think so?" Her voice purred with a mixture of sultry desire and fear.

He nodded. "I know so."

"So are you." She came to him, rising on her haunches. With a slow hand, she unzipped his fly, wanting to touch him. His callused fingers gripped her shoulders and she looked at him, the depth of his wanting capturing something inside her.

"Be careful," he said. "I'm ready to take you now. But I'm not going to unless I know you've been pleasured."

This time she swallowed and bit her lip. "What if I can't...you know."

A corner of his lip curved upward. "Watching you, I doubt that's true. I bet you're ready for me now. Except I won't try until I'm sure about you." He slipped his palm against her abdomen. "Remember you asked me to make love to you, show you how a man should love his woman." He edged his hand lower to the vee between her legs, allowing a finger to caress her nub.

She grasped his forearm, the sensation causing her to arch, bringing him closer.

"Not yet," he whispered in her ear, his other hand massaging her back. "You're wet." His words teased.

He slipped a finger inside.

She about buckled. Her breath caught. He held her steady with one arm, the fingers of his other hand within her, touching spots she never knew held such promising seduction.

Her body trembled. Soon, her only awareness became the searing fire in her loins. "Oh," she cried. Her ragged breaths raced, her thighs squeezed from a will of their own. She wanted him—now, and lifted her hips against his palm in anguish. He penetrated deeper, the luscious touch burning from her nub to those newfound points of sensual heat. She heard herself whimper, an act she couldn't prevent, and released herself to the pent-up tension within. Suddenly, the floodgates opened, and his touch became her only obsession. She came in delicious, splendorous relief and crumpled into his chest.

Using the arm he'd held around her, he tugged Rorie against him. "Well," her prince whispered against her ear, "I guess now we know the problem wasn't you." The hand that had brought her such pleasure shifted to below her buttocks and held her.

It took a few moments before she could regain her breath—and her sensibilities. "Oh, my. You didn't even..."

He smiled. "No, I didn't. But I still want to."

She fingered his dimples and kissed him, taking his mouth with the depth of her soul. "Well, then, I guess we're not finished yet."

He laughed. A hearty one this time. She treasured the sound. She'd just been made love to, had her first climax from a man, and they didn't even do *it*. She gazed at him and wondered—could she pleasure him in return?

Tom studied her as he picked her up and laid her against the pillows. What kind of ass could convince an intelligent woman she was devoid of passion? A damn stupid one, that was sure.

He laid half on top of her to distribute his weight so his body wouldn't crush her. Kissing her temple, Tom let his fingers graze over her shoulders. The moonlight poured through the window onto her ample breasts, her full hips. The glow lightened her creamy skin. He thought she looked like a statue of a Greek goddess, except her supple skin warmed with his touch, her heart beat faster with each stroke of his fingers.

A man would be lucky to have a woman so desperate for passion. Tonight, he realized, he'd been the fortunate one. Tom wondered if some arrangement between them could work, something that would take the loneliness away when he yearned for more than his job. But the reminder he shouldn't have a steady woman nagged him. Odds were any relationship would fail, leaving one or both of them crushed. Tom didn't want the kind of pain that came from abandonment. And failure wasn't in his vocabulary.

Embroiled in his thoughts, he kissed her milky shoulder, his fingers skimming over the back of it, and touched an odd ridge of skin. Lifting his head, he turned her shoulder slightly and frowned at the more than two-inch scar he saw marring her smooth beauty. "What happened?" he asked.

When he looked at Aurora's face, her eyes held a hint of fear.

Tom suspected he knew. Anger rose in him at the thought. He held the emotion in check, afraid she would misinterpret his reaction. Instead, he bent over and pulled the puckered skin into his mouth, tonguing the raised flesh. After placing a few gentle pecks, he looked at her, hoping she'd say something.

Unshed tears glistened in Aurora's eyes. Tom cursed inwardly, wishing he knew who the bastard was, knowing it better that he didn't, that this would end after tonight. He rubbed a thumb under her eyes, wiping some of the salty wetness away. "You know, real lovers tell each other these things."

She bit her lip. "But this isn't real." A solitary teardrop fell.

Tom wiped it away and wanted to say this couldn't be any more real. "It is for tonight," he said instead, meaning it. "It was your ex, wasn't it?"

She nodded.

"Talk to me about it."

"Why do you want to know?" Her tenuous look faded to one of caution.

"I'm your prince tonight, remember? It's my job to defeat the demons."

She giggled. He liked the crystal sound of her voice. She rubbed her hands along his chest. "You're incredible. Are you like this with all your women?"

Tom had forgotten how many women he'd bedded. Not too many—he liked to be careful—but enough, he was sure. He couldn't remember ever caring about another woman like this. "No," he answered honestly. "Tonight, it's just you and me, and it's different." He hoped she didn't ask how different. He'd already posed the question to himself and didn't know how to answer.

Aurora licked her lips. "He broke the bone in my shoulder. The scar is the result of the operation."

Tom would strangle the bastard if he ever found him.

"I know it's ugly," she continued.

No, he'd break his neck.

"Does it bother you?"

Her question halted Tom's spiraling need to beat the guy bloodless. He steeled himself, forcing his emotions to remain calm. Right now, Aurora needed someone to love her. "Why would you think a scar bothered me?"

She shrugged. "Thought it might turn you off."

"Aurora, there's nothing I've seen about you that could possibly do that."

Her smile grew as bright as the full moon. Reminding himself of his mission, Tom bent to kiss her, and this time when she reached for his jeans, he let her peel them off.

His bared erection hovered near her sex as he held himself off the bed. She used her feet to push his pants down when her arms fell out of reach. Tom obliged her by kicking the pants off the rest of the way, along with his shoes. She rose up on an elbow to reach his nipple with her mouth and licked it.

He let his head drop and placed soft nips along her neck. She arched again and her most sensitive spot touched the tip of his penis. "Oh, God," he groaned. "Wait here."

Tom pulled off his socks and reached over her to a drawer in the nightstand by the bed. Pulling out a foil packet, he tore it with his teeth, getting on his knees again to put the condom on.

Rorie looked at the package. She knew what it was, but she had never used one before. "Can I do that?"

His brow arched as a grin tugged his lips. "You know how?"

She smirked. "You can always show me." She took the condom from him. "But first..." She wrapped her other hand around his swollen shaft and stroked it, wanting to feel the hardness of it. "Geez." Sitting up, she positioned herself closer, rubbing her cheek against the soft skin covering the side of his penis. Letting her hair fall across the top, she fondled him and kissed the tip gently, licking the soft spot underneath.

"Woman, you're going to kill me." His hands fell on her shoulders.

She giggled and looked closer at the latex fitting. How hard could it be? Thinking she'd figured it out, Rorie placed it on his tip and held it there. When she looked at him for instructions, bare hunger showed in his eyes. Strangely, his reaction comforted her. "Well?" She smiled at him.

He nodded, panting roughly through his teeth. "You've got it. Just roll it down and leave some room at the end."

Eager, she did so rapidly.

"Ouch," he complained. "Watch it, sweetheart, that's my flesh you're pinching."

"Sorry." She released him.

He adjusted the latex and rolled the thing slowly the rest of the way. "It's okay. I'm still operational."

Rorie laughed as he lowered himself and spread his knees between hers.

"I need you tonight, Aurora." His gaze darkened, searched hers for some understanding.

"Why?"

"I just do." A pain showed in his eyes but quickly vanished. "Stay with me tonight. Make love to me like you mean it."

She brushed her hand over his cheek. "I'll be here," she whispered.

As he pressed his hardness inside her, her climax rose even higher. When she kissed him this time and drew him close, Rorie couldn't have meant it more.

Chapter Three

೩౦

When Rorie woke, the stranger's arms still cuddled her. Her back to his chest, he held her nude body tight against him, fitting perfectly along his frame. He'd folded his leg over hers as if protecting her. They'd fallen asleep like that, and, for whatever reason, she'd never felt safer. Odd she would be so comfortable with a man she didn't know.

She looked out the window. Only the brightest stars shimmered through the deep blue of the sky. It was early morning, not quite dawn, and throughout their night of lovemaking, her prince had held her. When her eyes drooped, he'd told her to go to sleep. Rorie hadn't wanted to. She didn't want the night to end. Yet, it had. And with the morning, came regret that she couldn't lay in his arms longer.

With a soft sigh, Rorie lifted the hand of the arm she rested upon and kissed it, listening to his even breathing while he slept. She imagined this was how a marriage should be, warm, comfortable—passionate at times. A shared caring between a man and a woman. She eased around so she could look at him. When she nestled her head into his neck and slipped a leg in between his, he stirred briefly, tightening his hold around her, her breasts snug against his chest.

His face held a hint of stubble. She brushed her nails lightly over the hair on his chin, kissing his cheek, inhaling his unique scent, trying to memorize every detail of him. In some ways, she did feel like a princess. Her fairy godmother had granted her one night. It was all Rorie could ask from her protector. Her two years of counseling had taught her to stand up for herself, that independence started from within. She couldn't depend on someone else to take care of her. Even if there was a possibility this man would want a relationship, he wouldn't be prepared for the emotional baggage she carried.

Still, she didn't want to leave. Placing a lingering kiss on his lips, Rorie eased backward, not wanting to wake him.

The arm he'd draped over her pulled her closer. "Where are you going?" His husky, soft voice rekindled her need for him.

She licked her lips. Rorie hadn't realized he'd been awake. "I probably should leave. It's almost daybreak."

His eyes opened and, in the pale light, she could see the different shades of green, the small specks of brown around his pupils. The color of a thick forest.

He took a deep breath and exhaled, brushing his thumb across her cheek. "Do you have somewhere you need to go?"

She shook her head, thinking her plane flight to her next photo shoot wasn't until late noon. "Not this morning."

"Then don't leave me, Aurora. Not yet." A corner of his mouth lifted. His smile looked haunting. Sad.

"I won't if you don't want me to." She rubbed her hand across his chest.

He pulled her closer. "We can just lie here if you want."

His burgeoning manhood pulsed against her leg. Her passion, her need for him, surged once more. This was her fantasy man. She would never again find anyone who would want her, need her like this. The night had been special, for both of them. She kissed him and let her hand slip lower. "We may never see each other after this." Grasping his hardened member, Rorie regretted the inevitable. "I'd rather not waste what time we have."

His gaze held her. She watched his throat constrict as he swallowed. "I'd like to know you better."

She bit her lip, trying to force the water in her eyes to recede, hoping he didn't notice. A relationship with him was impossible until she figured out her own life. "Make love to me, Prince." She thought she spied a glimpse of regret in his eyes.

He kissed her and pulled her over him. "You ever been on top?"

"No," she squeaked.

His broad smile dazzled her. "Then let me show you what we're going to do."

When he did, Rorie wondered if the neighbors could hear her groans of satisfaction.

Tom stayed awake, watching Aurora sleep, wondering how to ask her to spend the Sunday with him. Considering even if he should. This woman intrigued him. Her softness, her vulnerability, had him hooked. He'd already asked himself too many questions about her—what her real name was, what her family was like. And he had some driving need to tell her more about himself. That he'd gone to college on an academic scholarship. Dropped out after his father died from a heart attack, to care for his mother and his younger brother and two sisters. That he loved family, and loved the adrenaline-pumping job he had, believing it important in the scheme of things. And that he had a good income, enough to take care of a family. He'd decided last night that someday he'd like to have one himself.

Normally, he didn't talk about his desires with a woman. There was no need. But he wanted to talk to her. Discover her, and let her discover him. Get to know one another. He'd never felt the need to do such things with a woman. One night with this unique lady had him thinking funny things.

Tom sighed, figuring he thought too much. When Aurora fell asleep again, he'd set his back to the window, shielding her face from the encroaching sunlight, hoping she would wake as late as possible. He didn't want her to go, but he had the feeling she would. She'd made him no promises when he said he wanted to know her better. In fact, she didn't even respond to the question.

Just wanted him to love her.

'Course, she'd been on the verge of tears. Tom hadn't wanted her to cry. And he didn't want to pressure her. He figured she'd gotten enough of that already.

He placed a tender kiss on the crown of her head, trying to imagine what her life had been up to this point. The woman deserved better than the abuse she'd gotten.

So what makes you think you can do better by her?

The thought slammed his gut. He lived alone for a reason. His job. The stress of what he did tested relationships to the max. Tom knew few men whose marriages lasted. But what it did to the wives and kids when they left from out of the blue sucked. He'd never want to put someone through that kind of pressure.

Aurora took a deep breath. He closed his eyes, hoping she hadn't wakened. She moved, slowly at first, turning in his arms to face him. He kept his lids shut, praying she wouldn't leave, knowing it'd be better if she did. Her fingers glazed over the new tattoo he'd gotten high on his left shoulder. To remember Charlie. He could feel her looking at it as she traced the shape of the design—a wolf and an eagle, joined together with a banner that said "Brothers".

Aurora's soft lips touched his and she backed away.

Tom debated letting her go. He wanted her to stay. He heard her pick up her clothing. Cracking open a lid, he watched. Aurora forwent her bra and slipped her dress over her beautiful, naked breasts. Grabbing her other garments, she left the room.

In a few minutes, Tom heard the locks on the door click. The urge gripped him to go after her.

He stopped himself. What would his pursuit achieve? If they developed a relationship, Aurora would most likely get hurt. She didn't need more pain. It would be selfish of him to ask her to deal with the heartbreak.

Tom heard the soft swoosh of the front door as she exited. The small echo from it shutting sounded hollow in his home.

He sat up, wondering if the best thing to ever happen in his life had just walked out.

* * * * *

Rorie glanced at her tickets as she sat in the Fayetteville terminal. Once she left the States, she would fly to Mexico City then on to Panama. *World Wildlife Review*, a new publication, needed photos of the Darien National Park, a one-million four-hundred–plus-thousand acre preserve in the tropical outback bordering the dangerous country of Columbia. The huge area hosted several ecosystems, from swamps and coastlines to mountain ranges, the largest peak reaching seven-thousand five-hundred feet. Dr. Raúl Martinez, a local scientist and author of the proposed article, would meet her at the airport.

She'd checked out the forested area. Although there were rumors of guerilla squads from Columbia infiltrating the Panamanian park, if she stayed in the north and used the guide they'd lined up for her, she should be safe. No problem. Besides, Dr. Martinez would be there as well. He was an expert on the area.

As a freelancer, Rorie was lucky to get the assignment. She'd been working as a photographic journalist since she graduated from college, doing the more adventurous assignments the last few years. Her camera skills had improved tremendously. She'd been told that some of her handiwork even stunned the imagination. Now Rorie had the chance to capture a little seen universe with her lens. The tropical highlands hadn't been photographed in years, the fauna barely studied. She wasn't about to pass up the chance.

Rorie frowned, remembering her job had become Stephen's biggest contention with her. When she took an assignment more risky than a local social event, her pending departure led to his largest blowup, the one where he shoved Rorie against a steel post so hard it broke her shoulder blade. Stephen had wanted her to stay home and make babies.

That shoot was the one assignment she missed.

In college, an old accounting professor had shared a valuable lesson. "Once a bad investment, always a bad investment. Cut your losses and move on." His advice slammed into her harder than the post had. Rorie knew the time had come for her to make a change. It took two years—two long years. Stephen fought every step of the way, even soliciting their parents' help to manipulate her. For once, she didn't buckle.

He finally relented when Rorie promised to give him the inheritance from her grandmother, about a quarter of a million. The amount represented Rorie's total wealth in this world. Her grandmother had left the sum for college, and to invest in Rorie's dream of having a photo gallery someday. Mamie Jones Lindsay had been Rorie's only supporter when she wanted to study photography. The elder woman encouraged Rorie's pursuit of her dreams. Rorie knew her grandmother would understand the need to escape an overbearing husband and demanding family.

Rorie sighed, remembering their farce of a wedding. She didn't love Stephen. Never had, only it took a few years to realize it. Sex and love were two different things. Still, she'd tried to make a go of it. They'd married because their old, blueblood families decided the match would work. It was the next step in a life dominated by her parents. Rorie even liked Stephen at first. But she was sure the investment portfolio-toting Stephen had never loved her either. His affairs started soon after their marriage. What a sham those vows had been.

Yet no one knew of his abuse. Rorie had kept that to herself. She still did, even after her counselor advised her to tell her parents. But, knowing what a loving couple her parents made, she didn't want them to hear about the failure of their only child to garner the same affection, or of their unknowing culpability in supporting a violent union. The facts would hurt them too much. Only Sally, her best friend, knew everything.

And now the gentle stranger with whom she'd spent the night.

Sally only arched a brow when Rorie strolled into their shared apartment that morning. "Have a nice night?" she asked.

"The best," Rorie responded flippantly and walked into her room to pack. Sally didn't ask anything else. For that, Rorie was grateful. She wouldn't have known how to explain what happened. She still wasn't sure herself what went on. She *felt* something, some emotion she hadn't experienced in some time.

Her stranger was unlike any other man she knew. And in reality, she didn't even know him, except he was thirty-two, gorgeous—and made her feel better about herself than she had in years. He thought her beautiful. She liked that. It had been a long time since a man had said something so complimentary.

A voice over the speakers called her flight. She glanced at her tickets again, thrilled. A new life. One she would define. She'd done it—broken away, and she'd never need to depend on anyone else again.

Yet, an inkling of loneliness crept within her. Rorie not only divorced Stephen, she'd alienated her family. Her protector bridged the gap last night between her and emptiness.

She stood in line for the ticket taker and reflected on the enigmatic man, on what they'd shared. Rorie knew she'd forgotten what love was, but, she wondered, had the stranger's touch somehow seeped into her heart?

* * * * *

A Sunday night and Tom found himself seated at the same table at the bar he'd come to the night before. He didn't frequent places like this on a Sunday, but he'd hoped to see Aurora again. In two days, his team would rotate to a safe house in Venezuela. There they'd train the Venezuelan Army as well as help the Venezuelans keep out drug smugglers. He wanted to see Aurora before they left. Tell her—

Tell her what? Wait for him? She didn't know a damn thing about him. Why would she wait?

He looked at his team leader, whom he'd dragged out with him. Out of the guys in Special Forces, Captain Mark Garcia and his wife, Julie, were the only happy couple he knew. Mark was the one guy he'd trust to take on a weird excursion like this. Of course, Tom hadn't told his leader why they came here with the rest of the team.

"Everyone ready to go Tuesday?" Mark sipped his beer.

"Yeah." Tom scanned the room. Still no sign of her.

"So why are we here?"

"Huh?" Tom's head snapped up. He hadn't really followed the conversation.

Mark snorted. "Look. I know you better. You don't usually go on these junkets with the guys. And you've been searching the room every five seconds. Who is she?"

Tom shrugged and fiddled with the cap from his beer bottle. "Don't know."

"You don't know?"

Tom shook his head. "Met her last night. Her name's Aurora. That's all I know about her."

"Huh," Mark grunted. "And you slept with her."

Tom smirked. "All night."

"Her place?"

"Nope."

"Yours?"

"Yep."

"Whew. That's a first for you. Why?"

"Got lonely, I guess."

"Humph." Mark took another drink. "That good?"

Tom nodded.

He heard the captain chuckle. "Well, it's about time you found someone. You're getting old, man."

Tom quirked a brow at him.

"You know where she lives?" Mark asked.

"Nope."

"How about her friends? Know any?"

"One. Maybe two. Crawford and Hansen were out with her girlfriends last night."

"She's one of those?"

Tom frowned. "Not really."

"How do you know?"

Tom sighed. He didn't really need an interrogation. He just wanted to find this woman and tell her…

Hell, he didn't know what he wanted to tell her. "She just isn't, okay?"

Mark bit off a laugh. "Sure, Chief. Just be careful. You're still raw over Charlie."

His friend and commander eyed him. Tom understood Mark's concern.

"I need you one-hundred percent, Chief."

"I will be," Tom answered truthfully. "I always am."

"I know." Mark nodded. "Well, I'm heading home." He stood. "Unlike you boys, I have a loving wife waiting for me."

"You're damn lucky," Tom said and took a swig of beer.

"I'm lucky every day of my life." Mark winked. "You find a good woman, and you'll be lucky, too."

Tom grimaced. "Yeah."

He watched the captain walk out, realizing how great the son of a bitch had it. Julie was sweet, beautiful and loyal. They had one child and another on the way. Their relationship reminded him of his parents' life before his father died. What else could a man ask for?

He downed the beer and stood when Brodie came over.

"You leaving?" the sergeant asked.

"Yeah." He threw a few bills on the table. "But do me a favor."

"Anything, Chief. Almost." Brodie grinned. He had a new girl on his arm this time.

"If you see that chick you were with yesterday, ask what her silent friend's name is — and a phone number."

"The brunette?" Brodie said.

At the mention of another woman, the new girl Brodie stood with punched him in the arm and left.

The sergeant rubbed the spot and frowned. "Thanks, Chief."

Tom chuckled. "Anytime. You never know what you can pick up with one of those ladies. And you wonder why I keep reminding you not to play things too loose. The brunette?" he prodded.

"Will do, Chief. I can find her. Promise."

"Before we leave?" Tom asked.

"Maybe." Brodie grinned. "I'll try. Told you those girls come here a lot. Usually not on Sundays though."

Now the man tells him. "Thanks," he said and strode out.

Instead of going home, Tom took a brisk ride on his bike, speeding through the quiet countryside. The hour grew late but he figured he wouldn't get a wink of sleep tonight anyway. His thoughts would be filled with her.

* * * * *

Rorie mopped the sweat off her brow with her bandana as they headed back into El Real, a small town where the park's headquarters was located. She'd been in the jungle almost two weeks now with her guide, Luis Hernandez Cortes DeSoto something something Alvarez, using El Real as their base of operation. She glanced at Luis. She'd forgotten what other names were in his Christian designation. He'd told her a few times but the length of Hispanic names often baffled her. A jovial man, he just laughed when she tried to remember.

She sighed as they walked into the compound. Sometimes Dr. Martinez, the journalist of the purported article, even came with them on these treks. *What a treat.* Rorie huffed, wondering where the doctor had wandered off to again. She'd assumed, when she took this gig, the author would be with them to point out what pictures he wanted. But, no. Dr. Martinez left that up to her "good" judgment. Usually the man came out with their group, but, after giving his orders, she and Luis would hoof into the jungle alone. Today, the good doctor hadn't even left with them.

Rorie wondered if he'd come back. Normally Martinez returned to base camp by evening, wanting to take her out. After their first dinner, she realized he'd been more interested in seducing her than in discussing the article. Rorie hadn't gone again. Thankfully, she stayed at the only motel in El Real. Raúl had wanted her to stay at the state-run lodges like him, but she figured the farther away from him at nights the better. At least the motel had locks—cheap ones to be sure, but they worked. She even used the wooden brace provided to bar the door.

The trip, in regards to the doctor, had been a disappointment, but Rorie had to admit she'd gotten some striking pictures. The park, if you could survive the humidity and mosquitoes, exceeded the imagination. The trees created three levels of canopies, the tallest ranging to about one-hundred and sixty-five feet. The forest ceiling thickened so much that in some parts the jungle grew as dark as the last vestiges of dusk.

The spectacular wildlife included viable populations of some species that are endangered in the rest of the Americas. She'd even gotten a picture of a harpy eagle, one of the rarer species, when they'd visited some of the highlands.

And the people. Natives still lived pretty much as they had hundreds of years ago. They were fascinating. But apparently their numbers had dwindled, mostly due to the violence in certain areas of the forest and the resulting starvation the upheaval caused. Traders wouldn't trek to the settlements anymore, an income and food source the Indians depended on.

Some of the rumors Rorie heard were frightening. Kidnap and murder, hazing of the local population. And no one in Panama seemed to be doing anything about it. She wondered if they could. Panama had no army to speak of, only state police. They couldn't match up against the Columbian rebels and paramilitary infiltrating the southernmost part of the park. For political reasons, the Panamanian government found it hard to ask for help from any other country, especially the United States.

What a mess. Thankfully, Rorie had a great guide.

When they entered the town, they met up with another group coming from a different section of the forest. Dr. Christian Ferguson was a fellow reporter, a professional friend she'd made after her breakup with Stephen. He knew some of her past, of her failed marriage. They'd talked a few times since she'd been there. He'd arrived much earlier, working on an article for the *National Geographic* about native populations.

Chris stared at her a minute. With a somber expression on his face, he looked more disheveled than usual. As hot and humid as the air was, she figured she could say the same about herself. She waved to him and walked on behind Luis.

"Rorie," Chris called after her. "Wait." He ran up and caught her by the elbow.

"Must have been a long day," she said, noticing the dirt smudges on his clothes. He carried his photographer's camera case. She nodded at it. "Get some good shots?"

"That's the problem," he said, his white teeth gleaming against his tan. "My photographer is down and I'm lousy at taking pictures. We're sending Harrison home. But that leaves me hanging. I need another photojournalist. What if I take you to dinner tonight and we discuss a deal?"

"Me?" she squeaked and pulled at her new long layered cut. She'd gotten the style in Panama City while waiting for her transportation. Her hair still fell past her shoulders, but she thought the 'do gave her a more worldly appearance. She looked closer at him. "Work for the *National Geo*?"

"Why not?" he shrugged. "I've seen your work. It's great."

Rorie couldn't have been more flattered, well, except for when her stranger had warmed her the other night—but that was a different type of flattery entirely. Still, thinking about her one-time lover made her breath catch, and she thought about him way too often.

"What do you think?" Chris asked.

Chris was attractive—nothing like her mysterious man, but nice just the same. "Why not?" Rorie smiled. "I'd rather have dinner with you than Dr. Martinez."

Chris chuckled. He knew what a letch Raúl was. "Good."

"What happened to Mike?" she asked.

Chris shrugged. A flash of an unreadable emotion crossed his face, but the movement passed so quickly Rorie couldn't name it. "He got sick. Forgot to get the right meds before he left."

"That was stupid," she said. "He should know better."

"He thought he was covered. He didn't think his shots...had expired." Chris glanced between her and Luis.

Rorie recognized the look this time. Sadness and apprehension. She knew Chris had worked with Mike a long time. "He'll be all right," she said, placing a hand on his arm, hoping to console him. "What time do you want to meet?"

Chris pulled off his floppy hat and dusted the top of his head. "Thirty minutes? It'll give me some time to clean up."

She grimaced. "Make it forty-five. I need more time than you."

He kissed her on the cheek. "Deal. Meet you at your place." Turning, he ran off to join his guide.

Rorie watched him. The man was fit. He had to be to do the work he did. But he didn't stir her as her stranger had. Rorie wondered if she'd ever again experience the elusive sensation she'd found with her dark prince. Several times, she wished she'd asked him his name. She didn't like squirming from the erotic dreams she'd had every night with a man whose name she didn't know. But Rorie couldn't stop thinking about him, how his body fit with hers, how he made her feel inside. Her prince had said he wanted to get to know her better. Perhaps she should have let him.

Too late for that now. By the time Rorie got back, her unknown lover would have found someone new. Guys like that didn't wait when they wanted something. But Rorie couldn't help her jealousy of whoever the woman turned out to be.

"You go with him in the morning?" Luis asked with his thick accent, his pinched face interrupting her thoughts.

"I don't know. Depends on what he has to say. I'd still rather have you as a guide. Can you get us to the natives?"

He shook his head. "Dr. Martinez hired me and I have family to think on. I believe going with the *Señor* is not a good idea for the lady. What will Dr. Martinez say? This is a small place. The doctor will know you went with him."

Rorie grimaced. "Luis, Doctor Martinez hasn't come with us once. I don't even know if I'm shooting the right things. I promise, though, whatever I decide, you'll be paid the same."

The trusted guide shook his head, his gaze stabbing through her. "Miss Lindsay—" His voice grew hoarse, urgent. "Do not go with Dr. Ferguson. Promise me you will tell him no."

Luis' English seemed to improve. "I…" Her skin prickled as if one of the jungle's poisonous spiders had just crawled over her. Rorie reminded herself she needed to make her own decisions. No matter what this man thought, she needed to chart her own path. And what a great opportunity this would be. Her? Rorie Lindsay? A photographer for the *National Geo*? What a step up. Her life had finally taken a turn for the better. Besides, Chris was highly respected in his field and very well published. He would know what to do. "I'll think about it, Luis. Promise."

Her guide nodded and stepped toward her, standing closer than he'd ever been to her before. Nervously, Rorie held her ground.

"*Senorita*—" His voice dropped. If Luis hadn't been so near, she wouldn't have heard him. "I will not stop you, but I plead with you. There are other dangers you do not know in the forests of the Darien." Luis spun around and marched off.

The warning hung in the air around her.

Chapter Four

ஐ

Nonsense.

Rorie stood in the morning light and checked her watch, Luis' strange words banging about in her head.

"Ready?" Chris asked.

She nodded and shifted the bag on her back. "This is safe, isn't it?"

Chris hefted his pack. "Jorge hasn't steered me wrong yet. I trust him. Besides, who's the one who told me she thirsted for adventure?"

Rorie grimaced. She had mentioned the fact last night.

"We'll cover some of the habitat stuff today. Here's Mike's digital." He took the camera from his pocket, the small device protected by a thin, black leather cover. "I'd rather you keep it for me, if you would. I might ask you to take a few shots with it."

"Sure." Rorie shrugged and opened her hand.

"Let me put it in your pack. You're already loaded."

She turned so he could place the digital inside her overlarge camera bag, which doubled as a knapsack. She kept everything in there, even some survival stuff in case she got separated from the rest of the group. One couldn't take any chances.

Chris tugged the zipper to close the pack.

"Did you decide where we're going?" she asked.

"To Ipeluza. Have you been there?"

"No."

"It's almost due south from here. We'll take the jeep," Chris said as they followed Jorge. "Thought we'd get some shots in town first then trek into the jungle."

"And that's safe?" Rorie asked. "I thought everything south of here was off-limits."

As they approached the jeep, Chris stopped the guide then stood closer to her. "Listen, Rorie. I need you. Your shots are nothing less than spectacular. If anything looks dangerous, I'll send you back with Jorge. We should be fine to Ipeluza. While you're taking some photos of the village, I'll check with the locals on any activity. I can't promise, though, that we won't have trouble so, if you don't want the risk, stay here. I'll understand. But if we are stopped, separated or whatever, you stick to your guns. Tell them you're working for the *National Geographic* and nothing else. If, by some act of fate, we are kidnapped, the magazine will pay your ransom, okay? I talked to them last night before the line went dead. Everything's legit."

Chris looked at her. "Take a minute to think about it. The locals already know you've been working with Dr. Martinez. That should provide you with some protection."

"Really? Why?"

"Just trust me." Chris peered at her, some strange look in his eyes that seemed to say much more, but she wasn't sure what the gleam meant.

Rorie swallowed and wondered if she'd gone crazy. First, the sensual night she'd spent with a man she didn't know. Now, trekking into a jungle filled with terrorists. The thought exhilarated and frightened her at the same time. "I'm game." She nodded. "Just don't get me killed."

He smiled and kissed her on the cheek. "I'd never intentionally do that, gorgeous."

Gorgeous? She shrugged off his comment and the kiss then got in the back of the jeep. Chris's behavior had turned weird this morning. She chalked it up to the excitement he had for finishing this piece. Apparently, he and Jorge hadn't been able to locate many of the indigenous tribes that lived in the safer areas of the Darien. Now, Jorge had gotten news on where to find a small band of Chocoes who had moved, a tribe of Indians who still tattooed their bodies and lived as they once had along the river. Rorie grew excited, thinking what an adventure this had turned out to be.

But her enthusiasm waned when they reached the village almost two hours later. People stood about, listless. The shacks looked shabby. Rorie spent her time with Jorge, taking pictures of children with swollen bellies and the small, dilapidated huts. The recent incursions of the different factions of Columbians had taken its toll on this town. She wondered how close some of the fighting had actually come.

They had lunch with some people Jorge knew, some native dishes Rorie had been afraid to ask about, then in a few hours they took off along a trail by foot, Chris making sure she stayed between him and Jorge.

"We might spend the night in the jungle," Chris said after an hour or so. "Do you mind? We have the gear."

"No. Besides, I always come prepared. It'll be another new bold experience, I guess." Rorie glanced back at him.

Chris smiled. "The reason you became a wildlife photographer."

She nodded. "When I grow old, I want to be able to say I had a life. Like my father's mother."

"The adventuress you told me about."

"That's right." Rorie looked again at Jorge's back. "I have no intention of wallowing in my father's modest inheritance, albeit the money is generous by most standards. I love what I do. I wouldn't want to do anything else."

Jorge stopped and held up his hand.

She halted behind the guide as Chris sauntered close beside her.

"You don't want to settle down with someone?" her friend asked.

51

Her unnamed protector had asked a similar question. Rorie imagined if she ever did, it would be with someone like the first man in her life who'd made love to her—not that there'd been a second. Yet, anyways. "Yes." She nodded. "Eventually. I think it'll take me a long time to find the right guy, though. The next time I marry I don't want to make the same mistake."

Jorge disappeared into the undergrowth.

Chris lowered his voice. "So, for you, being with someone means marriage."

"Call me old-fashioned, but, yeah, it does."

He grimaced playfully. Realization dawned on Rorie that Chris actually flirted with her.

She laughed at his look, but quieted when Jorge reappeared, chattering something to Chris in rapid-fire Spanish. Turning, Jorge left again.

Rorie didn't like the face Chris made. "What did he say?" she asked.

"We're too late." Chris frowned.

"What do you mean?"

He took a deep breath. "I want you to stay here. Jorge and I are going to check the village."

"You aren't leaving me in the jungle alone."

"Jorge's running the perimeter. He won't be far." Chris's face grew impassive. "The place won't be pretty, Rorie." He paused. "Everyone's dead."

She stood rock-still for a moment then shook off her surprise. "How? Who?"

"Don't know. Whoever committed this atrocity is long gone. They won't be back." He rested his hands on his hips and dropped his chin to his chest for a moment. Looking up, he stared almost straight through her. "I hate to say this, but in a sick way, this is a photojournalist's wet dream."

She knew what he meant. "I'll go. Someone needs to cover this."

When they entered the small circle of huts, two mothers lay stilled on the ground with small children wrapped in their arms, the blood congealing in the gunshot wounds to their bodies. An elderly man rested on the steps to one hut, the side of his head blown open, flies settling on the mass of soft tissue protruding through the tattoos at his temple. The smell sickened her.

Rorie held her mouth to stop the vomit rising in her throat. For the first time in her life, she really despised someone—whoever did this. She hadn't felt this much disgust for Stephen.

"Here." Chris handed her his kerchief, which he'd doused with water from his canteen. "Use this to wipe your face. The views are only going to get worse from here."

She nodded and did as he instructed. Rorie didn't realize her knees were shaking until his hands held her up at the elbows.

"I'll be fine." She handed him back the bandana and pulled out her camera to go to work. She needed to document these people's torment. As someone once said, a picture was worth a thousand words. Trite, she thought, but apropos. The photos she took would tell volumes. And as ill sounding as Chris' words were about the job, the grisly scene could make her career.

She took a few shots outside then went inside a hut. A woman's body and her decapitated head were slumped over a bedroll. She lifted her camera to shoot when Chris rushed in.

"Let's make tracks," he said. "Jorge says someone's coming. I want to get you back to safety. I didn't mean for you to take a risk like this."

Rorie hurried out after him, rushing into the area between the huts and along the trail behind Chris.

"Move." He pushed her ahead of him. Jorge ran just in front of her.

A popping sound echoed in the jungle and a slug hit a branch over her head, splintering the wood. From somewhere, Chris pulled a pistol and fired back. Rorie hadn't known he was packing.

She took off. If anyone had asked her before the shots rang out if she could have run faster, she would have said no.

And she would have been wrong.

She raced harder. The willowy tree limbs growing over the path whipped her face.

"Hurry." Jorge stopped ahead and pointed to an opening in the forest. She ran through the gap, not knowing where to go. Chris grasped her arm as he fled past her, pulling her along in what Rorie guessed was the right direction, his gun still in his other hand.

A ray of sunlight broke through the heavy canopy in a small patch of cleared earth. Rorie guessed the area had been an old garden at one time.

Chris stopped at the far edge. "Which way?"

Jorge pointed to a cluttered thin line of dirt. Chris made for the trailhead with her in tow.

Another shot rang out, but this time Chris skidded to a halt.

Two armed men in tattered uniforms stood in front of them, their rifles pointed at Chris' chest. Others appeared, stepping through the forest around her group.

A soldier disarmed Chris and their assailants waited, watching their new captives. No one spoke.

Until Rorie heard the rustling of leaves behind her. Two more men, guns slung on their backs, strolled closer. Twisted grins appeared on their faces as they surrounded her, Chris and Jorge, relieving them of their packs and her camera case.

Then someone Rorie recognized walked onto the jungle trail and circled around one of the armed men.

"Hello, Miss Lindsay," Dr. Martinez said.

Her jaw dropped.

"I can see you are surprised to see me."

His oily smile irritated her. "Raúl, tell these men who we are. Tell them to let us go."

"Miss Lindsay, I believe these men already know those you are with. Probably better than you." He strolled in front of her and fingered her shoulder, letting his nails brush down her arm. "You should have listened to Luis, *querida*. He would not have steered you wrong. However, perhaps this is for the best."

"Let her go, Martinez," Chris demanded and yanked her to him by her britches. Chris slid his fingers into the back of her pants and hooked some object behind her belt.

She looked into her friend's face, getting the funny feeling something was going on here she knew nothing about. "You're not an ordinary reporter, are you?" she whispered to Chris.

The look in his eye confirmed her statement.

Raúl stepped to her and lifted her chin with the palm of his hand. "I will let her go," he pulled Chris's hand away from her, "when I am ready."

Raúl nodded to the armed men. Looping his arm through hers, they marched off.

* * * * *

Tom lay in his bunk, listening to the late afternoon rain pounding on the tin roof. It poured everyday and he grew tired of the noise pattering on the safe house. He looked around the room. Their location lay near the Columbian border. The concrete brick building had one sleeping area and a few other rooms used for operational purposes. They'd risen early and finished their training op just before midafternoon. This way, the exercise would be over before the downpour hit again.

Some of the other guys read or listened to music. Tom just thought. Although "daydreamed" might be a better word. He couldn't get Aurora off his mind, how her body shimmered in the moonlight, how she writhed underneath him in ecstasy. God, he wanted her, and felt himself stir just thinking about her.

A damn bad thing when you were in such close quarters and your only available release would be a cold spray in the open showers outside.

He kicked himself again for just letting her walk out. Brodie hadn't been able to get more on her. Tom grew afraid she'd be gone by the time he got back. She said she lived in Fayetteville—sort of. What the hell kind of answer was that?

One that brushed him off, he figured. Maybe she didn't want to see him again. But if that was the case, he wanted her to tell him flat-out and in person.

He needed to find her.

"Chief." Ken Talbot, the team's communications specialist, stuck his head in the door. "We got a heads-up from SOCSOUTH. The mission data is feeding into the computer now. Captain says to get your butt in here."

Before Ken could finish, Tom made it to the door. He strolled down the short hall and into the room. Mark looked at him. "We have a downed operative in the Darien Gap. Be ready to roll by zero three hundred tomorrow. A Chinook's on its way to take us to San Fernando for our flight out."

"When's the chopper's ETA?"

"They should be here by seventeen hundred. Right now, our biggest problem is the target. He's moving, using one of the new silent locators. Those things are sweet, but they're only good for thirty-six hours. I'm told the guy—a Chris Ferguson—already used about four. Hopefully, whoever's captured them will stop soon and we can get a read before we take off. Judging from the direction they're heading, they'll be in Columbia before we move."

"Understood," Tom said. "The operative our complete mission?"

"No. The man has some critical security info he tried to send the day before, but couldn't complete the transmission." Mark shuffled through his scraps of paper. "We'll need to secure that. Then there's his guide. And another guy, a civilian. They think his name is Roy Lindsay, but they're not sure. The line Ferguson used to report in went dead before he could finish. The man's some photographer working for *World Wildlife Review*.

Ferguson picked him up to legitimize his position, take some actual photos of some of the natives to satisfy his cover. Guess his original partner got shot the day before. They're not sure his partner's going to make it." Mark dropped the slips of paper on the desk. "Thing is, we're it. No one else is going."

"How many bad guys?" Tom asked.

"Don't know. The command center thinks about twenty." Mark shrugged. "You know SOCSOUTH. It's hard to tell with the jungle canopy. Their intel is sketchy, especially from the local talent."

"Great, that's all we need. Two to one odds. We have three to rescue and we're short two men. We don't know who has the security data either, I bet."

"Not really." Mark's lips thinned. "But that sums up the situation. A C-17's coming for our flight over. We need the plane to halo in. I'm guessing we won't have actual clearance to enter the country until we've landed—if we get it at all. We don't want the Columbians or Panamanians guessing we're in their jungle. A Chinook will pull us out. A KC-130 is flying from Miami to refuel the chopper in flight for the return. Get the men together." Mark scanned the data coming off the computer. "I want a briefing in the next thirty minutes."

"Yes, sir." Tom nodded, glad they had a real mission. He needed something to rid himself of his restless energy. Maybe the action would help him stop thinking about Aurora, of his dream of telling her what he wanted to do when he found her.

He walked out of the room, more than ready. Tom would see to it the men were ready, too.

* * * * *

Stuffed and trussed, Rorie felt like a turkey. She kept choking from the gag. Her wrists and ankles were raw from where the ragtag men had tied her to the chair, doing so after they jammed the back of the seat against the table centered in the tiny shack. She guessed they propped the chair to keep her from falling over, as tired as she was. She blinked, hoping to erase her weariness. Their captors had taken them by truck to some desolate location and forced them to walk over half the night, mostly uphill through a pass in the mountains, finally settling in this small site made with a few huts.

The worst part was she couldn't sleep. She kept hearing Chris' or Jorge's muffled screams in one of the other cabins, causing her to chill in the warm night.

The last few hours, though, had been quiet. Rorie wondered if her colleagues were still alive.

Another tear found its way down her cheek. How could this happen? Chris seemed so sure they'd be safe.

But her friend obviously had other things on his mind. Why had he brought her along? And what really happened to his partner, Mike?

Rorie tried to doze, her body stiff. She seemed to sit in stasis like that for some time—half in the conscious world, half out of it.

Footsteps sounded from far away. "Woman." Someone shook her. "Wake. I do not have time to indulge you."

Her eyes cracked open. The sky had lightened somewhat outside the window. Dawn had broken.

"Mmmm…" She tried to gain full awareness, but the pain in her joints begged her to go back to sleep.

"Wake up, *querida*. You have cost me enough time."

The shaking had to come from the person who spoke. A man's voice. A strong hand grabbed her chin and squeezed it hard. "Woman, do not test me."

"Ouch." Someone had removed her gag. Rorie's head shot up from the deep reclining position she had taken against the back of the chair. When she looked at her attacker, her memory came crashing back.

"Good morning, Dr. Martinez." Her voice cracked, her mouth had turned dry and tasted like cotton. Her nerves on end,

Rorie forced her face to remain impassive and unreadable. From years of abuse, she'd learned never to antagonize someone who had the upper hand.

"Much better." Raúl smiled at her. "Now —" He pulled a chair from around the table and sat, looking at her. "What did you take pictures of yesterday?"

She frowned. "Dead villagers. Where did you put my bag?"

He nodded to a weathered wooden cabinet in the corner of the room. "It's locked. I've already examined your case, along with what your friends carried. I did not know you labeled all your film. Of course, I will take the rolls to have them examined, just in case."

"Be my guest," she uttered. "They're for your article."

He snickered. "Of course. How about the digital cameras? I don't remember seeing them. Did you use them?"

Her blurred mind tried to remember. She had a digital, but the artist in her liked using real film. Had she used it? "No, I don't think so." Then she remembered Mike's camera. Oh, God, did it have a picture card?

"Why not?" Raúl asked.

"I don't like digital cameras." Rorie played along. "I only brought them because the magazine insisted."

Her answer seemed to suffice. Dr. Martinez stood. "That might explain why one didn't have a memory card in it." He hovered over her. "Can you tell me why you had two digital cameras?"

Rorie stared at him, unsure what to say. "One of them is mine. The other's the magazine's. I don't like using cameras I don't own so I didn't get any memory cards for the other. I didn't even look close enough at the camera to see what it needed."

"Really?" Raúl leaned forward, sliding both arms to either side of Rorie and resting his palms on the table behind her. His face came so close to hers she could smell his fetid breath. "And why is it I don't believe you?"

* * * * *

Tom glanced at the enemy's compound and gave the signal for his group to circle 'round. They'd split the team. He had five men with him, Jim Gutiérrez the ops sergeant, Eric Tanner a med specialist, Ken Talbot on the com, Brodie Crawford his weapon's sergeant, and Rick Hanson the intel sergeant. They were to charge the compound and free the hostages while the captain took the other three men and cleared the perimeter.

Hidden by the underbrush, Tom stopped several yards away. Ferguson and the guide knelt in a clearing surrounded by four huts. Two men held pistols to the prisoners' heads while one seemed to stand there and supervise. Tom had sent Jim and Brodie to check out the far buildings. Eric and Ken to get the other two.

Eric and Ken contacted him first. "The other guy's a woman," the com sergeant informed him through the headset. "They're in the second hut. Two soldiers and a guy in civvies. I think the civilian's unarmed, but he's batting the woman around pretty good."

"Hold your position," Tom ordered.

Seconds later, Jim and Brodie radioed over their headsets the all clear. After informing the captain of the number of men in camp, Tom put his guys in position for the attack.

Moving in, he set himself to make the kill of one of the armed men in the only occupied hut, giving Rick the other enemy soldier. Closer in, he heard a loud slap and a familiar voice. The man in civilian clothes moved, and what Tom saw caused his heart to stop.

"What the hell..." His gaze honed in on Aurora.

Tom shook the reaction off. Thinking about her now would only screw the mission up and get her killed. "On my count," he ordered and numbered down.

* * * * *

"Why are you doing this?" Rorie asked.

Raúl bent over and sneered in her face. "With how the United States devastated the Panamanian government with the overthrow of Noriega, some of us believe we should join with Colombia again." He stood and lifted his hand, the chair he'd sat in clattering behind him as it fell. "Your reticence to tell me what I need to know is irritating. Talk to me. And I can make your stay much more pleasant." He lowered his hand and rubbed it along her cheek. "Now speak." He raised his arm again.

Rorie flinched, anticipating another sting from Raúl's backhand. The last one had busted her dry lip. Thirsty and hungry, she eyed Chris and Jorge through the open doorway. Raúl had made them kneel in the dirt, the other rebels holding them up since, by her friends' haggard appearance, they couldn't kneel on their own. Chris looked almost dead.

Raúl threatened to kill her friends if she didn't tell him the truth. But what could she say? Yeah, she could tell Raúl that Chris gave her the camera, but what good would it do? Raúl had said the camera was empty. She didn't know where the memory card for it had gone. The only thing she knew for sure was Dr. Martinez would kill her for the pictures.

"Tell me now," Raúl screamed, grabbing her chin and squeezing her cheeks so hard her jaw ached. "Or you will have a similar destiny as your compatriots."

She licked the blood off her lip, sure this would be the end of her. "And why should I think you won't kill me? I don't believe you. I don't know what you're talking about and you're still going to kill us, one way or another."

He backhanded her. Moaning, she closed her eyes, a ringing sounding in her ears. Or was the noise that popping sound again?

She heard a thud. Then another. Something heavy fell on the floor. Opening her eyes, the two soldiers guarding her lay lifeless. Raúl rushed to grab a rifle from one of them and turned in front of her to fire out the door.

Before he got a shot off, she heard another pop. The doctor slumped against her, his heavy body in her lap, his slicked-back hair rubbing against her face, his hat sitting halfway on her head blocking her view. She screamed.

Several footsteps sounded on the wooden planks. "U.S. soldiers, ma'am," a male voice said and moved behind her. "We're here to rescue you."

Spitting out Raul's oily hair, she felt the weight of the dead man lifted off her.

Then she looked into the painted face of one of her rescuers and froze. The man's forest green eyes stared at her, a hint of laughter showing in the creases around them. Her mouth gaped open from shock.

Her mysterious protector and one-time lover let a smile crack over his painted face. "Hello, Aurora."

Chapter Five

ℰℐ

"Prince?" Her voice sounded meek, almost a whisper to her own ears. Why did her savior have to be him? And why should she even care?

"*Prince?*" one of the guys cracked as he examined a dead soldier.

"Shut up, Brodie." Her one-time lover frowned. "You okay?" His gaze grew intense.

Rorie swallowed. "Yeah, I'm fine." If she weren't tied to the chair, she would have crumbled from exhaustion. She looked for a nametag on his shirt. Nothing.

Her protector brushed his thumb across her cheek and stepped back. "Rick, get her to the chopper. Brodie, come with me." He spun and left.

"But…"

"Don't worry, ma'am, he'll be back." The man Prince had called Rick cut cleanly through the bonds at her wrists then came around to free her feet.

She looked at him and rubbed her chafed arms. "Don't I know you?"

"Yes, ma'am." His white teeth showed through his camouflaged face. "I was with one of your girlfriends a few weeks ago. Cathy? Cathy Bounds?"

"Oh, yeah." She remembered. God, how could she forget?

"Come on. We need to move. Can you walk?"

Rorie stood, her legs a bit wobbly. She heard more of the popping sounds farther away. "I think so."

Rick helped her down the short flight of stairs to the ground and held her arm, rushing her along.

"What happened to Chris and Jorge?" she asked.

"They're just ahead. Two of the men are carrying them out."

"They're okay?" Rorie swallowed.

"As far as I can tell. Can you run?"

She nodded, taking off as Rick pulled her along. When Rorie glanced backward one more time for her defender, he had disappeared. How would she explain this recent predicament to the unnamed man? And why did she feel compelled to even mention her compromised situation? Perhaps she didn't want him to see her as weak, someone who needed protection. After all, hadn't she learned to take care of herself?

Rorie panted as she ran, shrugging off her thoughts. The thick moisture in the air hampered her breathing. In a few minutes, the trees parted and she saw the helicopter, the large blades making a low whooshing sound. The chopper had landed in a field cut from the wilderness. Sharp stumps still showed along the edge. Apparently, the area had been here for a similar purpose for some time. Rorie wondered how long the Columbians had operated in the forest.

Rick hurried her inside. After talking over his headset, he spun and left, disappearing into the jungle. She scanned the tight interior. Two pilots sat in the cockpit, checking the equipment, one speaking over the radio. Two other men sat near the front, looking over some paperwork. Chris and Jorge lay on the floor in the middle of the helicopter.

"Oh, God." She rushed to Chris and knelt by him. His eyes were closed, but she could see his chest moving up and down underneath his bloodied shirt. Bruises covered his face. One arm sat funny against his chest and she thought the limb had been dislocated.

She glanced at Jorge. One of the soldiers worked on the guide. "Is he dead?" she asked.

"Not yet," the soldier said. "I'm trying to stabilize him."

"Rorie—" Chris opened his eyes and grasped her wrist with his good hand, his voice weak. "Your bag? You have it?" His eyes riveted into hers, panicked.

"No. But I know where it is." She held his hand and rubbed the back of it.

"Tell someone." He coughed. "Must get…it."

"Chris," she whispered. "You may not have noticed but there's a whole army of terrorists out there trying to kill us. It would be suicide for someone to go after it."

"No." He held her arm in a death grip. "Must have plans inside. Critical to defense. Tell man in charge…"

His voice faded and he passed out.

"Chris?" She shook him gently. He didn't move but the rise and fall of his chest let her know he still breathed.

God, now what should she do? She glanced around for someone who could make more sense out of what Chris meant. The pilots and crew were busy readying for a quick take off. The soldiers who had come for her were in the jungle except for the one working to save Jorge.

There was no one else to send. She bit her lip. Chris and Jorge had risked their lives for the information that was in her pack. If Chris needed her bag then it held something important. Still, she was frightened. Her sense of adventure had fled.

She glanced around the helicopter—studied Chris, Jorge and the man who worked to save her friends.

Swallowing, she steeled her resolve. Her safety be damned. She was a good American. These men had risked their lives to save her group. The least she could do was retrieve her pack— right?

Rorie backed toward the opening. Before anyone could stop her, she jumped out and sped for the hut.

More gunshots rang out. The firefight sounded near.

Keep going. Not far.

Fear kept her running.

Rorie found the hut and sped up the few stairs. Inside, she stopped, cringing as she tiptoed over Raúl's dead body, afraid he might jump back to life.

She stared at the jerk. "He's dead," she declared, reinforcing the fact in her head. Then she kicked him for good measure.

Rushing to the cabinet, she pulled the handles, shaking them when they wouldn't open.

She pounded the door with the side of her fist. "Shoot."

An explosion rocked the ground nearby.

"I didn't mean it," she spat out between her gritted teeth and hit the floor.

The gunfire grew closer.

"She's gone, Chief," the med tech reported over the headset.

Tom rushed for cover and fired a few return volleys. There were a lot more than twenty-odd men in the jungle. Unfortunately, the captain's group ran into them before they could exit the target area. One of the men in Mark's patrol had been injured. Another team member carried the wounded man in as Tom and the rest provided cover. What else could go wrong?

"What do you mean she's gone?" Tom ducked behind a tree, yelling over the mike.

"Your girl. She took off while I worked on the guide. The loadmaster said she went in the direction of the compound."

"And the son of a bitch wouldn't go after her," Tom spat out, disgusted. He followed his men, firing and again taking cover.

"Believe it or not, he jumped out to catch her, but she'd already hit the underbrush. You know he isn't allowed to stray from the bird. You want me to go after her?"

"Shit." The team needed all the men they had to deal with this mess. Tom glanced over his shoulder. They were close. He could hear the chopper.

Tom took a deep breath and glanced into the woods. He couldn't lose her again, especially not like this.

"No. Stay with the wounded," he ordered. "I'll find her."

Signaling to the ops sergeant to take over, Tom veered toward the compound.

"Stupid thing…"

Rorie hit the lock on the cabinet door repeatedly with one of the chairs, but the steel closure didn't budge. Her remaining option lay with the dead soldiers and she dreaded touching them.

Wincing, she squatted beside the one nearest her and rolled him over.

"Oh…" She grimaced. His dead glare arrested her. Shaking off the grisly image, she reached for his knife.

The noise in the woods came closer. Rorie hurried to the cabinet and inserted the blade in the slit between the doors to pry them open.

Shots sounded outside the window.

Frantic, Rorie dropped the knife and picked up the soldier's gun, hitting the hard butt against the lock. "Open, you stupid thing," she yelled, a mixture of cold terror and determination burning inside her. "I'm not going to let those people's pain be for nothing."

One of her hands slid along the barrel as she hit the door and her finger accidentally slipped into the trigger. The gun fired. Screaming, Rorie tossed the rifle away as her backside hit the floor.

The hard metal of the barrel clattered on the wooden planks. Footsteps sounded behind her.

No time to run.

Turning, she scooted back against the cabinet, apprehension freezing her there.

Her protector ran in and knelt beside her, his free hand patting different parts of her body. "Are you hurt?"

Expelling her breath, Rorie shook her head, relieved. "No."

"Good," he growled. Frowning, he grabbed her arm, pulling her toward the door and mumbling under his breath.

"No," she protested and yanked against him with no effect. "Chris said we need my backpack." Her feet slid against the floor as he pulled her. "It's locked in there."

Her lover stopped as she pointed to the cabinet. Shoving her behind him, he reached for his pistol with his free hand and quickly shot the lock off. "Grab it," he ordered and returned the pistol to his holster.

She took both Chris' and hers.

Her rescuer stared at her, his brows arched. She was sure Prince questioned her sanity.

"This one's Chris'." She held up the bag. "I thought it might hold something important."

The man grabbed Chris' pack and slung the bag over his shoulder. Going to the door, he scanned the outside. "Come on." He jerked his chin toward the opening. She followed close behind.

As they left the compound, more enemy soldiers entered on the other side. Quickly, Prince slipped her into the underbrush and followed unseen.

"Jim, we're on our way. Are we clear?" her savior asked into the small mike dangling near his mouth, grasping her by the arm to urge her on.

They ran and Rorie couldn't hear the reply. Only Prince's cursing as he pulled her off the trail. They sped through the brush, reaching another trail and running on. She heard the blades of the helicopter speed up and, after glancing through the canopy, saw their ride home rise in the air.

"Where are they going?" Terror settled in her throat. She tried to pull away and run after them, but the man held her, dragging her along with him.

"We need to meet them at a different point. Their position was overrun. Now keep quiet and do as I tell you."

It seemed like forever to Rorie, but in seconds they neared another open space. The helicopter lowered, a rope dangling out the side.

But before the chopper could descend, an explosion rocked the treetops. The loud sound deafened her and shoved her confidence into her boots. "Oh, my God…"

The copter lifted.

"Fuc—" Prince looked at her funny. She thought the men in the helicopter were telling him something.

Moments later, he grabbed her again and pulled her along a different path. "Run, and don't look back," he said, pushing her on.

As Rorie took off, she heard him fire.

Her lungs burned, her legs felt like jelly, but she still raced. Her life depended on it.

Suddenly, Rorie heard him behind her. "Move," he commanded. From somewhere inside, she yanked out the energy, and fled in a burst of speed.

Bark on the tree limbs overhead shattered with the pounding of bullets. Her defender turned and fired. She could hear him.

But she kept running.

Spying an opening to the path up ahead, Rorie charged into it—then skidded to a halt.

A deep gorge lay in front of her, a small, planked rope bridge of about thirty feet strewn across it. "Oh, my God…"

With her fear of heights, she'd never make it.

"Go," Prince yelled, running toward her.

"Bu…but…" She pointed to the bridge, her hand unsteady.

"Hell." Without stopping, Prince swept her up with his left arm, balancing her pelvis on his shoulder and flew onto the bridge, holding the rifle with his other hand.

"Oh, no." Rorie covered her face, mortal dread consuming her as the bridge swayed. Some shots brushed past her. "Oh, God."

When her rescuer turned, she peeked through her fingers and screamed. Her upper body had arced over the sisal railing and into thin air over the precipice.

Panicked, Rorie grabbed onto what she could of his shirt and belt. When he'd gone full circle, the planking came back into view. She heard him fire as he ran backwards over the remaining few feet to the other side.

Like an old film you manually cranked to view, she saw clips of the gorge through the narrow spaces between the slats. She gasped, holding her breath and trying not to vomit.

Then she saw dirt.

Her protector rushed along the path a few feet. Dropping her in some brush, Prince dashed back to the bridge.

Catching her breath, Rorie turned to watch him and rubbed her bruised bottom. As Prince ran toward the ropes, he pulled something off his chest. She watched him throw the item at the bridge then run back, falling on her to cover her with his body.

Rorie couldn't breathe under his heavy weight. Until he shifted with the loud explosion. The blast let her know what he'd thrown.

When her lover released her, Rorie looked up, timber still falling on the ground. "Wow." She'd never seen such a thing in her life.

Her protector jerked her up as shots echoed over the gorge. "Come on."

They sprinted, Prince pulling her along. Thankfully, the popping noise ended after a few moments.

But they kept running.

Finally, her stomach wouldn't tolerate any more and the stitch in her side grew to painful proportions. "Wait," she cried and put her free hand over her mouth.

He stopped. Sitting Rorie down, Prince shoved her head between her knees. "Don't pass out on me, babe. We need to make tracks."

"I'm...trying...not to," she said between pants.

"Take a deep breath," he ordered.

She took several until the wave of nausea passed. *Thank God.* Suddenly, all her emotions crashed in on her and she wept, her body shaking.

"Hey, it's all right." Her lover crouched and held her.

Rorie put her arms around his neck and cried in the crook of it.

"Shhh," he said and rubbed her back. "We'll get out of this, Aurora. I promise."

She felt like a baby—until he placed a lingering kiss on her temple.

She hiccupped. Looking at him, she let her fingers tease the short hairs along his neck then upward until she reached the floppy hat he wore. Her eyes drank him in and his seemed to do the same. "I don't even know your name."

The corner of his mouth rose. "MacCallum. Tom MacCallum."

"Tom..." She swallowed and touched his lips. "I won't ever forget you."

"Good." He let his dimples show. "With what I have planned, I would hope not."

What he had planned? What did he mean? Pulling away, she noticed a rip in his shirt and a dark splotch around it. "What's this?" She touched it lightly.

He cringed. "A flesh wound. It'll be all right until we get farther from the enemy." Tom rose halfway and looked around.

Satisfied, he straightened completely. "Sweetheart, blowing that bridge bought us a little time. But I don't want to guess how much. You think you can walk fast?"

She nodded.

Putting his hands under her arms, he lifted her. "Be as quiet as you can." Tom stared at her a moment then touched his lips to hers. When he ended the kiss, he studied her, the green in his eyes deepening. Rorie fingered his Adam's apple as he swallowed.

"C'mon," Tom finally said and tugged her hand a moment. Releasing her, he turned and walked ahead.

Rorie touched her mouth. Her skin burned with his tender kiss. Licking her lips, she followed before she lost him in the jungle, wondering if the kiss was a prelude to something more.

Don't lose her bag.

That was the last order Tom received before the connection faded. The flight crew wouldn't be coming back. Not right now anyway. The pilot needed to get the wounded medical care and Ferguson had some critical info. He and Aurora were on their own for the next eighteen hours.

Tom adjusted the strap of Ferguson's bag over the flesh wound he'd gotten while running over the bridge, hoping to seal the scrape until he had time to treat it. The bleeding had stopped. That was good. And it had bled enough to clean the puncture. Still, he ought to put an antiseptic on it.

But they needed to get to the secondary extraction point and he didn't want to hang around any longer. Who knew if those bozos called some of their friends?

Tom examined the global positioning unit he'd pulled from his rucksack. Using the GPS data, he designed a doglegged trek to get them to the preplanned area, a route designed to prevent the bad guys from following. About fourteen miles walking. Not far by normal standards, but normal didn't include the thick forests of the Darien and a woman untrained and unfamiliar with the terrorist-filled wilderness. Their trek would take all day and part of the night at this rate and they would need to cross another river. Then there was the thick jungle. He would have to hack through some of the vegetation. He hoped Aurora could make the distance.

Tom glanced back at her. She was still pale, but at least she moved. Her tan khaki shirt and pants fully covered her body and her boots seemed sturdy enough. Somehow, they'd make their way out of there.

He released a deep breath. He shouldn't have kissed her. Not now. Aurora and her pack were his mission. He needed to get her to safety.

He shook his head, thinking he'd gone off the deep end. That had to be it, because, in a weird way, Tom was damned happy he and Aurora were stuck in the jungle together. They were alone. They could get to know each other, sort of, if it became safe enough to talk.

Or maybe on the bird on the ride back. Before some CIA guy hauled her away to be questioned.

At least he could get an address and phone number. And was Aurora her real name? How the hell did intelligence mix that up with Roy? Was Lindsay her maiden name, or the bastard husband she'd had?

Tom took a quick look at her again. He couldn't very well ask her now. He watched her through the corner of his eye. She looked tired but kept up. With everything she'd been through, she actually did pretty well. He'd been impressed.

She hurried closer and he turned away. He didn't want Aurora to catch him staring at her.

She tugged his sleeve. Tom stopped and looked at her.

"I—" She started to say something and instead licked her lips. "Bathroom," she mouthed.

"Number one or number two."

She held up one finger.

He wanted to laugh she was so cute. Tom smirked instead. Taking her arm, he led her off the path a few feet to a tree with enough brush to provide her some privacy. Quickly checking the area, he stood on the other side of the trunk, wary, hoping like hell he could get her out of this soon and into his arms in a more secure location. He wanted her again, he knew that much. But getting involved scared him.

Still, he was ready to take the risk—to some degree anyway. At least he now knew what she meant about "sort of" living in Fayetteville. Aurora traveled, like he did. With their jobs, his idea might work. And when he got her out of here, he could talk to her about it.

Rorie rolled her eyes. God, how embarrassing. She hadn't wanted her first reunion with the sexiest man she'd ever bedded to be like this. With her broken lip and disheveled appearance, she'd been sure she looked a sight. Now, she had to pee. She couldn't hold it anymore.

"Hurry," Tom whispered from the other side of the large trunk.

"It would help if I knew you weren't listening." The burn of a blush crawled up her neck and into her cheeks.

Tom chuckled—albeit softly. "How about if I did the same over here?"

Rorie pressed her eyelids shut, flinching, positive she'd never get over the shame. "Sure."

When she heard him whizzing, she dropped her bag. Unzipping her pants, Rorie squatted and leaned against the tree. Finishing, she undid her pack and pulled out some wet naps to clean herself.

"Don't leave anything behind," Tom said.

Rorie glanced around to make sure he wasn't looking. "Oh, don't worry. I always pack my stuff out. I'm a good camper."

The low rumble of his voice soothed her. "It's so we don't leave any signs they can track."

"Oh." Seeing his straightened back to her, his alert position, she felt relieved. She didn't want him to see her in such a ridiculous posture, yet the way he stood guarding her had an odd tingling running through the lower part of her anatomy. She shrugged the sensation off. To think about sex now was stupid.

Rorie stuffed the soiled tissue in the foil packaging, putting the paper in a tight zippered section of her bag. Quickly finishing, she grabbed her pack, stood and came around. "Ready," she whispered, standing close to his side.

When Tom looked at her this time, his deep gaze stirred more than the tingling need she'd just repressed. His eyes told her he wanted her, too.

Swerving, his long strides took him down the trail. And she knew. This would be a long trek, in more ways than one. For both of them.

Tom checked the GPS data again. It'd been a few hours with no sign of the enemy. They went downhill most of the way, keeping off the trails as much as possible, but sometimes going downgrade was harder than going up. He could tell Aurora was dead on her feet.

"C'mon." He led her to a protected mossy area by a few large trees and sat her down.

"You mean we're actually taking a break?" she whispered.

Tom nodded and studied Aurora. Her bottom lip looked better, although the skin was still cracked and raw. He felt justified shooting the son of a bitch. Aurora hadn't deserved what the man had done to her. He handed over his canteen. "Take a few sips. I'll be right back."

"Where are you going?"

"To make sure this location is secure." He paused. "And to pee, maybe."

She blushed.

"Do you need to take care of anything else personal?" he asked. "I can dig a hole."

"No." Aurora looked away and sighed.

Tom had the feeling she hadn't been ready for the other kind of intimacies being alone in a deadly wilderness created. "I'll be right back. Stay here and don't wander off trying to find me. This might take a few minutes."

She nodded. "Promise. Are you going to give me a signal or something when you return? How am I going to know it's you?"

"Honey, you'll see me before you hear me."

Rorie watched him leave. In moments, she lost sight of Tom. He had blended into the woods. She lifted the canteen to her lips and stared at the empty forest. *You'll see me before you hear me*, he'd said. The comment gave her a chill. She believed him, glad Tom MacCallum was on her side.

Rorie recapped the canteen and set it alongside her. Somewhere along the way Tom had told her how long their hike would take. He said it'd be night before they got there.

They had a long way to go.

She rested her head on the bark and closed her eyes. The long hours and the crazy few days had taken their toll on her body as well as her nerves.

And then, there was Tom MacCallum. Being around him did more to stir her up than drain her. But the emotions that ravaged her when she was around him confused her. Did she desire him?

Oh, yeah.

Could she want more than sex with him?

She didn't even know him.

And since when did that have anything to do with love? Or was it lust?

Lust — had to be.

That and some primitive hormonal response to a guy who'd just saved her hide for the second time.

Rorie smiled, thinking of his hand brushing across her breasts. She could almost feel his touch, sense his arm tightening around her…

"Cripe."

She heard Tom cuss. Rorie jumped from her stupor in time to see the length of a huge snake wrapped around her chest, another part of the scaly creature tightening around her neck.

Tom slung the gun on his back, rushing to her with a knife drawn. He shoved his arm between the bark and the snake by her neck, then, with a clean swoop, hacked through the serpent.

Fluid from the incision squirted in her face. "Oh." Rorie banged her head on the back of the tree as the hold the snake had on her loosened. "When is this nightmare going to end?"

"What nightmare?" Tom said. "This is lunch."

"And I'm the bait?" The decapitated head dangled from his hand in front of her. "Ewww." She recoiled.

"Sorry." Tom tossed the head off to the side and chuckled.

She adored the sound. "Well, that's the third time you've saved me." And didn't she feel like an idiot.

"I guess I should have told you to keep your eyes open."

"Sorry." She shook her head. "I should have known better. It's just I'm so tired."

"I bet." Tom wiped the snake guts from her face then uncoiled the animal from around her. "How much sleep did you get last night?"

"Little to none. It was late when we arrived. Even when those creeps tied me up, I could hear Chris and Jorge screaming. I…I couldn't sleep." Wetness pooled in her eyes and she batted her lashes to make it go away, hoping he wouldn't notice. "Blast it." She wiped her face with her sleeve, glancing at him.

Tom moved away to sit down, skinning the snake, as if to give her some space.

"Are we really going to eat that?" She grimaced.

"Why not?" He smiled at her. "You ever have boa?"

"Never." She shuddered. "I think. I'm not sure what they fed us in Ipeluza."

His dimples deepened and Rorie couldn't help but smile at him.

"So is Aurora your real name?" he asked.

Rorie tried not to watch him slice the animal, but some sick fascination kept her glued. "Yes. Aurora Elizabeth Lindsay. Don't ask me where the name Aurora came from. It was my mother's idea." She bit her lip and studied him. "My friends usually call me Rorie."

"Rorie." He nodded. "That explains why they thought you were a Roy."

"Roy? Who thought that?"

Tom took a few more swipes and Rorie cringed.

"It was the intelligence we had. We were told you were a guy."

"Oh." She pressed her lips together. "I didn't know you were in the Army."

"Is that a problem?"

"No."

His head bent over the snake, but Tom peeked at her from underneath his hat. "You didn't even know my name."

"I should have asked." She rubbed her sore neck.

"I could have told you." Tom lifted his head and his gaze held hers. For a while, neither of them spoke, the remembered passion heavy between them.

"So, you're a Chief?" Rorie cleared her throat.

Tom went back to the snake. "Yeah."

"I never heard of a Chief. What rank is that?"

"Warrant Officer. It's a rank between the commissioned officers and the NCOs."

"NCOs?"

"Non-commissioned officers." He pulled the skin off.

"I see," she said, although Rorie really didn't. She knew virtually nothing about the military. "So what is it you do?"

"I'm the XO. I take over if the team leader goes down."

"XO?"

"Executive officer."

"Ah." She looked away before he saw the total confusion in her face. "You're second in command. Of a team." Gee, that sounded intelligent—not.

"Something like that."

She enjoyed the way his dimples appeared when he smiled, even if it was at something dumb she said. "And a team is?"

Tom looked at her, humor showing in the creases around his eyes. "Special Forces, ma'am. We're all in a team. Every guy has a specific duty, although we're cross-trained."

"Well, that part I guessed." Rorie blushed and looked away. "So what rank is the team leader?"

"A captain."

"I thought lieutenants were under captains?"

Tom shrugged. "They don't have lieutenants on teams. The captain's the only commissioned officer."

"Oh." Rorie crinkled her brows and sighed. "I guess you can see I have an extensive military background." She looked at him. "Sorry if I ask too many questions."

Tom actually laughed at that. "It's okay." He stopped working on the snake and his smile faded, something deeper showing in his eyes. "If you remember, I told you before I wanted to get to know you better. I assumed you'd get to know me better, too. You ignored me at the time."

His heady gaze arrested her. Rorie bit her lip. She remembered.

A sudden ache gripped her gut. One part of her wanted more from him than what they'd shared, another was afraid to take the chance. "How far away are we?"

"The extraction point is about nineteen clicks southeast of here." He chopped up the snake, putting the meat in a bag he'd pulled from his rucksack.

"Nineteen clicks? What's that in real people terms?"

"Kilometers," Tom explained as he cleaned his knife and stuffed the blade in his boot. Reaching for his canteen, he opened the container and dribbled a small amount of water over his hands. After putting the canteen away, Tom wiped his palms on his pants.

He studied her again. "You need some rest. Why don't you take a short nap? I'll make sure no more snakes bother you."

"Goodie. Then I guess we have enough to eat for the rest of the day, since I won't be used for bait."

He laughed again.

"Are you sure we don't need to keep going?"

Tom shook his head. "We'll make better time if you rest. The bird coming for us won't be at the rendezvous point until after midnight. We won't stay here long. Just don't get too comfortable in case we have to move quickly. In the meantime, the break will give me a chance to go through Ferguson's rucksack—and yours, if you don't mind. I'd like to get rid of anything we don't need—as well as find whatever Ferguson wanted you to go after."

"I thought we couldn't leave anything behind?"

"I'll bury whatever is excess. Besides, I need to hide the remains of the boa. No one will know we were here."

"Wow." She frowned. "Can we keep my cameras and film?"

"Probably." Tom pulled a poncho from his pack. "You can use this to lay your head on. Now, get some rest."

"Okay." Rorie handed him her camera case. "Here. Be my guest." Puffing up the poncho as best she could, she laid her head on the ground near him. "Wait a minute..." She bolted up.

"How stupid could I be?" She scooted next to him and took her bag back. "Chris gave me Mike's camera."

"Mike? Mike Harrison?"

Rorie nodded. "Chris' partner." She unzipped the main compartment. Finding the digital in the camera bag, she handed it to him. "With everything going on, I'd forgotten. Thing is, Raúl searched our packs. He was trying to find the card that goes into this, but I didn't have it."

Tom's brows furrowed. Opening the thin case, he pulled out the camera and studied the equipment a minute. Handing the digital to her, Tom fingered the case. "There's something hard in here." He turned the soft leather inside out. A small slit had been cut into the side near a seam. She wouldn't have seen the opening if Tom hadn't eased his fingertips into the tiny hole.

When he pulled his fingers out, he held a micro-thin card. Tom waved the digital recording in front of her. "I bet this is what the guerillas were searching for."

Chapter Six

ɞ

"Oh, my." Her mouth gaped open. Rorie lifted her hand to take the card, but Tom pulled it out of her reach.

"No," he said, and put the digitalized information back in the case.

Rorie held up the camera. "Don't you want to see why you went through all this trouble? I mean, really. You tramp through the wilderness then you get shot..." She held a hand to her mouth. "Here I am rambling and you haven't even looked at your wound, have you?"

"I was just getting to it." Tom took the camera from her and put it back in the case.

"But?" She pointed toward the digital.

"Whatever is in there is top secret. I'm sure you don't have clearance." He stuffed the camera in his pack along with the bagged snake, and dug for his first aid kit.

Rorie huffed with frustration over his decision, but she let her ire go. The man had just saved her hide. The information wasn't worth arguing about. "Let me." She unzipped her pack and pulled out a small kit of her own, trying to take control of her jangled nerves.

"I'll be fine, Aurora." Tom laid his hand on top of hers to stop her. "I'll take care of it."

"No." She needed to do something to help. All she'd done so far was run—or depend on Tom to carry her across the dangers. Not an auspicious beginning for someone whose main goal was to establish her independence. "I need to be useful."

"Okay." Tom nodded.

"You need to take off your shirt." Rorie licked her lips.

He brushed his thumb over her mouth. "Do you always do that thing with your tongue?"

She glanced away and fiddled with the first aid kit. "Only when I'm nervous." *Oh, God*. She hadn't meant to say that.

Tom leaned closer to her face, his hand scooping the back of her neck, massaging the small muscles he found there. "Are you nervous now?"

Rorie swallowed, thinking her body's immediate warm reaction to his caress proved she'd lost her mind. Here they were, missing in the jungle, terrorists at their heels and all she could think of was…

"Well?"

"Yes," she whispered.

He pulled her lips close to his. "Why?"

"Because…because of this."

She slid her arm around his neck and pressed her mouth to his, her tongue delving inside.

"God…" Tom pulled her against him and took over the assault.

Rorie broke away moments later and laid her head on the crook of his shoulder. "This is crazy," she whispered.

"Yeah." He rubbed her back. "I know. But I feel the same way."

Rorie straightened, reminding herself she had no time for a relationship. First, she had to figure out her own life—and *that*, Rorie needed to do on her own. Still, would there be anything wrong with seeing him in a sexual way again? "This probably isn't a good time to talk about our…attraction."

Tom thought there wouldn't be a better time. Except he was sure the talk he wanted with her would lead to other, more pleasurable, activities. "Yeah, you're probably right," he groaned, reminding himself their safety and the memory card was his first priority.

She grimaced. "Take your shirt off. I know your wound must hurt."

Little did she know. His worst pain resided in a place a mite lower. He hefted his rifle off his shoulder and laid it next to him. Her eyes followed his movements as he undid his top button. Her look made Tom hopeful Aurora would like the idea of spending more time with him. He wanted the opportunity to show her more of the intimate things they'd shared.

A corner of his mouth arched upward. Tom tried not to smile, but God she made him feel good. "We call this a blouse. It's part of my BDUs." Maybe if he talked he wouldn't have to think about his below-the-belt problem.

"BDUs?" Aurora glanced at him.

"Battle dress uniform."

"Oh."

As she looked into the small container she held, Tom threw off the blouse and his hat. He was in the middle of pulling off his T-shirt when she spoke. "Is this all right to use?"

He jerked the light material off his head and looked at her. Her eyes had widened and her breathing deepened.

He couldn't help but smile this time. Tossing the T-shirt on the ground next to him, Tom took her in his arms again, holding her breasts against his naked chest as he kissed her.

Aurora moaned before she eased back. "Your wound," she whispered against his lips.

"It never felt better." He kissed her again and she molded her body into his. "I like the way you treat your patients," he muttered against her mouth.

She giggled then used her palms to push him away. "Will this work?" She held a generic antiseptic, humor dancing in her eyes.

He nodded. "It'll do."

Aurora handed the antibiotic to him then ripped open a cleansing pad and scooted over to his right side, dabbing the wound. "At least it looks clean."

"Do you have some medical training?"

"Only first aid classes. CPR and all that."

Tom thought if Aurora didn't move away he might stop breathing. CPR would come in handy.

She wrapped the tissue in the container from which it came then took the salve from him. "Do you want me to put a Band-Aid on it?"

Her eyes turned light amber again. He knew more than she did about dressing a gunshot wound, but Tom relished the thought of someone taking care of him for once. "You probably need to."

Reaching over his lap, Aurora put the cream back and grabbed her kit. Getting what she needed, she knelt next to him, intent on finishing the job.

He put his arm around her waist and tugged her closer. "I still want you, Aurora."

To balance herself, she lifted her knee and placed it between his legs on the ground. Sitting on his thigh, she held some tape and gauze in her hands. The same desire burning in him shined in her eyes.

"I know." Her lips parted. Blinking, she peered at his shoulder and put the gauze on the wound, taping it down. "This should hold for a while."

Aurora wouldn't look at him and he didn't want to stop looking at her. "I'm sure it's fine." Tom closed the gap between them. She moaned as he kissed the soft skin of her throat. Tom continued along her collarbone until the small hairs on back of his neck straightened. "Shhh." He lifted his head. Looking around, he snatched up his rifle.

After pushing Aurora to the ground behind him, Tom swerved toward the rustling branches. A long nose poked through the brush. Then a larger, gray body pushed its way out, feeding on the undergrowth.

"A Baird's tapir," Aurora whispered. "Give me my camera. I've got to get a picture."

Crouching higher, she'd peeked over his shoulder.

Tom eyed her, thinking she'd lost her mind. "We're in the middle of a dangerous jungle and you want to take pictures?" He kept his voice low.

"It's my job," she whispered back. "Hurry," Aurora insisted. "He's leaving."

The hog-like creature walked along the edge of the small clearing, ignoring them while chewing leaves in the undergrowth.

Tom laid the rifle alongside him and dug into her pack. "This do?" he mouthed and handed a camera to her, taking up his weapon again. He'd been surprised the animal hadn't bolted.

Aurora took it and quickly snapped a few shots then inched closer. As the tapir returned to the woods, she scooted after him.

"Whoa." Tom jumped up and grabbed the back of her pants with his free hand, pulling her to him. "You're not going anywhere."

His quick reaction caused the tapir to rush into the jungle.

"Oh, now look," she said, keeping her voice low. Aurora slapped her hand against her thigh. "He left." She directed her frown at him.

"Aurora, your safety is part of my mission." Tom stood closer to her, trying not to be too loud, yet he needed to make his point.

"But, he's a baby," she insisted and pointed to where the animal exited.

"You got enough pictures," he whispered in her ear. "I don't want you lost in the jungle."

Aurora pulled her head back and glared at him. "You know how rare that animal is?"

"Not as rare as you're going to be if you're found by one of those guys who kidnapped you. I don't want you walking out on me again."

Her eyes deepened to a cinnamon. "What's that supposed to mean?"

"Nothing."

"Oh, no." She looped the camera strap around her neck and put her palms against his bare chest. "It means something."

Her touch inflamed his passion. "Fine." Tom cleared his throat. "Call it a Freudian slip. But you're still my responsibility. I have no intention of letting you get hurt." He pulled away and, laying his rifle down again, grabbed his T-shirt and slipped the material over his head.

"For your information, I can take care of myself."

"I'm sure you can. But my mission is to get you and that memory card to safety."

"And you always complete your missions." She planted her hands on her hips. "You told me that before."

Tom remembered. "Yeah." He stopped tucking in the thin shirt and just gazed at her.

Her look became a mixture of anger and want. "Tom, I'm not a mission. And I make my own decisions about things. You need to know I can take care of myself. I don't need someone telling me what to do."

When he didn't answer, she started up again. "I hope we have an understanding, because if we don't, we aren't going very far."

Tom opened his mouth to say something, but stopped. He figured she talked about him and her, not their trek in the jungle, but sometimes not saying what you think made more sense.

"You're very goal-oriented, aren't you?" she said when he didn't speak.

"Yeah. So are you from the looks of things." He grabbed the blouse, but stopped a second and stared at her. "Aurora, I want to get you safely home. That's my goal right now, and I intend to achieve it—especially since I hate it when I lose. Besides, the alternative sucks."

"Which is?"

To die. Although he didn't say that. "You want to stay in the jungle?"

She shook her head. "No. You think we'll get out of here?" Her voice grew edgy.

He nodded and donned the thick material. "As long as you do what I tell you." Tom knew that wouldn't go over well, but right now she needed to know he was in charge.

She licked her lips. "Look, Tom, we can talk about things, but I won't take orders, from you or anyone else."

"Stubborn." Tom buttoned the blouse. "That can be a good quality. I'll remember."

"You're not funny." She crossed her arms.

With her hair messed up, Tom thought she looked cute riled up. "I didn't mean it to be." He tucked the ends of the blouse in his pants.

"Look, not that I'm complaining, but throughout my life all I've done is listen to everyone else. I'm responsible for myself. No one else can do that for me. And I make my own decisions."

"Good." Tom hefted the strap of his rifle on his shoulder and walked over to her. "Then please make the decision to do what I ask."

"Why?"

She actually pouted, and damn if he didn't want to kiss her. "Because unless you're an expert on the jungle and jungle warfare I think it's best we trust my judgment."

Her rigid shoulders relaxed and she rubbed her temple. "Okay. Point taken."

"Look, if we're going to make it out, you need to work with me." He took her into her arms. "Don't get me wrong. I want you to make your own mind up about things. I said that when I first met you."

Aurora nodded. "You did. When you asked me to go with you."

He lifted her chin. "I'm glad you chose to come." He looked away for a minute, trying to think of what to say. "This is a hell of a time to romance a woman, so I'll just put it like this. I like you. I think you like me. I want to explore that."

She licked her lips.

Tom smiled. "You nervous again?"

"Yeah." She nodded. "You don't know what you're asking."

"Maybe not." He pulled her against him. "But that's the 'I want to get to know you' part. What do you say?"

She paused and fiddled with his collar. "Are you sure we shouldn't stick to unbridled sex?" The confusion in Aurora's eyes belied the flippancy of her comment.

Tom tried not to scowl. "We could, if that's what you want."

Her look grew pensive. "I don't know what I want. That's part of my problem."

He bent over and placed a gentle kiss on her lips then whispered, "Maybe your desires are something we could explore together."

"Somehow, I doubt it."

Tom thought she looked scared as she fingered his mouth. He kissed her again, letting his hands slide around her hips, his thumbs barely tucked into the waistband of her pants, his touch melding her hard against him. As Tom moved to the small of her back, he hit a small object hooked behind her belt. He eased his mouth from hers. "What's this?" He unclipped the object and held it up, immediately recognizing the locator.

Aurora looked at the unit. "Chris put that in my waistband when we were captured. I'm so used to it now I'd forgotten it was there." She bent to take a closer look. "What is it?"

"A locating device. I didn't realize Ferguson had the piece on you. I thought he'd have the instrument somewhere on himself. I'll at least give him credit for trying to get you out of this mess, dumb bastard."

"What do you mean? What happened wasn't Chris' fault."

"Like hell. He should have never gotten you involved."

"He thought we'd be safe."

"Yeah, my ass..." Tom cleared his throat. "Sorry, I shouldn't say that."

Aurora smirked. "I think you were more colorful when we were getting shot at."

"Yeah, well..." Tom shrugged. "I'm not perfect."

She laughed.

He liked it.

"I'm far from that myself," she said. "But the facts still don't change. I decided to go with Chris. I also decided to leave the helicopter and retrieve my pack. No one else is to blame for that."

"I'd bet Ferguson didn't tell you he was CIA."

"Well, no..."

"He shouldn't have brought a civilian into this."

She crossed her arms. "I still make my own decisions. Chris asked me to be his photographer. I decided to go along."

"Fine." Tom didn't want to argue with her. Instead, he spun Aurora around and returned the locator to her belt.

She glanced over her shoulder at him.

"It's a good place for it," he said and tapped her behind where he'd put it. "There's a few hours left on it. It might help." Remembering his duty, Tom glanced at his watch. "C'mon. I still want you to take that power nap."

He led her over to the poncho and made her lie down. In a few minutes, she went to sleep.

Tom looked through Ferguson's pack first and tossed most of the stuff out. Then he checked hers. He promised her they'd keep the cameras and film. Tom stuffed them in his ruck. He took out her passport and checked her wallet. Her driver's license gave an address in Fayetteville. *Good*. He'd copy it.

Then Tom pulled out a small sack of Kotex. Glancing at Aurora in her sleep, he wondered if she'd need them. Deciding it better not to ask—especially with the tension between them—he stuffed those inside his ruck as well, hoping at some point she would. They'd used protection, but nothing was foolproof. He figured her getting pregnant wasn't part of her plan, or his for that matter. Not yet, anyway.

Not yet? What kind of comment was that?

He stopped himself and rotated his sore shoulder, figuring Charlie's death had hit him harder than he thought. He'd started thinking again—a dangerous thing to do. Tom loved his job, but lately he wanted more from life. Maybe a good woman to come home to instead of an empty house? What had Garcia said? *Find a good woman, and you'll be lucky every day of your life.* Yeah, he wanted to be lucky.

He studied Aurora. She was the best woman he knew—not that Tom knew much about her, but hell, he knew more about her than any other woman. He liked her. Probably more than he should under the tense circumstances. His attachment distracted his concentration to the mission.

But she had heart. Aurora said she didn't know what she wanted, but hell, who did? He sure didn't at this point. He had too many things warring inside him. He'd die someday. That Tom knew. But would his death be because an enemy shot him or from old age? For that matter, he could be killed from crossing the street—

Or by a heart attack like his dad.

Tom frowned, thinking about the father who had been much more to him. Ben MacCallum had always been a stalwart man, an honest man who married his childhood sweetheart and worked hard to get Tom through school. Tom loved his dad, but, as a son, he'd let his father down. Tom was supposed to come home that weekend. His dad had asked him to. But Tom had too many things going on at the university.

Later, Tom got the call from his mom. He'd rushed home as soon as he'd heard, but the effort had been too late for him to do anything. Perhaps if Tom had been there, he could have saved his father. Somehow, he should have known his dad was sick.

Still, Tom did what he could to repair the damage his dad's absence made. Seeing what his father had left behind, it didn't take Tom long to decide what to do. To his mother's chagrin, he enlisted a few weeks later so his mom and his siblings wouldn't live in poverty.

After his father died, Tom decided he never wanted to fail someone again. He'd kept his promise to himself as best he could. He'd gotten Ben and Trisha through school. Maria had two more years. His mother and her Hispanic temperament were doing well. Teresa Maria Hernandez MacCallum still looked good for an older woman, and she contributed her wellbeing to her aristocratic lineage.

But Tom hadn't been there for his best friend, Charlie, either. And that bugged him. He and Charlie had gone through jump school together and ended up in the same unit. They stayed fast friends after that, even joining the SF teams about the same time. Then Charlie got transferred to another team.

Charlie's death proved how short life was. Tom had grown tired of living without something more than work. Thing was, what more *did* he want?

He glanced at Aurora's beautiful face and wondered if maybe she wasn't his answer. One night of passion and a fire had lit between them. At least he now knew she felt something, too. What, Tom wasn't sure, but the emotion was something she didn't want to acknowledge. He figured her last relationship had something to do with her response.

Tom brushed her cheek with his thumb. She looked like a sleeping princess—except for the bruises that had begun to show.

Which reminded him.

He took out his camo paint and a meal bar. When Aurora awoke, he wanted to camouflage her to help her blend in the jungle. She'd be easier to hide that way. He also didn't want to take the chance she'd see those bruises that had begun to show. There were some shiners.

Tom simmered thinking about the abuse she'd already suffered in her life. She didn't need another jerk slapping her around. And he'd been too late to stop it. Of course, there'd been no way to prevent it, but not being there for her still bugged him. A lot.

Scowling, he shoved the meal bar into one of his pockets. Aurora needed to keep her energy up. She could eat the bar along the way.

Tom glanced at his watch and kicked himself. They shouldn't have stayed this long.

Using his knife, he dug a shallow hole under a bush and buried everything. Then he went to Aurora and lightly shook her shoulder. "Hey, princess, time to get up."

She moaned and rolled onto her back. Blinking, she looked at him. "My father used to call me that."

"With a name like Aurora, I don't doubt it." He smiled. "Sit up a minute. I have a surprise for you."

She rose on her elbows first then pushed herself up the rest of the way. "I hope it's something good—and quiet. I don't think I can take anymore excitement."

"Hey, our day has barely started."

She groaned.

"Look." Tom shrugged. "All women like makeup, don't they?"

"Huh?" Her brows arched. "You're not going to give me a tattoo like the natives, are you?"

"No." He grabbed the camo grease and sat next to her. "This is better." He dabbed her nose. "I'm going to make you look like me. It'll only take a minute."

Aurora glowered. "Oh, goodie. As if I don't look a sight already."

"It won't hurt. Promise." He would be especially careful around the purplish hand marks on her cheeks.

Aurora closed her eyes to let him smear the stuff on her lids. "I bet this is great for the complexion."

Tom snorted, not wanting to say her face would probably break out. "Yeah, maybe it moisturizes or something."

She snickered, trying to keep her lips closed as he smeared paint over them.

Tom finished her face and her hands. Afterwards, he gazed at her neck. The vee in her shirt exposed the lightly tanned skin, plunging downward to imminent danger. He cleared his throat. Discretion, in this case, was definitely the better part of valor. "Here." Tom held out the paint. "I'll let you do your neck and, ah…" He pointed to her cleavage.

"Chicken." Aurora grinned and dipped her fingers in the different colors.

His knew his gaze smoldered. "Your khakis stick out. We'll put some streaks on them, too."

"So, I really *will* look like you." She'd finished with her neck and put some stripes of green and black across her chest then the front of her pants.

He watched her, knowing his below-the-belt friend would suffer. He would have liked to paint her front, but he was afraid the action would lead to something else. They'd already wasted enough time. "Stand up and I'll get your back." Tom took her hand and helped her. Dabbing some paint on her shirt, he worked lower, spending a little more time on her bottom than he needed. But, damn, touching her felt good. Finishing, Tom turned her around and nodded. "You'll do."

Aurora struck a sexy pose. "Now if I can do that 'you'll see me before you hear me' thing and learn how to shoot a gun, I can be just like you. I'd really find some adventure then, wouldn't I?"

"Maybe." He rubbed his chin, trying not to laugh. "Is that why you became a photographer? To find adventure?"

She nodded. "I wanted to experience life."

"Well, you can't say this isn't an experience." Tom put on his rucksack.

"This jaunt will be the capstone of my adventuring career — if we get out of this alive."

"We will."

"What happened to my bag?" Aurora looked around.

"I ditched it, but kept your cameras like you asked. You'll move faster without a pack." Tom glanced at his watch again. "We need to pick up the pace."

She gave him a two-fingered salute. "Yes, sir, Chief. Just point me in the right direction. I'll follow."

Tom pretended to frown as he adjusted the heavier ruck on his back. "I thought you didn't like taking orders." He picked up his rifle.

Aurora smiled. "Well, I *decided* you were right. For now, I'm following your directions."

He liked her persistence. "Good." Tom took out the meal bar he'd shoved in his side pocket, grateful he wouldn't have to argue with her. "Here." Unwrapping the bar, he handed it to her. "It may not taste like much, but at least it's something."

"Okay, Chief."

He shook his head and stuffed the wrapper back in his pocket. "Make sure you eat the whole thing."

"Aye, aye, Chief."

Tom pulled out his map and the GPS unit from his front pocket. "You're not in the navy."

"Oh."

"'Aye, aye' is naval jargon." He checked the data.

"I see."

"You're in the Army now."

"Got it, Sarge."

"That's Chief."

"I mean Chief."

"Or you can call me 'sir'." He smiled at her sarcasm.

"Got it—sir." Aurora grinned back.

He shook his head. She was right. With her disheveled hair and face paint, she looked a sight. And something about it stirred an emotion in him that had nothing to do with sex. He didn't just like Aurora.

He cared about her.

"By the way," he asked, trying to change the direction of his thoughts. "Do you know how to use a sidearm?"

She frowned. "I tried once. They scare me."

He sighed. "We'll have to work on that." Looking at the map, Tom studied the river crossing. There would be another bridge. "How long have you been afraid of heights?"

"It's more I'm afraid of falling." Her brows knitted.

He glanced at her and nodded. "We'll work on that, too. Soon."

"I don't think I like the sound of that." She planted her hands on her hips.

"You'll be fine." He thought Aurora looked worried.

"Well, just another goodie then. What fun we are having, being in the Army."

Tom smirked at her playfulness and folded the map, putting it back in his front pocket. "Let's go." He walked ahead. They still had a hell of a long way to go.

Steeling himself, he put his mission foremost in his mind. He needed to get Aurora and the memory card to safety. Hell, he *would* carry her if he had to in order to get to the extraction point in time. He couldn't fail her.

He glanced over his shoulder at the woman who meant more to him than he wanted to admit, and reminded himself—he would never fail someone he cared about again.

Chapter Seven

೫

Rorie hadn't really wanted to argue with Tom, but he needed to know where she came from. Her new life, her independence, was too important to her. She'd never let anyone control her again. Still, he'd been right. She was no expert in the jungle. And right now she needed him to get out of this mess. She'd decided that sometimes logic should overrule desire.

Thunder cracked overhead and Rorie stopped to see if it hit the trees. Globules of rain plopped onto her face. "Most excellent," she said, thinking the day would only get worse. She glanced at Tom. He held his gun in front of him as he marched along in his warrior way. She sighed. "Rain. Just what we need."

"Here." He stopped and fiddled with his bag, pulling out his poncho. "Put this on."

"But what will you wear?" She took the raingear. "Didn't you keep mine?"

"Yeah, but yours is blue."

"What's wrong with blue?"

"You see any blue leaves in this jungle?"

She grimaced. "Oh."

His dimples deepened as he gave her a moment to put the raingear on then he walked ahead. Rorie lifted the hood over her hair and watched his broad shoulders as he moved away. Tom was a strong man, in more ways than one. Besides his physical fitness, he had character. At least, he seemed to care about her welfare. Of course, she'd thought the same of Stephen when she first met him. Little had she known.

Rorie shrugged. So much for her judgment of men. Still, Tom had protected her, not hurt her, and she couldn't help but admire the sway of his backside as he walked the trail.

They had been going for several hours now, not speaking, just tramping through the jungle. It reminded her of some weird monkish order where the members took a vow of silence.

Except they weren't monks.

I like you. I think you like me. I want to explore that.

His words echoed through her head—frightening and exciting her at the same time. She did like him. Too much. With as much as she'd thought about him over the last few weeks, maybe she'd become obsessed. That wouldn't be healthy. But didn't Tom like her, too? Yet, she couldn't think of a good reason why a man like him would be interested in her.

Rorie studied him as he trekked through the brush, remembering how his hard body felt against hers. At least enjoying the sight of his physical qualities allowed her to think about something else besides what he'd asked her. Occasionally. Her mind wouldn't let her thoughts stay on just his body.

Maybe your desires are something we could explore together.

Her libido flamed every time she thought of what Tom had said. But he meant more than the physical. He wanted something to develop between the two of them, but what? She wasn't ready to get involved again. For one thing, Tom could be demanding. He had all the signs. For another, her self-esteem sucked. She still had too many dragons to wrestle, too many fears to conquer on her own. Another reason she chose to do the job she did. Her grandmother had told her to find her limits and exceed them, then do it again. *Learn to use your fear as a tool to make yourself stronger.*

Rorie still missed the soft touch of the elder woman's aged hands and the kind sound of her voice.

Another crack of thunder and the rain deluged them, pounding much harder. Her protector got soaked. She rushed to catch him.

"Tom?" She tugged on his arm.

He stopped and looked at her, a small rivulet running off his hat onto his shoulders.

"You're wet. Don't you think you should wear this?" Rorie pulled at the poncho. "I could wear mine. I mean, who else would be running around in these woods right now?"

"I won't take the chance they're still not trying to find us. They're used to this. They'll be moving. Trust me."

She didn't like that idea. "Won't you get sick, getting so wet?"

Tom pointed to the raingear she wore. "That thing keeps you dry only so long. Besides, the water's warm. As long as we keep moving, I'll be fine. Now, keep quiet. They can still hear us if we come up on them." He took off again.

She tagged after him, this time not happy about having to follow him. She didn't like the idea of terrorists still looking for the two of them.

In a few minutes, Rorie could hear water rushing in the distance. Her gut tightened. She wondered if they would have to cross another river.

Stopping, Tom turned around and lifted his finger to his mouth, telling her to be quiet. Then he moved her to some brush and had her hide within it. She decided to listen to him. After all, what did she know about terrorists?

"I'll be back in a few minutes," he whispered, leaning over to reach her ear. "No matter what you hear, stay put, okay?"

She nodded, trusting Tom knew what he was doing.

Rorie waited for a while, listening to the rain pattering on the leaves, wondering how long Tom would be, thinking she should have gone with him.

Minutes passed and the more the moments dragged on, the more her stomach knotted. Tom seemed to be gone a long time.

When the bush rustled and the limbs parted, her body tensed. Until she spied Tom. He waved to her to come.

"Next time, I go with you. Where were you? I thought something happened to you."

"Checking things out."

Rorie crawled out onto the muddy ground.

Tom helped her up, holding her arms when she stood. "You miss me?"

"Maybe." She scowled.

"Good." He lifted her chin with the crook of his forefinger. "You ready for another challenge?"

Rorie listened to the rushing water and swallowed. "Are we going over one of those bridges again?"

"Yep."

"Then, no. I'm not ready."

Tom sighed. "Aurora, I'm not giving you a choice. This bridge is a little different. It would be safer if you walked it yourself. We're in the open over the water. If someone sees us, you'll need to hurry."

She stood her ground. "You're being a little pushy, aren't you? What if I decide to go farther downstream?"

He scowled. "Then I'll pick you up and carry you. We'll miss our flight out of here if you mess around and I have no intention of us missing the bird. There isn't another way." He took a step closer. "The bridge is good. I've already crossed it. And the span isn't as long as the last one. Only about twenty feet. Both of our lives depend on you moving across as fast as you can. You can do it." He peered into her eyes. "I'll be right behind you."

She took an unsteady breath, knowing her options were limited. "Okay. But I don't have to like this."

"I didn't expect you would."

When he led her out of the undergrowth, the rumbling water got louder. Tom halted before he entered the opening, scanning the land and allowing Rorie to get a view of the bridge. She looked in horror at the intertwined maze of ropes strewn across the crevice. There were no wooden planks this time, only the ropes tied together to make a V-shape one could purportedly walk over.

She glanced at the white-water stream. The other fissure had been deeper by several feet. Still a good drop on one side, the water in this gorge moved much faster, spilling over a steep incline of rocks so that, in some ways, the motion made the stream look like a waterfall.

And then there was the bridge—if you could call it that. She gulped. "I can't."

"You can. Trust me, okay?"

She swallowed. "Trust is one of those things I've deleted from my vocabulary."

"You can add it back. Aurora, we don't have another choice. Look at the crossing as one of your adventures."

Trapped, and at the same time compelled to succeed against her fear, Rorie steeled her resolve. "I suppose you walk across the large cabling of rope on the bottom?" Did she squeak when she said that?

Tom nodded and slung his gun strap over his shoulder. "When I move, come quickly. I'll go over the ropes a few feet to show you how then let you pass me so you can go ahead. You're going to have to look down—just ahead of yourself—to check your footing, but try not to look at the water or anything else. Just focus on the main cable at the bottom. Slide your hands along the side ropes and don't let go of them. Use your instep when you walk across so the heels of your boots steady you. Understand?"

Rorie jerked her chin in a nod, water splattering around her.

"Ready?" he asked.

She shook her head no. "With all this rain, are the ropes slippery?"

"A little. But remember I'm behind you. If you lose your balance, I'll be there to get you. Just grab the ropes and move, okay?"

Her heart thumped in her chest.

Tom hugged her and kissed her temple. "Tell yourself you're going to do this, Aurora. Believe in yourself. You have nothing to fear. You're capable. Tell yourself you can."

She squeezed her eyes shut and mumbled, "I can, I can, I can, I can." Popping open her lids, Rorie looked at him. "It's now or never."

Tom chuckled before he darted across the open area to the bridge, running over the thick rope a few feet then stopping. "Come on." He turned to her and jerked his head toward the other end.

She went after him, but stopped abruptly at the edge, her insides hammering. "I can't do this," she cried.

"You can." Tom stretched his arm out and Rorie clutched his open fingers. "I've got you. Grab onto the rope with your other hand."

With a jittery grasp, she put a death grip on the side rope and walked onto the cable.

"Take another step and slide your hand along the rope."

Rorie looked into his face.

"You can do it."

She gave him an unsteady nod. Focusing on the cable, she slid one foot then the other and moved ahead. "Oh, God, the thing's wobbling," Rorie panted, her nails digging into the back of his hand.

Tom came to her. "It's supposed to. But the ropes aren't going to break. You won't fall. Trust me, Aurora. Please." His eyes implored her.

She hadn't trusted anyone in years. She'd been disappointed too many times, especially by Stephen. How many times had her ex promised her he'd change? Then in a few days or weeks, he'd beat her again. No, Rorie had learned the hard way the only person she could depend on was herself.

Except Tom had saved her three times already.

She studied him then looked across the way. Unless she wanted to stay and get eaten up by the jungle or captured and beaten, or worse, from the terrorists, she didn't have a choice. Rorie slid her boots across the wet rope until she reached him.

Tom slipped his arm around her waist and stepped around her. "Now go." He lifted the back of the poncho and tightened his hand around her belt. "I've got you. You're fine."

Having Tom at her back comforted Rorie. She slid her feet forward, refusing to pick them up, but she moved. As Tom promised, he stayed close behind.

The nearer they got to the center, the more the bridge swung. She stopped as the seesawing grew to a few feet on either side, her shallow breaths causing her vision to blur. "I can't."

"You're okay," he said.

"But I can't," she said, petrified.

"Don't say that." She felt Tom's strong chest against her back. "Tell yourself you can. C'mon, Aurora, we've got to move."

Rorie closed her eyes and swallowed, droplets splattering her face. "I can do this. I *can* do this. I can do *this*." She opened her eyes and took a step. "I *will* do this."

"Yes, you will," Tom told her. "You're strong."

"I'm strong." Rorie took another step.

"You're doing this."

"I'm doing this." She slid her feet more quickly against the cable.

"You're fine and safe."

"I'm fine and saf…" Rorie shrieked as her foot slipped off the rope.

Tom yanked her up and steadied her. "I have you."

She nodded.

"Take a deep breath. You're going to hyperventilate."

Her body quivered as she breathed in and out.

"Now, do it again. Give yourself permission to be brave. We're almost there."

If Rorie wasn't so scared, she would have laughed. "I'm brave?" she uttered strongly, the humor in the statement easing her tension a bit. She looked up. Less than half way to go. She moved faster, until Tom let her go.

She stopped. "What are you doing?" Rorie couldn't even glance over her shoulder at him. She stood frozen with uncertainty.

"You can make it, Aurora. Trust yourself."

Trust herself?

All of a sudden, she saw the truth in his statement. She didn't trust herself, either. Yeah, she'd come to rely on herself to get the basics done, but nothing else. She'd been more fearful of everything since knowing Stephen, all because she didn't think she could do whatever it was she wanted to do. In fact, Rorie realized, out of everyone, she trusted herself the least. Had her battered relationship done that to her as well? "Well, damn."

"Huh?" Tom came up behind her.

This time, Rorie did glance over her shoulder and nodded at him. "You're right. I *do* need to trust myself. I need to believe in myself again." Straightening her back, she lifted her foot and took a small step, then a bigger one. She inched along, her heart still pounding, but realized her only other choice was to give up.

She wasn't a quitter.

In minutes, Rorie reached the other side and hopped onto Mother Earth. "Oh, my God, I made it." She stared at her shaking hands.

Swerving, she jumped into Tom's arms when he stepped onto solid ground. Drawing her arms around his neck, she kissed him. "Thank you. I would have never crossed if you weren't there."

"No problem." Tom lifted her, wrapping her legs around him and walked into the safety of the woods.

"I did it," she said.

"I told you." His dimples deepened as he looked around. "Sweetheart, I hate to dampen your enthusiasm, but we need to keep going. Although, when we do stop, if there's time, I wouldn't mind continuing this." He probed the depths of her eyes.

She looked away. He wanted an answer—to all his questions, questions that asked a lot more than for her to spend the night with him. She didn't know what to say. With his encouragement, she'd conquered the bridge. But wasn't she supposed to be slaying her demons herself? She licked her lips.

"Nervous, again, huh?"

She took a deep breath and fingered his lapel. "Yes, but I'm brave and strong."

"Yes, you are." His lips moved closer to hers.

"I can do this."

"Yes, you can." His breath caressed her face. "The question is, do you want to?"

She gazed into his deep green eyes and knew the answer. "Yes."

His quicksilver dimples showed again. "Good." He lowered her to the ground. "Then we'll talk more about us later." He walked ahead.

"Right, Chief," she said.

Tom paused and she heard his soft chuckle. "Aurora, you're the funniest woman I know. Now, keep quiet."

Rorie smirked. The funniest, huh? She kinda liked that. As he trekked ahead, she watched him, hope and fear intermingling with her view of his derrière.

God was she confused.

* * * * *

Darkness encroached on the jungle and night sounds echoed around them. Tom figured the sun had gone down, but it was hard to tell between the overcast sky and the thick canopy. He pulled out the GPS unit and his map to check their position. They should be close. Good thing, because he didn't think Aurora could take much more, and he didn't want to march in this muck in the dark.

Mostly, he'd stuck to the trails, taking extra precautions—a risky move that kept them exposed. But he took the gamble to make up time, one that seemed to be paying off. He hoped the enemy's first priority had been to make tracks since the discovery of their base of operations, looking for another cover, especially since they couldn't come right after the two of them. Tom prayed they'd abandoned their search.

He glanced at Aurora and slowed, ensuring she stayed close, making certain she walked beside him. He didn't want to lose her—and he didn't want her to drop to the ground before he could catch her. The few times he cut through the undergrowth, Aurora had skidded on the rain-slicked jungle floor. She'd gotten muddy and wet. One time, she almost slid into the long, hard needles of a black palm. If she'd gotten those six-inch spikes in her, she would be hurting bad.

Aurora swayed and he grasped her arm. He'd pushed her—hard, stopping every so often so she could rest. Still, she hadn't complained. "You okay?" he asked.

She nodded and leaned on him for support.

"Another half hour, maybe," Tom said, holding her arm, afraid if they stopped again, he wouldn't get her going. "You hungry?"

She shook her head.

He'd given her small things to eat along the way, trying to conserve what they had. He only carried enough provisions for two to three days for one person and there hadn't been much in hers or Ferguson's packs. If the chopper didn't make it, he'd cook that snake in the morning.

He glanced upward and prayed the rain would stop. The onslaught had lessened, but if the downpour kept up, he knew the pilot would never take the chance and fly in this weather.

Thinking of their alternatives, he slogged through the mud until Aurora's hold on him loosened.

"No you don't." Tom grabbed her before she sat down.

"Can we rest? Just for a minute?"

He could barely distinguish the features of her face, but he could hear the desperation in her weak voice. "I'd rather not."

"I can't go any further." She started crying and he took her in his arms.

"It's okay. I'll carry you."

"You shouldn't have to," she blubbered softly. "I'm sorry. I'm such a liability. I should have never gone back for that bag. I should have told someone like Chris asked."

"You didn't know." He rubbed her back. "And it's too late to second-guess what you did now." Tom lifted her chin with the crook of his finger and brought her lips near his. "Aurora, we're going to get out of this. You have to believe that."

She nodded against his finger. "Okay."

"I'll carry you over my shoulder for a while."

She shook her head. "No, I need to take care of myself. You're right. We're going to get out of this. I'll be all right. I'm not going to give up."

God, he admired her determination. "Good." He found her lips with his thumb and kissed them. "We'll be there soon."

Tom locked his arm in hers and trudged on.

Somewhere along the way, the rain stopped. Twenty minutes later, after veering off the path, he found the target area. He halted just short of it, stopping in an area with plenty of cover just big enough for the two of them to rest. "We're here."

"Thank God." Aurora collapsed on the ground.

"Come on." He lifted her and, squatting, leaned her against the trunk of a large cativo tree. "Wait here. I won't go far."

She closed her eyes. "You'll have to teach me how to do this recon thing so I don't have to hide in the bushes all the time."

"Later," Tom said.

"Unless, of course, all you're doing is going out to pee." She yawned.

"Both, maybe." He stood. "Don't close your eyes."

"Yes, Chief." Aurora popped open one lid and smiled at him.

He wanted to kiss her again, but the action would be too distracting. Tom jerked a nod and spun on his heel, quickly covering the area. It didn't look like anyone had been around, but it was hard to tell with all the rain and the dark. When Tom returned, Aurora had fallen asleep against the tree where he'd placed her. He could hardly see her at this point. The night had finally come. "Hey, wake up, princess," he whispered and tapped on her shoulder.

She bolted up. "Huh?"

"It's okay. It's just me."

"Oh." She lifted her arm over her face and relaxed. "Sorry. I know you said not to fall asleep, but I couldn't keep my eyes open."

Tom sighed. "I'm going to set up a hootch so we can rest."

"A what?"

"A hootch. A small lean-to. But I need the poncho."

"Oh." She started to lift it off.

He stopped her. "Just hold it a minute while I create the support first." Finding a couple of usable long limbs on the ground, Tom slung his rifle over his back until he trimmed the branches and set them up so the poncho and the netting in his ruck would fit over them. The small, low-lying structure would be big enough so they both would fit and would provide them with some cover.

"Go ahead. Crawl in," he said, hearing her in the dark.

"How are we both going to lie in there?"

"I'll show you." Tom lifted the edge of the poncho so Aurora could move inside. When he crawled in after her, he adjusted his ruck so he could lay back on it comfortably and held his weapon to the side. "Now get on top of me."

"Get on top of you? Are you sure you don't have other ideas?"

"I assure you, darlin', my intentions are honorable." He took her in his free arm and helped her over him. Aurora's breasts were heavy against his chest. "Besides, I'm too damn tired for anything else."

"I know what you mean."

He smiled and kissed the top of her head. "I know you do. You did well today."

"You think so?"

He felt her head lift up, even though he was sure she could hardly see his face, it had gotten so dark.

"I know so." His lips searched and found hers. Tom kissed her then positioned his head back against the rucksack. "I don't know many who would have held up as well as you have. You're an incredible woman."

"Humph. I don't know about that." She laid her head on his chest.

"Why not?"

"Huh?"

"Why don't you know how incredible you are?"

Aurora lay quiet a moment. "I guess abuse does that to you."

Tom churned inside, wanting to beat her ex again. "Don't let him win, Aurora."

She spread her hands across his chest. He felt her nod an agreement against him. Then she shivered.

"You cold?"

"A little."

"Wetness can cause that. Here." Tom rolled to his unarmed side, taking her with him, keeping his weapon away from her. The action caused his banged-up shoulder to ache, but he didn't care. He wanted to protect her.

She cuddled next to him and Tom wrapped his arm around her, folding his leg over hers. "We'll need to stay close so our bodies keep each other warm."

Aurora rested her head on his biceps and fingered his face. "Hard to imagine getting cold in a tropical jungle."

"Yeah? We'll, believe it or not, I've known some guys get hypothermia."

"Really?" Her voice grew soft.

"Really."

Her hand rested on him and she stayed quiet a moment. He thought maybe she'd fallen asleep. "How much longer before they get here?" she said.

"A few hours. You should get some sleep."

"Are you going to sleep?"

"No. I'll stay awake and wait for the chopper."

"Then I should keep you company."

"There's no need. I know you're exhausted."

"And you're not?"

Tom snorted. "I'm used to it. Aurora…"

"Don't you think it's time you called me Rorie?"

He shrugged. "I guess. Why did you tell me your name was Aurora in the first place?"

Her breath warmed his neck. "Because with what we were doing, I thought Aurora sounded more…attractive."

Tom chuckled. "Then maybe I should call you Aurora all the time."

"Why?" Her soft panting caressed his chin.

He rubbed his face against hers. "Because I think you're beautiful all the time." He covered her open mouth with his. Aurora encircled his neck with her arm and lay flush against him. Her response excited him and his lower member hardened, making him forget how tired he was.

Until he felt a tear against his cheek. Tom stopped and fingered her hair. "Are you crying?"

She nodded. "Sorry." Her voice cracked. "I don't know why. It's just there's been so much."

Aurora had become tender, vulnerable. "Don't worry about it. It's been a long day. Get some rest."

She sniffed a few times. "Tom?" she whispered.

"Yeah."

"Will I see you once this is over?" The tiredness came through in her voice.

"You can bet on it."

"You know, that scares me—maybe more than crossing that bridge." She fingered his collar.

"We'll work on that."

"Why?"

Damn good question.

"Because..." He rubbed her back. "Something special happened between us. I want to know what it is, don't you?"

He heard her sigh. "With everything I carry around, you'd be better off staying away. Look what I've already gotten you into." She snuggled her cheek into his chest.

"Why don't you let me decide that for myself?"

For a while, she didn't answer. "I like being with you."

"Good. I like being with you."

"I might scare you off."

"I don't scare easy."

"I hope not."

Tom kissed the top of her head.

"Thank you," she said.

"For what?"

Aurora lifted her head and trailed kisses up his neck until she found his lips. He pulled her close and drank in her sweetness, capturing her mouth with his.

When she pulled away, she took off his cap and ran her hands through his hair. "For this. For staying with me. For being a friend."

Tom swallowed. "What did you expect?"

She paused. "I don't know. Stephen would have—"

"I don't give a damn about Stephen." He sighed and held her close. "By the way, is Lindsay your maiden or your married name?"

"Maiden, why?"

"Good."

She snickered. "If you met Stephen without knowing it, you'd probably like him. He's very charming. Charmed my mother off her feet."

"Then he should have married your mother." Tom cleared his throat. "Sorry, you don't deserve that. Neither does your mother."

She giggled. "It's all right. I know you didn't mean it."

"Why'd you marry a jerk like that?" he whispered, wanting to have taken back all the bad things she'd experienced.

"I didn't know any better at the time. He'd been a friend. Both of our mothers decided we'd be a good match. Our dads had similar business interests. What more could a young girl ask for than a good-looking, well-established husband to take care of her?"

"They married you off?" Tom hoped the shock stayed out of his voice.

"Not exactly. My parents made the suggestion. I went along with it. My parents were matched. They fell in love with each other eventually."

Tom cleared his throat. "'Similar business interests' sounds like you were brought up privileged."

"I was. Private girls' school and everything. Very conservative and old-fashioned. My family has money—not a lot, but enough."

"Not a lot is relative. Sounds like your family had more than enough." Aurora hadn't shown any signs of wealth. Would she reject him for having a simple life? "Chiefs don't make a lot."

Aurora lifted her head. Tom assumed to gauge his expression although he knew she found it hard to see his face. "I don't care what you make. I care what you are inside. I like everything I've seen so far." She rubbed his chest. "I think I told you before I gave everything I had to Stephen. And in divorcing him, I alienated my parents. You have a nice house and two vehicles. You have things. I'm just starting to get those again."

"Why did you do that, give him everything you had? You deserved to take everything." The thought she'd become destitute irked him.

"Because I didn't want my parents to know of the abuse—at least, not through Stephen's eyes. Everything would have been my fault and they would have believed him. I didn't want to tell them myself because I didn't want them to feel guilty for the kind of marriage they coerced me into having. And I didn't want to take the chance I'd be condemned by my mother because I didn't get Stephen to love me. I got tired of being judged, of being the inept person in our relationship. I used the money to pay him off so that he would leave me alone for good. It was worth the price."

"Jesú. No wonder you're confused about yourself."

"I should have told you I carry a lot of baggage."

Tom thought about what crap he carried around – Charlie's death, his father's. "We all have something, Aurora. I just know I want to be with you. I'm not sure of anything else. Just don't shut me out."

"I don't know if I can help it."

"Why?"

"Fear, I guess."

Tom smiled. "You got over the bridge."

"Only because you pushed me."

"Okay, then I won't let you shut me out."

"Tom, I need to conquer my fears myself."

"You don't need to do it alone."

"Why?"

"Because people need people. And friends help each other. In the army, it's called teamwork."

She laughed. "Oh. Sorry, Chief, I forgot I was in the army." She paused. "You have a way of putting things, don't you?"

"I'm trying." He didn't know what else to say. "Why don't you get some rest? You need it." And he wanted time to think. He pulled the crown of her head underneath his chin.

"Okay." Aurora sighed, and in moments he heard her soft, deep breathing. Tom covered her with as much of his body as he could. She'd told him she didn't know what she wanted and pushing her could create a challenge he wasn't ready to face. Still, if he let her run with her fear, where would he be?

Nowhere, that's where.

He didn't want that and he didn't think she really did, either. He wanted some kind of relationship with her. What, Tom wasn't exactly sure. A few dates, at least. If it seemed they were getting along, maybe have her move in with him. But would she want that? Or would she rather play the field, like her friends were doing? Would he help her and she reject him in the end?

Tom wondered about his own feelings, whether or not he was being selfish. He didn't think so, not if Aurora wanted the same thing, too. He just wanted her to give them the chance, not reject him out of hand. But how would he get her over the fear of building something with him? Especially knowing a relationship scared the hell out of him, too?

He looked up and said a small prayer, hoping like hell he could figure this out. Begging that the chopper would come to get them — soon.

Chapter Eight

‰

A fire crackled nearby. Rorie worked to open her heavy lids, patting the empty space where her protector and lover had lain. "Tom?" she murmured, her voice heavy with sleep.

"Over here." He sat a few feet from the small lean-to. His broad shoulders were slumped and he roasted something on some sticks over a small fire. Tom had pulled his hat over his forehead, but she could still discern his haggard face.

"What are you doing?"

"Cooking the snake."

Blinking, Rorie realized predawn had come. She could see his shadowed form, highlighted by the flames from the small pit he'd made. Tom wore only a T-shirt, his other, the blouse he'd called it, hanging on a pole he'd erected near the fire. "Where are they?" She started to panic. "Did we miss them?"

"No." Tom bent toward her and lifted the netting. "Come out and we'll talk."

That didn't sound good. "What happened?" She crawled under and came next to him, noting the hint of stubble on his chin, the dark circles under his eyes. The space they camped in was so small, she had to sit so their bodies touched.

"Sit down." He dropped the netting and nodded toward the ground. "Here." He handed her a piece of cooked meat. "Have some breakfast."

Rorie screwed up her nose and took a bite. "Mmmm. Tastes like chicken."

Tom grunted with half a chuckle. "It's nourishment. I want you to eat several pieces."

She stared at him. She didn't know if her stomach could handle that. "They aren't coming, are they?"

His gaze penetrated her. "The weather probably held them up. We'll wait a while longer. If they don't show, we'll have to move. The enemy is in the mountains. We'll go into the valley, back into Panama."

"Well, a lot I know. I thought we were in Panama."

Tom shook his head. "They took you to Columbia. Just over the border."

"Oh." She swallowed, fortifying herself for what might happen. "How long are we going to wait?"

"Not long. We'll see. If things stay quiet, we should be all right."

Rorie took another bite of the strange tasting meat. She wanted to cry again, but she wouldn't let herself give in to it. She could do this. She had to. "Do we get to talk?"

He nodded. "Yeah, sure. Quietly."

She licked her lips, wanting to know about this stranger who made her pulse race, who seemed to care. Whom she didn't know a thing about except she felt closer to him than any other man she knew. "How long have you been doing this?"

He shrugged. "Been in the Army for twelve years. Doing this the last six, almost seven."

She did a quick calculation. He must have been twenty when he signed up. "What made you join the Army?"

"Family."

"Your family made you?"

Tom smirked. "Not exactly. My mother hated the idea. But the Army appealed to me at the time."

"Why?"

He paused and studied her a minute. "My father passed away. My family had little money. Someone needed to support my mother and the rest of the kids."

"You were the eldest?"

"Yeah."

"Didn't you already have a job?"

He stared at her then rubbed his chin. "Not exactly." His gaze peered into her.

He wasn't very forthcoming. "And?"

"And what?"

"Well, what were you doing?"

"I was in college."

"Oh."

"The Army seemed like my best option."

"I see." Rorie nibbled on the meat. "You like what you do?"

Tom paused. "Yeah. Love it."

"Why?"

He took a deep breath. "It's important. What I do makes a difference, although most people don't have a clue. After you see the things I've seen, you count yourself lucky. Sounds corny, but you're glad you're an American. You're willing to fight to keep your freedoms — for yourself and your family."

Family? What family? She swallowed. Could he be married? "Do you have a wife, children?" Rorie bit her lip, almost afraid to ask, thinking that sleeping with a married man would be the sin of all sins she'd committed to date.

His dimples deepened until he had a full-fledged smile. "No kids of my own. Just my brother, Ben, and two sisters, Trisha and Maria. I've never married — or had any kids otherwise."

"Ah." The knot that had formed inside her with the idea eased. She hadn't thought he'd been married, but one never really knew. Look at the games Stephen had played.

Rorie puffed her cheeks, reminding herself she shouldn't care, but she couldn't help wonder why he'd never wedded. A good-looking guy like this? And nice, too. She cleared her throat. "Ever serious with someone?"

He shook his head. "Not really. Thought so, once. I was wrong."

"What happened?"

He lifted a brow. "Came home from a mission. She was in bed with someone else. Apparently, she didn't like to be left alone for any length of time."

"Oh." Rorie wished she hadn't asked the last question, but something inside her compelled her onward. "You, ah, lived together?"

Tom nodded, his keen gaze making her aware he studied her reactions to everything he said. God, she hoped her face didn't reveal too much—like how deeply she desired him, how much she thought of the two of them together. What a fantasy world she'd developed.

She looked away. His life was none of her business. She shouldn't want to care about him. She couldn't afford to. Already he took possession of her every dream. Now, being around him, well, thinking about the two of them during the day made her obsession with the idea worse.

Tom studied her a while. "You cut your hair."

"Yeah." Rorie fingered the ends. "I wanted a new look. You know, for a new me."

He nodded. "I like long hair. It's all right, I guess."

"Gee, thanks." She frowned, trying not to react to what he thought, yet glad he noticed. Then she remembered he had buried his hands and face in her hair the night they...

She cleared her throat. "It's still long." Rorie turned sideways to him, arching her back, barely able to grasp the ends. Before the cut, she could do that easily.

Tom glanced up, one dimple deeper than the other as he lifted a corner of his mouth. "Yeah, I see." His gaze captured hers, desire smoldering in his eyes. He took a deep breath and looked back at the roasting snake. "How much of a new you are you going to make?"

"I…" She hadn't really thought about it. "I don't know yet. I need to find myself again. The last few years have taken a lot out of me."

He nodded and looked her up and down. "I like the woman I met."

Rorie swallowed, unnerved by his scrutiny. "The wild one who picks up guys whose names she doesn't even know?"

He snorted, then the depth of his heady gaze intensified. "No. The honest one. The passionate one who could make a man want for more."

She bit her lip, breathless, his words soothing and stirring something deeper than her sensual desires.

"Don't change too much." His countenance softened. He looked away. "You have any more wild nights like that?"

"None." She smiled, glad to know he'd thought about the two of them. "You?" The question came out before Rorie could pull it back, but, God, she wanted to know. Like him, she needed to think that what they'd shared was special, although she wouldn't admit it to him.

He rotated a stick over the spit. "No. We left for Venezuela a few days later."

She hoped he didn't hear the soft release of her held breath. She didn't want him to know how good his response made her feel. "I left for Panama that afternoon."

"There are men in Panama."

His focus stayed on the snake, but she knew he wanted to know if she'd been with anyone else—the way they'd been with each other. Rorie sputtered, her ego wanting him to know the truth. "I wouldn't consider Raúl much of a man."

"Raúl?"

"The man you pulled off me. He was the journalist I worked with."

"Oh," Tom grunted. "What about Ferguson?"

"He's just a friend. Besides, I only tagged up with him the day before yesterday. He—"

She shook her head, still finding it hard to believe Chris was more than he seemed. "I didn't know what he did. I've known him for a while, professionally. I always thought…" she shrugged, "he was a reporter."

"It doesn't surprise me."

"Why?" The soothed, yet stirred need inside her ached to know where his thoughts were taking him, what he had in mind.

Tom frowned. "You've been through a lot. I just don't want to see you hurt. I wondered that night if you knew what you were getting into. I meant what I said then. You should decide things for yourself. Don't let your friends do that for you." He looked at her. "Or me, either, although I'll warn you now, I'll be trying to convince you of…" he shrugged, "things."

She swallowed, wondering what "things" he had in mind. "I will."

"Good." He went back to the snake. "Do you…"

"What?"

"Do you want to be like your friends? Finding a new guy every night?"

Rorie almost choked on her bite of meat. She stared at him a moment, catching a glimpse of his pained expression. Shaking her head, she looked away. "I needed to be with someone. Sally just took me out so I wouldn't sit in the apartment alone and mope."

A look of relief breezed across his face and she grew stupidly hopeful. "Why?"

He shook his head. "I'm trying to figure out why you left me that morning. You didn't have to, you know."

"Oh." She licked her lips and cleared her throat, wishing she could tell him she felt something for him, too. "Tom, I don't think I'm ready for a relationship with anyone."

"Why? Because of your ex?"

"Something like that."

"I'm nothing like him."

"I know." She fiddled with the stick of meat. "At least, I think I know. Obviously, my judgment about men sucks."

"I doubt that."

Rorie studied him. Even though she desired him, she'd decided last night when this adventure was over, she needed to stay away from Tom. She had the feeling when he decided to do something, not much could stop him from doing it. His good intentions could be her undoing, set her back from the independence she'd developed so far. If he decided to help her, then where would she be? She needed to defeat her dragons herself. No one else could be responsible for that.

Still, she couldn't forget the incredible night she'd spent with him. Tom obviously had a hard time forgetting, too. Would she ever find someone who could please her so again?

"I think you need to remember you didn't choose Stephen," he said.

"No, but I went along with the choice."

"But that doesn't have anything to do with your judgment of men. It has to do with you not listening to yourself."

Tom was right. She hadn't. She'd known Stephen had a temper. She had thought she could change him. Boy, what a mistake that was.

"Your clothes still wet?" He ate a bit of snake himself, a warm look in his eyes capturing her as he scanned her body.

"They're a little damp." She tried to still the need burning in her.

He nodded toward the pole, breaking the hold his look had on her. "If you want, I'll give you some privacy. You can hang your clothes here." Tom finished eating and dropped the stick in the fire. Rising, he grabbed the blouse and donned it. "I need to check our perimeter. I dug a hole behind that tree you can use to, ah... Well, you know. Your stuff is in my rucksack. I'll leave it here. If you could break down the hootch and pack it, I'd appreciate it." He picked up his gun, which had lain next to him. "I'll be a few minutes."

"What happens if the helicopter gets here and you're not back?"

"I'll hear them coming. Don't worry. Just hurry with that stuff in case we need to move. It's getting lighter. We'll need to put out the fire soon, but I'd like you as dry as possible."

"Check, Chief."

Pausing a moment, Tom smiled wistfully then disappeared into the jungle.

God, what was he doing? When Aurora arched her back to show him her hair, her breasts pressed against the buttons of her shirt. Tom thought the fastenings would pop, as much as her cleavage strained against the blouse. He must be crazy, otherwise he would be focusing solely on how to get them out of there.

Releasing a breath, he tried to concentrate on his task, but he'd grown tired. He'd stayed awake all night, thinking as much as waiting for the chopper. Wondering how he could help her, debating whether he should. Figuring he'd lost his mind, getting involved with a woman he could ill afford to have. Aurora wasn't the fun-girl-for-a-night type. Thank God, she didn't want to be. But Tom suspected she needed more permanence. Would she consider living with him?

He rubbed his tired eyes, thinking again, wondering if that was what he wanted. He'd been a sergeant the last time he cohabitated with a woman, still new in his career on a team. Almost asked the woman to marry him. It was an amicable breakup and he didn't blame her entirely. It wasn't as if he'd had a lot invested in the relationship. He'd realized then he was already married to the Army. A woman was merely a convenience. They'd had an agreement. She broke it. That was that.

Still, he wondered if he couldn't have something more. Captain Garcia found happiness with a faithful wife. Why couldn't he?

Wife? God, now what was he thinking.

Tom looked at the canopy, changing the direction of his thoughts, ideas he couldn't afford to think about right now. The bird should have been here hours ago. He was sure they weren't coming and the locator Rorie wore was probably dead by now. They had no choice but to move on.

He bit the inside of his cheek, taking inventory in his head of what they needed. He still had some ammo left. When they'd covered the captain's backside yesterday, he'd grabbed some extra from Brodie. But it still might not be enough. He also had the pre-designated escape route through Panama. Maybe the guys could find them from the exit plans before anything else happened.

If not, he and Aurora could make it to civilization, someplace where he could contact his unit. It would be tricky. If they got out of the jungle, they'd have to fit into the public, pretending to be tourists or something. Tom wished he had the radio. All he had was the headset he'd jammed in one of his pockets.

He scanned the area, mulling over the morning's conversation. Whether Aurora wanted to admit it or not, she liked him. She'd cared whether he'd slept with someone else, hadn't she? She'd sighed and her shoulders relaxed when he'd told her he hadn't. There was something between them.

He was too scared to guess what. But he'd be damned if he wouldn't find out for sure. He didn't like these odd sensations he'd been having—ones that made his life seem empty. He needed to resolve this for his own sanity. Figure out what these feelings were for sure. Aurora may not like it, but he wouldn't let her go unless he knew for a fact she didn't want him.

After making the decision, Tom cleared his mind and focused on ensuring they were alone, deciding he needed to cool it with her until they got to safety. They should have left more than an hour ago. But he'd enjoyed watching her sleep. She needed the rest. Hell, at this point, he did, too. Exhausted, Tom wondered how much good he would be for her now.

His ears perked at the muted sounds of rustling leaves. Stopping, he crouched and inched in the direction of the noise.

Conversation. Spanish. Soldiers complaining about their lack of comfort. Looking for two Americans.

The voices came closer.

Tom ducked into the underbrush, praying the delay he'd taken to let Aurora rest hadn't cost them their lives.

Rorie ran her fingers through her hair to unknot the strands then glanced at her broken and battered nails. After yesterday, no trace of the manicure she'd gotten in Panama City remained. She'd always kept her nails short because of her job, but she'd kept them neat, not caked underneath with dirt.

She wiped them on her pants and looked around. She felt weird—exposed, sitting half-naked in the middle of the forest. Rorie pulled out some mosquito repellent from Tom's pack and applied it liberally. Returning the lotion, she reached for her shirt hanging on the pole to check how dry it had become. The fire was almost out and she didn't plan to add any more wood to the embers. Hopefully, the helicopter would be there soon, but she wasn't counting on it. Something about Tom's behavior told her the good guys wouldn't be coming. She even took the locator device off and shoved it in her pocket. No need for it now.

She drummed her fingers on her lap. Rorie hated waiting. She hated feeling helpless and useless. Surely there was something more she could do?

She ticked off the few ideas she'd listed in her head. She'd already taken care of her morning ablutions and filled the hole Tom had dug, covering it up so he wouldn't have to. Then she'd tossed the sticks he'd used to make the hootch, shaking out the raingear and packing it in his rucksack, as he called it. Finding a clear pouch, she'd stored the cooked meat, too, thinking they could eat some later if they needed.

Rorie looked at his camouflaged pack and debated whether to pull out Chris' camera and take a peek at what secret had put them in so much danger.

She decided against it. "You don't have clearance, soldier. Remember, you're in the Army now."

And, God, so was he.

She wondered if she could live with what Tom did for a living. Talk about dangerous.

She kicked herself for even thinking such a foolish thought. That kind of idea meant she'd considered having a relationship with him—which would be totally out of the question. Hadn't she already decided that?

Rorie hummed to break the strong hold the idea of being with him had on her. The tune soothed her. "Besides, we still have to get out of the jungle," she said, interrupting herself. She wondered how they would accomplish that.

At least Tom would have an idea. She needed him to survive this mess—a problem of her own doing—and she felt guilty getting him involved. If she hadn't been so ambitious, so stupid to go back after Chris' bag, they wouldn't be in this predicament.

God, she could hear her mother now. "Aurora, I warned you all this nonsense would only lead to trouble," Rorie quipped. Then the quiet sound of her grandmother's voice overcame the doubt. *Rorie, dear, you were born to have a life. Don't let anyone else live yours for you.*

Her grandmother's faith in her had been the only thing that pulled her through the rough times. She sighed, missing the older woman.

Sniffling, Rorie fingered the pants she still wore. They were pretty dry, enough so she wouldn't take a chill. She wiped a tear from her face and glanced around, hoping to see Tom.

Loud screeches sounded overhead, breaking the stillness of her thoughts. She jumped and looked up. Howler monkeys pranced and hopped from limb to limb. "Where did you guys come from?" Monkey poop dropped on the ground in front of her. They were throwing their feces at something.

Then she heard movement in the distance. Listening to her gut for once, Rorie kicked the pile of dirt from the pit on the dead embers and stomped on it. After spreading some rocks and foliage over the top, the area appeared untouched. Grabbing her shirt, she knocked the pole down over the covered fire pit as a final touch. Throwing her shirt over her shoulders, she scurried into the brush, crouching underneath the heaviest part of the undergrowth.

Seconds later, two men in fatigues walked into the clearing, raising their hands to protect themselves from the monkeys' projectiles.

Good girl, Tom thought, almost making it back to camp before the guerillas walked through, getting there in time to see Aurora rush for cover on the other side.

The men maneuvered across the glade, stopping to fire a shot at the monkeys making so much noise over top of them, talking about women, saying something about a storm coming.

When the soldiers were far enough away, Tom moved stealthily toward Aurora, staying in the brush and coming up behind her.

She gasped as Tom put his hand around her mouth and turned her head toward him.

Recognizing him, Aurora relaxed. As Tom released her, she sagged against him, burying her face in his chest. He put his finger to her lips, reminding her to be quiet.

They remained frozen for several moments. He wanted to ensure the men had moved on.

After a while, he bent over and whispered in her ear. "Relax. We'll sit here a while. I want to make sure they're gone."

She grabbed his collar and yanked him to her. "Don't leave me again," she ordered, barely mouthing the words.

"I won't." He held Aurora and placed a sweet kiss on her mouth. Looking up, Tom scanned the canopy, waiting for the monkeys to move on, hoping the men wouldn't backtrack to find them.

Until he felt cold steel against his neck.

Chapter Nine

ಬಾ

"*Levántense*," the soldier demanded.

Tom looked Aurora dead in the eye, hoping she got the hint to stay put. Dropping his rifle, he turned slightly to cover his right side to retrieve the knife in his boot, lifting his left hand as if he'd surrendered in order to cover his action.

In a flash, Tom grabbed the barrel of the man's rifle and yanked him downward, slicing the rebel deeply behind the knee, causing him to buckle. Tom slit the man's throat before the soldier could utter a word.

Wiping his knife on his pants, Tom studied the corpse. The man was young, younger than what Tom had thought from the voice. Had the kid even turned twenty? With some regret, Tom shoved the blade back in his boot.

Picking up the rifle he'd dropped, he rose halfway and scanned the area, alert. The soldier appeared to be alone. Maybe the others were used to him straggling behind.

Crouching, Tom took what ammo he could see from the body and stuffed it into his side pocket. When he finished, he shoved the corpse into the underbrush.

Tom donned his rucksack and grabbed the dead man's rifle, looping it over his back. "Let's move." He picked up his weapon and looked at Aurora.

She'd turned pale, staring at the dead man underneath the brush. Covering her mouth with her hand, she started to retch.

"God, not now. We've got to go before they come looking for him." He yanked her up. "Now stay low." He pulled her along, letting her lose her breakfast along the way.

He cussed inwardly, thinking this was the most fucked mission he'd ever had. But it was his own damn fault. Instead of concentrating on the objective, he thought too much about Aurora and what he wanted to do with her. If he was going to get them to safety, he'd needed to think with the head on his shoulders, not the one below his belt. He'd have to concentrate only on getting them out, not how good she felt in his arms.

Committed to keeping her safe, he ran them harder, ducking under branches, jumping over fallen tree trunks. Tom angled southeast away from the enemy. They ran for several minutes until she tugged on him.

"I've got to slow down."

He nodded. "Not too slow, though. We need to keep moving."

"Okay," she panted, working to button her shirt. Even now, her cleavage affected him. He waited until she finished, regretting the lost view.

Then they ran deeper in the jungle until he felt they were far enough away. The area had thickened and they were going downhill. "We'll stop here." He needed the break himself. He'd been up the last thirty hours or so at this point. "Stay in the brush while I check our perimeter."

She shook her head. "No. I'm going with you. You can show me what to do."

"Aurora, you should rest."

"And what about you? I know you were up all night. Look at you. You're tired. When people are tired, they make mistakes."

She was right. He should have heard that guy sneak up on them. His laxness almost cost them, but she didn't know how to do what needed to be done. "I'm trying to protect you."

She planted her fists on her hips. "I know you are. Granted, we're in the middle of the jungle and you're more equipped to deal with that, but there are some things I can do. One, is to go with you. Two, is to stay awake while you get some sleep.

You're not invincible, as much as I'd like to think so at this point since it would ease my worries, but lying to myself would be stupid. I did that the first few years of my marriage. I'm never going to lie to myself again. Now, you can either take me with you to check the perimeter, whatever that is, or I'll follow you to make sure you don't drop in your tracks. I don't care which."

He bit the inside of his cheek to prevent himself from laughing. "You rebelling?"

"No." She crossed her arms. "Just making up my own mind about things."

"I see." After putting the safety on the dead guerilla's rifle, he held it out to her. "Here. You might as well get used to carrying it, since you want to pull your own weight."

"But…" She lifted a finger, looking him in the face. A hint of laughter showed in the upturned creases around his eyes. She'd told him she was afraid of guns. He was testing her.

Fine. She could take a challenge. She did the bridge, didn't she? And it wasn't as if she would shoot the dang thing. She lifted her chin. "Okay." She took the weapon and looked at it a minute, trying not to shake. "Why'd you take his gun, anyway?"

"I've already used a lot of ammo. I might run out before we make it through. It's an insurance policy."

"But you took the bullets. Isn't that enough?"

He shook his head and took the thing back. "This is an AK-47. It uses different ammo than mine. That's why I needed the rifle. See this?" Tom pointed to a handle on the side. "Leave this alone. I have the safety on so it shouldn't fire."

"Okay." Rorie nodded. "What's your gun called?"

A corner of his mouth rose. "My rifle? Normally, I call her Betty, but I'm thinking about naming her something else. Officially, it's an M-4, modified for SF use." He handed the AK-47 back to her.

"You name your gun after a woman?"

"Most guys do, if they decide to name it. I'm from the old school. I still do. And it's a rifle, not a gun. A gun is something else."

She arched her brow. "What's the difference?"

He looked at her a moment. "Never mind."

Rorie wondered if she should press the issue. Deciding against it, she studied how he carried his weapon. "Can I just sling it over my shoulder?"

Tom nodded. "Sure. Since you don't know how to fire it, yet. I'll show you how to use it when we get back." He started to walk off.

"I can pull a trigger," she said, miffed, falling in step behind him.

"There's more to shooting a weapon than that, and I really don't want you hurting yourself or accidentally shooting me in the back." He stopped and turned to her. "Or on purpose for that matter."

She paled. "I would never do that."

He lifted her chin with his hand, stroking her cheek with his thumb. "I know that," Tom said. "I was just joking. Now keep quiet. And step where I step." He turned and walked on.

Rorie followed, stretching to put her shorter legs in his footsteps.

In about twenty minutes, they were back in the space where they'd started. She wasn't sure what they'd accomplished except they didn't see anyone. He dropped his pack and sat then pulled out the map and GPS unit.

"What are you doing?"

"Revamping our escape route."

"We had an escape route?"

"Yeah. We set an escape before the team hit the ground. If we stick close to it, they might find us along the way."

When Tom looked up, a lock of hair flipped over his forehead. The sexy, rough look he had started her thinking of things she'd tried hard to avoid.

"I see." Rorie took a deep breath, working to change the direction her thoughts took. She studied him. "Maybe I should look at your wound? You probably need a new dressing on it."

And doctoring him would give her a chance to touch his magnificent body again. *Ouch.* Why'd she think that?

Tom shook his head. "I already took care of it this morning while you slept."

"Oh." Rorie calmed herself, thinking it was better this way. Here they were in the middle of the jungle trying to survive, and what does she think about? Sex. *God, Rorie, what an idiot you are.*

She concentrated instead on the movements of his fingers on the instrument, her mind wandering to how those fingers had caressed her. She kneaded her arms, trying to forget.

Tom rubbed his tired eyes.

"Don't you think you ought to get some sleep?" she said.

He glanced up. "I will as soon as I set this. Do you think you can keep watch well enough?"

Rorie nodded. "Tell me what to do."

"You'll need to use your ears as well as your eyes and stay quiet. I want you hidden, too."

"Okay."

"You see, hear or smell anything, get me up. Even if you suspect something, wake me. Anything."

"I understand. Are you going to set up that hootch thing?"

Tom shook his head. "No. Takes too much time. I want to be able to move if we need." He crawled underneath some growth and made a rudimentary bed. "Give me thirty minutes then wake me. And I mean only thirty. There's a storm coming, but I don't know when it'll be here."

She looked around the upper canopy, trying to see the sky. "How do you know?"

"I heard some of the soldiers complaining about it. Sounds like a big one, though, and I want better shelter by then."

"You understand Spanish?"

"Fluently. Portuguese and French, too. Thirty minutes?"

"Gotcha." Rorie sighed, focusing her mind on her new task. "You know, I thought they had you back there, since you didn't return right away."

Tom stopped making a bed and eyed her a moment, an intense look she couldn't interpret. "I won't let you down, Aurora. I promise you'll get out of this, even if I die trying."

She knew he meant it. She licked her lips and whispered. "I don't want you to die."

A corner of Tom's mouth lifted. "I have no intention of letting that happen. I've got too many ideas with you I want to work out." He sat and patted the ground next to him. "Come over here and keep me company."

Holding the gun in front of her, she slid into the brush and snuggled her back against his large body. "Are you still going to teach me how to shoot this thing?"

Looping his arm over her, he covered the opening with some leafy limbs to hide them. "I'll tell you the basics, just in case. We won't actually fire it. Don't want to give away our position." He lay on his back, resting against his pack. "Remember. Thirty minutes." He lifted his head. "Your watch is still working, isn't it?"

She nodded. "Thirty minutes. Got it, Chief."

He chuckled and closed his eyes. In moments, she heard his deeper breathing.

Moving slowly, Rorie laid the gun she held down and turned toward him. His rifle rested on his other side in front of him. She studied his face, the cut of his chin. God, Tom MacCallum was handsome. How could she have found someone like him?

She placed her head on his chest, lying next to him, putting her leg slightly over one of his, dreaming that maybe they could have something together, too, some strong emotions telling her not to give him up. She'd have to analyze that.

Tom put his arm around her, interrupting her thoughts. Rorie lifted her head to look in his face. "I thought you were asleep," she whispered.

One dimple peaked. "I was. With you so close, it's hard to accomplish that."

She tried to back away, but he held her next to him. "Tom, maybe I should leave you alone."

He opened his eyes and peered into her face. "Don't. I want you near me."

She swallowed, curious as to what else his statement meant. "Promise me you'll get some rest? I'm not starting the thirty minutes until I know you're asleep."

He chuckled softly. "Demanding. I can see life with you will be interesting." He closed his eyes again.

"Tom."

"I'm sleeping."

"Closing your eyes doesn't count."

"Now is not the time to argue with me, Aurora." He opened one eye and peeked at her. "You keep talking, and I'll find something else for us to do." Opening both eyes, he stroked her face. "I want you. If we're going to get out of here, I really can't think about that right now."

She licked her lips. Little did he know how much she desired him, too. "Okay." Rorie sighed. "Get some sleep. You have thirty minutes."

"Make that twenty-five."

"What?"

"We've already used five. I mean it, Aurora. We need to move soon."

"Okay." She relented, figuring an argument with him right now would only cut into his rest. Talk about stubborn.

"Stay awake," he ordered.

"I will. I'm not tired. Promise, Chief. I'll be a good soldier."

A dimple showed again and Tom closed his eyes.

She looked at him for the longest time, watching him sleep, wondering if maybe she could do this thing with him—some kind of a relationship, whatever their togetherness would be. But it scared her.

Her grandmother's words came into her head, again.

Learn to use fear to make yourself stronger.

Mamie had urged her to get beyond her anxieties, not let her insecurities cage her. Beyond anything, Mamie wanted Rorie's life to be Rorie's own.

Dear, you were born to have a life. Don't let anyone else live yours for you.

She looked at Tom. Would she let her fear stop her from finding happiness? Could she really find love with this man? Rorie had lived alone for two years. More, if she counted the times Stephen stayed away.

Biting her lip, she realized, maybe the time had come for her to take up the challenge to her heart.

* * * * *

Another gust blasted over the treetops. Rorie looked at her watch. There were still four minutes to go before she needed to wake Tom, but the viciousness of the wind worried her.

She licked her lips.

Another blow hit, stronger this time. "Tom." She nudged his shoulder.

He jumped, pushing her into the ground as he covered her, his gun ready.

"We're okay," she whispered, rubbing his back.

He sagged. Lying on top of her, he took a deep breath. "Sorry. I should have told you to be careful waking me. A guy gets a little edgy under these circumstances."

Tom eyed her a moment and she thought he would kiss her. Instead, he rolled to the side and looked at his watch.

"I woke you a little early," she said as another gust blew. She looked up. "I think the storm's coming."

He nodded. "I'm glad you did. Stay here a minute." Moving over her, he left the small copse and crouched in the lighter part of the brush.

He took a few moments to look around then Tom held his hand to her. "Come on."

Rorie picked up the gun she carried and slid from underneath the branches.

Tom helped her up then pointed to the AK-47 she held. "Keep that available."

She frowned. "Maybe I'll call it George."

He snorted and bent to reach for his rucksack. "I guess that's fair."

"You know any Bettys?" she asked.

"Nope."

"Then why'd you name your gun Betty?"

"It's a rifle." He stood, adjusting his pack on his back.

"Okay, rifle."

"I liked the name. It was simple." Tom stood closer to her. "But I'm thinking of changing it to Aurora."

"Oh." She licked her lips, thinking of some way to change the subject. "Why don't you call that thing a gun?"

Tom smirked. "Because in old-school boot camp, they drilled in our heads a gun had something to do with the lower male anatomy."

"Oh." Heat seared her cheeks. And here she thought she'd tried to change the subject. God, she'd never make that mistake again.

"Here." Tom took her weapon. "As I said before, this lever controls the firing. Right now, it's in safety mode. Click it down one, it's on automatic. Click it again, it's single shot. God forbid you'll need to use this thing, but if you do, go ahead and put the control on automatic since I'm sure your aim could be improved. And hold the rifle with both hands, settling the butt of the stock against your shoulder. This weapon has a kick but you should be okay. Just don't drop it. If you do want to aim, hold the weapon up and look through these crosshairs, okay?" He pointed to the vee-shaped piece of metal on the barrel. Checking the safety, he held the rifle out to her.

Instead of taking it right away, Rorie wiped her palms against her legs. "Okay."

"Use it if you need to. I mean it, Aurora. These men will kill you in a heartbeat. Just make sure I'm out of the way."

She stared at the rifle and nodded. "I will." Grasping the weapon, she slung the strap over her shoulder.

God, he wanted to hold her. But he couldn't. He couldn't afford to think like that until he got her home. He'd screwed up too many times already. Taking a deep breath, Tom stood and marched on, wishing someone would be here to kick him in the butt and make him concentrate on the mission.

Instead, he made a promise to himself to keep his hands off Aurora until this was over.

He glanced at her, her hair disheveled, the paint he'd put on her face smeared. She looked a mess, and something about her tousled appearance allured him even more.

Sighing, Tom looked away, and hoped like hell he could fulfill his promise to get her to safety.

* * * * *

The storm raged around them, the wind gusting with such strength Rorie needed to stop sometimes and hold on. Every time lightning struck, she would jump, the thunder cracked so loud. They were both soaked, even with Tom's poncho she'd put on.

"We're going over that rise," he shouted. "There's a rock outcropping there, maybe some caves if my notes are right. I'm hoping we can find shelter there."

Rorie nodded. They moved forward, slogging through the mud, working their way up a steep incline. Tom had told her he didn't want to go this way because the altitude exposed them more to the elements, but the path was better than getting trapped in a flash flood or mudslide in the valley. And this way was shorter to Panama.

Another light flashed—close this time. The boom made her ears ache. Covering them, she failed to watch where she stepped and slipped, hitting her shoulder on a large boulder. She tried to steady herself, but the effort made her slide farther.

Rorie screamed as she bumped along the rocky ground, landing a few yards down.

"Oh." Her whole body ached as she pushed herself to her knees.

"Let me help you." Tom rushed to her, steadying her as she got up. "You okay?"

"Fine."

He frowned. "You've got some good scratches." The poncho had flipped up and he pulled at some loose fabric on her upper arm where a rock had ripped her shirt. The rain washed the blood away from the deep cut.

"Yeah." She glanced at her sore palms then pressed her hand down against the gash in her arm.

He jutted his chin toward the ridge. "Walk ahead of me. I'll catch you if you fall again."

"That isn't necessary." It had been her own stupid fault for not paying attention.

"Just do it, Aurora. I'd rather not argue now."

She huffed, thinking his overprotective behavior would be her undoing. It certainly tried her patience, especially under these circumstances. "Tom, I'm fine."

He looked at her and jerked his thumb up the hill, telling her to move.

Rorie bit her lip, upset with his demanding behavior. She wasn't one of his soldiers and she'd be damned if she'd follow orders like one. Hadn't she already warned him?

Another bolt of light struck, this time hitting a tree not too far away, the electricity arcing and burning a circular path down the trunk.

Deciding this wasn't the time for a good fight, she hurried up the mountain.

When the two of them reached the ridge, they ducked under a low overhang.

"Stay here," Tom ordered. "I'll look around."

"I can do that too," Rorie insisted.

"Just stay here," he commanded and took off.

"Ooooh." She gritted her teeth. "That man still doesn't get it."

Not five minutes later, he came back. "We're in luck. There's a cave deep enough we can get out of this wind."

He helped her up, holding her arm and hurrying her to the entrance.

She stepped through as another bolt of lightning briefly lit the dimness. The cave veered to the right and burrowed into the rock, providing a broad niche and rock wall to protect them from the pounding rain.

Grateful, she shivered, the wetness finally getting to her.

"C'mon." He entered behind her and tugged her arm toward the cozier interior. "There's firewood. Someone's used this place before."

Entering the oval chamber, Tom dropped his pack. He slung his rifle over his shoulder and took out a flashlight, pointing the beam to the middle of the room. "See, there's even a fire pit. The cracks in the wall near the top must provide the ventilation."

Rorie looked upward and saw water seeping in through the small slits in the upper corner.

Tom looked at her and cleared his throat. "We should stay until the storm passes. With those winds, I have the feeling we might be here a while. I don't think we've gotten the worst of it yet."

"Fine," she spat.

"Ah, you should get out of those wet clothes, too. And I want to check that gash in your arm."

"I can do that myself."

He paused. "You're mad at me."

Rorie put her hands on her hips. "That about sums it up."

"Why?"

She crossed her arms. "Did it ever occur to you I'm not an invalid? Neither am I an idiot."

When Tom frowned, his brows knitted. "What makes you say that?"

"What? How about the way you've been treating me? Go here, do that. You know, even if there's something you think I don't know, you could show me. Then I could get something to take away from this mess."

"Aurora, I'm only trying to protect you. You're part of my mission. It's my job."

She huffed. "I am *not* a mission. I am a human being. And I can take care of myself, thank you very much."

He frowned and knelt in the dirt. Putting the flashlight down, Tom took out a small container from his rucksack. "I'm too tired to argue the point now. If you want to do something, you could make a fire." He handed her the waterproof container that held some matches. "I'll leave the ruck and flashlight here."

"That sounds an awful lot like an order. I am not one of your men."

Tom's gaze examined her from head to toe and back again. "No, you certainly aren't. I'll be back in a minute."

"And just where are you going?"

"Out. To pee. Is that okay?"

She licked her lips. "Fine."

"You need to go?" he asked.

"No."

He stared at her a minute. "Aurora, we're both tired. I don't want to fight."

His softened voice took away her angst. She rubbed her head. "Just don't tell me what to do anymore."

Tom frowned. "I can't do that. Not yet. I have to get you out of here, first."

"What if I don't obey your commands?" She crossed her arms.

The muscles in his jaw tensed. "That's up to you. But if it's a safety issue, I won't give you a choice. I'm going to get you out of here whether you work with me or not."

She rolled her eyes, and held up her palm as if to stop him. "Fine. I know. I'm a mission. Got it, Chief."

He frowned. "You know you're more than that to me."

Rorie turned her back on him, not wanting him to see the humongous tear rolling down her cheek.

He came behind her and wrapped his arms around her. "We've both been through a lot the last few days. I'm worried about you, okay?"

"Why? You hardly know me." She turned in his arms and watched him swallow.

"I know enough. I care about you. Can't that suffice for now?"

"Maybe." She laid her head on his chest and slid her arms around his waist. "You scare me."

"I don't mean to."

"I know." She looked at him. "It isn't your fault. Part of it's me. I'm trying to discover who I am. I can't do that with someone who's going to constantly tell me what to do."

Tom looked away, trying to think. God, he only wanted to keep her safe. "Can we work on this?"

"Maybe." She pressed her lips together. "Why are you so overbearing?"

"I didn't think I was."

"You probably wouldn't." Rorie gave him a weak smile, remembering he'd only gotten less than thirty minutes of rest. A debate about his behavior now wouldn't be fair. "You're right. We're both tired. Maybe now is not the time to talk about this. Go to the bathroom."

He paused. "I was really going to check the area."

She let her head fall against his chest and laughed. "Okay, soldier. Go do your job. I'll see if I can be useful."

He nodded and left.

Rorie watched him go, studied his tall form, his strong presence stirring her.

She looked away, trying not to think about how his body felt against her. He was exhausted. He was trying to protect her. Maybe she shouldn't be so hard on him? Perhaps she overreacted. Control was a big issue for her.

Leaning the rifle she carried against the back wall, she picked up some kindling lying in the corner of the room. She placed the wood chips and some larger pieces in the fire pit and lit them. Rorie didn't want to make it too big. She didn't know how well the ventilation worked.

Still, a larger fire would be better in order to dry their clothes.

Pausing, she ruminated on that thought. The best way to dry them would be to take them off. Hadn't he said as much?

And he'd mentioned they would be there a while. Tom said he wanted her. God knew, she wanted him. She needed his warmth right now, the sense of safety and comfort lying in his arms would provide. Her grandmother had told her to live her life. At this rate, they might be dead tomorrow. Somehow she didn't want that to happen before she made love to this magnificent man at least one more time.

She made up her mind. Going to Tom's rucksack, she pillaged through it to find her blue poncho. Taking it out, she laid it near the fire then stacked some wood close to the pit as well.

Removing all her clothes, she spread them across the wood she'd piled and laid his poncho out to dry.

Getting some medical stuff, Rorie sat on her raingear and wrapped part of the plastic around her legs, trying to ward off the chill. Opening the first aid case, she pulled out some antiseptic. Her bleeding had stopped, but the cut could reopen. She started to apply the ointment, until she felt someone else in the room.

Looking up, Tom stood there, staring at her, heat in his eyes.

"You told me to get undressed." She smiled at him as she put some salve over her wound then covered the scrape with a bandage.

Tom's gaze wandered over her and his mouth slightly parted.

Rorie laid the salve aside and straightened the poncho over the ground, exposing her body fully to him. "Now it's your turn."

Chapter Ten

ഇ

I'm a dead man.

Tom couldn't take his eyes off her. God, he wanted to touch her, yet his promise to stay away kept beating itself into his head. He watched her breasts rise in the glow of the firelight. The nipples peaked so hard they looked like they ached for a mouth to caress them. His mouth.

Aurora licked her lips, her eyes hungry. What made him take such a stupid oath?

Her safety.

And that was more important to him than laying her down and finding the warmth in her body. "That won't be necessary. I'm fine." He looked away, saw his poncho laid out before him near the fire. Maybe she meant for him to sit there?

He glanced her way again. With the look she had, he didn't think so.

"God." Looking away, Tom groaned and plopped down on the empty poncho. Laying his rifle to his side, he tossed his hat on the pile of wood she'd put her clothes on.

"I'm trying to get that to dry," she said, pointing to where he sat.

"It'll be all right." Tom lay down, exhausted, and studied the rock crevices in the ceiling to get his mind off her.

"Tom, you need to get out of those wet clothes before you get sick. What good will you be if that happens? I certainly can't carry you out of the jungle."

She paused. He eyed her from his peripheral vision.

One of Aurora's dainty brows arched directly at him.

Tom quickly closed his eyes.

"You said yourself we'll be here a while," she said, continuing the assault. "The wind's picking up. Sounds like hurricane force to me. At best, we're in a tropical storm."

"You ever been in a hurricane?" He made the mistake of looking at her.

"Yes." She raised her brows, smug with her response. "Now get your clothes off or I'll take them off you."

"I won't let you." He closed his eyes.

"You won't have a choice when you're sound asleep. And it's drier over here."

He looked up. She patted the area next to her. "Come on."

Tired or not, his lower member pulsed in his pants. "Aurora, I think its best we're not naked together." He looked away, concentrating on the cracks in the rock.

"Why? It isn't like we haven't been before."

"That's the point. I don't think I could stop at just holding you. I'd rather not tempt myself."

She licked her lips. "What if I don't want you to stop?"

Her breathy voice made a gulp of air catch in his throat. "Aurora, I don't pack condoms with me. What would I have to protect you with?"

She huffed. "Do you have something I can catch?"

"Hell, no." He sat up straight.

"Then stop trying to protect me. All I want to do is take care of you instead of you taking care of me. Besides, what good are you going to be if you get sick? You need rest and I'm cold. I thought we'd keep each other warm. I'll make sure you don't get too amorous if that's what you want."

Tom closed his eyes and laid back again, his tortured body in pain. He heard her rise to come toward him then felt her unbutton his blouse. "Aurora…" he warned.

"Just go to sleep. I can't imagine how exhausted you are at this point and still you're trying not to show it. At least let me do something." She undid the last button and reached for his sleeve. "Can you sit up so I can take this thing off?"

He sighed and opened his eyes. "You aren't going to leave me alone, are you?"

"No." Humor danced in her face as she undid the button at the cuff.

Huffing, Tom sat up. Looking away, he unbuttoned the other sleeve and yanked his blouse off. She laid it over some of the wood she'd set up.

"T-shirt." Aurora held out her palm.

He gazed at her breasts then closed his eyes, almost ripping the cloth as he pulled it over his head. "I'm not taking off my pants."

She giggled, putting the T-shirt with the blouse. "You can keep your underwear on, if that'll make you feel better, Chief."

He stared into her face. "You're asking for trouble."

"No, I'm not." She bent over, unbuckling his belt. "You're soaked."

"Aurora."

She unbuttoned his fly.

Tom put his hands on her shoulders. "Aurora," he whispered.

She slid her fingers into the back of his pants and pulled downward. "What?"

He wanted to tell her to stop, but he couldn't find the words. "My boots. I need to take them off."

She lifted her head, her mouth inches away from his. Her eyes turned golden and she smiled. "I'll get them."

Sitting, he watched her struggle with the wet laces. It took her a few minutes, but she got them off and, with his socks, put them near the fire.

"Your pants, Chief."

She knelt near his feet, the contours of her body highlighted by the flames. He soaked in the sight. She was beautiful.

"Your pants?" She arched a brow at him.

Sighing, he lay back and lifted his hips to take the fatigues off then handed them to her as he sat up again. "The underwear stays on."

She grinned as if she'd just won a battle. Maybe in a way, she had. "You are one good-looking man, Tom MacCallum." She put his pants with his other clothes.

Tom frowned as he watched her firm buttocks bend over the woodpile. "I'm glad you appreciate it."

"Oh, I do. Trust me." She sat on her heels next to him. "Now, are you going to join me over there so this one can dry? I am cold. When this one dries, I want to cover us with it."

For the first time, he noted the goose bumps rising on her arms. Tom looked in her face to avoid gazing at her full breasts. "No sex. We'll just keep each other warm."

She frowned. "Have you all of a sudden taken a vow of celibacy?"

"No." *Not what he wanted to say.* "Yes. I mean..." He released a pent-up breath. "Look, Aurora, I want you in more ways than one. But most importantly, I want to see you safe. If I think about you this way," he ran a hand through his hair, "we'll never get out of here."

"Hmmm," she purred. "Sounds promising."

"Aurora." He used a look that had warned many men in the past. When she placed her palms on his shoulders and looped her leg over him to sit in his lap, Tom knew she wasn't buying any of it.

She pressed her breasts against him, her soft bottom stirring his erection. "Come and keep me warm or I'm going to seduce you. Then you *will* never get me out of here."

He gulped. Sighing, he let his head drop against her breasts. With a will of titanium, he forced himself not to take each of her nipples on his mouth. "You win. Go over there and let me calm down."

With deliberate movement, she brushed the vee of her bottom across his erection and, lifting his chin, nibbled on his lower lip as she kissed him. "Thank you." Rising, she left for her side of the fire.

Tom looked at her, lying there like the queen of Bohemia in all her splendor. He couldn't take it. Bolting up, he went out of the chamber to take care of his need in private, resting against a corner of the other room.

Rain spilled horizontally through the opening chilling him, the darkened chamber bursting into light when the lightning struck.

"I could do that for you."

He heard Aurora speak from the opening to the inner sanctum, her lair of seduction, if his summation was correct.

"God, woman, you're killing me."

She came to him and touched his back, her fingers spread, caressing as they brushed around his torso and went lower.

He didn't say a word as she pushed the thin cotton covering him out of the way and touched his manhood, his need rising, drowning out the sound of the storm. Tom braced himself against the wall, his body tense as she moved her hands over him.

In minutes, the tightness in his body released. He listened to his own panting as he grew spent.

"Feel better?" she murmured against his back then kissed it.

"Yeah." His voice sounded rough.

"Now maybe you can sleep," she said, releasing him and straightening his drawers.

His breathing ragged, he looked at her. Aurora's eyes held more than passion. She cared about him, too. He was sure she did.

Encouraged, he lifted her in his arms. Carrying her across the threshold to the next room, Tom laid her on the dry poncho, not caring what would happen next.

She wanted him. For now, that was enough.

Rorie fingered the cross hanging from the chain of his dog tags as she lay on his chest, his arms holding her against him. He'd made love to her. Differently this time. He didn't want to penetrate her, didn't want her to get pregnant if she wasn't ready for that. He just didn't want to hurt her. Still, he'd made her come.

How different he was from Stephen. Stephen would have taken everything she'd offered and then some. Some sense of honor held Tom back.

His deep green eyes watched her, studied her every move. He wanted more than physical intimacy from her. Strangely, she needed more from him as well, but she didn't want to define the emotion. Still, he'd asked her not to shut him out. Right now, she didn't want to.

"Have you always worn this?" Rorie asked, breaking the stillness of her thoughts as she outlined the intricate etching in the sacred symbol.

He nodded. "Always."

"Catholic?"

"Yeah. Both sides. My father was Scottish, my mother Puerto Rican. You?"

"Presbyterian. Descendants of British bluebloods, both of them. What's your family like?"

"Close. Crazy. My brother, Ben, is an investment analyst. He was named after my dad. He's doing pretty well. Trisha was married last year. She has a Bachelor's in nursing. Maria has two more years in college, but she's yet to pick a major."

"You saw them all through college?"

"Yeah. I helped. They got student loans, a few small scholarships. It worked out."

"You're the eldest, why was your brother named after your father, not you?"

"I was named after my maternal grandfather, Tomas Alexander. Mom wouldn't have it any other way. After that, Dad made sure he got into the act. He didn't think a Hispanic first name sounded right with a Scottish surname, so he had to approve of everyone else's."

She giggled. "They loved each other, didn't they? Your father and mother."

"Yeah." His voice sounded distant, broken. "When my dad died, it really broke Mom up."

"What happened?"

Tom shrugged. "Dad had a heart attack. Apparently, he'd been sick for some time, but he didn't want me to know. He wanted me to come home that weekend, but I had other things to do, although now I don't remember what. He'd died before I got there."

Rorie studied Tom. He held something in. "You feel guilty about it, don't you?"

He stared at her and nodded. "If I'd known, I would have been there. Maybe I could have done something to stop it."

"You don't know that."

He clenched his jaw. "No. But I feel it."

"You can't help what happened." She brushed her fingers along his cheek.

"Maybe not." He rubbed her back and held her closer. "But I can't help thinking I could."

She sighed against his chest, glancing at the rifle he'd laid next to them, pondering what he said.

"What about your mom and dad?" Tom asked.

Rorie looked at his face. He needed to sleep, although she didn't think he'd admit it. "They met in college. I guess they liked each other right off. They socialized in a small group. Both of them agreed with the match when their fathers proposed it. Like I said, they eventually fell in love. Mother said she had to work at their relationship. She was proud of that. She thought I needed to do that with Stephen. She likes to run my life. Thank God, I had my father's mother. My grandmother never believed in arranged marriages. She encouraged me to break away, rebel. I finally have."

"Have you?" He eyed her, his look delving, searching.

"Mostly," she admitted, her voice a whisper.

Tom pulled her head to him and kissed her. "Good. Because I want more with you, Aurora, and I don't think I'm in your social class."

"I don't have a social class." Her gaze flicked over him. "What more could you want?" She could barely hear the question herself.

He studied her a long time before replying. "Something. I'm trying to figure it out. All I know is right now is I want you in my life."

Didn't she want that? "Okay," Rorie said, a sense of freedom and satisfaction overcoming her. "But no promises."

He smiled. "I'm glad you agree. I wouldn't want to get pushy and you get mad at me."

She chuckled. "Just don't tell me what to do."

"Mmmm. You said that before." He kissed her again then ran his hand through her hair. "You're beautiful."

"I'm glad you think so. Don't you think you should get some sleep?"

"Not yet. I like the feel of you in my arms."

"I'm not going anywhere."

"Yeah, but I don't know how long we can do this."

Talk about stubborn. Nibbling on his chest, Rorie moved across it until she came to his arm, kissing then tonguing the tattoo. Pulling back, she fingered those figures, too, examining the eagle and the wolf, reading again the banner joining them. "Brothers," she murmured. "This must mean something. I wondered about it our first night together."

She studied his face. Tom's pupils widened, the dark green of his irises deepening, making his eyes look almost black. Some mixture of emotions flittered across his face.

His Adam's apple rose as he swallowed. "It's for my best friend."

"Mmmm. Which one are you? The wolf or the eagle?"

He grunted. "The eagle. My friend was always more grounded than I was."

"I see. So what does he do?"

Tom paused a minute. "He was killed in combat six months ago. I'd released his ashes over the Smoky Mountains the night I met you. It was his final wish."

His confession took her by surprise. She didn't know what to say. "I'm sorry." She stroked his cheek with her fingers, thinking on the charge of emotions the night their meeting had brought.

He shook his head then kissed her palm. "Not your fault." He smiled grimly. "But meeting you eased the pain." He rubbed her back. "I'm glad we got together."

Rorie nodded and focused on the tattoo, not wanting to admit she was glad they met as well. "What was his name?"

"Charlie. Chief Hartman."

"He was a chief, too?" She glanced at him.

Tom pressed his lips together. He nodded this time. "We went through basic together."

"Basic?"

His dimples deepened. "Boot camp. First level of training for a soldier."

"Oh."

"Anyway." Tom sighed and stared at the ceiling. "Charlie and I fought together. Was on my team until he finally went to Warrant Officer School and got his own. A terrorist in the Middle East shot him. Charlie died alone. No family. We knew what each other wanted. For our burial."

He glanced at her and looked away again. "I was on a mission then. The Army had him cremated by the time I got back. I took the ashes until I could deal with his burial. Spread them over the Smoky Mountains like he'd asked."

His eyes looked glassy. Sliding over him, Rorie kissed him, the touch of her lips soft, her heart going into it, wanting to comfort him, not able to understand how deep his pain dwelled. The only person she'd ever lost that she'd loved was her grandmother. But she'd been sick a long time.

Tom's thumb stroked her cheek. "I needed you that night."

"I'm glad I was there for you." She kissed him again and rested her head on his chest, thinking of what she could do to ease his torment. "You're not alone, Tom. You have family. Friends."

"Yeah." He looked at the ceiling while he ran his fingers through the locks of her hair. He'd grown distant, as if he'd fallen deep in thought about something.

She didn't know what else to say. "Why don't you get some sleep? I don't think any bad guys are going to look for us for a while."

He took a deep breath and stared at her. He opened his mouth to say something then stopped and nodded, looking at her.

She smiled. "You need to close your eyes to sleep."

"Ah. But I can't help looking at you."

Rorie pretended to grimace. "Sleep first. I'll be here when you wake up."

"Naked?"

She nodded. "If you want."

Tom snorted and closed his lids. "I'll dream about that. If the storm slows, wake me." He popped open one eye. "And don't leave this room unless you have me with you."

"Hmmm," she said. "Overprotective to the end."

He huffed. In moments, he fell asleep.

She snuggled against him, the room quiet now except for the crackling of the flames and the storm raging outside.

Rorie thought about how much pain he'd gone through, about how much he'd done to help his family. Tom MacCallum was an unusual man.

She glanced at the rifle beside him, and wondered if what he did in the army wasn't a reflection of his pain, his attempt to protect the ones he loved from leaving him.

* * * * *

A loud bang jolted Tom from a solid sleep. With rifle in hand, he bolted up, still groggy, his eyes adjusting to the dim room, looking for the enemy.

Aurora walked through the entrance, carrying some wood, the tails of her shirt flapping around her from the stiff wind blowing through.

He released a pent-up breath, lowering the barrel. "I thought I told you not to leave the room."

She halted when she saw him. "We were getting low on firewood. There are plenty of small pieces being blown through the entrance. A bunch of leaves, too. I thought I'd pick some of the wood up and let it dry." She dropped the load near the fire.

"I could have shot you."

Aurora eyed him a minute, some emotion crossing her face. "You didn't."

He ran a hand through his hair, realizing she'd put his poncho on top of him. "You should have woken me. With this wind, what if you were hurt?"

"I wasn't. I was careful. And you needed the rest. You were right, though." She sauntered over and sat next to him by the fire. "We're going to be here a while. It's hurricane season. I suspect we might be in one. I'm glad you found this place."

Tom glanced at her meager attire. She only wore the shirt. "I thought you were going to stay naked?"

She rubbed his arm. "It's colder away from you."

Laying his weapon on the ground beside him, Tom lifted the poncho. "Then maybe you should crawl in with me?"

Aurora eased underneath. He covered her as she snuggled next to him. "You should still be sleeping."

Another bang sounded in the outer room. "How can I do that with all this noise?"

"The tree limbs and debris are hitting the cave entrance." She leaned into him. "You hungry?"

"No, but I bet you are."

She frowned. "No. I ate some more of that gross-tasting snake."

Tom stroked her cheek. "Good. I don't want you to starve. Although we'll need to conserve unless I go hunting."

"Yum. I wonder what other delectables you can find. Maybe some of the poisonous frogs they have. Can you eat those?"

"No." He nuzzled her neck. "There are always grubs, if we get desperate."

"Oh, yea. My fav."

He chuckled. "You're funny."

"I'm glad I have some redeeming quality."

"There's a lot about you I like."

"Like what?"

"You're beautiful."

"Great. So I can seduce you easy enough. At one time, I probably wouldn't have been able to do that."

"What are you talking about?"

"I gained a lot of weight when I married Stephen."

"I'm sure you were still beautiful."

"Doubtful."

"Why are you talking like this?"

Aurora frowned. "It's just I can't seem to do anything right around you. I can't get over a bridge without you, you won't let me help with anything, and I can't even go get firewood without you complaining."

"I commented. It wasn't a complaint."

"Sounded like one to me."

He sighed. "I went to sleep thinking you'd stay put and anything coming through that opening would be dangerous."

She eyed him a minute. "You didn't tell me that."

"I told you not to leave without me."

"That doesn't tell me what you thought. It would have helped if I'd known that. Then maybe I would have woken you."

"Why didn't you just do what I asked?"

"I told you before. I'm making up my own mind about things. I don't need you to tell me what to do."

He bit the inside of his cheek. "Aurora, until we get out of here, I'd appreciate it if you'd do what I say."

"Not if what you say doesn't make any sense."

"Aurora."

"No."

"Dammit." He cursed under his breath.

Aurora moved to pull back, but he wouldn't let her. "Don't go. Please," he whispered.

"You're scaring me." Her eyes darted away from him.

Tom released her immediately and she backed away, sitting on the edge of the plastic bedding.

"Why?" he asked, keeping his words soft, calm. He could have kicked himself for losing his temper.

"Why what?" Her breathing had grown erratic.

"What did I do to scare you?"

"Nothing." She looked away, hugging herself, shaking.

"Does my cussing bother you?"

"It isn't that so much, as…" She shrugged. "I don't know."

"My cursing wasn't exactly directed at you."

She glared at him. "It sounded like it."

Tom swallowed. "Did Stephen yell at you before he hit you?"

She nodded, hiccupping over the tears she worked to control.

"I may say things from personal frustration, but I won't hit you or try to hurt you. Ever."

Aurora looked at him, her eyes wet. One drop rolled down her cheek and she licked it off as it hit her upper lip. "I know it's perfectly normal to get frustrated, even to curse. I do it. But when you get upset, I'm oversensitive. Now you see the kinds of problems you're asking for. How can you think of having a relationship with me when I have so many issues?"

"Why?"

"Why what?"

"Why are you oversensitive when I get upset?"

She wiped her face. "None of your business."

He sighed. "I can help you if you let me."

She shook her head. "Don't you understand? There are some things I need to do on my own. It's my problem. This is why something more than sex between the two of us won't work."

"Don't give up now just because this happened."

"Why should you care?"

"Because—" Hell, he hadn't had time to examine his feelings, but he suspected he already knew.

Tom ran a hand through his hair and sat up. "I do. You're a brave woman."

"One who can't take care of herself."

"That's not true."

"Isn't it? You think I'd get out of here alive if it wasn't for you?"

"This is different." He touched her hand, wanting to hold her, but afraid the contact would push her away, not bring her to him. "You've been through more crap these past few days than most people will ever go through in their lifetimes. You're not only doing it and surviving, you're doing it with a sense of humor. Don't be so hard on yourself."

She looked at him a while, assessing him, shivering. Tom could tell she thought about what he'd said.

"We're working this together," he urged. "What about when you stood watch while I slept?"

"That didn't take much."

"No? You were right. I needed to sleep before I fell over. What if I was alone and exhausted and the boa found me instead?"

"You would have probably jumped up and ate him alive." She sniffed and bit her lip, the corners of her mouth twitching upward.

Tom smiled. "You know better. I can't do this without you, either. You're cold. I promise I won't bother you. Come here and let me keep you warm. Good soldiers get rest while they can. You should sleep, too."

"No. I am not one of your soldiers and I know you're disappointed with me."

He grimaced. "I know you're not a soldier. You're an intelligent woman perfectly capable of making up her own mind. But right now, we're in a situation where I'm better equipped to make the decisions. If it means so much to you, you can be in charge when we get home."

"In charge?" She laughed. "Of what? I already control my own life, thank you very much."

"I'm talking about whatever happens between you and me."

She quirked her brow. "What makes you think there will be something?"

Tom paused. "I'm going to ask you out. It'll be up to you whether or not you go."

She stopped fuming a moment. "You won't push?"

He took a deep breath and listened to the storm outside, thinking. "I'll try not to."

Aurora stared at him a minute. "Tom, I meant what I said. I need to defeat my own dragons. I can't do that with a domineering man around."

"All I ask is that you let me help." He lifted the poncho. "Please don't shut me out. Not yet."

She licked her lips then came to him. "You wouldn't really balk if I made a decision on something?" She cuddled into him.

He covered her up and wrapped his body around her. "You stick around long enough, I'll prove it to you. Of course, I still may not agree—especially if you decide we shouldn't be seeing each other."

Her cinnamon eyes studied him. "You really want me to?"

"To what?"

"Stick around."

He nodded. "Yeah." And he meant it in more ways than one.

The crackling fire and the gusting winds took up the moments of silence. After a while, her tension eased. She rolled over and pushed her body flush with his, her sweet behind lying against his hips.

"Tom?" she murmured, her voice thick with sleep.

"Yes."

"Stephen pointed a pistol at me the last time we argued. I knew at that point I had to leave."

Tom froze. "I didn't know it was you until you walked through."

"I know." She rolled onto her back, her breath warm against his chest. "Even when you pointed your rifle at me, something inside told me you wouldn't shoot. You think that would be more upsetting than our argument, but it wasn't. I don't know why. It's part of what I need to understand about myself. You make me mad when you get so demanding, but I've always felt safe with you. Even now, it's just... Maybe it reminded me of too many things. I want you to know that." She'd closed her eyes. The firelight created a golden glow around her face.

"Thank you." He held her, treasuring the feel of her.

"Mmmm." She half opened her lids, her eyes shimmering. "For what?"

Tom stroked her face and placed a chaste kiss on her mouth. "For trusting me."

She fingered the dimple in his cheek. "You're welcome."

"Get some rest."

Aurora nodded and closed her eyes. When she stopped shivering, he was pretty sure she slept.

He watched her breasts rise, wondered why he couldn't think to tell her just now of all the incredible things he'd thought about her. The fact she was funny, caring, sensitive. She was more than beautiful outside, she was beautiful inside, too. That he loved her.

Oh, God. He finally admitted it. When did that happen?

Tom stared at her for the longest time, reflecting on the direction his mind had taken. He did love her. He wanted to protect her from anyone who would harm her. And he wanted to beat the crap out of that bastard ex of hers. No wonder pistols scared her.

She said she had demons to defeat. He wanted to help. That was the problem. She didn't want him to. Still, he admired her independence and tenacity.

Then there was the intimacy, the closeness he had with her. Tom had never had that with another woman and he wanted it, needed it like a drug.

His mind raced, trying to find an answer, a way to solve the dilemma between them. How could he make her see they could do this together? That he could help?

Without being overbearing.

He thought about that. He could do it if he had to. And he did have to. If Tom pushed too hard, she would run. She wanted to do this herself. How could he help her to do that?

Sighing, he lightly kissed Aurora's forehead so she wouldn't wake then picked up the cross he wore and rubbed it, praying.

How could he gain more of her trust?

Chapter Eleven

80

Rorie woke to the smell of dirt. Opening her eyes, she realized her nose lay near the edge of the poncho. She rubbed the tip to brush off the smudge of earth she'd gotten on it and scanned the room. The fire had died to a few embers. Fully dressed, Tom sat on the ground at her feet, watching the entrance, his rifle in hand.

She stretched. "What time is it?"

"Early morning. I'll get you some breakfast and then we need to march."

"I can get my own breakfast."

"You know how to make an MRE?"

"What's an MRE?"

"Meal-ready-to-eat."

"You mean I don't have to gnaw on the snake?"

He lifted a brow. "I ate most of it. I don't think it's going to keep."

"Okay, no. Then I don't."

"I'll show you the first time. You'll be able to do it on your own after that." He paused a moment. "You know, taking care of yourself in a jungle involves training."

She sat up, letting the poncho slip to expose her torso. "So you're going to train me?" She smiled.

Tom rubbed a hand over his jaw, his stare roving between her breasts and her face. "I'll do what I can."

"Thank you." Rorie knew she beamed, grateful he'd given up at least that much. Showing her what to do would help him as well as her, since then she could do things for herself and he wouldn't have to worry about her all the time. Like what he'd said about teamwork, right? Although she wasn't sure he saw things that way. "What's it look like outside?"

Tom shook his head slowly and glanced at the entrance. A smile tugged the corners of his lips before he spoke. "A mess, from what I can see. The debris from the storm partially blocked our exit. I cleared some of the mess away. I hope this thing hit the forces following us. That would be nice. At least it would throw them some curves and buy us some time." He rose. "Get dressed. I'll give you some privacy."

"Why? What are you going to do?"

"Make sure no one who cares is out there." Tom studied her body a while.

Rorie knew she tempted him. "You sure you don't want to wait until I'm dressed?"

His dimples broke out again. "Positive. I'll be back in a few. Be ready." He turned and left.

Rorie sighed and rose quickly. Tom was right. They needed to leave.

After donning her clothes, she packed everything then sat in the dirt to look through Tom's rucksack. The gash in her arm looked better this morning, but she redressed it anyway. After spraying some bug repellent, she rummaged through the sack looking for the MRE things. Instead, she found hers and Chris's cameras. It hadn't hit her until now that she should have taken more pictures. My God, here she was, a photographer, and she'd lost a great many opportunities.

Her digital was smaller than her other camera. Making sure it had a card, she shoved it in her back pocket then studied Chris's camera. Biting her lip, she wondered if she could just take a peek.

"Maybe you ought to give me that." Tom held out his hand.

She jumped. She hadn't even heard him come in. "I didn't look at anything," she protested and slowly held it up, eyeing him, noticing he'd repainted his face.

"No," he took the proffered instrument, "but you were thinking about it."

She blew a puff of air. "Well, what do you expect? Here I am carrying around all this top secret stuff, being an unwilling participant in some undercover operation, and I have no clue what this is about. Not to mention, our lives are at risk because of said information. Besides, I was just curious."

"Sweetheart, better you don't know." Tom shoved the small unit back in his waterproof ruck.

Rorie frowned. "How's your shoulder this morning?"

"Fine. How's your arm?"

"I already bandaged it. And the only reason I'm in your bag was to look for those MREs things. Well, besides packing the ponchos."

"I'll get them." He looped the weapon over his back and unsnapped a different section of his rucksack. "What do you feel like? Beef or chicken?"

She looked at the cardboard box and pressed her lips together in confusion. "Chicken?"

"Coming right up."

He fixed it, using another plastic packet to heat the meal. When he finished, he handed it to her. "The sun's almost up. Eat quickly."

"Yes, sir." She held up two fingers and saluted him.

Tom shook his head. "One of these days, I'll teach you how to do that right—and when to do it."

"Oh, joy." She took a bite of her meal. Compared to the snake, it tasted like heaven.

He took the camo paint out of his pack. "Come here. I'll do this between bites."

Rorie squinted and chewed another piece. "I was afraid you'd insist on that."

"We need to be as stealthy as possible. You can't do that with a white face traveling through the jungle." He spread some paint on her cheeks.

"Ouch." He'd touched a sore spot and she screwed up her face.

Tom winced. "Sorry."

She studied his reaction. She hadn't looked in a mirror in days. "How bad do I look?"

Tom eyed her. Her voice sounded soft, but her eyes told him she wanted a straight answer. "You have a few bruises." He dabbed some more paint on.

She took a ragged breath. "And you had the audacity to say I was beautiful."

He worked lower, along her jawline and neck. "You are. What's wrong with saying it?"

Her eyes brimmed with unshed tears. "With black and blue marks all over my face?"

"Yeah." He rubbed some paint across her lips then kissed them.

"I can't believe you think that," she whispered against his mouth.

"I do." Tom took some more paint and spread it over her chest and cleavage.

Rorie glanced downward, watching him spread the grease then looked him in the face. "Tom?"

"Yeah." His voice grew hoarse.

"Are you —" She pressed her lips together.

"What?" he murmured.

She gave him a weak smile. "Never mind. Just thinking crazy right now."

He sat back and capped the paint. "Go ahead. Ask. I'll tell you."

She shook her head and finished her meal. "No. Forget it." She stood and brushed the dust off the back of her pants. "Point me to the bathroom and I'll be ready to leave."

He gazed at her and took a deep breath, half-relieved she didn't ask, half-wishing she had. Yeah, dammit. He loved her. But how would Aurora react if she knew? Would she run, or would she embrace the idea?

Shoving the paint in his ruck, he stood and maneuvered it on his back. "Come on. I'll show you."

He grabbed the foreign rifle and handed it to her. Securing his own weapon, Tom swerved and walked outside the cave, upset with himself that he couldn't have saved her from the beating her captors gave her.

* * * * *

Rorie mopped her brow as she trudged in the muck, glancing around the humid, steaming jungle. The moisture had thickened so much you could smell the water in the air.

She looked upward. The winds had blown the bulk of the foliage away. You could actually see through the tallest trees to the clear sky. The hot sun shone down on them, the ground for once exposed to the sunlight. With the reduced cover they had, Tom hurried.

She watched him march ahead. He wanted them together. But how? What did he want? He liked her. They had great sex, why wouldn't he like her? God forbid a man like him would be in love with her. She was a mission to him—with some side benefits. That was it. There couldn't be anything else. Her fantasies had taken over again and she needed to crush them.

But, oh, did she wish…something. She didn't know what. She liked him. He made her feel good about herself. But was there anything more?

Rorie refused to think about it. She had to deal with her demons first.

"We're almost to the river." Tom stopped and studied his map.

Rorie readjusted the rifle she'd slung on her back, listening to the water rushing in the distance. "This may sound like a stupid question, but are we crossing another bridge?"

"If it's still there. If not, we head downriver, but I really don't want to get too low in the valley. I'm sure it's flooded and it'll be a bitc— ah, tough to get through." He cleared his throat. "This stream should take us to the Tuira River, which will lead us to the Pinoganga village and onto Yaviza. From there we can phone or hit the Pan American Highway to Panama City and get to the embassy. I'll decide once we get there."

"Won't we go by El Real? We could call from my motel room. And I could pick up my stuff."

"Too chancy." Tom shook his head. "Some from the group that kidnapped you might still be around. Your first guide came from there, right?"

"Yes. But he seemed decent enough. He'd tried to warn me not to go with Chris."

Tom lifted a brow. "That's what I'm talking about. How would he know what Ferguson was up to? In fact, I wonder if he hadn't told the man you worked for."

"I see what you mean." She hadn't thought about Luis' participation in any of this. Welcome to the world of espionage. "I didn't think the rebels operated that far north. I guess I was wrong."

He studied her a minute. "Did they tell you anything when they questioned you?"

"Like?"

"Anything about themselves. The CIA will want to know."

She shrugged, trying to think. "Besides being angry, Raúl said something about Panama and Columbia being reunited."

A muscle twitched in Tom's neck and he nodded. "They weren't rebels." He turned and walked on.

She caught up with him. "What are you talking about?"

He stopped, his gaze boring into her. "The men who captured you weren't rebels. They're a new Colombian paramilitary group that's trying to reunite Colombia and Panama."

"Oh, my God." Her eyes narrowed. "Doctor Martinez belonged to the Panamanian government. Actually, he was rather high-ranking."

Tom nodded. "Some have infiltrated certain levels. It's a problem. Panama didn't reestablish a military after we ousted Noriega. They need one to protect themselves."

The civilization of Panama just became more dangerous to Rorie. She'd never believe another travel brochure again.

"You ready?"

Tom's voice interrupted her thoughts. She bit her lip. The thought of crossing another rope bridge unnerved her, but what choice did she have? She pasted on a smile. "Sure, Chief. What are we waiting for?"

"You can do this," he reassured her.

Rorie took a deep breath. "I know. But I'm glad you're doing it with me."

He smiled. "Then let's go."

A few minutes later, Rorie stared at the stream. The muddy, debris-filled water raced around a bend before it reached their location. The banks overflowed, but the bridge still stood. Fortunately, this one had planks and sat lower to the water. No deep gorge to go over, which pleased her. This would be easy.

"The ground is really wet around these supports." Tom dropped his pack and slung his rifle over his shoulder. "Let me check them to make sure they're going to hold."

Approaching the thick wood poles, he kicked and tugged first on one then the other. "They're weakened but they should be fine." Tom yanked on the main lines strung over the water.

"Ropes look good." He stepped onto the first few planks. "Aurora, watch the poles across the way to see if they move."

"Okay," she confirmed.

He tugged again, using his full weight against the braided cable.

"I don't see anything," she said.

He studied the length of the bridge. "I think it'll do." Tom picked up his pack. "Look, I want you to move first. You're lighter than I am so you'll put less strain on the planks. Step on the edges of the wood so your weight's more distributed on the bottom rigging and keep a death grip on these side ropes. I'll grab you if anything breaks. I don't want you tossed in the water."

"I'm a good swimmer."

He shook his head. "Your abilities won't matter if a rock or some other large debris knocks you out. The stream is moving too fast for anyone to swim. I don't want to pick up your body downstream."

"Gee, nice thought." Rorie crossed her arms, amused. "Anything else, commander?"

"You're not worried?" he asked.

She let her hands drop. "No, Chief. This bridge isn't that high. It's the height that gets me."

"I thought you had a fear of falling."

"The higher you are, the harder you fall."

"I see." He smirked. "Okay. Let's go then. I'll be right behind you. Make sure you test the board before you step on it."

She lifted a brow. "Overprotective to the end."

He came close to her, brushing his hand across her cheek. "I'm going to get you home."

"And what are you going to do when that happens?" Rorie didn't know why she blurted that out, but now that she had she wanted to know. She studied him.

He glanced away for a second. When his gaze came back to her, the color in his green eyes deepened, his look stirring her. "Make sure we can be together more often, for one thing." Tom jerked his head toward the bridge as he strapped his rifle to his back. "Let's move. I don't like being in the open."

She agreed. Walking to the bridge, she stepped to the edge of the first plank, gripping onto the supporting ropes. Rorie sensed he stood right behind her. "So, Chief. What exactly did you have in mind?" She took a few more steps.

"About what?"

His voice sounded close. She looked at the ropes. His hands rested near hers. She glanced over her shoulder at him. "How are you going to make sure we're together more often? Between your job and mine, I think we travel a lot." The planks seemed sturdy. She walked faster.

He chuckled. "I'll find a way."

The rushing water grew louder as they traveled across the bridge. "You're very insistent on this. You must have some idea what you want," she yelled, wanting suddenly to know what he thought, thinking she'd better ask while she had the guts.

"What would you think of moving in with me?" His breath warmed her ear.

"What?" She swerved, forgetting the planks, and bumped into him as he took another step forward.

Tom grasped her around the waist and pulled her close. "I know it sounds crazy, but it isn't like we haven't slept together. With the little time we'll have, we could get to know each other better."

She arched her brows, hoping the shock didn't show on her face. "I don't believe in doing that." Living with him wasn't what she wanted to hear. She wanted to hear...

What? That he loved her? Get real.

She straightened her back and turned, putting her feet on the edges of the planks to hurry across, working to avoid the subject.

"Why not?" he asked.

She stopped and swallowed, thinking of a good answer. "We hardly know each other." Satisfied with her response, she quickened her pace.

"We know each other better than most couples." He caught up to her.

"No." She shook her head. "I can't. I'm reestablishing my independence."

"I could help you."

"I don't need help."

"Why?"

"Because I…" She stopped and turned on him. He studied her, ready to measure her response. God, she wished she understood men. What was he after? "Why do you want me to live with you?"

"Like I said, we could get to know each other better."

"What else?"

"If you keep moving, I promise to tell you when we get to the other side."

With nervous anticipation, she walked on.

"If you're worried about a commitment of some kind, please don't be. You could leave anytime."

Did she want that? For some reason, no commitment made the whole thing sound even worse. Still, he'd said he cared about her. But obviously not enough for something more than physical intimacy.

"Aurora? What do you think?"

She glanced at the other side. A few more boards and she'd be off the bridge then maybe she could avoid this subject. "Sounds like a convenient way for us to have sex more often."

"Is that all you want?" he shouted over the earsplitting rush of the water.

She turned, looking over her shoulder at him. "I told you before I don't know what I want."

"Then live with me and let me help you figure it out."

"No, I…"

Her eyes widened as the roof of a hut came floating around the bend and headed for the end of the bridge they'd just come from. "Tom?" Her voice rose as she pointed.

He swerved, spying the oncoming disaster. "Run," he yelled and pushed her along.

She took off, feeling the jolt to the ropes right before she hopped onto the bank.

When she turned, Tom had weaved himself into the sisal as the bridge swayed, the water swelling and rushing over him from the impact of the roof.

"Tom!" Oh, my God, she couldn't lose him now.

When the water cleared, he still hung onto the lines. He ran for her as the supports near her creaked. She sat and locked onto the wooden poles to keep them stationary as the roof uprooted the poles on the other side, tossing her protector once again.

"Oh, please God, don't lose him." She saw him pressed against the ropes as the water leveled and the roof passed through. The far end of the bridge headed downstream. Hand over hand, Tom worked his way along the ropes, his progress hindered by the water rushing over him.

The pole on the upstream side near her took a pounding. Rorie strained against it. She knew she would lose the support soon. "Hurry," she screamed.

Another step and…

One support gave way. Rorie locked onto the remaining pole. The jolt had loosened Tom's grip and he slipped, catching the rope farther down. Water covered half his body. He sputtered as he put his full weight onto the last stable rope. "Let go before you're pulled in."

"No," she screamed. The pole leaned toward the water. She dug her heels into the muddy bank, her arms tired from holding the pole steady. "Hurry…up, dammit." Putting her knee in front of the pole and gripping the rope, she scooted around and pressed her back against it.

Rorie could see the strain in Tom's face as he pulled himself along, the rushing stream weighing against him. He came closer.

The tug of the water on the rope worked against her. She yanked on the line, pulling it to her as best she could, trying to keep the tension on the sisal until Tom got on the bank.

"Erggg." Her arms ached. Her heels buried deeper into the muck on the bank, Tom an arm's length away.

The pole jerked and the slick rope slid through her fingers, burning her palms.

"No…" she screamed as the pole snapped, hitting her in her sore arm and laying her flat into the mud.

"Oh, God," she whimpered. Had she lost him?

Chapter Twelve

❧

Tom's heavy weight landed on her, holding her down as the load of the bridge snapped the line out of her hands. His hard breathing on her face reassured her he was safe.

"Thank God." She kissed his stubble-roughened chin then found his mouth. His arms slid around her as his tongue separated her lips and penetrated her. She became rapt in him for a moment. Relieved, she pulled back. "I thought you were gone."

"Not yet." He placed a small peck on her mouth. "You won't lose me that easy. How's your arm?"

She rubbed it. "It hurts, but I'm fine. The pole didn't hit me that hard."

Rolling off, he sat in the mud next to her.

She pushed herself up on her elbows, eyeing him. Sludge coated both of them.

He brushed a speck of muck off her cheek and helped her sit up. "That pole could have dragged you in."

"It didn't. And I don't want to hear any complaints about not following orders."

"Yes, ma'am." He smiled. "Your turn to save my life?"

"Well, I guess it's about time." Rorie stood and wiped her backside, getting more mud on her hands. "I've lost track of the number of times you've done it for me."

He stood alongside her. "We make a pretty good team. It's what I was talking about. Teamwork. Sure be a shame to break us up."

"Don't you ever give up?"

"I try not to."

"No."

"No about what?"

"About living with you."

"Why not?"

"Because you're too overbearing."

"You can help me solve that." He put his arms around her.

"No."

"Why?"

"How can I find myself when you're always telling me what to do? In your place, it would be even worse. Forget it. Besides, I'm not living with anyone outside of marriage, which, Chief, I'll never do again. Especially until I solve some of my own problems."

"That doesn't sound like 'never'. Which problems do you need to solve in order to get serious with someone?"

"Argh." She pulled away and stomped along the trail.

"Aurora?"

She swerved toward him, frustrated with her own lack of direction in her life. "How about my fear of falling?" She knew that would never go away. She wasn't even sure where the anxiety came from, not that it had something to do with her relationships, but her falling problem was the first one that came to mind.

"Okay. When will you know you're over it?"

When? How the hell would she know? She didn't even understand it. She planted her hands on her hips, irritated with herself that she couldn't outright tell him to leave her be. Then another thought hit her. Did she really want to be without him? "When I jump out of a plane."

"Done." He pushed ahead of her.

"What do you mean 'done'?"

"I'll help you with that."

"That's the point, Tom. I don't want your help." Why couldn't she get him to understand she needed to do this on her own?

He stopped her. "Aurora, you pulled me out of a stream. I'd have been swept away if you hadn't held on. Don't you see we can work together on our issues? It's what teamwork is all about. It's part of being a couple, along with the more intimate things."

She licked her lips, warming with the thought of those more intimate things, wondering if maybe he could be right. "I don't know if I want to be a couple."

"What are you afraid of?"

Tom stood close. She wanted to pull him to her, stroke the stubble on his chin, grateful he was still alive, thankful he cared enough to save her so many times. "I don't know. My first marriage was such a failure."

"A person learns from the mistakes and moves on."

She sighed. "Well, maybe I'm still learning about failed relationships. Let's face it, the one with my mother isn't the greatest, either. Could be I'm not good at them. But I meant what I said." Rorie paused, thinking, realizing she wanted him in her life, but she wasn't ready for the type of live-in arrangement he had in mind and might never be. She certainly wouldn't settle for something like that without any commitments. "Can't we just be friends for now?"

"If that's what you want." He scowled.

"Thanks." She kissed his cheek. Even with the mud, the greasepaint, the rough look of him, he exuded maleness, a sexiness she found hard to avoid.

Breathless and even more confused, Rorie focused on the trail leading away from the bridge, not knowing where to go in the jungle, not knowing where to go with her heart.

* * * * *

They walked a path that followed the general direction of the stream. Every so often, Tom could hear the water in the background. The storm had blown the jungle cover away, so he'd decided to use the trails. The one they were on would take them to the Tuira River. Tom stayed even more alert.

Listening to Aurora's footsteps behind him, he could have kicked himself for the thousandth time. He knew better than to ask her a stupid question like "let's live together". She needed time before she'd be ready for something as drastic as moving in with him. She had to develop a deeper sense of comfort with the idea first.

Tom knew the thought of losing her had made him do it. He'd let her go once and regretted it. He didn't want her to leave again, at least until they got some things straight. Something more than a sexual interest went on between them, even if she didn't willingly recognize it. She cared for him. He knew it even as he knew his own name. She wouldn't have been saying her prayers for him on the bank otherwise, would she? And for sure, he'd fallen for her. Otherwise, he wouldn't be making such an ass of himself. Now, if he could just get them the hell out of here.

He stepped on another fallen log, analyzing what Aurora had said. What did she mean she'd never marry again? Didn't she say she wanted a family? He didn't believe she meant to stay single, didn't believe she only wanted to be friends. The type of friends she referred to didn't sleep with each other. And if he knew one thing about her, she at least wanted sex from him.

He grumbled, trying to unravel this puzzle of a woman. If she wanted to parachute from an airplane, he could help her. He'd trained as an Army jumpmaster, for God's sake. And he had plenty of friends in private business he could set her up with, ones he'd jumped with himself.

"Can we take a small break?" Aurora's sultry voice sounded tired.

Tom looked at her.

"I know you want to move fast," she said, "but I'm almost running trying to keep up with your long legs."

"Sorry." He glanced around for some small trees or bushes that would provide some protection from unwanted eyes while they rested. He spied a patch of green on a small cliff by the river. "Over there." He jutted his chin toward the area. "Follow me. Maybe we can do some training while we rest."

"Hmmm. I'm overcome with the prospect."

He headed toward the spot. "I thought you wanted me to teach you?"

She sighed. "I do. I'm just pooped. My personal trainer back home would be thrilled with the workout I've been getting. I'm waiting for the part where we go swooping through the trees on some vines."

"The training will give you something else to think about other than being tired." He stepped into the cover of the smaller trees. "We'll start with small arms."

He heard her stop a moment behind him. "Oh, joy."

Tom chuckled. She wanted to get over her fears. Might as well start with this one. He unsnapped his holster and pulled out his Beretta. "Sit down."

Aurora dropped under one of the thin trees and squished the features of her face together, obviously not comfortable with the ensuing discussion.

He held the weapon flat in his open palm. "This is a 9mm Beretta, model 92F. Standard issue for the U.S. military. I have the safety on so it won't fire."

"Good." She eyed him skeptically. "You know I don't like this."

"Don't expect me to let you off that easy. You want to get over your fear of firearms, especially small ones, then knowing about them is the first step."

She glared at him. "Thanks, Chief, but I don't remember me saying I wanted to do it right now."

"You said you wanted to be trained to take care of yourself in the jungle. That's what I'm doing." He crouched beside her and her eyes widened as he held the pistol nearer. "You like swimming?"

"Yeah…" The hesitation in her voice lingered.

"But water can be dangerous, especially if you don't know what you're doing, right?"

"Right." She nodded, frowning. "I think we just proved that a few hours ago."

Tom stopped himself from laughing at her sarcasm. "Think of firearms the same way. What you don't know *can* hurt you." He sat next to her. "How have you felt about carrying the AK on your back?"

"This gun—I mean, rifle?" She pointed to it.

"Yeah."

"I've gotten used to it, which is different from actually firing it."

"True, but you're comfortable."

She squinted. "I've had this funny feeling me carrying it was an intentional ploy to make me comfortable."

Tom lifted a brow. "It worked, didn't it?"

Aurora rolled her eyes. "I guess. You didn't really give me much choice."

"Look, if you want to protect yourself in this environment you need to know how to use a weapon."

She frowned. "Isn't it funny how I have this fear of guns and now I get the chance of a lifetime to get over it?"

"Very funny." He bit the inside of his cheek. "Open your hands."

Slowly, she unraveled her fingers. When he placed the Beretta in her palms, her whole body shook. He put a hand under hers to steady her. "You aren't hurting anyone and no one is hurting you. You're just holding this, okay?"

She bit her lip and nodded, calming herself.

Slinging his rifle strap over his back, Tom moved behind her and pulled her back into his chest. Slipping his palms along her arms, he took the back of her hands in his to control them then worked her fingers to pick up and properly aim the Beretta. "Get the feel of it, Aurora," Tom whispered in her ear. "You aren't going to hurt anyone unless you need to. You're doing fine."

She nodded. Tom watched her eyes glisten. He knew she was scared, but she had to get over this. "See this notch at the top? Use it like the crosshairs I showed you on the AK-47 to aim. This has a bit of kick, so you want to hold your arms out and brace yourself if you need to fire it. Or you can lie on the ground and extend your arms. This is a close-range weapon. It can go about seventy-five feet, but with your inexperience, you want to make sure what you're aiming at is a lot closer, okay? Probably within fifteen feet."

Aurora glanced back at him. "We aren't going to fire this, are we?"

"No." He smiled to reassure her. "I don't want to announce our location and we need to save the ammunition."

"Thank God." She looked upward, leaning her head against his cheek. "Can I put this down now?"

"One more thing." He removed one hand from hers and pointed. "This is the safety for this weapon. Move this here to fire. If you suspect someone is coming who might hurt you, make sure you've taken the safety off." He let go of her other hand. "Get the feel of it."

"It's heavy." Aurora glanced at him and licked her lips.

"A little." Tom nodded. Her shaking started again, but it wasn't anywhere near as bad.

"Can I put it down now?"

"I'll take it." He gently pried it from her hands. "This is loaded right now, so if you need to use it, do. Once you're more comfortable with it, I'll show you how to load and clean it."

"Clean? How often do you do that?"

"After every use, preferably. Before a mission, you want to make sure everything's working properly. It's harder to keep things maintained when you're on the run in a jungle. You do it when you can. You at least keep it oiled."

"You've used yours since you came to get me."

"Yeah. I cleaned all the weapons as best I could while you slept."

"Oh."

She stared at him a moment and he couldn't keep his mind off her moistened lips.

"You killed that boy without using this." Aurora pointed to the Beretta.

"Yeah." She would have to bring that up. "If I'd had a choice, I wouldn't have."

"How many people have you killed?"

He didn't want to talk about that either, didn't want her to be scared of him. "A few."

"Do you ever feel bad about it?"

Tom studied her a minute. Would she be afraid of him now, knowing he didn't always feel remorse? "Sometimes, not always. Regardless, it takes something away from you when someone dies. I've only killed in battle, Aurora. Only when I've needed to. With the boy, we couldn't afford capture."

"I understand." She glanced at her lap.

"How do you feel about it?" he whispered, hoping she didn't hate him for what he did.

She looked up and pressed her lips together. "I'm glad I'm alive. I saw firsthand what those men were capable of doing. I'm sure they would have killed us in time. Still, I don't understand how people can act like that."

"You'd be surprised." Again, he wished he'd gotten to the enemy earlier to prevent the beating she'd gotten. He rubbed her chin with the thumb of his free hand. At least her bruises had started to fade. "I'm glad you weren't hurt too badly."

"Me, too." She paused, giving him a weak smile. "Thank you," she whispered.

"For what?" Tom put the sidearm in his holster, hoping she'd dropped the discussion.

"For helping me. For coming to get me." She turned and slipped her hand around his neck and pulled his mouth to hers.

The kiss lasted mere seconds, but the tenderness and vulnerability Aurora conveyed bored into his very soul. How could she let this warmth between them pass unrecognized?

He cleared his throat. "I'd better keep watch. Go ahead and rest. We'll work on more of this later." Tom stood and took a post that kept the drop to the river at his back, figuring nothing would come that way. With this position, he got a better view of the sloping landscape leading to the bank. He hoped he could keep his mind off her.

"How long can we stay?"

"Not long. Try to sleep if you can. It'll be a long day. We're going to travel while the sun's up."

She sighed then lay on the ground, watching him. Soon, she closed her eyes.

Tom studied her from the corner of his eye, noticed her chest rising with each breath. *He loved her.* Yeah, the feeling was still new. He didn't know where or how that happened, but her refusal to acknowledge their attachment provided a challenge to him—especially to his ego. Could he admit his affection to her? Would she accept his love, or would his confession push her away? He wanted time to see if a relationship with her would work and he didn't think she'd allow them that. Aurora had fears to work through, lots of them. But who didn't? God knows, he had his own. Jump out of an airplane? Fine. Drop into a hot zone? No problem. Love someone?

God, that scared him to death.

He shivered, gazing at Aurora's peaceful face. Without knowing it, she had thrown down the gauntlet to her heart.

No matter his fear, he'd be damned if he wouldn't pick it up.

* * * * *

Rorie moaned as she raised herself on her elbow. The hard ground made her stiff all over.

Solid arms grabbed her from behind and covered her mouth. She struggled. "Shhh," Tom whispered in her ear.

She stopped, glancing at him over her shoulder. He put his finger to his mouth then to hers. Shouting sounded near the river.

Tom released her and pointed to himself then at the place the voices came from. Motioning to her, he directed her to stay put.

After picking up the foreign rifle she'd laid beside her, Tom replaced it with his and leaned toward her ear. "I'm low on ammo, but there're still a few bullets in my M-4. Use it if you have to."

"Buuuutttt…" She swallowed. "You haven't shown me how to use an M-4 yet. Not really."

The lines in Tom's face deepened with worry. He handed her his pistol. "Then use this. Don't forget to take the safety off and make sure you see exactly what you're shooting at. Be back in a few."

Rorie frowned before he disappeared into the jungle. Crawling to the edge of the thicket of small trees, she lay down and watched him. Even with the reduced cover, she found him hard to spot.

The yelling grew louder. Spanish.

She inched higher, trying to glimpse what went on. The small knoll Rorie lay on swooped down to the riverbank. An elderly tattooed man stood on the sandy edge by the water, a young boy with him, another half-clothed man on the ground in pain. Three soldiers had surrounded them. More shouting from one soldier who held a gun on them. The boy hovered between the standing man's back and the bow of a small canoe resting on the edge of the river.

The soldier spoke then bashed the old man in the jaw, knocking him down, forcing the boy to bump into the boat. The soldier yelled again.

Putting the pistol down, Rorie removed her camera from her pocket and took a few pictures, thankful her digital hadn't sustained any damage from the washed-away bridge.

Tom appeared suddenly, crouched in the brush, startling her. His brows arched as he pointed to her to back into the safety of the trees.

She quirked her mouth, knowing he'd be upset. With regret, she put the camera away and picked up the pistol, doing as he asked.

Rolling into the copse, he lay next to her, primed to shoot and whispered, "What the hell were you doing? Trying to get yourself killed?"

"No," she mouthed. "I was taking pictures. I'm a photographer. It's what I do."

He rolled his eyes.

She leaned toward him. "Are they the ones trying to find us?"

Tom nodded.

"What's our next move, Chief?"

"Stay here." His lips moved, but he made no sound. A shot fired and he covered her head with his upper body.

When the yelling started again, he let her up. Rorie looked over the scene. The man on the ground no longer moved. "Oh, my God." Salty tears stung her eyes.

Tom clamped his hand over her mouth. He leaned next to her ear. "Don't give away our position."

She gave him a brisk nod.

He released her mouth and focused on the action in front of them.

Rorie pressed her lips together. She'd thought he meant only for her to stay put, not both of them. She poked his arm and mouthed, "Aren't you going to do something?"

Tom shook his head.

She grew annoyed. "Why not?" she lipped again.

"My mission is to get you out of here. I won't risk that."

She didn't want someone else to suffer for her. "They're looking for us, aren't they?"

He nodded once, his chin set, and pointed to his eyes then the riverbank.

What he said got to her. She tugged on his sleeve again to get his attention. "If you won't do something, I will." When she pushed to get up, he snagged the crook of her arm and made her fall facefirst into the ground.

"No," he mouthed, eyeing her as he swallowed.

Another shot fired.

Rorie spat dirt from her mouth. "But…"

He leaned near her ear. Keeping his voice low, he said, "Look, I'd like to help them, too, but I won't risk capture or worse. My mission is to get you out of here and get that memory card to Ferguson's people. I need you to understand that. Besides, the only way for me to stop them is to kill them."

She licked her lips. The old man's arm bled. One of the soldiers pointed their rifle at the boy's head. "Do it," she said.

He took a deep breath, his eyes peering into her, analyzing her.

"Tom, I have to do something. I can't have their lives on my conscience."

"Fuck." He took a deep breath. Looking back, he found his forgotten M-4 and placed it near her, pointing to it. "Keep the weapons beside you." Crawling, he snuck below the small brush toward the riverbank.

Rorie watched him disappear. She inched on her stomach to the edge of the trees and said a small prayer, hoping he'd get there in time, wanting him to be safe, guilt enveloping her for making him do something she abhorred.

The lead soldier yelled again. This time he aimed a pistol at the boy. Pops echoed behind the soldiers in the brush to her left. The lead man fell first then the soldier with his rifle drawn. The last one lay dead before he could bring his weapon around.

Rorie sighed and dropped her head on her folded forearms. The natives would be safe. She took a deep breath, relieved she and Tom were out of danger.

In the ensuing quiet, she heard the crunching of the underbrush nearby, some mumbling from new voices.

Not again, she thought, spying two other soldiers walking by her position, darting behind some trees.

Rorie froze. Had they seen Tom? They had to have, she reasoned, otherwise, why would they hide?

She scooted under the foliage, watching, holding her breath. The events by the river had her so wrapped up she hadn't seen the other soldiers coming. Tom would head right for them. How could she warn him?

Dread consumed her. A strange fear grabbed her heart.

Realization dawned on her. She couldn't lose Tom. Not now. She had to save him and let him know…

Rorie glanced at the pistol. There was only one way to stop him from walking into a trap.

When she removed the safety, her hands quivered.

Chapter Thirteen

෨

The report of his Beretta echoed through the woods, causing Tom's stomach to clench. "Damn, she is trying to kill herself." He took off, firing at the approaching soldiers, heading in a direction away from Aurora to lead the enemy away.

What the hell had he thought, allowing her to be alone? Yeah, he tried to do the noble thing, but if anything happened to her, he would never forgive himself for being so goddamned stupid.

From the corner of his eye, he watched the Indians pick up the injured man and jump into their canoe, paddling with some effort on the flowing river.

Aurora fired again.

"Crap." He scanned the higher ground. One of the soldiers went down, but he couldn't tell if Aurora had hit the man or if he'd ducked for cover.

"Dammit." He turned and took aim, covering himself as he went toward her. His ploy to distract them wouldn't work now.

Tom worked fast. Ducking and firing, rushing ahead, rolling in the dirt when needed. Anything to keep the men at bay. At least, the two directions of fire he and Aurora had confused the small retinue of troops.

The paramilitary fired again, in both directions. He tried to draw their volley, making himself a more obvious target, and looped to their other side.

Tom took cover behind the trunk of a large tree. It grew on a short knoll and gave him the advantage of a better view. One of their men was definitely down. Two more soldiers had come from the direction of the trail. The enemy was now stuck between him and Aurora. That left three standing.

Scanning the grove of trees, Tom saw bits of Aurora through the leaves. She'd tucked herself well under the foliage. Was she okay?

Fear crept into him. She had to be okay. He couldn't accept anything less.

The gunfire stopped. One man approached Aurora's position. Tom heard her shoot — and watched her miss.

"Thank God she's alive," he mumbled. He exposed as little of himself as he could to take the man down. Drawing fire, he rushed toward Aurora, sending bursts at the men. Their return shots sent debris flying around him. Shards of wood smacked into his face. But nothing would stop him. Aurora needed him. He raced.

Rorie watched Tom run, ducking behind the trees when he could. Fear made her heart pound in her chest. As the men exposed themselves, she shot, trying to control the shaking in her hands. She hit the tree right next to one of their heads. She was definitely getting better at this, although her shoulders ached from the kick the pistol had. She'd gotten one of the men shooting at her. She still saw the soldier wriggling on the ground.

The guerillas fired again. She glanced at the pistol and wondered when she would run out of bullets.

Sticking her butt up, Rorie pushed her upper body along the ground. She wanted to take a spot behind a lip of earth beneath the thick branches of the tree where she'd taken cover.

One of the soldiers aimed at her and fired.

"Ohhhh." A burning sensation ripped into her raised rear end. Had she been hit?

Rorie waited for the new round to stop before she looked at her wound, wanting to pee her pants.

The armed force shot at Tom again. One man stepped farther out. Firing, she winged his arm.

Then Rorie heard another pop. The soldier fell. Tom had to be somewhere nearby.

One man left.

The last soldier scattered the area with bullets and ran. She pressed her hand against her wound and scanned the grounds. She couldn't see Tom.

Oh, please God, don't let him be dead, especially before…

Tom slid into the ring of trees surrounding her.

"You're safe." She closed her eyes with relief, trying to ignore the pain, thinking the bleeding couldn't be too bad. When she opened her lids, Tom lay flat on his stomach near her side, gun at the ready, tracking the one man left.

The single soldier turned to shoot.

Tom fired, and the man dropped.

Her gut lurched to her throat. "Was that necessary?"

Tom glowered at her. "You want him to go back and get reinforcements?" He took the pistol from her and stashed it in his holster.

"Well, no." Her trembling stopped.

"What the hell did you think you were doing firing on a patrol of men?"

"A patrol? I only saw two."

"There were four of them." His thinned lips hardened.

"Well, I didn't see the other ones at first and you told me to use the pistol if I had to. Besides, things turned out fine, didn't they?"

"Fine? They could have killed you."

"They didn't."

"They could have. You exposed your position."

"I did not. I stayed under the branches like you taught me. Even had this mound of earth to protect me." She patted the pile of dirt.

"They pinpointed the direction you fired from. That was enough. If I hadn't reacted the four of them would have been all over you."

"No they wouldn't. They were after—" She didn't want to say "him". "The Indians."

"Exactly. Until you gave them something else to shoot at. Those men didn't even know you were in this thicket. They were focused on what happened at the river."

"And you. They saw you. What do you think they were doing, hiding behind the trees?" She grew angry. Did he think she had no consideration for her own safety?

Tom pointed his finger at her. "They didn't see me. They were going to shoot the natives. Probably thought the old man killed their men."

"Well, then I did the right thing," she snapped.

"No. You didn't. You risked yourself and this mission. My primary concern is to get you home."

"Oooh, you stubborn man. I couldn't let the boy and the old man be killed, too. Especially on my account."

"So you sacrificed yourself?"

"I didn't."

Tom rolled his eyes upward a minute. When he looked at her again, his jaw had that stubborn set about it. "You took an unnecessary risk. From now on, when you use a firearm, you do it *only* in self-defense. You let me handle the dirty work."

She arched a brow. "So, I'm not supposed to get blood on my hands, is that it? You can't live with that, can you, me taking care of myself? Look, Prince Charming, I don't live in a tower."

"Dammit, Aurora, that's not it. But protecting you *is* my job. It's what I'm paid to do. I don't want you setting yourself up again. And that," he jabbed the finger in the air at her, "is an order," he growled.

She blustered. "You pompous ass. You can't order me around."

"I just did."

"Well, Chief, don't expect me to listen. Damn." She looked away a moment, working to get her temper in check. Hells bells, she'd been afraid for him, that's all. As much as it scared her, she made the decision to put her life on the line to save him. She knew she took a risk, but could she live, knowing the only man who'd ever cared for her died doing something she'd asked?

Rorie trembled, thinking of what could have happened. Taking a ragged breath, she rested her chin in her cupped hands. "I thought they were going to shoot you." She swallowed, looking at him, forcing the desperate tension she'd felt when she thought him in danger to go away. "I couldn't let that happen."

"Shoot me?" He released a slow breath through his clenched teeth, the tightness in his shoulders abating as he calmed. "Honey, if you watched what went on, looked at where they were aiming, you would have seen them watching the old man and the kid. I'd gotten yards away by then."

"Well, I'm not the expert you are. Besides, I couldn't see you and if you remember, you kinda indicated you didn't want me hanging my head out of the bushes."

"You're damn right I didn't."

"Well then, make up your mind, Chief. I can't follow two opposing orders."

Tom's head slumped. Sighing, he glanced at his hands. When he looked back at her, Rorie read the mixture of fear and relief in his gaze. "You scared the hell out of me."

She allowed herself a slight smile. "No more than you did me."

He took her hand and stroked the back with his thumb. "At least I know you're not afraid to use a firearm—even if it still makes you nervous."

She sighed. "Thanks. I'm sorry, Tom." She frowned. "Being here is all my fault. You would probably be out of here by now if I wasn't along."

"Don't talk like that. You did what you thought was right." He shook his head. "No, the fault's mine. I knew better than to leave you alone." His gaze captured her. "Being around you does poor things to my judgment."

She bit her lip, not sure how to react to his confession. "At least the boy and the old man are alive." She winced from the injury to her rear, but covered the pain with a small grin.

"Yeah." He nodded, smirking in response to her smile.

"What about the man on the ground?"

"Don't know. He was shot up, but breathing. They might save him. The old man and the boy took him with them." Tom brushed his hand across her cheek. "I'm sorry, Aurora. I won't fail you again. Promise."

"You didn't fail me this time. I don't think you ever will." Her voice turned breathy. She studied him. Something troubled him. Deeper than what she could discern.

He shook his head. "No, I should have thought about it more. I knew we shouldn't have interfered. You didn't know better. I did. Look, I don't want you hurt. I'm going to get you home in one piece—alive and kicking."

Rorie wondered how to tell him about her rear end. "No one asked you to."

"Yes, they did. The government sent me here to get you. You and the film are my mission."

She swallowed. "I thought I was more to you than a mission."

The green is his eyes deepened until the color turned almost black. "There's a lot of truth in that statement. I don't want you running away when I tell you how much."

She bit her lip. She didn't want to know. Not yet. She wasn't ready.

His jaw set again. "Until we get out of this jungle and I get you on a plane home, don't take any more chances. Just do what I tell you, understand?"

He'd turned dictatorial again.

"Fine. You're the expert. But don't piss me off."

"I'm not trying to. I'm trying to keep you alive." He stopped derailing her a moment and brushed his hand over her cheek. "Why couldn't you let me get shot?"

"Isn't it obvious?" She swallowed, not wanting to tell him she cared too much for him already.

"Not really. I'm a big boy. Didn't you think I could handle myself?" His green-eyed gaze pierced her hardened shell. "Or could it be you really do care?"

"I—" Rorie shut her mouth. No, not now. She didn't want him to know what she thought. She didn't even want to recognize her need for him. If he knew, he would use the information against her. Make her want him more than she already did. Wouldn't that be disastrous to her plans for independence?

"You said it yourself. I need you to get out of here. I'm your mission." She took a deep breath, hoping he'd buy the excuse.

Someone else wouldn't have noticed the disappointment in his eyes. But she was no longer someone else. She loved him.

Oh, God. The acknowledgement rolled through her in waves of delight and fear. She loved him. Rorie bit her lip trying to keep her composure. She couldn't let him know, not now. She needed to get control of her life first, and before she did that they needed to get out of the jungle in one piece. But deep within, her heart knew there was no turning back. And she'd be damned if she'd let the man she loved risk his life when there was something she could do about it.

He paused as if he wanted to say something more about the two of them, then his look hardened. "Then, please, do what I ask," he said. "Otherwise, I promise, I'll make you. Even if it means you'll hate me the rest of your life."

"We'll see," she finally replied. She didn't have any intention of crossing him, but if his life was threatened again, she wouldn't back down.

Rorie rolled her wounded side away from him. Now that he'd calmed, she didn't want him to see her torn skin. Not yet.

Tom pulled off his hat and ran a hand through his hair. "Why do I listen to you?"

Rorie thought he spoke more to himself than her. "Sue me." She'd kept her voice low but her retort had more bite to it than she intended. She didn't know who she was more upset with, Tom for caring so much, or her for letting him get to her heart?

He set his jaw, pressing his lips together, not saying what he thought.

She sensed frustration boiling beneath his surface. She knew she confused him. But, hell, she'd tried to warn him. She confused herself.

Standing, he slung the M-4 she'd left forgotten onto his back. "Don't let weapons lie around anymore."

"Yes, Chief." She eyed him. "Is this our first official lover's fight?"

He smirked. "I hope so. It means you at least recognize we have a relationship."

She licked her lips, not sure what to say. She didn't want to recognize a relationship with him yet—but here she had.

Tom shook his head and spoke before she had to respond. "Let's get out of here before more of them find us."

Rorie cleared her throat. "That may be a problem." The time for confessions had come. Putting both hands on the ground, she struggled to stand, gritting her teeth from the ache in her butt. Unsteady, she glanced at her bloodied hand, particles of dirt sticking to her palm.

"Oh, God." He grabbed her fingers, examining her hand, then he stared at her.

"I think they were using my backside for target practice." She grimaced.

Kneeling, he examined her rear end. "Why didn't you say something?"

"We were fighting."

"Still." He stood and loosened his pack, looking inside, she guessed, for medical supplies.

"Shit," he muttered.

She looked at him and watched his Adam's apple rise and fall, disappointment springing into his face. "I don't see an exit wound," he said. "I bet the slug's still in there." He exhaled through his clenched teeth and pulled out some gauze. "I know that hurts like a bitch."

"It wasn't your fault," she said, wanting to placate his sense of guilt.

He inhaled slowly. "Yeah." Nodding, he studied her. "Yeah, it was."

"How can you blame—"

Spanish shouts sounded from the direction of the trail.

Tom snapped his head up, glancing through the cover. "Cripe. More of them. A lot more." He glanced at her wound. From what he could see, the bullet had grazed the outer skin and ripped into her dermis. The wound was deep, but not serious, and the bleeding had lessened. He damned himself for letting this happen.

No time to consider your stupidity, MacCallum. "Can you move?"

"Yeah."

Tom stuffed the gauze through the hole in her pants, covering her wound. They'd be overrun in moments if he didn't hurry. "Come on." He closed his pack and tightened the strap to his hat. Picking her up, he slung her over his shoulder and ran for the edge of the cliff.

"Wait. What are you doing?" she protested. "I thought we were hiding in the trees?"

"Not now. I'm sure they heard us. They'll be covering every inch of ground. There's too many of them to defend our position. Even with your sure-shot skills."

"Ha, ha," she said to his back. "Funny. Very funny. You know I missed most of the time."

"You hit at least one guy. I think two." He perched on the ridge. "You said you like to swim," he yelled over the sound of the water, setting her down.

The voices grew louder. Rorie glanced at the denuded forest then back at the drop. "Yeah, but—"

"We're at a lower elevation. The river's still fast but not as dangerous. By now, most of the debris is downstream. I think we can navigate it."

Rorie dug in her heels. "That means jumping."

She was afraid. He knew she would be. "It's either the river or the enemy, Aurora. You can do this."

Shots rang out, breaking some branches overhead. She latched onto him. "Okay, Chief, I'm all yours."

"Tell me that later." He interlocked his arm with hers. "Hold on. Tight."

Tom pulled her with him as he jumped off the short cliff into the fast flowing water.

Rorie's scream filled the air—until she hit the cold river. Tom's hand clamped onto the back of her collar as she sank, water painfully going up her nose. He yanked her to him. She stroked and kicked her legs along with him until they reached the surface, breaking through the silted water like bobbers on a fishing line.

"God, it's cold," she shivered as the current pulled them along. She glanced at the retreating cliff, noting how far she'd fallen—and survived. "We made it." She snorted muddy fluid from her nostrils.

Tom locked an arm around the ribs under her breast, getting her to float. "You okay?"

"Yeah." She spat debris from her mouth. "I'll live."

A wave splashed over them and she heard him cough from behind. "Kick for me, honey, would you? We need to turn around. Point our legs downstream."

"Sorry." She put her legs and arms in the effort, the cold water numbing the pain from the wound. When they turned, the trunk of his body floated somewhat underneath her.

She heard a thump. "Argh…" he complained.

Rorie wanted to glance back, but knew the tenuous hold he had on her could break. A large log floated past. "You okay?"

"Fine. I'm going to grab onto the next thing that comes by. Be ready to hang on."

She nodded, hoping he understood.

"Now," he yelled and loosened his grip on her, forcing her body as best he could upward and over the end of a small tree trunk. She latched onto it.

Somehow, Tom got himself around her and clamped his hands next to hers. "Can you pull yourself up?"

Rorie struggled and grabbed a hold of the rough bark. His knee came up underneath her buttocks to push. "Oww," she complained when he hit her damaged muscle.

"Sorry."

Gasping, she rested her chest over the top of the trunk, the water swirling around them. "No problem," she gasped.

Tom lifted his upper body and took a better hold on the wood. "Let's see if I can set us down on the other side. Not too far." He kicked and the log inched toward the middle of the river.

The pounding sound of the rushing water increased. Dread seared into her. "Tom?" she shouted.

"I hear it. Rapids. Help me, sweetheart."

She kicked as hard as she could, using one hand to paddle with, hanging on with the other. The log moved faster, but not fast enough to avoid the dips and peaks of the white water. The sound grew louder. Rorie glanced downstream, her eyes fixated on the disappearing edge. "Oh, God. It drops off."

Tom lifted himself enough to peer over her. "When I give the command, let go of the log. Keep your feet downstream. Better a rock breaks your leg than gives you a concussion. Understand?"

She swallowed as the river sped faster, the water's drop coming closer. "Yeah, Chief." She glanced at him briefly, afraid she'd never get the chance to tell him she cared, that she wanted him, too. That she needed more time.

"You can do this, Aurora." He'd bent to speak into her ear, kissing her cheek, making her aware of the depth of his passion in the short space of his touch. He believed in her.

The decisive moment approached. She realized the truth.

The time had come for her to believe in herself.

Then Tom gave the order to let go.

Chapter Fourteen

൭

Tom's arms clamped around her. Water tumbled around them, the thrumming sound of the river deafening her ears. A jolt hit Rorie and the raging water pushed them apart, submerging them. Tom was lost to her.

Faith. She had to believe this would work. That she would find him alive again.

Falling water pounded her back, the stream pulling her downward. She couldn't see her hands in front of her face, the view through the liquid thickened by the violent motion and mud. Rorie's lungs burned. She stroked to get away, the pull of the current calming as she swam at an angle upwards, away from the falling water.

Panting, she surfaced. "Tom?" Treading water, she glanced around. They'd landed in a large pool, a respite to the raging water. "Tom?" Panic rose in her. She couldn't find him.

He rose, several feet from her but closer to the bank, gulping deep breaths.

"Thank God." Tom swam for her, taking her in his arms when he reached her. He kissed her forehead then her neck and lips as he kicked to keep them above water. "I went under looking for you."

She ran her hands over his hair-roughened face. "I got caught in the undertow. I told you I was a good swimmer."

"Yeah, but with the damage to your—" He stopped, looking at her a moment. "Let's get out of here. Can you swim to shore?"

"Yes. I'm fine. Really. It's only a few feet."

"Okay, you go first. I'll follow just in case."

Releasing her, they swam away from the side of the river they'd jumped from. When she felt the sandy bottom of the opposite shore, she stood. The extra weight on her wound crippled Rorie. She bent over and crawled toward the bank, pain shooting down her leg and into her hip.

When Tom reached her, he helped her up, carrying her the rest of the way across the flooded embankment in his arms.

Rorie looped her hands around his neck, wincing from the throbbing hole in her backside. "You know, you keep saving me like this and I might *have* to keep you around." Her attempt at humor helped to keep her mind off her aching butt.

His dimples deepened, his grin brilliant. "Sounds like a deal I can't pass up." He placed her on her good side under a tall tree. "Let's take a look at this." The bleeding had stopped, probably an effect from the cold water.

But before Tom could patch her, he noticed some movement across the water. "Crap, they followed us. C'mon." He picked her up, throwing her over his shoulder and ran through a wall of brush—right into a handful of men.

The soldiers were armed and ready, as if they'd been waiting for the two of them. For once, fear rocked him.

"You're surrounded, *Señor*." The lead man walked around the ring of men, his knockoff Makarov pistol drawn. "Please do not give us any more trouble, eh?"

Tom noted the shorter man wore no insignia, no rank. The guerilla looked like a man comfortable with authority.

The one in charge circled behind Tom. Bending over, he looked into Aurora's face. "*Buenos días*, Miss Lindsay."

Glancing over his shoulder, Tom watched Aurora lift her head, using her hands to push against his back. "Luis?"

Rorie's former guide gave a few orders in Spanish. One of the soldiers left and she heard the man call across the water to the others.

"Set her down," Luis ordered, a strength in Luis' voice she hadn't heard before.

Tom held her a moment then let her slide down his body, holding her against him. "She's injured."

Rorie looked at Tom. The only sign of emotion she detected was the twitch of a muscle in his jaw when he spoke.

"I see." Luis circled back around, examining the rip in her britches. Then his dark, intelligent eyes analyzed Tom and her.

An eerie chill seeped through Rorie's skin, as if her guide knew every secret she kept within her—especially the ones about her and Tom. This side of Luis she'd never seen. And here, from the comments she heard from him over the last few weeks, she thought him a benign family man—one who avoided controversy.

Rorie gulped as his firm grip took her arm and pulled her away. Supporting her, a corner of Luis' mouth peaked. "I hope you don't mind if we take the weapons." He nodded to a few of his men. "*Desármenlos y tomen su mochila.*"

"*Si, jefe,*" one of the men responded. "*Manos pa' rriba,*" the soldier said to Tom, jabbing the point of his rifle into Tom's upper arm.

With a scowl, the only man she'd ever cared about gradually raised his hands in defeat.

"So, you were Aurora's guide," Tom said to Luis as the men took the two rifles he carried, his pistol and the pack.

"Yes." Luis sneered. "You may call me Major Alvarez."

"Major?" Tom addressed Luis as a soldier pulled off Tom's hat and stomped on it.

"Yes, *Señor.* And you are?"

When Tom said nothing, Luis spoke a few words and one of the guerillas in the process of patting Tom down reached to rip open his blouse.

Tom's steel grip around the man's fingers stopped the soldier. Rorie noted the pain in the Columbian's face before another man pounded the butt of a rifle to the back of Tom's head, causing Tom's face to jerk forward. Tom pressed his lips together and took in a deep breath.

"*Basta*," Luis ordered. Dragging Rorie with him, her ex-guide stepped forward and held out the palm of his free hand. "No more trouble, if you please. I do not think you would like Miss Lindsay to witness something unpleasant."

Tom unbuttoned his blouse and gave Luis his dog tags.

Luis first jostled the metal chain in his hand then sneered and read the etched surface of the tag aloud. "*Tomas* MacCallum." He studied Tom. "Of course, *yanqui* dog tags do not have rank. Your level?" he asked.

"CW2."

Luis pulled Rorie into him, his arm locking around her waist like a lover. "Which is a Chief Warrant Officer 2, am I correct?"

Tom's glare hardened before he nodded. A soldier searching him checked Tom's pant leg.

Luis spoke to his men. He must have explained Tom's response because the others seemed very pleased with themselves, laughing and slapping each other on the back.

"Not bad," Luis told her, loosening his hold on her waist. "To capture someone at his level so highly trained. We would like such training. Do you think your friend would help us?"

"Doubtful," she spat.

Luis snickered and spoke in Spanish again, glancing around the group of men. Although Rorie couldn't understand the words, she knew Luis passed their conversation on to his subordinates, causing another round of hilarity.

The pleased face her former guide wore irritated her. This did not seem like the man who'd guided her the last several weeks in the jungle. How could she have read him so wrong? She could kick herself for being gullible. And Tom said she wasn't a poor judge of men.

When Luis finished showing off, he gazed at her and said, "A woman like you could do better."

Rorie looked away. What did he mean she could do better? Better than what? Was he speaking about Tom? Did he know Tom and she were lovers? How could he? Unless he only prodded her, trying to find something he could use to manipulate her. The explanation was the only one that made sense. Stephen had done that plenty of times. She'd never fall for that trick again. Little did Luis know, she wouldn't tell him a thing.

Another soldier found Tom's knife stashed in his boot. Throughout the search, Tom watched her, his countenance growing darker, deadly. Rorie wondered what he thought and guilt assailed her. If she'd listened to him from the beginning, they wouldn't be in this mess. But no, she had to do things her way. She wanted to cry, but refused to do so in the face of adversity. She wondered if Tom would forgive her for putting them in a position to get caught.

Then again, he'd promised not to fail her. Would he believe this was his fault? She peered into Tom's eyes, thinking how determined a man he was. Would he forgive himself if they were hurt, or worse, killed? She didn't think so, and the blame cut deeper into her.

When the men finished, one of them nodded to Luis.

"Chief," Luis said, "if you would do the honors of helping Miss Lindsay, I would appreciate it. My men have enough to do carrying your weapons and guarding you. You are quite deadly."

"It's my job."

Luis beamed. "Yes, I understand. And I am sure you understand what I must do. Now, if you please?"

Tom stepped forward and picked her up in his arms, cradling her. "I'm sorry," he whispered in her ear as the men surrounded them and urged them along.

"Not your fault. I should have listened to you more and not complained. I'm the one who's sorry."

A younger soldier shoved Tom in the back, apparently not satisfied with his pace. Tom turned and stared hard at him. Rorie watched the man flinch and back away.

The group entered a clearing. A jeep and a larger truck were parked at the end of a rutted dirt road.

"The forest service built this road years ago during a more civilized age," Luis said. "It leads to an abandoned outpost. Our army now keeps it cleared, making it much easier to work in this part of the jungle. Your people did not know of this, did they?" He glanced at Tom.

Tom's absent stare answered the major.

Luis chuckled. "No, I can see that they did not. If you had known about our camp, you wouldn't have come this way."

The armed men forced Tom to put Rorie in the back of the jeep. Before the soldiers let him crawl in beside her, they bound Tom's hands behind his back. When they finished, the men left to join their comrades in the truck.

Sitting in front, Luis turned toward her as they took off. "Miss Lindsay, I am sorry you were hurt. I will have someone look at your injuries."

"I'll do it," Tom growled. The jeep lurched forward.

A black brow on Luis' face arched. "And you are a doctor, too?"

Tom scowled at her recent guide. "No."

Luis settled into the seat and chuckled. "Interesting."

From then on, the men in front involved themselves in their own conversation. Rorie leaned into Tom, trying to keep her injured hip elevated, but every time they hit a rut, the jerky motion would cause her backside to hit the seat.

"Oomph." A particularly nasty jolt caused her to flop over Tom's lap.

"Why don't you stay there?" he said. "Hold onto my legs, so you can keep your wound from getting pounded. I'm afraid it'll start bleeding again."

She looked askance at him and considered what he said. As awkward as her position lying over him looked, she liked the idea. At least her backside would get a break. "Thanks." She smiled at him as a gesture to reassure him she was fine.

His eyes drooped and the look he gave her back conveyed his concern.

Aurora sighed and closed her eyes, letting the enormity of their situation sink in. He had every right to be concerned. Still reeling from the shock of Luis' deception, she grew frightened of what her former guide would do with them once they arrived. Would they make it through the night?

She swallowed. Fact was, the word "concern" didn't begin to describe what she felt.

She was scared to death.

The drive to the guerillas' encampment didn't take long. When they slowed, Tom watched Aurora sit up and brush the hair from her face. She looked pale and clammy, her lips tightened with pain. Tom gave her credit. She didn't complain. He studied the few shanties in the compound. As long as he breathed, they had a chance. He had to get her out of here. The question was how.

The driver stopped the jeep in front of the smallest shack and got out. The major gave a few orders, and the men from the truck scrambled, spewing forth from the back like refuse shot from a cannon.

Stepping out of the vehicle, Alvarez had one of his men cut the tie at Tom's hands. "Please help her inside," the major asked him. "I will let you attend to her then we will talk *hombre e hombre, si?*"

"*Si,*" Tom said. When he turned to Aurora, she held her stomach. "You okay?"

"I feel sick," she complained.

Tom lifted her, carrying her like a baby. "Where are we going?" he asked.

"Here." The major pointed to the hut in front of them. Alvarez studied Aurora. "I will see about medical attention. Follow me."

If Tom hadn't known better, he might think the major showed some care for Aurora. However, he knew these people. There was another reason the man kept them alive. Tom could only guess what that reason could be.

He followed Alvarez inside. A twin bed replete with a blanket and pillow sat in the corner. It and a chair were the only furniture in the room.

"The facilities are over here. Please make use of them." Alvarez pointed to a tiny bathroom. "The water is good to wash with, but do not drink it. I will see about getting you proper drinking water."

From what Tom could see, there were no windows except for the curtained one near the door and a small barred one in the bathroom. "If I could get our canteens—"

Rorie moaned, interrupting him. "Is there some place I can throw up?"

"Yeah." He carried her to the toilet and held her over the porcelain bowl.

Alvarez followed him.

"Can I at least have the medical supplies from my pack?" Tom asked the major while Aurora lost the contents of her stomach.

"I will have them brought to you—and water. This, perhaps, does not need to be said, but you, Chief MacCallum, are a prisoner. There will be guards posted. Please do not make things difficult for them. I would not like the *señorita* to be hurt more than she is already. *Comprende?*" His stern look conveyed his warning.

"I understand."

Alvarez swerved. Tom heard the major's steps click on the wooden floor, giving a few men orders to search the rucksack Tom had carried.

"Ugh." Aurora unleashed another shot at the toilet then, relaxing against him, wiped the back of her mouth. "That's horrible."

He rubbed her back. "Feel better?"

She nodded.

"Let's get you to bed." When Tom lifted her, he realized her cut bled again. Drops of red fell on the grungy tiles. "When's the last time you had a tetanus shot?"

She shrugged. "I don't remember."

That bothered him. With the pollution in these waters from the storm, that could be a problem. Infection was always a probability with a wound. He had salve for that. But lockjaw or something worse? She needed a tetanus booster.

Frowning, he carried her into the bedroom and, steadying her, removed her shirt. "Let's see about getting your clothes to dry."

"Okay."

Aurora seemed too weak to argue. Tom unzipped her pants and pulled them down to her knees. Turning her, he laid Aurora on her stomach, her bottom bare and her pants-bound legs dangling over the edge. Tom threw the blanket over her upper body. Kneeling beside her on the floor, he pinched the wound together and applied pressure.

"Oww," she complained.

"You're bleeding again. I'm trying to stop the flow."

"Well, can you do it softer?"

"No." He cursed under his breath, wondering where the damn person was with his stuff.

Finally, a man entered with the first aid supplies and some peroxide. "Took you long enough," Tom barked and covered Aurora's behind as the young soldier came closer.

The man jumped, looking confused.

"*Tráigalos aquí.*" Tom ordered the guard to bring the items to him.

The soldier took uncertain steps, tossing the cache on the end of the bed.

"*Lo siento, señorita.*" The soldier glanced at her backside as he apologized then ran out the door.

"Poor guy," Aurora said and raised herself on her elbow.

"What's so poor about him?" Tom growled. He quickly sorted through the supplies, tearing open some gauze and pressing it against the wound.

She held a glint in her eye. "You scared him half to death."

"Good." The bleeding slowed and he put a quick piece of tape over the gauze to hold it in place. He cleared his throat. "Let's get your pants off the rest of the way."

"Wow, is that an invitation? Nice to know you still want me."

"Funny." He smiled at her. "I just thought you'd be more comfortable if you could lie on a dry bed."

Even though Aurora smiled back, she seemed shaky. Her skin had paled. He touched her clammy forehead. "How do you feel?" He untied her boots, quickly tossing them off, thinking she might be going into shock.

"I could take my own boots off," she said, her voice weak.

Stubborn to the end, he thought. "You're the patient. Now, lie down and behave."

She rolled to her side and watched him. "I hate to ask a stupid question, but what will they do with us?"

Tom took a deep breath and pulled her pants off her feet. "So far, your old guide's been fine. They'll break apart every inch of my pack. Probably find the film, although if you didn't know what to look for…" He shrugged. "You, they might ransom. I think Alvarez knows you didn't have anything to do with this. That should help."

"What about you?" She lifted her head to look at him more closely.

He rolled her back on her stomach. "Don't know. I'm officially a prisoner. That was clear enough. Although I'm surprised the major let me stay with you."

"Why shouldn't he? We're both prisoners, aren't we?"

"Technically. But I don't think he feels you're as deadly as I am."

"Oh." She put her chin on her fists.

"I'm surprised they haven't bound me," Tom continued, "although Alvarez knows I want to take care of you. That may be why. You would get them more money being alive and well than sick and injured."

"Nice thought." She pushed herself up and turned to look at him, jutting her wounded side toward him. "So when am I going to get the chance to take care of you?"

Tom held his breath. He probably wouldn't get out of this alive. "When we get back would be good with me."

"Hmmm." She studied him.

"Now stay still and let me clean this." He made her lie flat. He didn't want her to think about him. If Tom had been paying attention to his job instead of his dick, they wouldn't be in this mess. When it came to trouble, his instincts had never let him down—until now.

He poured some peroxide in the wound and watched it fizzle. "I'm going to tell them I came back for you, act like you hadn't been on the bird already. I want you to tell them the same thing. After all, it's mostly the truth."

"Yeah." Her voice broke. "I'm sorry, Tom. I thought I was doing the right thing when I went after Chris' pack."

"I know." His voice softened. "Whatever happens, Aurora, don't look back."

"What do you mean?"

She tried to move again, but he put his hand on her back to stop her. "I mean, if you get the chance to get out of here, you do that. Don't think about me."

"How can I do that? If you think I'm leaving you behind, you're crazy."

"Aurora, the government will get me somehow." He didn't mention it would probably be when he was dead.

"Fine. I won't argue with you now, but—Oh!" She sucked in a breath through her teeth when he opened the wound more and let the peroxide seep deeper.

"This will hurt for a while," he said, knowing the cleansing needed to be deep, satisfied the action had gotten her to stop thinking of him. "All the bleeding you did should have helped wash the germs out."

"The bullet's still in there, isn't it?"

"Yep. But it isn't near any vital organs. That's good." He rinsed the wound a bit more then cut some tape to knit the edges together. Using the gauze, he bandaged the injury as best he could. "Don't move too much. When I'm sure the bleeding won't start again, maybe I can get you a bath."

"Okay."

"Tired?" Tom asked.

"Yeah." She rested her head on her crossed arms.

"Then get some sleep." He covered the rest of her body as she nodded off.

Standing, Tom removed his blouse and went to the bathroom to clean up as best he could.

A knock on the door caused him to stop and leave the bathroom. A guard walked in. The old man from the river stepped in behind him—the one who had been with the boy and wounded man that Tom had saved. Tom's nerves went on alert, wondering how the old man had gotten here — and why.

The Indian's eyes darted shrewdly around the room then rested on Tom. The elder nodded once at him, their eyes meeting in silent recognition.

"*Tú.*" The guard pointed to him. "*Ven conmigo.*"

Come with him? "No." Tom shook his head. "The girl needs me," he said in Spanish.

"*El viejo es un curandero. Él cuidara por ella,*" the guard insisted.

The soldier implied the old man was a medicine man, that he would now care for Aurora. But was he skilled in caring for a gunshot wound?

"*Vamonos, ya,*" the guard ordered and pointed his rifle at him.

"Come. Now," the armed man had said. He wouldn't allow Tom to find out. Looking at Aurora one last time, Tom grabbed his blouse and walked to the door.

The old man's hand on his arm made him pause. "The girl will live. Or it will be my life sacrificed," the elder croaked in broken Spanish, his eyes drilling him with the message.

Tom followed the guard, wondering exactly what the old man meant. When he stepped outside, five men surrounded him, rifles drawn. These men were larger and better armed than the ones who had found them only an hour earlier. Each one had the look of a hardened soldier.

"*Muevete.*"

Move, he'd told Tom. One pushed Tom from behind with the butt of his gun toward a truck where Alvarez stood, waiting for him.

Alvarez scanned his body, as if studying him to see for himself how deadly he could be. "You will be transported to another place, *Señor.* We will question you there. We do not want to disturb Miss Lindsay. Agreed?" A corner of the major's mouth quirked upward, but his dark eyes contradicted the humor in his smile.

Tom swallowed, sure his time was up.

Chapter Fifteen

એ

"Tom?" Rorie bolted up, irritating her wound. She groaned and laid her head on the pillow. A loud noise sounded at the door. Shouting?

"*¿Está usted bien?*"

She looked to the nearby voice. The native from the riverbank sat in a chair at the foot of the bed, staring at her. She pulled the sheet tighter around her. Drawing on the little Spanish she knew, Rorie thought he asked if she was okay. But what was he doing here? Was he a prisoner, too?

"I'm fine. Where's Tom?" she asked. Getting no answer, she tried to rise.

The elder pushed her down. "No." He shook his head. "No. *Hombre* okay. *Él regresa aquí.*" He pointed to the floor.

Tom would come back? Rorie shook her head, wishing she'd learned more Spanish before she came to Panama. Tom wouldn't be fine without her, she was sure. What would they do to him? "No. I need to get to him."

"*No. Usted lo vera más tarde.*" The elder pointed to his eyes then made a movement with his hands for her to stay put.

Rorie didn't entirely understand him. Turning to her side, she lifted her body by bracing her trunk on her elbow. She might be able to make the door.

The native stood and blocked her path. She moaned. He stuffed a leaf in her mouth before she could protest and made her chew. Putting a wooden cup on the side of the bed, he put some leaves inside and lit them, causing them to smolder. Picking up the cup, he held it under her nose.

"Oooh." She backed away from the stench, but it stuck to her.

The old man pushed the cup closer.

"Neeeuuuoooo." She pursed her lips and waved her hand in front of her nose. "Yuck."

"No *youk*." He botched the word. "*Medicina. Te sentirás mejor.*"

She recognized the word medicine. Was he a healer? To satisfy him, she inhaled the fumes. She had to admit, it didn't take long for the pain in her rear to feel better.

Breathing in another draft, she got a little lightheaded. "What is this stuff?"

She looked at him, but the old man only smiled. "*Le vas a gustar a tu hombre esta noche. Ya veras. Todo estará bien. Sueña, niña. Acuna te cuidara, okay?*"

"Okay" she understood. But what else did he say? Tom would like her tonight? What did he mean? Her vision blurred. She began feeling funny, amorous even, as she thought of Tom. "Who are you?" She pointed to him. "Ah, *quien eres?*"

"*¿Yo?*" He nodded and jabbed a thumb in his chest. "*Mi, Acuna.*"

She became a bit dizzy. "What happened to the man and the little boy?"

Acuna lifted a grizzly brow.

"Boy. *Niño.*" The word sounded slurred to her. She held her hand about three feet off the floor.

The elder smiled. "*El hombre lo rescato.*"

Rorie squished the features of her face in confusion and tried to focus. "He saved them?" She got a big hit of the smoke. "Wooohoooo, this stuff is something." She held onto the bedpost and pulled herself into a crooked sitting position, resting on her good rear cheek.

Pulling a gourd from the satchel he carried, Acuna chanted and rattled the dried pod over her body.

"What are you doing?" she asked, dropping her feet over the edge of the bed.

"*Medicina.*" He put his hand on her arm and made her lay her head on the pillow, her feet dangling from the side. Rolling her on her stomach, he put her legs on the bed and lifted the sheet, inspecting Tom's handiwork. "*Bien. Tu hombre sabe lo que hace.*"

She crooked her head to peer at him. He said something about Tom being hers, that he was a good man—she thought. "Thanks. I think." Did he believe Tom and she were a couple?

Outside, Rorie heard the squeal of brakes. A truck stopped in front of the building. Through the window, she saw a soldier jump out. Spanish words permeated through the door.

"What's going on?" she asked.

The old man looked at her as the guard burst through the door. With her eyes, Rorie tried to convey a message to the healer. Would he help?

* * * * *

Why hadn't he told her he loved her?

Stripped to his waist and on his knees, Tom studied an ant in the black dirt of the jungle floor, willing his mind to deaden against the pain inflicted by his captors.

As much as he tried to focus, his thoughts came back to Aurora, and his concern for her safety. Watching the ant work, Tom analyzed his life. Wondered why he'd let his past hurts, his perceived failure to his father, prevent him from finding joy in his life, prevent him from committing his heart to a woman. His father wouldn't have wanted that.

Now, Tom didn't either. For once, it mattered to him that he lived to walk away from a mission. It mattered that he loved.

"Why are you here?" Alvarez asked, pulling Tom from the struggle of his thoughts.

Ignoring the question, Tom tried to relax, a difficult thing under the binding of the pig pole they'd put across his shoulders and lashed to his arms. They were in a glade close to the compound. Tom guessed Alvarez didn't like getting his buildings dirty. Tom wondered how Aurora was.

"*Señor.*" Alvarez's voice grew harsh. The major had asked this question a thousand times already.

Tom glanced around the open area, trying to think of another bogus detail to satisfy him. "Uh…"

The rifle butt to Tom's back told him he hadn't responded quickly enough.

"Tell us where the film is, *Señor*. We know your spy had the information." Alvarez grabbed Tom's hair and jerked his head up. "Please, *Señor*, I do not want to hurt Miss Lindsay's *amante.*"

Tom bit the inside of his cheek, trying not to glare at him. "You have things wrong. I'm not her lover. I was sent to return her to the United States."

Alvarez bent over and stared in his face. "If you are not her lover, you want to be. Have you slept with the *chica*?"

Tom gritted his teeth, trying not to say anything, reminding himself a good interrogator designed such superfluous questions to goad their victims.

Alvarez laughed and nodded at one of his minions. Tom saw the strike coming and jerked his head away as best he could. The butt of the soldier's rifle glanced off the side of his head and busted his lip.

"How is Miss Lindsay involved?"

"Involved in what?" Tom grunted when the strike hit his back, knowing his response would get him another pounding. He bent over, thinking he had at least one cracked rib.

"Do not play coy, *Señor*. We know Ferguson was a spy." The major squatted and jerked Tom's head up again. "I want to know how involved Miss Lindsay is." Alvarez quirked his brow. "You may save her life."

Think. Tom bit the inside of his cheek. One wrong word and they would terminate Aurora. "My mission was to rescue two American hostages." Tom lowered his voice. "Look at her, Major. I seriously doubt she's a spy. She doesn't even know how to use a weapon."

For a mere second, Alvarez's harsh look softened. Did the major believe him?

A truck had left before. Now Tom heard the same grind of the engine as one returned. Alvarez stood. "We shall see."

The deuce and a half came into view and two soldiers got out.

One carried a half-clad Aurora in his arms.

"Look, *Juan*, be careful where you put your grubby paws." Rorie tried to move the soldier's palm off her good butt cheek, a hard thing to do while the creep cradled her to him. He gave her a toothy leer, drooling over her bra-covered breasts, which protruded over the edge of the sheet. "Ooooh." She couldn't move him. Instead, she glanced at where they had brought her.

"Oh, my God." She stared at Tom. His left eye had swollen and blood had dried on his lip. Pain showed on his face. She kicked her legs and punched the shoulder of the man who carried her.

The soldier's grip tightened. He spat out some Spanish cuss words, at least one of which she understood.

"I will be a bitch if you don't let me down." She pushed her hands against the soldier's arms without much of an effect then glared at her ex-guide. Seeing what Luis had done, she derided herself again for misjudging him. What a fool she was.

"*Tráigala aquí*," Luis ordered.

The soldier walked to Tom and lowered her in front of him.

"Humph." She stumbled slightly, still suffering the effects of the drug the healer gave her—if one could call what she felt suffering. Lifting her chin to regain her dignity, Rorie wrapped the sheet tighter around her. They'd only given her enough time to grab her underwear, which she had to don on the way, hiding herself under the bedsheet while the two men ogled her. "Bastard."

The soldier showed his grimy teeth. *"Creo que le gusto, jefe. ¿Puede ser mía?"*

The soldier leered at Rorie. Did he say he wanted her? She looked at Luis and stilled.

Luis glared at the man. *"Es prisionera, idiota. Y es peligrosa. Te morderá tus aguacates mientras duermes."*

The soldier paled.

Rorie lifted a brow, afraid Luis might have told the guerilla she was fair game. "What did he say?"

Tom's soft grunt brought her attention to him. "The major told him you were dangerous. Said you would cut off his testicles in his sleep."

Rorie glared at the man who had held her. The soldier stepped back some as Luis talked to him.

Moving slowly so as not to reopen her wound, Rorie knelt in front of Tom, oblivious to her own pain. "Are you okay?"

He lifted his head and looked into her face, a longing in his eyes. "Better, now. Thanks." He cleared his throat. "Isn't your bum hurting?"

She shrugged. "Whatever that old man gave me did the trick. I feel no pain. No pain at all." She wobbled a bit and steadied herself by grabbing his shoulders.

He winced and she jerked her hands back. "Sorry. I didn't know."

"No problem." He looked her up then down. "I thought you looked a little high."

"High?" She opened her eyes as wide as she could then blinked. "You think I'm high?" She giggled even though his statement confused her. "Are my pupils diarated? I mean dilatered." She shook her head, wishing she could think more clearly. "Wider than normal?"

"Yes."

"Oh." She thought she detected a hint of humor in him, even with the pain he must be suffering on her account. God, did she feel guilty about them being caught. If she hadn't convinced him to save the natives, they would still be hidden.

She shook her head. No time to think about that now. They had to get out of there. Gingerly, she sat on her heels, trying to act nonchalant. "Why did they bring us here?"

Tom eyed her. "I'm not sure why they brought you. They brought me out here for questioning. Maybe scare me with the hole they'd dug a few feet behind my back."

"Hole?" She glanced behind him and through the legs of the soldiers standing around. The deep pit looked body size. What he said hit her then. "They can't kill you," she whispered. "That's…against everything. Geneva Connection and all that."

"It's the Geneva Convention and they don't subscribe to any document that civilized. They made that clear."

She swallowed, wondering how they would get out of this. "Are you in a lot of pain?"

He took a moment before he answered, but his eyes never left hers. "Some."

Rorie glanced at Luis. He'd finished his conversation with "Juan", a name she made up for the creep. Luis just stood there, watching them. "You need some of the stuff the old man gave me. You'd feel fine. I think the healer wanted to put me out, but these guys wouldn't let him."

"Mmmm." Tom looked her up and down. "They should have left you there."

She cut her eyes to Luis who still studied them then looked back at Tom. "I'd rather be with you."

"No, you wouldn't."

Tom sounded so insistent. She wanted to hold him, tell him she cared, that she...

God, even now, she couldn't say the "L" word. But in her heart, she knew. And seeing Tom abused made her angry. "Why are you doing this?" she demanded of her old guide.

Luis scoffed. "I do not want to, Miss Lindsay, but I need the information you ran off with."

"Information? Pah, as far as I know, we were ambushed by your people for no damned reason."

"No need to lose your composure, my dear. Perhaps you are innocent, as you say. But if you could tell me anything that Mister Ferguson told you, you could help save this *yanqui* soldier's life."

Tom eyed her harshly, as if not to say a word.

"You wouldn't dare kill him. He only came to get me."

Luis shrugged. "I would have no choice. I, too, have my orders."

"Ohhh." She rubbed her numb face—until a thought hit her. She looked at Luis. "So if I can tell you something, you'll let us go?"

Luis nodded.

She wasn't sure if he lied or not, but she didn't want Tom beaten anymore. She certainly didn't want him killed. She took a deep breath. Should she risk telling him?

"Wait a minute." She lifted her index finger in front of Tom's face. Hopefully, he wouldn't speak up and blow this.

Tom frowned, the creases in his face deepening. "Aurora, no," he whispered.

"Chris did give me something." Rorie saw the shake of Tom's head, but the slight movement would have been imperceptible to anyone else.

She just smiled. "Chris gave me a camera." She lifted her brow and looked at Luis. "Of course, I left it in my *other* pair of pants." She flipped the edge of the sheet at him.

Luis glared at her. "The camera is in your pants?"

She nodded.

The arch in his brows deepened. "Where are your pants?"

When she shrugged, she nearly unbalanced herself. "Your *fine*—and I say that in the loosest of terms—soldiers wouldn't let me put them on. I barely had enough time to put on my underwear." She squeezed her eyes together and lifted her index finger into the air when she opened them again. "Hey, that's funny. Barely, as in, I'm dressed—barely. Funny."

Luis smirked and stared at her a moment. "*Metanlos en la camioneta. Muevanse,*" he ordered.

The soldier who had carried her put his arms under her breasts and lifted her.

"I told you to watch it, *Juan.*" She elbowed him, satisfied when she heard him grunt.

"*Puta,*" he sputtered in her ear and lifted her into the cradle carry again.

"Same to you, buster." She tried to slap him, but he just jerked his head back out of the way.

She heard Tom groan when two others helped him rise.

The men put them in the back of the covered vehicle and two of them took posts at the tail end. Rorie kept her injured cheek raised and leaned her head carefully against Tom's shoulder, avoiding the pole they'd left strapped to his shoulders. When they took off, their two guards watched the passing scenery as if looking for something.

Tom studied them. Rorie seemed sure his quick mind worked to find an escape. In her drugged state, she certainly couldn't think of anything. She'd been surprised she thought of any diversion at all, much less sending them to her battered camera. Between the water and the hits she took from the rock face of the falls, her camera had to be ruined. She put her hand behind her back and crossed her fingers. As the jungle rolled by, Rorie wondered if her deception would work.

* * * * *

Tom groaned as they shoved him through the door of the hut and pushed him to the floor. The soldier Aurora called Juan carried her in and put her on the bed. The old man had disappeared.

Alvarez marched in behind them. "Where are your pants?"

She pointed to the bathroom. "The medicine man hung them in there with my shirt." She plopped back on the bed.

Tom had an idea what Aurora thought. At least Alvarez's search of the digital would buy some time. It was obvious to Tom they hadn't found the chip in the hidden compartment of Ferguson's camera case. Question was, how could he get Aurora out of there and get the chip back?

Alvarez ducked into the room and in a moment came back, pants in one hand, Aurora's camera in the other. "Is this it?" He walked over and held the digital in front of her.

"Looks like it to me." She nodded.

He sneered at her. "It's ruined."

Aurora shrugged. "Jumping over the falls probably didn't help it any."

Alvarez's jaw tightened. "What was on it?" He dropped the pants on the bed.

She shook her head and rolled onto her side, supporting her head with her hand. "I can honestly say the Chief never let me take a look. Every time I tried, he stopped me."

The major glared at her. "Why would he let you keep it?"

Aurora paused. Tom prayed she wouldn't say anything stupid. So far, her story sounded plausible, even to him, but she couldn't think straight with the drugs the old Indian had given her.

She cleared her throat. "He didn't know I had it. I tried to look at it while he was away."

"Why?"

"Because—" She pressed her lips together and stared at him. "Somehow, I remember someone warning me not to go with Chris. I wanted to know what got me into this mess. I figured I at least deserved that much."

"And you saw nothing?"

She shook her head. "The Chief would always be back before I had the chance to look."

The corner of Alvarez's mouth twitched. "Always the curious one. I knew that about you." He held the camera up and analyzed it. "Did the Chief look at this?"

"No."

Tom thought she held her breath.

Alvarez glanced at him briefly then back at Aurora. "Why would your boyfriend leave you in the jungle alone?"

She quirked her brow. "My boyfriend?" she squeaked.

Alvarez nodded.

"If you're referring to the Chief, him being my boyfriend isn't even a remote possibility," she said more quietly.

"Why not?"

"Because—" She laid her head back on the pillow. "First, I don't know him that well. Second, I still have too many things to figure out for myself."

Alvarez glanced his way. Tom wished he could interpret the strange look the major gave him.

"So." Alvarez turned his attention back to Aurora. "The Chief, then, where did he go when he left you?"

She huffed. "To the bathroom, I guess."

"Don't be impertinent, Miss Lindsay. It does not become you," the major snapped.

Aurora licked her lips. "I didn't mean to be. He hid me a lot and took off, to check things I guess. He never told me what he did."

Good answer, Tom thought. So far, everything she said could keep her out of trouble.

The major nodded, seemingly satisfied. "We will check this." He held up the battered camera. "I hope you are telling me the truth." Alvarez ordered one of his men to take the digital. "Soon it will be dark," he told Aurora. "I suggest you get some rest. Perhaps you can think through those things you want to straighten in your life." Alvarez glared at Tom. "Before it is too late."

Tom didn't like the "before it's too late" comment. He hoped the major didn't have another meaning hidden behind that statement.

A jeep screeched to a halt outside. A new voice echoed from that direction, a commanding, authoritative one. Tom heard boots on the steps to the hut and the snap of the two soldiers guarding them as they came to attention.

"Colonel." Alvarez nodded briskly to the man Tom sensed behind him.

"These are the prisoners?" the colonel demanded in Spanish.

"*Si*," the major said.

The colonel grabbed Tom's hair and jerked his head up. Cold black eyes penetrated him. "Kill them. Tomorrow at daybreak as a show for the troops," the leader said in Spanish. The colonel shoved Tom's head forward when he released him.

They both would be killed? Tom's gut tightened.

Alvarez argued they could get ransom for Aurora, but the colonel only shook his head.

"No." The new man in charge pointed to Tom then spoke in perfect English. "You will be punished for the tears of the mothers and the widows, *Señor*." He bent over and peered into Tom's eyes. "Tomorrow, you will die."

Chapter Sixteen

&

"No, you can't," Aurora shouted.

The man she called Juan held Aurora down and covered her mouth with his hand.

The colonel sneered at her then swerved and walked out.

Tom's shoulders slumped. There would be no reprieve for them. The worst possible scenario had happened. Aurora had been condemned to death. He had failed to protect her.

Alvarez ordered his men out. Juan released Aurora and walked dejectedly outside.

After closing the door, the major crouched in front of Tom. "I do not want Miss Lindsay to hear." He spoke softly in Spanish. "You killed Colonel Montero's favorite nephew. They found him in the forest with his throat cut, his rifle missing. I assume it was you."

The kid that had snuck up on him, Tom thought. He still remembered the boy's face. Tom's only answer was the blank stare he gave Alvarez.

The major sighed. "I was hoping—" He glanced between Tom and Aurora then took a deep breath. "I will see what I can do for her. I do not hold out hope for you."

"I understand," Tom said in the same tongue. "Why are you doing this?"

A wrinkle between the black eyebrows of the man's passive face belied Alvarez' feelings. "I do not want an innocent woman killed. I, too, had a woman I loved once. Colombian revolutionaries killed her. I will do what I can to save Miss Lindsay. I thought you would want to know."

The major pulled Tom's dog tags from his pocket and jangled them. Giving Tom one last look, he dropped them around Tom's neck. Standing, the man patted Tom on the back and walked out.

When the door closed behind him, Tom tried to rise.

Aurora dropped the sheet and hobbled over. "What did Luis say?"

"He's trying to help you."

She sniffed. "God, I'm so sorry." She fell on her knees and flung her arms around his neck, kissing him.

Tom tried to ignore the aches in his body her touch stirred, especially the one in his heart. "Forget it. You think you can get this off me?" Escape was imperative now. He had to think of a way out of there.

She nodded and fumbled with the ties, freeing one of his hands. Tom helped her untie the binding on his other wrist then rubbed his chafed forearms, letting the pole drop behind him.

The wooden rod tapped on the planked floor. Tom wondered if they'd forgotten he could use that as a weapon. He picked up the staff and glanced at the door. Armed guards stood outside. He knew that. But why didn't the guards keep them under constant surveillance?

Tom guessed those boys felt safe enough. There were two ways out of the building—either through the front door or through the large window by it. Guards stood at both.

What else could they do? There was a bed, a chair, the curtains at the window, sheets...

"Tom." Aurora put her hand on his chin and turned his head to face her. "Let's take that shower you promised. We have a few hours." Her hand shook. "I want to spend them with you." A tear glistened down her cheek.

He wiped the moisture with his thumb then cupped her face. Grown men cried. He wanted to do that now—cry about his failure to protect the person he loved, weep about the fact his time had run out before he had the chance to love. He was scared. He didn't want to die. But Aurora needed him strong now more than ever. "We have to find a way out of here."

"You thought of something?"

"No. Not yet. We need to wait for dark anyway."

"Which would be soon," she said.

"Yeah." He swallowed. Bending toward her, he placed a short, sweet kiss on her mouth. "This might scare you," he said, his lips a breath from hers. "But no matter what happens to us, I want you to know one thing."

"What?" Her lower lip trembled.

Tom touched his forehead to hers. "I love you," Tom whispered against her lips. "I have since our first night. I wanted you to know."

Her tears fell. She fingered the creases near his eyes then played with his cheeks where his dimples would be. "Something special did happen that night, didn't it?"

"Yeah." His voice grew hoarse.

She stared into his eyes. "I love you, too," she said. "I've just been too afraid to admit it."

He gave her a sad smile. "That's more than I've ever had from another woman." Briefly, he touched his lips to hers. "Aurora, I'll take any morsel of affection you'll give me."

"Oh, Tom." She hugged him. "This can't be happening."

"Believe it, sweetheart." He grunted as she touched his bruised ribs. "Careful, babe. I think I have a few battered bones."

"I'm sorry." She loosened her grasp and stared into his eyes. "They're going to murder both of us, aren't they?"

Tom unwrapped her arms from his neck and looked at her. He couldn't lie. "Yeah, if I can't think of something else first."

Rorie leaned her partly nude body against him to soak up his warmth. She'd finally found something special in her life. Now, it would be yanked away before she could sort through her fears. She couldn't let that happen. But what could she do to prevent it?

She backed away from him and rose. *Think*. She looked at the bed. The medicine man's juju stuff was still on it. With a limp, she walked over and took a sniff of the burnt leaves he had in the cup. "Yuck." The smell was still strong within it. "I wonder—"

"What are you thinking?" Tom asked as he came behind her.

She shrugged. "Taking inventory, I guess. This stuff will knock you out. It's part of what the old man used to drug me earlier. It could be useful."

Tom smiled. "It could be. Now you're thinking like a soldier."

She cringed. "Do I have a choice?"

He snickered. "Not really. And I can use this pole as a weapon until I get my firearms back."

"I think I could fit through the bathroom window if we can get it open."

"That'd be good. If you can, hightail it out of here."

"Not without you."

"Aurora…" He ran his fingers through her hair. "I'll die to protect you. Don't let my sacrifice be in vain."

She swallowed, for once realizing how deep his conviction ran. "We can get out of this if we work together. Teamwork, I think you told me."

He nodded with grim determination. "Teamwork, then. But first, let's see about this window."

Tom helped her along as they walked into the bathroom. He jiggled the opaque levered window open without too much noise then tested the bars. "They seem pretty solid." He tried to close the panes again, but they wouldn't budge. "Wouldn't you know it?" he grumbled as a breeze blew through.

"We could probably use the fresh air." Rorie sighed and glanced to the shower, hoping she could make love to him once more before they met their end.

"Go ahead, if you want. Maybe a bath will relax you." He'd come behind her and rubbed his hands across her bare midriff.

The urge to cry again gripped her, but she refused to give in to it. "I was thinking a shower was something we could do together. Tom, if we can't get out of here…"

He brushed her cheek. "I'm not giving up yet. Not as long as there's a breath in me."

"Then I won't either."

He nodded. "Let's see if there's some hot water." Tom turned the tap. In a few minutes, steam rose. "Looks like we're in luck."

Rorie watched the vapor curl against the flaked, peeled paint on the ceiling. "Tom?" She pointed up and looked at him. He'd already taken off his blouse. She'd come to appreciate the view of him in the dark tan T-shirt, his biceps bulging against the cloth when he moved his arms.

"Yeah?"

She cleared her throat. "What about up?"

"What do you mean?"

She pointed to the loose plaster. "Through the ceiling. These buildings are old. Maybe…"

"Yeah." For the first time that day, he gave her an honest smile, one filled with hope. "Honey—" He grasped her chin and lifted it for a quick, searing kiss. "I always thought you were brilliant. I could use the pole to break through, provided we could do something to cover the noise."

"And I bet the ceiling has a vent in it somewhere," she said.

"I bet you're right." He turned off the water then reached for the light switch on the wall. "I wonder if the electric…" Before he could finish, the light came on. "Bingo."

"Bingo?" She looked at him like he was crazy. "How is the light going to help?"

"I don't know. I'm thinking here." He shrugged. "They aren't going to do us until daybreak."

She squished the features in her face together. "Do us? Gee, that sounds like I'm only getting my hair done, not being blown to kingdom come."

He chuckled. "The colonel wants a big show for the troops. We'll be the entertainment."

"How pleasant." Her rigid smile mocked Tom's comment.

"Yeah, but that means we have tonight to escape. Let's save the shower for later. I think I have a plan."

"Thank God." She touched the bruise around his eye. "They left the antiseptic. While you plan, why don't you let me tend to your wounds?"

He lifted a brow as he held her in his arms. "You have a deal. Although I warn you, get too chummy and other things might pop up."

"We have some time before dark," she said soberly. "I want to love you once more before we die."

Tom cupped her cheek in his palm. "Aurora, you're a fighter. I admire that about you. You broke away once from an intolerable situation. You'll do it again. Don't give up. Don't ever give up. Promise me."

She held back her fear and nodded. "I promise."

Under her protests, Tom lifted her and cradled her to him, carrying her to the bed.

He laid her carefully on her side, listening to her cry softly. Removing his T-shirt, Tom crawled next to her on the bed. Covering them, he held her. She nestled into the crook of his neck, her tears wetting his skin. He swallowed, treasuring how she felt in his arms. If their escape didn't work...

He couldn't think about it. The plan had to. He rubbed her back. "Aurora?"

She looked at him, her movement against his chest causing his ribs to ache.

"Yes."

"If we get out of here—"

"When," she interrupted. She sniffed and lifted his palm to kiss it. "Like you, I'm not giving up, remember?"

"When, then." He thumbed her mouth and felt her upturned lips. "I want to tell you—" He didn't know how to put what he felt into words.

"Tell me what?"

He breathed through his parted lips. "I love you. I don't know how else to say it. I don't know how I got so lucky as to have you in my life, but I don't want to lose you now that I have. As crazy as it seems, no matter what happens come morning, I'm glad I found you again. You've made me realize what I've missed in life."

She brushed the tips of her fingers over his face. "I know what you mean," she whispered against his lips. "Right now, all I want is to show you how much I love you." She reached for the buttons on his pants.

"Aurora, I don't know if…"

"You said we have time."

"Yeah, but…" He groaned as she touched his member. "Jesus God, I want you." He buried his head against her neck, breathing in her scent.

"Then take me. Take all of me while you can."

Oh, he wanted to. "Remember, I have no condoms."

"God, Tom, stop protecting me for once and make love to me." She paused. "There might not be time tomorrow."

He raised himself on his elbow and looked at her, his gaze intense in the dimness. "Aurora, I want you in my life. If I make love to you now, I want you to know it's as a man to his woman—for real. Not just from two needy people who met in the middle of the night." He sighed. "I don't mean to push," he said, "but when we get back, I'll do my damnedest to convince you to stay with me."

Rorie knew Tom meant everything he said. Could she take the ardor and commitment his affection would bring? Did it matter? They might be dead in the morning.

With the thought that there might be no future for them, Rorie sobered. The rest of her life might be made of the few hours they had left until morning. What else was there to fear?

Her decision came quickly. "Tom, make love to me now. I want to be your woman, your only one."

He kissed her. "You will be." With desperate ardor, he held her as if he'd never let her go, his lips devouring her as a hungry man would his meal. She savored every taste of him.

As he removed her bra, she'd determined she was more than ready to deal with tomorrow—should it come. The important thing in her life right now was Tom, and being loved by him.

When they both were naked, they joined in reckless abandonment.

When they finally peaked, they climaxed together.

Nothing in the world could have prepared Aurora for the taste of such sweet beauty.

* * * * *

No one bothered them when darkness came. Rorie figured the troops were tucked into their sleepy little beds. At least, she hoped so.

Bits of light trickled through the fabric of the curtain from a floodlight on one of the other buildings, the shades of gray highlighting Tom's strong face. She loved him. She knew that now. But when he came to ask her again to live with him, could she tell him yes? She didn't know, but some strong urge in her wanted to find out. She wanted to test the boundaries her fears made. Somehow she thought happiness could be found on the other side of those imaginary borders she had in her head. But would she have the time to find out?

Their escape had to work.

She lifted herself and sat gingerly on the edge of the bed. Earlier, Tom had shoved the only chair under the handle of the door to give them some privacy. Then he made the most exquisite love to her again, and nothing else but the two of them mattered.

Afterward, she'd treated his wounds, gently kissing each one, smearing some of Acuna's burnt juju stuff on them to take away the pain. She'd ripped up the pillowcase to bandage Tom's ribs. Then she dressed. He put on his T-shirt and pants and she let him get some rest. She'd already had a nap that day. Although she'd grown spent, he needed sleep more than she did. At first, he argued with her, but she insisted.

Thankfully, he caved in. He needed to be as strong as possible to get them out of this.

The most amazing thing about his acquiescence to her request was, in such a perilous situation, he trusted her to do what she said she would. Wake him up one hour after dark. To date, no one in her life—except her grandmother—would have trusted her with something so important.

Miraculously, she smiled. They were near death and here she was smiling. How incredible. All because of Tom and his respect, his love for her.

She hit the button for the blue light to her watch. The time had come for them to make their move. She reached for him in the semi-dark and placed a soft kiss on his mouth. "Time to wake, sweet prince."

His arms came around her before she could pull back and deepened the kiss, teasing her mouth with his tongue. "Hmmm, so in this fairytale, the princess awakes the prince?"

She giggled. "Yea, verily. Have you been up this whole time?"

"No." His slumber-roughened voice warmed her heart. "I slept. Promise. I just wanted to stare at you for a while."

"Hmmm," she spoke softly against his lips. "Sounds like I have you under my spell."

"A sweet one, to be sure." His hand slid along her back and caressed the good side of her bottom.

"Ah, enough of this, Prince. Time for you to get up and go slay the dragons. We need to split."

His soft laughter penetrated her soul, reminded her that they had to get out of there. She couldn't die until she knew what love really meant with this man.

Tom rose. In his bare feet, he went to the large window and eased back one of the drapes, turning his head as he glanced through the opening he'd made.

"The guards are half asleep," he whispered when he came back to the bed. After shoving the juju medicine in his pocket, he picked up the pole, his sock-stuffed boots and his blouse from the floor. "Be right back."

She frowned, thinking he'd want to carry her again. "I can make it to the bathroom myself. You're hurt. You shouldn't be picking me up."

He bent over and kissed her. "Stubborn, but can I take a piss first? The flush of the toilet will alert the guards we're awake, but they'd find that out when we turn on the shower anyway."

"Fine." She crossed her arms.

"Get the blanket," he ordered. "It'll provide some protection from the elements. I know how cold you can get. I'll be back to help you in a minute."

She could barely make out his powerful back in the few beams of light intruding into the bathroom. Outside, she heard the guards stir.

When he returned, he helped her up and they walked to the shower together.

"There's enough light coming through the window, although I wish I could close the damn thing. I don't want to make too much noise. The guards might get suspicious." He kept his voice low. "I think I can see what I'm doing though. I'll turn the water on. Hopefully, the noise from the shower will keep them from hearing. If not, things could get ugly. You keep watch. Listen for the doorknob turning. If you hear or see someone, let me know."

"Right, Chief." She slung the blanket over the bathroom door and steadied herself against the doorjamb.

"Aurora…"

"Yeah, Chief?"

"It's Tom to you." He stepped toward her and brushed her cheek with his thumb. "After everything we've shared, I'd rather you talk to me like a lover."

She kissed his palm. "Yes, darling."

He cleared his throat. "When we get out of here, I want to have a good talk about you and me."

"You've said that before. I—" She paused. "I want to talk as well."

He nodded before taking two steps to the shower. Pointing the showerhead toward the wall, he turned the water on. Tom's gentle but rhythmic tapping on the ceiling alerted the men. She heard them stir. Words from one man sounded like a question. Rorie thought she heard one of them rise.

Someone jangled the knob. *Think.* What should she do?

She moaned like a woman in ecstasy. Tom stopped his pounding as she limped to him, getting droplets from the backlash of the spray over her in the process.

"What the…" he complained.

"They tried the door," she whispered.

Tom put a finger to her lips, his head poised toward the window. "Someone's coming around the side."

"Pretend you're screwing me." Rorie threw her arms around him and pressed her chest against his spray-moistened top, sighing with sensuous abandon.

"What?"

"Hold me and knock me into the wall like we're having sex standing up. Do it. The window's too high for them to see what we're really doing. They can think the noise is from us hitting the wall with your thrusts."

"Jesus." His first look at her in the gray light said she'd gone crazy. Then he groaned—loudly—into her neck.

Lifting her legs and wrapping them around his waist, he held her rear and backed against the wall. Repeatedly, he drove into her with his hips, taking the pounding of the wall on the back of his hands—damp clothes to damp clothes and everything.

"Ah, ahhhhh," she said, letting her voice raise a pitch higher, hoping this ruse would work. Rorie heard another set of footsteps outside the window. "Oh, God, Tom."

From outside the window, she heard one of the guards chuckle. Some Spanish words flew from one of their mouths then both men laughed. Rorie wished she could understand what they said. She moaned again and whimpered against Tom's neck.

"Jesus, God," he cried softly, panting as he held her, stopping the rhythm of his hips into hers. His member pulsed against her.

For several seconds, Rorie only heard the falling water and their shared breaths.

Then the men, their jovial voices hushed, moved away.

"I can't believe that worked," Tom mumbled.

"What'd they say?" she asked.

"You don't want to know. Though I'll tell you, we're going to try this some time for real. Naked."

She blushed, knowing he couldn't see her reddened cheeks.

He eased her down along his body and held her close. Now, both of them were damp with water. "I'm almost through," he whispered. "Stand watch some more."

She nodded, although he probably couldn't see her do that either. Still, she moved away and leaned against the doorjamb again, watching him. Tom pointed the jet of water toward the ceiling, softening the plaster. Then he pulled down pieces of the wet wallboard.

Within minutes, a gaping hole appeared — big enough to get them through. He turned off the tap and felt for her in the scant light, grabbing her arm and pulling her to him. "Be quiet. I'll push you through then come up after you. Make sure you stay on the rafters. The plaster crumbles pretty easily."

"Okay."

Tom grabbed the blanket and looped it around her neck. Taking her arm, he supported her as she moved beneath the hole. Letting go, he positioned her underneath. "When I push you up, grab onto the beams on either side of you."

"Gotcha."

"Ready?"

"Ready."

Tom set himself behind her, putting his arms around her thighs. A sudden thrust upward and the hole was within reach. She grasped the beams as Tom's shoulders then hands moved under her hips. In moments, she was through.

"Stay on the beams," he whispered, reminding her and handed her the pole.

Rorie sat on one of the wood supports, her legs dangling out of the hole. "Will you need help?" she asked in hushed tones.

"No." He moved away from the breached wallboard and Rorie watched him sit on the toilet to put on his socks and boots.

When Tom stood, she moved away, laying the pole over two beams farther in to help balance herself as she sat on them.

After brushing himself off, Tom pulled his body through. His strength amazed her. With the injuries he sustained, Tom shouldn't be able to move.

On his knees, he balanced on the beams on either side of the hole and glanced around. Rorie had already noticed vents set on both sides of the walled area underneath the trusses. Tom took the blanket and threw it over his back, then reached for the pole she'd left on the beams. He tucked the wooden staff under his arm. "Follow me," he said as he carefully made his way toward the rear of the building, away from where the guards were posted.

Rorie inched along behind him, refusing to recognize the pain she felt in her rear. When they reached the vent, Tom tested the seal it had.

She sat on a beam near him.

He leaned over to talk quietly to her. "I don't think I can move this without making a lot of noise."

"Oh, God." She rested her head on the pressed wood board that made a wall between them and the outside. "What do we do now?"

"I wish I had a screwdriver," he said.

"Wait a minute." Rorie patted her pockets. Slipping her hand into one of them, she pulled out the tracking device. "Can you use the clip on this?" She handed it to Tom.

"That's funny—" He stared at the device. "I'm surprised Alvarez didn't find this when he searched your pants."

"Well, I don't know why he didn't, my knight in shining armor, but let's not look a gift horse in the mouth, okay? I'd put the camera in another pocket. Maybe he searched that first. When he found what he wanted, why would he look further?"

Tom snorted and removed the clip. "Right. Now be quiet and listen for the enemy." Stuffing the rest of the instrument in a blouse pocket, he went to work.

What seemed like hours was probably only twenty minutes. Still, Rorie continually checked her watch.

Finally, with little effort, Tom pulled off the small vent. Nudging his head out, he studied the landscape.

"What do you see?" she asked.

He put a finger to his lips. After a few more moments, he leaned toward her to whisper, putting a hand on her cheek. "I'm going to lower you to the ground. You'll have to run about twenty feet into a patch of woods. And I mean run. I know you're hurting, but work through it. Just beyond the few trees, there's some scrub brush. Hide in there until I get to you, understand?"

She nodded in his palm.

"Ready?" His lips were close to her face.

"Ready," she muttered against his cheek.

"If you hear gunfire, don't look back. Just run for your life, okay? You know how to find north?"

"Yes." She nodded.

"The river is to the west of here. Find it and follow it. Maybe you'll hit a village and they can help you. It's your best bet."

"But…"

He kissed her lips. "Promise me. I need to know you're freed."

She paused, wanting to tell him she wasn't leaving without him. But he'd said he'd sacrifice himself for her—and he didn't want his death to be in vain. She held back her tears. No one had ever put her first in the scheme of things. And here, he talked about the ultimate sacrifice. "I love you, Tom." She kissed his lips, grabbing onto him like a lifeline.

"I know," he said when he pulled away, dumping the brown wool blanket over her shoulders. "Promise me, Aurora, you'll do everything to keep yourself safe."

"I promise," she said, and meant it.

"Let's go." Scanning the outside once more, he helped her in front of the hole. "Put your legs out first." He held one arm while she grabbed onto the edge of the opening with the other.

He lowered her as far as possible then she dropped to the ground the rest of the way, wincing when she hit.

Glancing around, Rorie took off for the jungle. In seconds, she hit the brush, the pain in her rear exploding into her leg, and turned to watch for Tom.

She caught a glimpse of him as he jumped with the pole and made for her position.

Rorie sighed when he finally grew near and crouched beside her.

"You all right?" he asked.

His hushed voice, combined with his warm palm on her face, comforted her.

"A-okay."

He nodded. "C'mon." Tom lifted her in his arms before she could protest and ran several feet into the jungle.

Finding another patch of brush, he hid her underneath, covering her with the blanket. "I want you to stay here," he said. "If I'm not back in an hour or you hear an alarm from the camp, you go on without me."

"No."

"Yes. Aurora, I have to get Ferguson's camera case. Plus, it would help us a lot if I can retrieve my weapons and rucksack."

"Tom, please don't. We have to be near some civilization. Don't leave me. We can make it out together."

"You're going to be fine. I have my orders," he whispered and brushed his thumb over her lips. "Besides, it's me they really want for the show. You're just an extra."

"An extra? Damn you, Tom, this is asking too much."

"I promise I'll be careful. Remember what I said. Make for the river if I'm not back in an hour or if there's trouble."

He kissed her quick then took off with the staff as his only weapon, disappearing into the heavy growth of the forest.

* * * * *

Confident Aurora would be safe in her hidden position, Tom circled around the small, but neat compound. He'd noted earlier there hadn't been much damage this far down the mountain. On his second sweep, he studied the camp for his best move, still not able to identify where his things were. Although seemingly well kept, the plant growth allowed around the buildings surprised Tom—bushes big enough that someone could hide in without detection and with much of the area unlit.

He took advantage of the slight. Hiding in some scrub growing against a dark side of the barracks, he watched as the butt of a cigarette burned red in the blackness. The smoke lifted in the air. He stood close enough that he could smell the rancid odor—marijuana, definitely.

The armed soldier who smoked the weed stood a tad shorter than Tom. The spare tire on the man's gut almost matched the width of the soldier's back. Still, the man had come out alone. For what Tom needed, the man would have to do.

Tom lay down the pole, not needing it for this maneuver. Inching forward, Tom got as close as he could. When the soldier turned his back again and leaned on the side of the building, Tom made his move.

Grasping the man's head from behind, Tom twisted it, hearing the sickening crunch of bone on bone, signifying the man died quickly. Pulling him into the cover of the bushes, Tom snuffed out the lit stub and patted the dead man down.

Vacant eyes stared at him. Tom decided there were some things he had to do he would never share with Aurora. She might understand, but she would never like it. He wanted to protect her from the ugliness.

Removing his blouse and rolling up his pant legs, Tom stripped the body. He put on the man's outer clothes, a jungle uniform different from his, and put on the military cap the man had worn. When Tom finished, he stuffed his blouse underneath his newly acquired top, making it seem like he had a paunch on him.

He checked the pockets. In them were a lighter, more stogies and some Columbian money. Tom checked the body again and found a knife hidden in the man's boot. He took the blade and stuffed it in his own jump boot where his knife should be. After making sure he had every useful thing he could find, Tom covered the body with the forest's debris. Picking up the rifle, he crawled from under the cover.

Hunching his shoulders and pulling the hat down on his brow, Tom stood and lowered his chin. Another man came around the building. Tom turned his back to him, facing the bush. The soldier called to Tom in a rough-hewn variety of Spanish, hailing his friend.

Tom leaned the rifle against the hut, ready to grab it if need be, and bent to slip the knife from his boot up his sleeve. This was no time for gunfire—especially outside the main barracks. The whole camp would be up in arms from the noise.

"Manuel, you cannot sleep, huh?" The soldier approached his back. "Me, either." The new man released a slow whistle. "I think about the chica. What a waste her death will be."

Tom grunted.

"Hey, you should have heard them going at it," the soldier continued. "*Bang, bang* on the bed then in the shower."

Tom heard him smack his hands together.

"The *yangui* soldier will die happy. Should I be so lucky if I am captured."

Tom grunted again, realizing the soldier had been one of their guards. The watch must have posted new men.

"Hey, you there, amigo?" The man patted him on the back.

Tom had finally gotten both pants flies open and took the opportunity to piss, hoping the guy would leave.

"Ah, why didn't you say something? You stoned?"

Tom nodded. The man laughed. Through the corner of Tom's eye, he saw the soldier lean against the concrete block building.

"Ay, ay, ay. The colonel, he is plenty angry. They could not find what they looked for in the *yanqui's* things. He and Major Alvarez argued in their little hut. We heard them from our post. The major, he stomped off. Took one of his walks in the woods. He likes the woman, but the colonel, oooh." The man whistled as he sucked air in through his teeth. "He will not let him have her. Hey?" The man slapped him on the back.

Tom went rigid, tried to pee as long as he could, holding himself with one hand while fingering the knife in his sleeve with the other.

"You got anymore of your *special* cigarettes?"

"Shhh." Tom roughed his voice and turned his head away from him.

"Okay, okay. No one needs to hear. But you know, man, you owe me."

Tom slid the knife deeper into his sleeve and pulled out a marijuana joint, handing it to the man over his shoulder.

"Thanks, man." The soldier smacked him on the back again. "No wonder you are in the dark. Care to join me, *amigo*?"

He shook his head and buttoned up both flies. *Can't this damn man leave*? Tom let the knife slip into his palm as new footsteps approached. His gut knotted.

"Hey, Santos, the colonel wants you."

"Oh." From the corner of his eye, Tom watched the man Santos shove the joint in his pocket and straighten to salute. "*Si*, Sergeant. How may I be of assistance?"

"For your loyalty to the Columbian people, you will have the honor of marching the firing squad to their duty at dawn."

Tom heard Santos pause. "Thank you, Sergeant."

"Finish with your business and do not keep the colonel waiting."

"*Si*, Sergeant. I will be right there."

Tom heard the crunch of boots recede. Santos confirmed the sergeant's exodus when he leaned nearer Tom's back and said, "Oh, shit. Who the hell wants to shoot a pretty woman? I can think of better things to do with her."

Tom huffed, thinking maybe he should put the knife in Santos anyway.

Before he could reconsider, the man slapped him on the back again and took off.

Turning around, Tom followed Santos to the edge of the building and watched him run across the front of the compound to a hut on the far side. From the way Santos talked, the camera case had to be with the colonel.

He rubbed his blouse where the cross he wore dangled against his skin. Some angel watched over him tonight.

Glancing upward, he prayed the heavenly being would guard his back once more.

Then he skirted around the rear of the huts to the colonel's cabin.

Chapter Seventeen

ﻬ

Rorie hated to wait. And this kind of waiting only made her nervous. *Where was he*? She glanced at her watch again. Six minutes to go. Tom should be back by now.

Her clothes were almost dry. Still, the night air gave her a chill. She tightened the blanket around her, glad Tom had thought to take it, and listened carefully again for any disturbance. She'd heard nothing at all but the seductive calls of the night. Nodding with weariness and the remnants of the drug she'd been given, she forced her eyes open again. She couldn't afford to fall asleep. Tom might need her.

A bird called. She wondered what kind it was. The song reminded her of why she'd come to the jungle. The seemingly innocent jaunt to photograph wildlife had turned into an adventure of the nth magnitude, one she didn't want to repeat.

Except she found Tom, discovered more about herself, tested her fears beyond limits she had unknowingly made in her head.

No matter what came of this, she knew she had changed — and she would never go back to being the old Aurora.

She thought about her birth name. It sounded different when Tom said it. Not like a pampered little girl, but a mysterious, seductive woman. She'd grown to like how the word rolled off his tongue. And she couldn't stop thinking about him.

Frustrated, Rorie looked at her watch again. Four more minutes and she would head for the river, leave Tom — maybe forever. Those were her orders from him, and she'd agreed. Why did she make such a stupid promise?

Because he'd asked her to make sure his sacrifice wasn't in vain. She swore she would keep herself safe, but…

She huffed. How could she ever forgive herself if she let something happen to him? Especially when this predicament was her fault for not following Chris' request in the first place—the one that asked her to get someone else to get his pack.

Instead, she'd botched one thing after another. Every time, Tom came to rescue her. Now, it was her heart at risk. Would he be able to save her now?

Rorie had never loved anyone like she did Tom. She knew that was part of her problem—she loved him. How could she let him make a sacrifice that she herself wasn't willing to risk?

"That does it," she mumbled. "Turnabout is fair play, Tom MacCallum. You've taught me a thing or two about jungle warfare. I can't just sit here."

She got on her knees to crawl out of the heavy undergrowth, halting when she heard the soft thud of footsteps approach.

Two bare feet stopped in front of her, the leaves rustling as a limb lifted in the air.

"*Señorita?*"

The faint outline of a person's upside down head appeared in front of her in the dark. She froze with fear.

Suddenly, a tiny iridescent flashlight shined, the beam directed at the top of body's head.

Rorie jumped, hitting her temple on a thick branch.

White teeth flashed in front of her, the odd-looking mouth seemingly sitting atop the nose. "*Señorita.*" Acuna nodded. "*Te encontré.*"

She sighed with relief.

"*Vienes.*" He waved to her.

She crawled out and hugged the brown blanket to her, finding the old man wasn't alone.

Several of his native friends had come with him.

"Praise the Lord and pass the mashed potatoes," she said, echoing one of her grandmother's sayings. Hope filled her. The chance of getting Tom back alive just raised several notches—in her favor.

* * * * *

Looking through the opened slats of the shuttered windows, Tom counted four possible rooms to the larger hut. Two bedrooms, probably a bath and a main living area. Right now, Colonel Montero had Santos in the big room, both men enjoying a cigar and liquor from a bottle that looked like whiskey.

The bedrooms were dark, but the windows were open. Going to the larger of the two, Tom pulled the knife he'd appropriated as he balanced the rifle in his other hand and slid the blade between the closed shutters to lift the latch. He assumed the bigger room would be the colonel's. Hopefully, the sleeping area would hold Tom's things.

The opening was screened. Afraid he'd make too much noise by pushing the wire mesh up, Tom cut a hole along the edge of the frame large enough for him to crawl into. Putting the knife between his teeth and placing the rifle quietly inside, he inched through, moving to the closed door and putting his ear to it to listen to the men in the other room. They still seemed engrossed in their own conversation.

Tom shoved the knife in his boot, picked up the AK and scanned the area in more detail. Beside the bed stood a table. Strewn across it were tactical plans. Tom thought those might come in handy. A hutch stood against one wall. Tom went to the wooden piece and tried the door. *Locked.*

He checked under the bed, to be sure nothing was there, and went back to the hutch. If his stuff was in the room, it had to be in the wooden upright dresser.

Taking the knife, he swung the strap of the rifle over his shoulder and pried the metal clasp on the soft wood. The lock popped open without much noise and he thanked his guardian angel. Opening the hutch, he found only clothes hanging in it—expensive ones to be sure. Cussing inwardly, Tom quickly checked a bit more of the room.

Hearing the scraping of chairs in the other room, Tom ducked behind the door, the blade ready in case the colonel entered.

Footsteps echoed on the floor, heading away from the bedroom. Tom heard the squeak of the front door. When the two men walked outside, he released a silent sigh of relief.

Glancing over the papers on the table, Tom noticed some plans involving chemical weapons from some Asian supplier. The information irked him. Who would supply these guys with this shit? And how could the guerillas afford them?

Tom bet the data on Ferguson's disk documented some of this. No wonder the CIA was so hot to get the info. Probably why Ferguson willingly risked Aurora's life—the weapons were too deadly.

Laughing sounded outside. Tom didn't have time to think about this now. Aurora was waiting. Besides, the gook stuff was Ferguson's job.

He took a few of the documents he thought important and stuffed them in his shirt, shuffling the remaining plans to make the area appear undisturbed.

Going to the door, Tom listened again. Both men sounded like they'd moved toward the next building. Putting the knife away, Tom unhitched the rifle from his shoulder and readied himself. Easing the bedroom door ajar, he scanned the hallway and what he could see of the main room.

A narrower door stood off the passageway. A closet?

Tom opened the bedroom door further. Crouching low, he exited and silently shut the entrance to the colonel's quarters behind him. Going to the closet, he opened it and peeked in.

Nothing.

The voices of the colonel and Santos drifted through the window from where he'd spied on them earlier. Staying low, Tom moved to the end of the corridor. The room reeked of an expensive brand of tobacco. Holding his breath, Tom plastered himself against the wall, using it as cover. He peered around the corner toward the window.

Damn if some of his things weren't spread over a small bench underneath. With the big room brightly lit and the two men outside, how could he get to them?

Tom glanced at his watch. His time had run out. Aurora should be headed for the river by now.

Deciding he had no choice, Tom low-crawled across the floor past the table—until heard Alvarez's voice by the front door and froze.

* * * * *

"No." Rorie shook her head at Acuna, who tried to lead her to the river. "We—" She pointed her finger between her and the small contingency of men. "Need to get *hombre*. Man. Soldier. *Americana soldado*. *El hombres* name *es* Tom MacCallum. He's still in camp." Rorie pointed toward the compound. "He saved your people." She wouldn't leave without Tom and looped the blanket she'd roughly rolled over her shoulder for emphasis.

The elder sighed and said something to the others in a language which sounded like one other natives used while she was in Ipeluza.

A larger man, younger than the medicine man but one who looked to have some years of experience, spoke, his hands moving. He pounded a fist on his chest then pointed to the compound.

Rorie crossed her fingers.

Some of the men grunted. The man who had spoken turned to lead the group to the camp. One of the men broke off and took her arm, trying to take her to the river.

"No." She shook her head. "I go with you." She pointed to herself then the direction of the guerilla group.

The larger man, whom she assumed was the leader, stopped and looked at her then whispered orders at the medicine man.

The other native released her. Acuna looked at her and held a finger to his lips. With her and the old man in the rear, the group went toward the compound.

* * * * *

The colonel called for Alvarez.

Thank God.

Tom crawled closer. Ferguson's camera case sat in plain view. When Tom reached the window, he leaned against the wall and picked up the case, feeling for the chip.

It was still there.

Shoving the case in his side pocket, Tom took a few deeps breaths and waited. The enemy spoke very near the window.

Slowly, Tom picked up the extra ammunition for the former AK-47 they'd carried, knowing he could use it for the rifle he'd just acquired. He stuffed the ammo in another pocket, along with his GPS unit. Then he picked up his belt and the holstered Beretta. Leaning the rifle against the bench, Tom slid the holster on the belt and eased it around him. When he had it fastened, he picked up the rifle again.

Deciding he could leave the rest, he listened more closely to the discussion outside. Santos had left. Only Alvarez and Colonel Montero remained.

Tom sat motionless, ready to move, depending on where the men went.

The voices drifted away, seemed to go toward the back of the cabin.

Inching upward along the side of the window, Tom peered gingerly through. His line of sight was clear in the one direction.

Moving just enough to look toward the men speaking, he saw the colonel and Major Alvarez nearer the rear of the next building. Alvarez raised his voice. As Santos had indicated earlier, their discussion seemed to have garnered some heat.

Tom thought there was no better time to split. With the two men arguing, he decided he could make it out with his pack. Tom shoved Aurora's other cameras inside and made for the entrance to the cabin. He hoped the loud disagreement the two officers had would cover the noise from the hinges when he opened the front door.

With Tom's stealth, the door made little sound. Tom hopped out, foregoing the stairs, and hit the ground running.

Making the cover of the nearby canopy, he slipped into the undergrowth and worked his way around the cabin. Tom needed to get to where he'd hid Aurora. He could track her movements from there.

As he came around, Tom heard the officers still fighting. Alvarez seemed to be on the losing end, Montero threatening him as a traitor to the cause.

Tom hastened away as a silence hovered between the two men.

Several minutes passed before he came to a clearing big enough where he could view the sky. Tom pulled out the GPS unit and checked the landscape to get his bearings, the blackness of the new moon ensuring he could see several stars through the narrow glimpse the trees provided.

Looking up, he studied the constellations. Aurora would be somewhere farther north by now. Tom pegged the direction. Where he'd hidden her was several more feet northwest. Figuring she wouldn't have gotten far, he crossed the glade.

"Stop, Chief MacCallum."

Tom heard the click of the safety released on the Makorov pistol before he could reach the edge of the glade.

Exposed, Tom ducked and rolled into the brush, trying to get a bead on his unknown assailant, hoping the enemy wouldn't be able to see well enough to fire back at him.

His ploy worked. Tom peered from his hidden position. Whoever called him had dodged behind the trunk of a tree. Tom wondered if he should have fired at the target. Normally, he would have, but he didn't think Aurora had gotten far enough away. A shot could have stirred the whole camp, bringing the small regiment of men sleeping there after both of them.

Now though, he had an armed enemy to contend with — one he couldn't see.

Moving in the darkness around the grassy opening, Tom made a silent path toward his would-be attacker. Tiny hairs on his neck stood on end as he edged closer. Tom stopped and dipped lower into the bush, eyeing the tree where the man had been.

No one there.

Tom didn't like that. He got an odd feeling whoever came after him had more skill tracking and hiding than the rest of these goons. Was the man lying in wait for him?

Glancing upward, Tom tried to peer into the dark canopy. He couldn't see much, but in this patch of woods, he decided someone would have to be pretty damn good to shimmy up the wide trunks without a rope or something, especially without him hearing it. The guy had to be on the ground nearby — and after him.

Or would he have slipped off toward the camp? That would have been the smart thing to do. Get reinforcements.

But that should have been the first thing for the guy to do as well. Why go into the jungle alone after someone who could kill you, when you could overpower the person with numbers?

Sloppy soldiers. Or simply untrained. Tom thought much of what happened at this camp didn't make much sense militarily — an oversight of theirs he'd use to his advantage.

Regardless of the reason, Tom needed to go after the perpetrator. Taking a wider berth, he circled around the last spot where he'd seen the man. As he neared the point again, a shadow darted between the bushes.

Always careful, Tom pressed his rifle to his chest and moved closer, thinking he would much rather be the hunter than the hunted.

And that anytime with two skilled opponents, the situation could change.

* * * * *

Her backside too sore to make the whole way, Rorie hunched under the blanket in some bushes, the medicine man next to her. They sat in an area near the camp while the others searched. The natives' ability to blend in the woods amazed her. They hadn't made a sound and their disappearance reminded her of Tom.

You'll see me before you hear me.

Although it'd only been a few days since he'd said that, the time that had passed seemed like eons. Funny, but she had lived more in these few days with him than she had her whole lifetime.

Rorie swallowed, thinking of the torture Tom might be going through, what he'd already gone through for her. He had to be okay. He just had to. She had things she needed to tell him.

And she needed to come clean with her soul.

In the distance, some twigs snapped. She buried her body under the blanket, Acuna reminding her to be quiet.

A shot echoed in the quiet night. Rorie lifted her head. What direction did it come from? Was it…?

She quivered with fear, hoping Tom remained with the living.

Acuna motioned her to stay put then left their leafy cover and disappeared into the night.

Now she was alone, worry eating at her.

For several moments, the night air filled with the chirping of crickets and frogs—probably the poisonous ones. Then the sound of someone rushing came closer. Rorie peered through the branches. A uniform-clad leg passed, one that seemed in a hurry to get away. Was it Tom?

She bit her lip. The person could be him. If it was, how would he find her in the jungle?

She had to be sure.

Scooting out of the bushes, Rorie wore the blanket like a shawl and followed, mimicking the silent step she'd seen Tom and the natives make—only she wasn't anywhere near as quiet.

When she passed a large tree, a man's rough hand clasped around her mouth and yanked her into his body.

"Tom?" she tried to mumble through the fingers.

The cold metal of a handgun to her temple let her know she'd made the wrong choice again.

* * * * *

Shit…

Scant beams of light from the camp filtered through the trees, enough so Tom could see the colonel's form. Tom watched Montero ease into the open with a hostage, glancing around. He'd almost had the colonel when Montero squeezed off a shot. He knew the officer had run with fear.

Now, Tom's blood ran cold. Montero pressed the pistol against the other figure's head, hiding as much of himself as he could behind the smaller body. Tom didn't need to see the new person in this fight. His gut told him who it was.

Aurora.

He ducked behind a tree, thinking. *Too dark to get a clear shot. Might hit her.*

"Give yourself up, *yanqui.*"

Montero's voice sounded different this time.

"I will spare the woman."

Tom inhaled a deep breath.

"I will kill her now if you do not show yourself."

Pressed against the trunk, Tom moved enough to glance at Montero, making a quick assessment. An expert marksman, Tom could shatter his elbow. But could he fire before Montero killed Aurora? He said a silent prayer. "I want your word as an officer you'll let her go unharmed."

"You have it."

Hoping his angel stayed with him, Tom stepped around the tree. Montero swiftly shifted the aim of the pistol toward Tom.

"No…" Aurora screamed and struggled with Montero.

The jungle echoed with the Makarov's report.

Chapter Eighteen

🙞

Rorie knocked the colonel's arm, shifting the direction the guerilla officer fired, but her action wasn't enough. She watched Tom fall. "Oh, God, no." The man she loved couldn't be gone. As hard as she could, Rorie elbowed the colonel's ribs. She needed to get to Tom.

Her enemy's hold gave way and Montero crumbled behind her.

Before she could rush to Tom, another arm shot around her and pulled her into the brush.

"Stay here," Luis whispered. "Your friend is not dead, I think."

Confused, Rorie looked through the limbs. Colonel Montero lay unmoving a few feet from them in a heap, the blanket she'd dropped in the struggle lying half over him. "Tom?" She couldn't see him.

Suddenly, Luis pulled her up. "Over here, Chief MacCallum. Please do not try to shoot me this time."

"Why not?" Tom's voice came from the darkness.

"Because I'm going to help you."

"Your colonel dead?"

"*Si.*"

"Let her move to him. I want to keep you in my sights."

Luis nudged her.

"Tom, thank God," Rorie mumbled as she saw him rise from the undergrowth. Relief flooded through her.

Keeping his aim on Luis, Tom walked to the colonel and rolled the limp body over. The yellow floodlights from the camp revealed a dark stain spreading over Montero's back. "Why?"

Luis nodded. "No time to speak now. We need to get to the river."

"But…" Rorie wanted to ask him what was going on, but she heard the men in the camp moving about.

"Agreed," Tom said and jerked the blanket free from the dead man, wrapping it around her shoulders. Luis grabbed the colonel's feet. He and Tom dragged the body into the underbrush.

As Luis took off, Tom hoisted her over his shoulder and ran after him.

"You shouldn't carry me," she protested. "Your injuries—"

"We need to move."

"Talk about stubborn. You're the most pig-headed—"

"Be quiet or our attempted escape will be short."

Before Rorie could say another word, Tom had caught up to her former guide.

* * * * *

Tom listened to the flow of the river as they neared. After breaking through some bushy leaves, they hit the bank. A native stood guard over a few canoes. Tom couldn't believe their luck.

Alvarez spoke to the Indian in what Tom recognized as a Choco tongue then the half-clad man took off into the jungle.

Alvarez turned to Tom. "When the chief returns, these men will take you to their camp on the other side of the river. You will be safe there for a day or two. Then you must make your way out on your own. Stay away from Pinogana and El Real. If you make it to Yaviza, call your embassy. You should be okay."

"Thanks." Tom lowered Aurora. He knew better than to ask, but he couldn't help himself. "You stopped me in the glade."

The major nodded. "Yes, but I hadn't realized Colonel Montero followed me. Sorry, but consider it the mistake of a tired, old man."

"I'm surprised you came into the jungle alone."

Alvarez took a deep breath and looked around impatiently as if waiting for the return of the Indians. "I'm more astonished Montero followed me without his loyal supporters, but he is insane. I believe he thought himself invincible. As for me? I took the risk. I needed to find you. I knew you were gone when I checked the holding cell."

"And the natives?"

The major frowned. "We press them into service when there is a need. No one questioned my use of them to treat Miss Lindsay's wound. As far as the other assistance they give?" He shrugged. "Anyone who would know they work for me is dead. You are safe."

Tom studied him. "Why the help?"

Alvarez gave him a pained smile. "I told you before. I had a woman I loved, too."

Tom nodded, feeling his bruised ribs. "I'll consider us even then."

The major grunted then looked at Aurora. "Best of luck to you, *Señorita*. If you let this man, I think he will take good care of you." Alvarez winked at her.

Someone from the distant camp called loudly for the major. Alvarez glanced over his shoulder. "I cannot wait longer. I must go and settle the men before they become suspicious. Things will happen soon enough in the morning when they find you are not there. Here—" Alvarez handed Tom a small white envelope. "Give Ferguson my regards."

After nodding to Aurora, the major disappeared.

Surprised, Tom palmed the unexpected gift. Crouching with Aurora in the brush, he fingered the sealed paper. The lump in the wrapper felt like the chip in the camera case he'd recovered. Could Alvarez have replaced the original?

"So is Luis a good guy or bad guy?" Aurora whispered.

Tom shrugged. "Hard to tell. I'm just glad he helped us get out of there. He seems to have the natives' trust. He knows Ferguson."

"So maybe my judgment about him wasn't so bad?" Aurora's breathy voice still questioned herself.

"No, I don't think it was bad at all. You should trust your instincts." He kept his voice low.

"But if he's a good guy, why did he beat you up?"

"If he tried to keep his cover, maybe he had no choice." It reminded Tom of Ferguson's use of Rorie. He still wouldn't forgive the man for that. "My interrogation could have been worse."

"But—" Aurora said.

"Stay quiet." He hushed her. "We could still be caught." Tom decided it best not to dwell on the odd situation. If Alvarez worked with Ferguson, he was in deep.

Activity from the camp droned in the distance. In a few minutes, most of the noise subsided. He heard the soft drumming of running feet on the path before the natives showed. The men moved in a hurry.

Tom pulled Aurora up with him as he stood before them. While the others readied the canoes, the old man who'd treated Aurora stomped up to her and scolded her, wagging his finger in her face.

She licked her lips. "What's he saying?" She leaned toward Tom.

Annoyed himself with her disregard of his instructions, Tom took a deep breath, inhaling her musky scent as he did so. The smell threatened to distract him from the grilling he intended to give her. "Do you really want to know?"

She pouted in response.

"Why didn't you take off like I told you?"

She grimaced. "Would you believe I got lost?"

He frowned. "Not in this lifetime."

The medicine man still raved. She looked to him. "*Lo siento*, Acuna," she told the witch doctor. "*Lo siento mucho*," she said, trying to apologize. Holding the blanket closed around her with one hand, she placed her palm over her heart with the other. "I won't do it again. Promise." She held up three fingers.

Tom bent near her ear. "Haven't I heard that before?"

"No." She glared briefly at him. "Okay, so maybe I promised you, too, but I promised you I'd keep myself safe—not stay in the bush."

"You were supposed to head north."

"Well, plans change. When Acuna showed up I figured the odds were in my favor. Besides, they were going to cart me off and I couldn't leave without you. You would have never found me."

"Uh-huh," Tom sneered.

Tom watched the old man shake his head, waving to them to come to the canoe, telling her in Spanish to listen next time. Aurora sighed and stepped in the middle of the boat, pulling the wool coverlet tighter around her. As she sat, she held her hurt side off the bottom.

Even in her pained state, Aurora looked cute. Tom smiled inwardly. He couldn't help himself. He just thanked God she was safe. That they were closer to home.

Relieved, he eased behind her and settled her on the crook of his bent leg to lessen the pressure on her rear. The old man still ranted under his breath. Tom leaned into her soft hair, letting the strands caress his face. "You know, I'll have some similar things to say when we get to their place."

She looked over her shoulder. A twinkle seemed to gleam in her eye.

Tom tried to shoot a scathing glare at her before the men pushed off from shore.

His attempt failed miserably when Aurora simply smiled at him.

* * * * *

Night sounds on the river echoed off the complacent water. The gentle movement of the canoe lulled Rorie. Just yesterday, the waters of the river had roared turbulent from the storm. Now, the dark path seemed to meander through the shadows of the forest, the stars winking at them from the heavens.

What a difference a few miles along the river made.

She snuggled into Tom and the arm he had around her adjusted to her change in position. His left hand had held her the whole way, his other occupied with his rifle. She knew he stayed alert. Knowing he sat behind her comforted her in a way she'd never felt before. A feeling more than safety enveloped her.

She was loved. She knew it. But how could she come to him with the half of a woman she'd become over the years? Her fears held her back from being able to give to him as he'd given to her. He deserved better.

Before she realized it, they pulled into a side stream, some of the canoes ahead of them disembarking along the shore.

"We're here," Tom whispered into her ear.

Rorie looked over her shoulder and kissed him on the cheek. "I know."

"Did you sleep?"

"Some." She nodded as their boat nudged the bank.

"Good," he said and helped her up, carrying her over the side to shore. She circled her arms around his neck and snuggled into him. "And your excuse for carrying me now would be?"

"I like holding you."

"I see." Too exhausted to fight, she nestled into his strong chest and glanced around. A fire crackled in the center of the circle the grass shacks made. The habitat looked thrown together, as if the natives moved into it quickly.

Unexpectedly, Tom stepped downward. The jarring motion irritated her backside. She groaned from the pain.

"Sorry," he whispered.

Acuna looked back and eyed her with worry. After saying something to Tom, they followed the medicine man to a hut Rorie could only assume was his.

Tom ducked through the hole and laid her sideways on a grass pad made for one. Covering her with the blanket, he dropped his pack next to the mat.

After lighting a candle, Acuna picked up a cup and came to her, but Tom stopped him.

After what seemed to Rorie like a brief set of instructions, Acuna left, putting the muck of whatever was in the coconut cup in Tom's hands.

Tom watched him go and closed the palm-lined door. Then he came to her, his deep scowl more ominous on his face from the play of the candlelight. "Let's get your pants off."

"Hmmm," she purred and lifted the blanket. "Just what a girl wants to hear from a guy like you."

Tom bit his lip, Rorie thought to suppress a smile, but his grin still showed through.

Putting Acuna's cup near her, Tom unzipped her pants. When he lifted her hips and bared her bottom, he grimaced. "I'm sorry, Aurora," he said, his voice rough.

"For what?" She rose on her elbow and stroked his cheek.

His Adam's apple bobbed as he swallowed. The desolate look in his eyes captured her soul. "For not keeping you safe. You would have been killed by Montero. There would have been nothing I could have done to prevent it."

"Tom." She leaned back on her good rear cheek and took his face in both her hands. "It wasn't your fault. I love you, but it isn't your job to save me. Some of the things that happened to me were because *I* made a decision about them—like firing on that patrol. You couldn't have prevented that. And there was no way you would have known their camp was just over the hill. Give yourself a break."

He shook his head. "I should have trusted my instincts and not gone back to the river. I should have stayed with you."

"Which would have accomplished what? Throughout this whole affair, you've stood by me—even when I was being unreasonable. I realize now my actions were driven by my insecurities. But you helped me see through that. You explained things to me, encouraged me instead of making me do them. You've done the right thing."

"Not always." His steely gaze chilled her. "My stupidity got us caught a few times—like when I killed that soldier who snuck up from behind me. Then at the river."

"If you hadn't gone to the river, Acuna and that boy would have been killed." She shook her head. "I saw all I wanted of the innocent dead when I was with Chris. Besides, you can't protect me all the time. Doing that would mean running my life. I thought you didn't want to do that."

"I don't, but I don't want you hurt, either."

Rorie frowned. "You can't always prevent that. My errors are my responsibility." She rolled onto her stomach, biting her lip as she looked at the wall. "Besides, that's part of the problem with me as it is. Everyone else makes decisions for me—to keep me safe. The only thing that's ever accomplished was keeping me caged." She looked over her shoulder at him. "Can't you see that's the last thing I need?"

"This is different. Out here choices—good or bad—mean survival."

"I understand that, believe me. But some things just happen, whether you like it or not. You couldn't have known there were other soldiers in the woods."

Tom shook his head and picked up the cup with Acuna's juju stuff in it. "I don't buy it. I messed up. Bad. And I'm sorry for that. If it hadn't been for your quick thinking and Alvarez's help, we would have never gotten out of there." He stared at her and Rorie had to wonder what went through his mind.

Looking away, Tom sniffed the cup and jumped back from the smell. "God, what is this stuff?"

Rorie snickered. "It'll make you feel better. Trust me."

"If you say so." Tom picked some of the gunk up and rubbed it between his fingers.

Rorie thought about what he said, about his doubts. She worried about him, about his need to protect her—and what it might do to their future. "I thought us working together was the teamwork part you insisted on," she said, hoping he'd see, in the real world, she could take care of herself. "Stop beating yourself up. You did what you needed to do."

She wanted to pound some sense into his thick skull before it was too late. Couldn't he see what he was doing to himself? To them? Tom wanted to protect the ones he loved—especially her, she realized. But he couldn't prevent every bad thing that happened.

She lowered her voice, hoping her angst over his pain wouldn't show in the shakiness of her speech, hoping that bringing the issue out in the open would help him. "Why do you feel the constant need to save me?"

"I…" Removing the enemy cap he still wore, he ran a hand through his dark hair and released a breath through his clenched teeth. "A long time ago I swore I wouldn't let anyone I loved die on me again."

She puckered her brows. "And just how, Tom MacCallum, do you think you're going to prevent that? You're not God."

"I know." He cleared his throat.

"Why do you think you need to save everyone you love?"

He paused then stared into her very heart. "I lost my father and my best friend because I wasn't there for them."

Somehow, she felt the depth of his loss. He didn't want the ones he loved to leave him again. "You were here for me."

Tom shook his head. "Not like I should have been."

Rorie heard the unspoken guilt. Somewhere inside herself, she understood. Tom thought he'd let each one of them down. "You're the only one blaming yourself."

Tom brushed her cheek with his thumb. "I don't want to lose you, Aurora. But I'd rather lose your love than have you end up dead. From now on, just do what I ask and don't question me anymore."

Rorie bit her lip. Now that she knew what drove him, it pained her to see him hurting.

Yet, there was one thing she knew. She couldn't live with a man who wouldn't let her live her own life.

"Only until we get out of here." She could concede that much.

"Promise?"

She nodded. "Promise. I won't renege or change the game plans this time."

Sending her a weak smile, Tom took his first aid supplies from his pack then cleaned and redressed her wound. The last thing he did was smear Acuna's gook on her then plaster a bandage on top.

"Your turn." She raised herself onto her good side and took the cup from him.

He frowned at her. "I'm fine."

She dipped a finger in the stuff. "Let me see your wounds."

"It's been a long night."

She smeared some goop on his nose. "Tom, I mean it."

He sighed and unbuttoned the blouse he wore. When he pulled a wadded-up top off his stomach, she realized he'd worn someone else's uniform. "How'd you get another set of camouflage?"

He tossed the extra blouse on the ground. "You don't want to know."

"Why?"

"I don't want to talk about it." He removed his top.

Her gut ached watching him. He was trying to protect her again.

Then it hit her. She couldn't expect him to change. He wanted to be her protector, her prince, but how could she become her own woman if she let him?

She just wasn't sure. She didn't want to lose Tom, but as persuasive as he could be, would he interfere with her life if he thought her safety was threatened? She couldn't let him, not in the real world. As much as she loved him, she couldn't be with him if he couldn't let her live her own life.

Yet, part of the problem was her. How she perceived things. In a relationship, she needed to hold her own ground. With Tom, could she?

Hoping to hold back the tears that threatened to come, Rorie swallowed. These last few nights might be her last time with this man—if she couldn't find a way to stand up for herself.

She lifted his brown T-shirt, running her hands over his muscled chest. Tom held her, nestling his head on her breasts. She breathed in the scent of him.

"I love you, Aurora." He lifted his head and kissed her temple.

"I love you, too," she said, leaving unspoken the fact she couldn't live with him right now. She wasn't strong enough to fight his possessive instincts.

Rorie pulled the T-shirt off his arms. Lifting the cloth over his head, she dabbed Acuna's muck on his shoulder and bruised ribs then put down the cup near the bed, her heart breaking. She fought back the wetness in her eyes. "Make love to me tonight, Tom."

His eyes held her. Then he took her in his arms and put his lips to hers.

When he kissed her, his touch seared her very soul.

* * * * *

Tom listened to the quiet hours before dawn, his mind racing, jumbled from the events of the last few days. Aurora lay naked in his arms, her breasts pressed against his bare side. Thankfully, she slept.

Gently, he brushed his fingers over her dark hair. He treasured this moment. He never wanted to let her go. He had plans for them—long-term ones he'd never made with a woman. If she'd let him, he wanted to be a permanent fixture in her life.

But he grew afraid he might not have a choice in the matter. She wanted her freedom, and he didn't know if that would include him—not with as insistent as he'd been. He recognized she needed space, that his need to protect her left her caged.

Still, he couldn't help himself. Wasn't some protectiveness normal from a man, a mate?

He didn't think she would see it that way. How could he make her understand?

Tom gritted his teeth, his head pounding with the mental overload that came with a difficult problem.

He wanted her in his life. He wanted to keep her safe.

She didn't want someone controlling her. Who would? He certainly didn't want to treat her like a puppet—and didn't want a woman who would want that. He wanted her to make her own decisions. Yet she saw his actions as dictatorial and her perception pushed her away.

Was he overbearing? Yeah, he had guilt over his father's and friend's deaths. It made him a bit overprotective. But here in the jungle it was different, wasn't it?

Or was Aurora right?

He grimaced. If he was so overprotective, then why had he listened to her so many times?

Maybe because some of what she'd said made sense. He hadn't wanted the old man and boy killed either.

A broken twig outside interrupted his musings. Someone stirred in camp.

Tom glanced at his watch. Still an hour before daybreak. Earlier he'd noticed the natives who stood guard over the camp. Were they changing the sentry?

Easing out of Aurora's arms, Tom pulled the pistol from his belt by the mat and went barefooted and buck-naked to the entrance, readying the Beretta.

Moving a palm leaf in the door, he gazed around the settlement. The fire had died to embers. With the exception of the bluer predawn sky, the area was darker than before. Tom blinked then narrowed his gaze as he studied the perimeter, sharpening his view of the dark.

Shadows moved along the dim edge. Tom looked for the sentries and couldn't see them.

Then a native walked into the clearing and glanced around. Turning back toward the path where he'd come, the native waved to someone behind him.

The barrel of a gun poked through, moving the brush. A pause ensued.

Then a camouflaged soldier stepped into the dim clearing, his rifle ready.

Chapter Nineteen

ॐ

Shit. Not again.

Tired, drained and thinking they were finally safe, Tom had let his guard down—to his regret. His heart pounded in his chest.

Before he could get back to Aurora, he caught the flash of movement from the corner of his eye. Someone rounded the hut.

Easing behind the door, Tom waited, sweat beading on his forehead. He hoped these soldiers were as sloppy as the rest had been. If only one man entered, Tom could disarm him without alerting the others. Then Tom could cut a hole in the back of the hut and he and Aurora could escape.

Without a sound, the portal inched open. No head, no rifle showed around the edge. The man was careful.

Tom wished he'd pulled his knife. The maneuver needed now called for stealth, not the noise a pistol would bring. Checking the Beretta and putting it on the ground, he held his breath, ready to grab the man from behind and break his neck.

"Tom?"

Aurora's soft, sleep-filled voice broke the silence. The mat rustled and he saw her outline as she sat up.

Suddenly, the door fell open and a heavily camouflaged man stepped through, leaves and twigs plastered to him.

Aurora screamed. Tom jumped before the soldier could turn.

The man lifted his arm, blocking Tom's attack, but Tom got around it. Another man rushed in. With the first man in a headlock, Tom swerved.

"Chief." The second man's voice stopped him. "It's us."

"Brodie?" Tom looked from Crawford to the man he held, pushing him around to see his face. "Ken, what the hell are you doing sneaking around? Why didn't you identify yourself? And, hell, just jumping in here like that. I thought I taught you better."

The communications tech only coughed and tried to catch his breath.

"Chief," Brodie said, "we weren't sure if these were friendlies or not."

"Jesu…" He ran a hand through his hair. "I could have killed you, dumb shit."

"I'm glad you didn't." Ken Talbot finally found his voice and sat on the ground to recover.

"Tom, what's going on?" Aurora held the blanket close to her.

Tom huffed. "Our rescue team."

Brodie eyed Tom's naked butt. "Nice outfit."

"Shit…"

Before Tom could finish, the captain stepped in. "I see you found 'em," Mark Garcia said.

Tom scowled when Ferguson came in behind him, his arm in a sling, the other holding a light pistol.

After eyeballing Tom, the CIA man holstered the sidearm and rushed to the blanket-clad Aurora, checking on her. The rest of the team gathered outside the door.

"The enemy get your clothes, Chief?" Tom caught the humor in the captain's voice.

"Naw," Brodie said. "He's undercover. You know, trying to blend in with the natives."

A couple of the men chuckled loud enough for Tom to hear.

"Hmmm," Garcia commented and cast a quick glance at Aurora. "That right?"

Tom squinted and ran his tongue over the front of his teeth. "No, sir." His skin chilled from stupidity in the warm morning air.

"Rorie's wounded," Ferguson interrupted. "She won't be able to walk to the extraction point."

"It isn't bad," she protested.

"I'll get Tanner to look at her," Garcia said. "I'll radio the bird, too. See if those jackasses will do us the honor of flying closer." He turned to Tom. "Get yourselves dressed. We'll wait outside."

Ferguson rose and shot Tom a questioning glare. Then left.

Rorie looked at Tom. He stood naked as a jaybird, but she thought he looked magnificent. "Is this going to get you into trouble?"

"No," he spat out. Finding her clothes, he handed them to her then picked up his pants and put them on.

Rorie lifted her bra and watched him dress. She treasured the view of his naked body, memorizing every nuance. Last night, she'd thought more about them, about her and the strength she'd found with Tom. He had been right. They had acted as a team to get out of the jungle. But if she needed to stand up to Tom, it would be a fight she would have on her own.

Finally, Tom tossed on his blouse.

Rorie sighed and buttoned her shirt, praying. They were going home. But if she couldn't find the strength to defeat her inner demons, she'd decided she would never see Tom again.

* * * * *

Rorie rested her head on her fists, her elbows digging into the grass mat. The medical sergeant worked on her bare derrière. She gritted her teeth from the uncomfortable probing.

Outside, the faint sound of helicopter blades whirred in the distance.

"The bird's here," Tom called from the entrance, fully dressed, armed and dangerous. Even now, his rugged voice still caused Rorie's pulse to race. How would she live without him? Without the encouragement he always gave her?

Without his warm arms around her at night?

She swallowed, pushing back her despair, wondering how she could do this. She had to break away from Tom—at least for a while, for her own self-image. Until she was a whole woman again, she couldn't confront his need to always save her and help him overcome his guilt. She was useless to him, and to herself.

He would be hurt, she knew. Might even find someone else. But it was a risk she needed to take. There was no turning back now. She had to do this—for herself.

The med tech bent his head and leaned forward to get her attention. "I'll dress your wound better when we get on board."

"On board? In front of all those guys? It's bad enough I'm baring my butt to you."

Eric Tanner blushed.

Tom came to her. "The bird won't wait, hon. We need to move. We don't want the bad guys finding us. Acuna and the rest are already breaking camp."

"Great," she grumbled, listening to the sound of the helicopter grow louder as their ride approached.

The med tech started to lift her.

"I'll take her." Tom stopped him.

"Just keep her still," Eric said. "The wound's opening up again. I need to put some temporary stitches in it." The med tech knocked some of Acuna's gunk off Aurora's behind. "I'd be interested to see what was in this native stuff."

"There's some by the bed and I have some other stuff in my pocket. I'm sure the old man won't mind."

"Cool." Eric put some of the gunk in a plastic bag and stuffed it in his pocket.

Picking her up, Tom hauled her over his shoulder. She propped herself up against his rucksack. "Is this really necessary?"

"Yep." He shifted her weight and ducked out of the opening.

She sighed as Eric followed. A smile tugged at the corners of the med tech's mouth.

She could have walked, but she decided to let Tom's insistence go. It wasn't worth arguing about. Besides, it would be the last time he would hold her for a while—maybe forever. And right now she needed all of him she could get.

Chris stood outside when they exited. He smiled when he saw her. "So, darlin', you get enough adventure?"

Before she could derail him, Tom took the option away from her. Swerving toward her friend and presenting her backside to Chris, she knew Tom shot him a fierce look.

Chris cleared his throat.

The helicopter came into view. Floating over the center of the huts, the sound grew deafening. Aurora wondered how they were going to land the thing.

Then men inside dropped a ladder. "Ah." The others began shimmying up. "You're not going to walk me up, are you?" she asked Tom.

"No," he yelled back.

He turned around and she saw them lower a metal stretcher to the ground. "I'm not an invalid," she yelled.

Tom shrugged. "Easiest way to get you on board."

When the stretcher neared the ground, the med tech went to the thing and readied it.

"Great," she grumbled as Tom crouched and loaded her into the steel crate. "Wait, I…"

She wanted to say goodbye to Acuna. Somehow, the old man must have known. He came to her. "*Esto es para ti, Señorita.*"

He handed her an amulet. *"Para protegerte."* He said a short chant over both her and Tom.

"What did he say?" she asked Tom.

"It'll keep you safe. He's saying a prayer for us."

"Oh," she said, knowing they needed as many prayers as they could get. She took Acuna's hand when he finished and pulled him toward her, kissing the old man on the cheek. *"Gracias, mi amigo.* For everything." She looked to Tom, who translated the rest for her.

It was the first time she'd seen the old man flustered. Blushing, he lifted his hand and gestured goodbye then departed.

"Let's go." Eric had strapped her in as they talked. Now, he sat on the edge of the stretcher.

"Are you coming on this contraption?" Rorie asked Tom.

He shook his head. "I'll walk up."

"But your wounds—"

"Are fine."

"You need something looked at, Chief?" Eric questioned.

"Later," Tom said. "Right now, let's get out of here."

The med sergeant nodded. Looking up, he waved his arm in a circle. The stretcher raised as Tom got on the ladder.

Rorie sighed. "What a lovely way to start a day," she spoke to herself.

"What'd you say?" Eric asked.

"Nothing," she yelled over the sound of the blades. "Everything's just perfect." She glanced over the side as they rose. Almost heaving from the height, she laid back, shut her eyes and took an unsteady breath. She should be happy they were rescued. They were going home.

But she'd lost her heart in the jungle—and knew she'd never get it back. She glanced at Tom as he lifted himself in the transport and sniffed back her tears.

Just then, she wondered what her mother would say about this. Vivian would have a field day when she found out. Rorie could hear it now.

The metal cot thumped against the side of the helicopter. Startled, Rorie jumped. Eric hopped off and he and Tom reeled her in. Closing the doors, the helicopter began its flight home.

Freeing her from the stretcher, Tom carried her to the back of the chopper, where Chris and the captain waited.

She tried not to look at the men who stared at her as she passed by. She could only imagine what they thought after finding Tom and her in such a compromising position. Then with her rear wound… Sheesh. Boy, did she feel like an idiot.

Tom set her down, leaning her against a pack on the floor and rolling her on her stomach. "I forgot to tell you. I think she needs a tetanus booster," he told Eric, who followed.

"I'll take care of it, Chief. Meanwhile, let's get this bleeding stopped."

Chris came next to her and held her hand. "How you doing, love?"

Tom glared at Chris again.

Angry for once, Rorie wished her eyes could really shoot darts at both of them for being so ignorant. She glared at Chris.

"That good, huh?" Chris chuckled.

"You could have warned me," she seethed.

Chris sobered. "I'm really sorry, Rorie. I promise to make it up to you."

Tom released a low harrumph.

"Meanwhile," Chris continued, undaunted after glaring back at Tom. "I need to ask you some questions."

"Can't that wait?" Tom growled.

"Ease off, Chief," the captain ordered.

Tom took a deep breath.

"Uh, Sir?" The med tech spoke to Chris, interrupting their tête à tête. "Can you interrogate her later? I need to get her pants off."

"Lovely," she commented. "Why don't we blast that over the intercom?"

She heard a few of the guys chuckle.

She jerked her head back to Eric, wanting those darts again. "Is taking my pants off really necessary?"

"Well, I can cut through them if you want." He sounded apologetic.

"Maybe the two of you could sit in front of her," the captain suggested, "to give her some privacy. The rest of you. Look someplace else."

The two men who had taken her through this debacle glared at each other then sat shoulder to shoulder with their backs to her.

"Do you need some help pulling them down?" Eric whispered in her ear.

She stared back. "I think I can manage."

With what little dignity she had left, she unzipped her pants and dragged them over her butt.

"Ouch." She felt a sting in her backside. She looked at the med tech, who had a syringe in his hand. "Just something for the pain." He smiled at her.

Tom put a hand on her hair, stroking it. "You're going to be fine," he whispered.

She looked at him. All of a sudden, her world blurred.

* * * * *

"She out?" Garcia said.

"Yes, sir." Tanner put in another stitch. "Just like you asked."

Tom looked at his captain and friend. "You wanted her knocked out?"

Mark nodded. "So we can talk. We found the guerilla camp and stormed it first," Garcia said. "Captured a few guys and sent them on with the state *policía*."

"You find Major Alvarez?"

"He escaped," Ferguson said, looking away.

Tom studied the CIA man. "This is for you." He pulled the envelope out of his pocket and handed it to him. "And I have your camera, although I'm not sure you need it. Have a few tactical plans, too. Some info from the colonel's desk, the guy who'd been running the place. Showed some outside involvement."

"Yeah. I'd like to see those." Ferguson frowned as he took the packet. "I'll get the rest of the stuff from you later. I can't tell you how important this information is, but a lot of American people will be safer—thanks to you and Rorie." Ferguson jerked his chin back to her. "She's quite a trooper."

"Yeah." Tom thought his voice sounded rough.

Garcia stared at him. "Crawford seems to think she's the one you were looking for that night at the bar," he whispered. "Is that right?"

Tom nodded, not wanting to say too much, especially in front of Ferguson.

"When did you know it was her?"

He studied his folded hands. "When we first attacked the compound."

"You should have sent someone else after her."

"I know." He eyed his friend dead on, not wanting to discuss the tactics of the mission in front of the CIA operative. There were some things Ferguson didn't need to know.

Garcia pause a minute then smirked. "Okay, Chief. Play it your way. We'll talk more later." He moved to speak with some of the other men.

"You almost finished?" Tom spoke to Eric but he looked at the sleeping Aurora. He wanted to take her in his arms, talk to her about the things they only hinted on, straighten some of her misperceptions out.

"Yeah," Tanner said. "Just a few more stitches. That bullet's in tight though. Thought I could get it from the look of the wound, but it's worked its way deeper. You guys must have moved around a lot." He arched a brow and bit off a grin.

"Yeah." Tom ignored the sexual innuendoes in Eric's comment. From the corner of his eye, he caught Ferguson staring at him.

"You want to talk to me now or later?" the CIA man said and glanced at Aurora.

"About what? The idiot you were, getting a civilian involved?"

"Ah, no. Your mission." Ferguson swallowed. "I honestly didn't think there was a risk to Rorie. The last contact from…" He cleared his throat. "Let's just say I didn't think there was a danger. Other things happened I was unaware of."

"Yeah?" Tom frowned. "Later would suit me just fine."

Ferguson eyed Aurora again.

"Leave her alone," Tom warned him.

"I'll be easy on her," Ferguson said. "After all, she's been a friend a long time. Now you? You're another story. I can grill you up until you're well done."

"Fine with me." Tom took the challenge.

Ferguson chuckled. "Take it easy, Chief. I like her. Now that she's divorced, I wouldn't mind getting to know her better. But I think she already knows what she wants, and it isn't me."

"What do you mean?" Tom shot him a look that had quelled many men.

Ferguson leaned closer. "I'm not in love with her. Nor is she with me. But I care about her. We were good friends. I hope we still can be."

"Finished." Eric interrupted and pulled up her pants. Ferguson stood then and moved to sit near the captain, leaving Tom with his thoughts.

He was in love with her. Was it so obvious to everyone?

Eric sat against his rucksack and closed his eyes. Tom looked away and scanned the row of his men. Some of them slept, some talked. They'd caught him in an awkward position with Aurora, but he didn't really give a damn.

He stroked her hair and took a deep breath. After all they'd been through, it would kill him if he lost her now.

He swallowed and studied her restful form. Somehow, he had to find a way for them.

* * * * *

Rorie heard a moan. She thought it came from her own lips, but she wasn't sure.

"She's waking up, Captain," someone said. She recognized the voice. Not Tom, though. She felt uncomfortable. Where was she again?

"Good. We're almost there."

Was that the captain? She thought so. "Mmmm." She tried to lift her head, but it felt heavy and ached liked a bitch.

"God, what did you give me?" She ran a hand over her face.

"Aurora?" Now that was Tom.

She tried to look up, but everything still looked fuzzy. She blinked her eyes, Tom's handsome face coming into focus. "Yeah." She smacked her lips. Her mouth tasted like cotton.

"We're almost there." Tom rubbed her back.

The helicopter lurched. She caught her breath and grabbed onto Tom's arm.

"We're on our descent," he whispered. "You're okay."

The copter swerved then lowered as they made their approach. She slipped her hand into his and kissed his knuckles.

"They'll separate us when we arrive." He'd leaned to within inches of her face and gave her a wan smile. "Don't worry. I'll come to see you in the clinic."

She nodded, still disoriented.

When the copter touched down, it jerked against the hard surface. The smooth, rolling sound of the doors opening brought her senses back to her, the light flooding into the small compartment. Some of the men jumped out.

"Where are we?" Her groggy voice sounded unreal.

"Venezuela. San Fernando Airbase. Last stop for you before heading home."

"Will you be coming with me?"

His green eyes clouded. "Can't yet. We have another month here. But I'd like to talk with you before they ship you out."

She nodded. "I would like that." Rorie bit her lip. Could she pull off saying goodbye?

"Chief, there's a gurney outside," the captain said. "Let's get her into it."

"Yeah." He let go of her hand, and with the captain, they lifted her and carried her out, putting her facedown on the rolling mattress, giving her a view of the helicopter that had returned them.

She lifted her head as Eric pushed her, Tom and the captain following along the side. The bright light blinded her, but she could see Chris talking to someone new as they passed him. When he saw her, he came over. "Rorie, sweetheart…"

"Sweetheart?" she interrupted. "Chris, darling, right now, you don't have the right to call me that. I'm still mad at you."

He sighed and put his hands in his pants pockets, strolling along the opposite side from Tom as another soldier from the copter joined Eric to cart her off.

Chris looked at her. "Well, hopefully, you won't be angrier after I tell you the news. Your parents sent someone to meet you."

"You think you could back off, Ferguson?" Tom said.

"Look, MacCallum." Chris leaned over her back and got into Tom's face.

"Chief." The captain put a restraining hand on Tom's arm.

Rorie sighed, too tired to stop their bickering, glad the captain was there to take control. "Chris, how could my parents be allowed to send someone here? How did they even know?" she asked.

The CIA man frowned. "It's standard policy to notify kin when someone is kidnapped."

"Great," she said.

Chris shrugged. "With your dad's money, he could pull the political strings. It isn't that hard. Reporters come all the time."

"Geez." She rubbed her face.

The gurney stopped and the others looked past her. A shadow loomed over Rorie's head.

"Well, there's my little soldier."

The voice from the past made her skin crawl. She didn't want to look around.

But the shadow wouldn't let her go. The clicking heels of well-soled shoes reverberated on the tarmac and circled around.

Gritting her teeth and steeling her resolve, she looked up at the figure in front of her. The sun glared around his head, but even if a thousand years had passed, she would still recognize the stench of his expensive cologne.

"Tsk, tsk." Stephen gripped her chin and turned her face to look at either side, frowning.

She slapped his hand away.

Her ex had the nerve to look hurt. "Oh, darling, see what happens when I'm not around to see you through these wild escapades of yours? Now look at you. See what you do to hurt yourself? What will your parents say? Vivian will be furious." Stephen peered at her, the actor in him giving her his most concerned look, a face filled with false pain. "You know, this happened all the time while we were...together, Chief MacCallum. I understand I have you to thank for getting my wife back. I was told of your bravery." Stephen looked away from her.

Rorie glanced back at Tom. When he looked at her, the brief question that crossed his face seared her gut. Did he believe Stephen's lies?

She closed her eyes and buried her head in her hands. Would her ex-husband's lies ruin her again? "Go to hell, Stephen."

Her ex huffed. "Well, dear *wife*, maybe someday."

Rorie raised her head. Stephen rocked back on his heels, leering at her as he scanned her body. "But now?" He possessively touched her chin. "Time for me to take you home, back to your duties as my wife."

"You lying son-of-a-bitch," she growled, jerking her head away. She worried about the clenched fists by Tom's side. "I am *not* your wife."

Stephen sneered and patted the breast pocket of his button-down Armani shirt. A crinkling noise came from a roll of wadded papers stuffed inside. "Per these babies..." he leaned into her face, his teeth gleaming like a large cat's, "darling, you're still mine."

Chapter Twenty

ဢ

"What?" Unbridled fear gripped Rorie, making her hands quiver. Something was up. But what could it be? She'd given Stephen everything of value. She lifted her chin in defiance to her trembling. "You are a liar and have always been. What in this world makes you think I'd *ever* go back with you?"

"Your parents, for one." He put his palms on the gurney and leaned toward her. "For two, there's a problem with the settlement."

"What problem?" She tried to shimmy away, but he leaned closer.

"Seems your grandmother had a stinger in her will." He straightened and stuck his hands in his pockets. "I revoked my signature."

"You…can't…do…that…" Her voice wobbled.

Stephen sneered. "Try me."

Tom jumped for her ex, but before he could follow through, the captain stopped him.

"It's between them," Chris said, stepping between her and Stephen to stand in front of Tom. "He has some kind of documents."

She looked at Tom, at his aggravated stare and reminded herself she didn't need him to fight her battles. Hadn't Tom told her she was brave? Strong?

She could do this.

Stephen chuckled, turning his twisted face to Tom. "And just what, pray tell," he told Tom, "do you intend to do about it, mister? You're nothing. A peon."

Rorie swallowed. No one would talk to someone she loved like that. "He…doesn't…have to do a thing," she sputtered. "I'm not going with you. Ever."

Stephen pushed his face into hers. "Don't be bold with me, you little tart. I overheard some of these guys. I know what you've been doing in the jungle these last few days. Don't think you can fool me. Adultery is still a sin in the state we divorced in—and I'll make sure everyone who matters knows about it. I have your traveling papers—orders from these men's superiors to take you home. And I control everything you have. You'll do what *I* say—or pay for it." The sadistic gleam in his eye told her he'd fulfill his promise to hurt her, no matter what she did.

She bit her lip and dared to look at Tom, hoping he didn't believe any of this nonsense. The captain still held him back, but Tom didn't fight. Only the twitch in his jaw and the intensity as his rich eyes studied her let her know how upset he was. Would he save her again?

No. Because she would do this herself. Glancing down, she caught sight of Chris' pistol sitting in its holster.

"I have a plane waiting," Stephen bit out. "And I'm *not* in a good mood. I've had enough of this third-world hellhole. I want to leave now."

"She needs medical attention," the captain said.

Her ex scoffed. "I'll find someone to care for her."

"You bastard." Tom struggled and a few more men grabbed him from behind to hold him.

Before Tom could break free, Rorie grabbed Chris' firearm. "The hell you will…" she muttered. The thing shook in her hands, but she pointed the barrel at Stephen's heart.

Her ex backed away, surprised for once. Then relaxed. "My, my, the kitten has grown claws."

The others stopped struggling.

"Not claws," she said. "Just common sense. I don't need to put up with you."

Stephen narrowed his eyes to slits. "You wouldn't dare use that. You're afraid of guns."

"This…" she cocked her head, "is a pistol. And I'm not afraid anymore."

"I don't believe you." Stephen sneered and took a step forward.

"Fine." She released the safety, and her action made a resounding click. "Take another step, and I'll have no choice but to defend myself."

"Ah, Rorie?" Chris asked. "Why don't you give that back to me?"

"Can you get the jerk out of here?" She looked at Chris from the corner of her eye.

"Consider it done."

She handed the pistol to her friend, who clicked the safety in place and put the weapon away.

"Mistake on your part, *darling*…" Stephen stepped to her and slapped her hard across the face.

Rorie blinked. Through the haze, she saw someone crawl on Tom's back.

Then the most amazing thing happened. Chris punched Stephen with his good arm. Tom broke away, and with someone still on his back, landed a solid jab to Stephen's chin, knocking him down. A few men pulled Tom back then two of the men on the rescue team jumped on top of her ex and pounded him.

Soon, a few others were there, some pulling the ones fighting off the top.

In minutes, the skirmish settled.

Someone yanked Stephen up from the tarmac. Her ex wobbled as he stood, his once crisp shirt now torn open and dirtied, his face cut.

She smiled. "Well, *darling*, I guess that's what you call teamwork. A concept I'm sure you know nothing about."

Still shackled by a few men, Tom chuckled beside her. The tender look he gave her this time warmed her soul.

"You'll pay for this." Stephen pointed his bony finger at her, his lip bleeding.

"I think not, puppy," she said, more confident than she had been in years.

"I'll let Vivian know what happened. She'll make sure you're cut out of their will."

"I don't care. Besides, I doubt they'll have much to say to you when I finally tell them about your abuse."

"They won't believe you. They never have."

"I have proof." She rubbed her scarred shoulder. "Stephen, get on your private jet and go home. I don't need you. I never have."

"You'll be hearing from me."

"She better not be," Tom piped up. His friends had released him. Now he stood next to her. She liked the warmth his presence brought.

"Don't threaten me, you low piece of shit," Stephen said.

Rorie grabbed Tom's hand to ensure he didn't jump on her ex. "Go home, Stephen."

Lifting his chin, Stephen stumbled off.

Rorie released a ragged breath and listened to some of the men curse at the jerk under their breaths.

"You okay?" Tom's brows creased and he put his fingers to her cheek to examine it.

"I'm fine." She captured his hand in hers and kissed the back of it.

"All rightie, now." Eric stepped close to her, working his jaw back and forth from a punch he must have received. "Now that we've had fun, can I get my patient some medical care?"

"Sure." Tom smiled at her and pushed the gurney along. Rorie thought her heart would break. He and his friends stood up for her. How could she leave him now?

* * * * *

Shrugging off his blouse, Tom lay back on the bunk and brooded. The captain wouldn't let the debriefing wait—and the med staff wouldn't let Tom get near Aurora until the doctor knew she wanted to see him. As promised, Chris had made the grilling intense. Going over the details of their trek reminded him how cluster-fucked he'd gotten everything.

He could have gotten Aurora killed.

No one else had thought that, though. Captain Garcia was there. He'd applauded him for his skill and ingenuity, for the ability to get out of the situations he and Aurora did.

But Tom didn't agree. How could he go to her? Tell her he'd love her for all time, when he knew he couldn't control the events that could cause her harm?

And control was the issue. Taking off where her parents left off, Stephen had manipulated her whole life. The issue was a giant among the things she couldn't live with. So, how different did that make him from her ex?

Not much, he figured. But he wanted to protect Aurora, not hurt her. Still, she wouldn't have him if it meant him interfering with her life's plans.

"Chief." Brodie stepped through the door to the sleeping quarters. "Doc says she's awake. They converted an office in the medical building into a private room. They're taking her there now. Thought you'd want to know."

"How's she doing?" Tom jumped up and donned his blouse.

"Great, I guess. Considering." The sergeant leaned against the doorjamb. "Took them a bit to get the bullet out. Whatever that old witch doctor gave her helped. Per Eric, Doc says she'll be fine in a few days. Told her she'd probably need a week or more before she goes on another excursion like this last one. She assured him she wouldn't be traveling for a while."

"Humph." Tom doubted that. Not with Aurora's spirit. He closed the last of the buttons and straightened his BDUs then marched past Brodie and stopped in the hallway. "Well?" He eyed the sergeant.

"Well, what?" Brodie smirked.

"You going to show me where they put her, or am I going to have to break your arms first?"

Brodie sprung into one of his ear to ear grins. "I guess I could manage." He stood and walked ahead. "Besides, the girls kinda like my arms where they are—not that you'd care, seeing as you're out of commission." He shot a heckling glance at Tom.

"Funny," Tom groused, knowing only how true his statement was.

When they got there, Brodie left. Ferguson had already arrived. He sat on the bed next to her as she relayed some of their exploits.

"Haven't you gotten enough for one day?" Tom asked the CIA man.

Ferguson turned to him. "Just leaving." He picked up Aurora's hand and kissed it. "I'll call you when I get back to the States."

"It's a deal," Aurora told him. "Thanks for everything."

Chris stood and turned on his heel. After giving Tom a two-fingered salute, he walked out.

Tom frowned. "You two kiss and make up?"

She smiled and her face glowed. "You could say that. We're still friends anyway."

"I don't know if I like that." He sat in the place Ferguson had retreated from.

"I'm not giving you a choice."

He pressed his lips together. "Got it."

She frowned. "He told me Mike didn't make it. I felt sorry for him. He and Mike had been together a long time."

"Sorry to hear that," Tom said.

She smiled. "Chris said Jorge would be okay, though."

"Good."

She licked her lips. "Tom?"

"Yeah?"

"You said when we got back home I could be in charge."

"We're not home yet."

"Close enough," she countered. "Tom?"

He gritted his teeth, thinking this was it. She would cut him loose—but his heart couldn't afford to lose her. "Yeah?"

"I love you."

Relieved, his shoulders slumped. He took her hands then closed his eyes and pressed the backs of her fingers against his forehead. "I love you, too. Aurora…" He bent over and kissed her with the depth of his soul. "I need you in my life. You loving me that first night made me realize I had more to live for than this job."

She fingered his lips. "I want us to have a chance together. But it won't happen if you smother me. I'm not strong enough yet to fight your protective instincts. I'm not even sure I'd want to. I just know I need my own life, one I control."

"I want that for you, too."

"I know you do. But not enough to let go of your guilt over some action you couldn't prevent, your fear of losing someone you love. I realize that now." She swallowed, tears in her eyes. "I…I don't want to see you again until I know for a fact I can set my own destiny."

"But…"

"Please, don't make this more difficult for me than it is. I love you. But I won't live with a man who won't respect my boundaries."

He let his forehead drop against her chest. "Maybe we can talk about this later."

"There will be no later." Her soft voice broke. "Chris tells me you guys are leaving in a few hours. Tomorrow, I'll be on a transport home."

He sat up, the pain visible in his face. "We have a few hours then. At least give me that."

She smiled sadly. "I'd like that."

He kissed her gentle lips. "I'll always love you, Aurora."

"And I, you. I'll never forget what we had."

Tom kissed her again, this time knowing he'd lost her for good.

* * * * *

The ride back proved to be the longest of Tom's life. Most of the team chattered. Some slept. Normally, he'd talk along with the rest, still feeling the adrenaline from completing a job well done. Now, the noise distracted him.

Tom dropped his head against the metal wall of the chopper, wishing he could be alone and find some peace. With Aurora's absence, the boys stood ready to give him hell and ribbed him over finding them both naked. Instead of taking it gracefully, like he would have, he barked at them. Now they knew for sure something went wrong.

But he couldn't help himself. Inside, he felt empty, alone.

He squeezed his eyes shut, hoping to banish the moisture in them the desolation brought. The one thing he really wanted in life, he found he couldn't have.

A lump formed in his throat. He rubbed his forehead. Someone sat down next to him.

"You okay, Chief?" Garcia kept his voice low.

Tom looked at him. He rarely saw his friend this concerned. "Fine." He blew some air through his puffed cheeks then blinked. "Who the hell am I kidding? She dumped me."

The captain rubbed his thumb over his chin—not a good sign, if Tom wanted his privacy. Garcia would wait until Tom stood ready to talk.

"You two seemed pretty close," Garcia said.

"Thought so." Tom worked his jaw.

"What happened?"

He shrugged. "She wants her independence after living with that bastard for so long. I guess a person can understand that."

"You could still be friends."

"She doesn't want to see me."

"I doubt that."

"It's what she said."

"Yeah, but I don't think she means it." Garcia cleared his throat. "Do you know her phone number?"

"No."

"Where she lives?"

He cut his eyes toward him. "Yeah. Got it from her driver's license."

"Not like you to give up, Chief. You fought like hell in the jungle for her, and now, you say okay and walk away. Guess I'm confused."

"Sir, you've never been confused a day in your life. What are you saying?"

"Tom," Mark whispered. "You want something bad enough, you fight for it. But right now, you're not. You're punishing yourself for some reason. I want to know why."

Tom rolled his eyes upward. He couldn't deny it. "I made some mistakes that could have gotten her killed."

"I see." Garcia folded his hands. "Which ones were those? The one where she ran off after Ferguson's crap? Or the one where she decided to start shooting at a bunch of guerilla soldiers?"

Tom winced. "I should have been there to stop it."

Garcia took a deep breath. "That's bullshit and you know it. You can't be everywhere and do everything. Yeah, you can try. Hell, you did try. But if you've done everything you can, you have to forgive yourself for what follows. You can't help everything that happened over the last week, and you can't help what happened to your best friend, Charlie, six months ago."

Just like he couldn't help what happened to his father, Tom thought. Garcia didn't say it, but he knew.

"I'm going to see about getting our rotation cut early. We've seen action—you especially. It shouldn't be a problem. When we get back, I want you to use that counseling option and get this figured out once and for all. I need you one hundred percent. I won't have that until you've let your troubles go and tried to patch things with Rorie." The captain laid a hand on his shoulder and whispered. "You deserve your happiness, Tom. Don't blow this because you have a hang-up you're unwilling to work through."

Tom rested his elbows on his thighs, his throat constricting, and nodded. "All right."

"Good." Garcia leaned back and closed his eyes.

"Thanks, Mark." From somewhere, a glimmer of hope entered Tom's soul.

"No problem."

Tom leaned against the wall of the bird and folded his arms. "Yeah, guess I want to be like my captain when I grow up. One lucky son of a bitch."

Garcia opened one eye and scowled. "What do you mean?"

Tom cracked a smile. "It's what you said the night I pulled you out to find Aurora. Find a good woman and I'd be lucky the rest of my life."

Garcia snorted and rested his head back again. "Yeah, but I didn't say you wouldn't have to work hard for her first. Women are like that."

"Hell, now you tell me."

The captain snickered.

Feeling better, Tom closed his eyes. He had a lot to think about. He'd lived with the guilt over his father's death for so long, the lack of having it scared him.

But not as much as losing Aurora.

This would be a battle within himself — one that he refused to lose. As long as there was a breath in him, he had to get her back.

* * * * *

Rorie sprawled on the couch in the apartment, resting her tush. She'd had a lot of time to think over the last few days. As expected, Stephen's line had been bullshit, a piece of junk he made up to manipulate her. Their divorce was legal — whether her ex had signed it or not. Her lawyer made sure of that by pushing the judge for a ruling.

Then there were her parents. Stephen had gotten to them first. They met her at the airplane, a scowl on both their lips. She'd sent them packing after telling them how abusive Stephen had been.

And she'd told them everything. Showed them the scar on her shoulder. Told them they could do whatever they wanted, believe whatever Stephen told them, she still loved them. As her counselor had predicted, the act cleansed her somehow, freed her soul.

Her father, when he finally believed her, responded with his usual blustering. Why hadn't she told them? Yada, yada, yada...

She revealed her reasons. The pressure on their marriage, her mental state. The fact she didn't want to alienate them.

But her mom? She wouldn't have predicted Vivian's reaction.

"Aurora, did you hear me?" her mom said, interrupting Rorie's thoughts by putting a tray filled with cucumber sandwiches and dishware on the coffee table. "Are you ready for tea? I think it's time we talked about your relationship with this man who rescued you."

But maybe she should have guessed.

It hadn't taken long for Vivian Lakehurst Lindsay to come to Fayetteville and her only child's rescue. Rorie had to admit, the woman had grit. She even submitted to staying in Rorie's teeny apartment to take care of her little girl, offering to pay Sally to move out for a while so she could take her room.

Fortunately, her friend only smiled at the proposal and said she had a place to spend the time. Before Sally left, she hugged Rorie and wished her good luck on the way out.

Rorie looked at her mom. She needed all the help she could get with her. Vivian had already rearranged the whole apartment—now she again stood ready to rearrange Rorie's life.

"Aurora? Are you all right?" Her mother touched her arm.

"I'm fine." Rorie shook her head to clear the thoughts away. "Mother, where did you come up with that name, anyway?"

An unusual line formed between Vivian's smooth brows. "What name, dear?"

She huffed. "My name. Aurora? It's…odd. Like something left over from the Seventies."

"Oh, my, no. It's an old name." Her mother relaxed her normally rigid back. Then moisture formed in her eyes. "You were always my princess." She patted Rorie's arm. "We'd already had a name picked out, but when the time came to make it official, you were asleep in my arms. Your father said you looked like Sleeping Beauty. I always liked that fairy tale, so we named you after the princess instead."

"Sleeping Beauty?" Rorie wanted to laugh, but bit her lip, not wanting to offend her mother.

Vivian took a tissue from the box on the table, one she'd placed there just that morning. "Yes. That was the princess's name, you know."

"Oh, my gosh." She sat up, realizing the name was perfect for her. She'd slept through her whole life, letting others care for her like a doll—until she met Tom. Her prince had kissed her, and she'd finally awakened to her life.

What was supposed to happen next?

She grimaced as she remembered. They both lived happily ever after. How could that happen when Tom was over a thousand miles away and she'd told him she didn't want to see him? "Mom, God has a funny sense of humor."

Vivian frowned. "What do you mean?"

Before she could answer, the doorbell rang. Vivian rose to get it, looking through the peephole first. Then she cracked the door open.

Rorie heard their voices. A woman questioning if Aurora Lindsay lived there. "Who is it, Mom?" Rorie couldn't see the person from where she sat.

Vivian opened the door the whole way. "I couldn't make her whole name," she murmured. "But apparently she's a Contessa."

In the entrance stood a beautiful, dark-haired woman. Well-kept, older, now that Rorie saw her more closely. But the lady glowed. She had a warmth around her that shined.

"You do not know me, Aurora," she said in a hesitant Hispanic accent, "but I believe you know my son."

"Your son?" Rorie had one of those eerie, gut-grabbing feelings one gets when their life is about to change.

The woman smiled and nodded. "Tomas Alexander MacCallum. He said he was in love with you, and you with him. I can see why. You are beautiful. I came to meet you. To talk about my son and why you should give him another chance."

Rorie shouldn't have been surprised — but her mouth gaped open anyway.

Vivian turned to her with the most astonished look. "Aurora? Does he call you Aurora?" She beamed and tilted her head.

Rorie blinked at her mother's strange reaction, nodding in answer to her mother's question.

A sudden light dawned on her brain. Her life was hers to decide, always had been. She just never realized it until this moment. No one could make decisions for her without her permission. Well, damn…

When Fate knocks on your door to correct your errors, you shouldn't shut it in her face. Rorie smiled at Tom's mother. "Hello, Mrs. MacCallum. Why don't you come in?"

For once in her life, Rorie knew exactly what she wanted.

Chapter Twenty-One

⁊

The quiet in the house was deafening. Tom lay on his bed, fully clothed. Even had his shoes on, ready to go should he get the call. He glanced at his watch for the thousandth time that night. He had been home for twenty-four hours now. Aurora had had plenty of time to call if she wanted to see him. His mother told him she'd left his telephone number and when he was supposed to return. Left his cell phone number, too.

He'd asked for her to call—if she wanted. His mom thought she would. He wasn't about to push.

But the waiting drove him crazy. Maybe he should have gone out with the guys? It was Friday night. He could see if she'd gone partying with her friends, see if she'd ended up in the bar where they first met.

It would disappoint him if he found her there, but it wouldn't matter. He would see her.

Maybe get down on his knees and beg. He'd never felt so helpless in his life.

The loud ringing of the phone jarred him. Tom sat up and grabbed the receiver, dropping it before he could get a good grasp on it. "Hello?" he said as he finally put it to his ear.

"Ah, hello? Is someone there?"

"Yeah." He panted into the receiver. He didn't recognize the woman's voice. His brows furrowed in confusion.

"Is…is this Chief MacCallum?" She sounded older.

"Yeah?"

"Chief MacCallum, I'm…"

"Look, ma'am, if you're trying to sell something, I'm not interested. I'm kinda waiting for a call here. Gotta go. Sorry." He started to hang up.

"No! Hello?"

He swallowed. The woman seemed panicked. "Ma'am, are you in some kind of trouble?"

He heard her raspy sigh. "No, it isn't me. It's Aurora. I'm…I'm afraid she's in danger."

"What?" Surprised, Tom jumped up and stood at the side of his bed, fumbling for his keys in his pocket. "Where is she? Is she in town?"

"Oh, yes, yes. She's asleep right now."

Tom released his pent-up breath.

"I stepped outside the apartment so I could call you in private," the woman continued.

"Is…this…Mrs. Lindsay?"

"Oh, my. Yes, I'm sorry, I forgot to introduce myself. I met your mother. She's a lovely woman. Speaks very highly of you. Said you'd gotten your Master's in Engineering after joining the Army."

"Thank you, ma'am. Now, about Aurora…"

"Oh, I love the way you say her name. Like a real prince."

"Ma'am, your daughter?"

"Oh, yes. She's going to be so upset when she finds out I called you. She's warned me not to pester her anymore, but I'm so worried. I don't want to lose her. She's all I have. But she's *never* done anything this crazy."

"Crazy?"

"Yes, absolutely insane. Harold, her father that is, told me not to interfere. Said Aurora knows what she's doing. But she's going off the deep end—literally. And I think you're the only one who can stop her."

"Mrs. Lindsay, I don't understand. What is she going to do?" Tom's patience ended. If Aurora's mother didn't say something soon that made sense, he was hanging up and going over there—whether Aurora got mad at him or not.

A long pause ensued.

Tom heard her sigh. "She'd decided the only way she can get back together with you is to jump out of an airplane. Tomorrow of all days. I told her that wasn't necessary. All she needed to do was talk…"

"What?" Had he heard her right? "Aurora's petrified of falling." Then he remembered. She'd told him in the jungle the only way she would live with him was if she jumped from a plane.

"I *know*," her mother emphasized. "That's why I'm so worried, but she insists this is something she needs to do—especially by herself. She won't see you or talk to you until she does. I told her this was insane, but she won't listen to me."

"Mrs. Lindsay…" Tom tried to reassure her.

"Just keeps insisting this is something she *has* to do. For her self-esteem, she says—and to complete some crazy promise to you. Do you know what she's talking about?" Aurora's mother tsked. "Oh, I'm sure you don't. She's just talking crazy right now. Oh, my, and her injury isn't even healed completely. Can you imagine? I begged her to wait for her wound to get better. What if it opens again? But she said it was healed enough and she couldn't wait anymore. She had to do this for herself before you came home…"

"Mrs. Lindsay…"

"I thought you could talk her out of it. After what I've done to her life, she won't listen to me. And I don't blame her." Aurora's mother began crying.

"Ma'am, it'll be all right. I promise." Aurora's mom might be upset, but he was ecstatic. "What jump school did you say she went to?"

"Oh, dear. I don't remember. Wait a minute. She has the information just inside. I'll go get it."

"Do you know where and when she's jumping tomorrow?"

"Ah, yes. It's just outside of your little Army base there— someplace along Yadkin Road. They're going through some kind of checklist and then taking off early. Supposed to jump around nine, I think. She wanted me to come and see her, but I just can't. What if, what if…"

"I understand. Look, I know where the place is, and who runs the program. They're top-notch. I'll give them a call. Meanwhile, don't say a thing to her about talking to me. Are you sure she said she'd see me after she jumped?"

"Oh, yes, yes. Said she'd call you when she finished. She just doesn't want to be pushed into anything. You know how she is when she makes up her mind."

Stubborn. He knew. But in this case, he loved the idea. "Thanks, ma'am. I'll call."

"Will you try and stop her?"

Tom couldn't lie. "No, ma'am. Not if it's what she wants. But I assure you she'll be fine. Please don't worry. I'll be on the ground when she gets there."

Mrs. Lindsay sighed. "If you say so. And young man, after everything that has transpired, perhaps you should call me Vivian."

Tom smiled. "Thanks, Vivian. For calling."

"Bring me my little girl safe and sound."

"I will." He figured that was one promise he could keep.

* * * * *

The small plane lurched in the wind. Rorie held her stomach and tried not to think about the drop. Thank God, she only had dried toast for breakfast.

"Hope ya'll are ready," the jumpmaster said. "We're almost over our target."

She'd seen him around the training area supervising, but Rorie hadn't worked with this instructor so far. She twisted her hands together. She wished she could remember his name. It'd be nice to know who she'd jumped with, especially if she happened to run into the Almighty today.

No. Using a distress method she'd learned through therapy, she put her mind in another place. Nothing would go wrong today. God wouldn't bring her this far only to let her fail. No matter what happened—with the jump or with Tom—her determination would bring her through.

Besides, she had Acuna's juju amulet he'd put on her before she left. She rubbed her hand over the zipped pocket she'd put it in. Although she didn't believe in magic, she wanted the reminder of what she and Tom had shared.

The pilot signaled the jumpmaster. Whatever-his-name-was gripped the lever to the door. "Ladies and gents, prepare to take the best thrill ride of your life."

The side door opened and a blast of icy wind hit Rorie in the face.

Her body trembled, more from fear than the cold air. "You can do this," she muttered, shutting her eyes. "You're brave. You're strong…"

She glanced around the plane. There were a few others who'd signed up when she did. Only one person had dropped out of the program. They'd gone through a check and review that morning. She was ready. At least as ready as her brain would let her be.

"You can do this," she uttered to herself.

One of the men in the class, Brad, she thought, walked over to her. "You jumping?"

She nodded.

"You don't look good."

She studied his color. "And you're as pale as a sheet."

He laughed. "First time is a killer, they tell me."

"Ha, ha." She tried to think his comment funny, but her quivering hands belied her. To bolster her resolve, she lifted her chin, and tried to joke back. "And here I thought it was only the last time you jumped."

He snorted at her response and stared oddly at her. "What if this is your last time?"

She took a breath. She only had this one lifetime to live — and being caged by her fears wasn't living. She wanted her mental freedom — the ability to determine what she wanted.

And with whom.

The jumpmaster grabbed onto a support and studied the drop through the open portal. His suit snapped in the wind.

He stepped back and looked at them. "Line up."

Oh, God. She licked her lips.

The rest of the group stood.

"Hook up your static line," the instructor said.

You can do this, she reminded herself. She had to. She rubbed the amulet and thought of Tom. Of his arms around her on the bridge. She wanted him back, but she wouldn't have him if she couldn't at least conquer one fear herself.

Standing, she got behind Brad, and became the last in line.

The jumpmaster stood by the door and pointed to the first jumper. "Go."

"Yahoooo…" The guy jumped out.

"Go." The instructor signaled again.

"Wait for me, baby…" The first guy's girlfriend jumped after him. Rorie held her breath.

"Go."

The younger girl hesitated.

The instructor looked in her face. "You can do it, Ann."

She nodded and smiled at him. Then jumped. Rorie heard her screaming on the way down.

Brad went next. He stood in the opening, his face intense, the wind reddening his cheeks. "Where did Ann go?"

"Down there. Her parachute opened. See?"

Brad nodded and went pale. Then lost his breakfast through the opening of the plane. "I-I...I can't..."

"Step down." The instructor unhooked him and pulled him away. Sitting Brad down, the jumpmaster shoved Brad's head between his knees.

Rorie felt sorry for him. And knew she sure as hell didn't want to look like that. Her shaking eased to a small quiver.

"Ready?" The instructor grasped her elbow.

She bit her lip and looked at him. Was she ready?

"You can do this, Rorie."

Hadn't Tom told her the same thing? She gazed at the open doorway. Her new life waited just outside. All she had to do was step through and grab it with everything she had.

Determined, she nodded. "I'm ready."

The instructor smiled at her. "That's my girl. Give us a few minutes to get over the jump zone again."

She took some cleansing breaths to calm herself. In a few minutes, the instructor waved her over. She stepped into the opened hatch. The wind lashed against her, whipping her face and smashing her jumpsuit against her body. Her breathing grew uneven, her hands sweated against the cold metal. She glanced down. The dots on the ground were really people and things far away.

"You're ready, Rorie. You can do this," the instructor said from behind her.

He was right. If she didn't believe in herself, trust her own abilities, who would? "Yes sir, I can." She squeezed her eyes shut. "Tell me when to go."

"Go," he yelled.

Looking out, she held her breath.

* * * * *

Tom paced in front of his motorcycle, waiting with the recovery team, hoping Aurora would make the jump. He'd called Kenny McPherson last night, a friend of his, waking him out of a dead sleep. Kenny was the head jumpmaster for the school Rorie had signed with. McPherson said he knew her and confirmed she was scheduled to jump today. Although someone else was to do the jump, Tom talked Kenny into taking it. Told him about Aurora, and why it was important to him.

An ex-Ranger, the guy owed him.

The plane came into position again. One by one, the colored chutes had bloomed out of the hatch. Now two more came.

He recognized the last chute. His friend's colors. He looked again. The jumpers were still too far up for him to recognize any of them. Kenny had said there would be five new jumpers. Tom counted only four.

Had Aurora stayed behind? As the chutes neared, he grew more nervous.

The first two jumpers neared. He heard them calling to each other—pumped with the thrill of their first solo jump. He knew how they felt. He assumed they were the couple Kenny told him about.

Next came a smaller body. Tom held his hand over his shades to get a better view. A young girl grabbed her risers, but dropped faster than she should have. When she hit, she hit hard.

Tom winced, knowing how that hurt. She rolled well, though, and the recovery team ran to her. When she stood, Tom knew she would be fine.

He looked at the sky again. There were only two more chutes, and one was his friend's. Would Aurora be the other?

They were still pretty far up. The plane had to circle around again before the last jumpers exited. The unknown person's chute drifted to the far side of the field.

Tom hopped on his bike and revved it, taking off to where he thought the chute would drop, nervous that it might not be her.

* * * * *

At first, Rorie couldn't comprehend why people did this for fun. What enjoyment could be had by possibly breaking your neck? But after the first few seconds of fear, when she had stepped out on faith, she found out for herself. There was nothing like the freedom parachuting gave. No ties, no one to bother you. The view was astonishing.

From this height, the countryside looked like green velvet, occasionally dotted with a bauble or two. As she got closer, she saw people moving about. The rest of the new jumpers had landed. They looked to be safe. That was the hard part, she thought. Landing, touching down on your feet.

Across the field, a dark motorcycle roared. The sound echoed upward to her.

The ground approached. The Earth seemed to move faster the closer she came. Ignoring everything else, she concentrated on her decent. "Stop, drop and roll," she voiced aloud. "Just like a fire drill."

She could do this. She had no choice at this point.

The land rushed to meet her, the dark Earth coming faster. Her destiny awaited. She would either start a new life—hopefully with Tom if he would have her after how lame she'd been—or be flat as a pancake.

"Here goes," she muttered, a sense of helplessness invading her.

Then she took control. *Stop, drop and roll.*

The balls of her feet touched down and she rolled to the side. "Whoohooo! I can't believe I just did this. This is incredible…" The silk canopy billowed around her, blinding her view of the landing site.

Then a gust took her by surprise.

"Whoa!" She grabbed the risers before the wind-filled parachute pulled her along. The force yanked her arms and she figured she was destined to be dragged along the rough ground.

Until a pair of strong arms encircled her and pulled her back.

Whoever had grabbed her tumbled with her over a bump in the earth, the parachute tying them together.

"Oh, my gosh," she said when they finally stopped. "Are you all right?" She pushed the fabric out of her face—with the assistance from whoever had tried to hold her.

And stared into Tom's smiling eyes.

"I thought you might need some help." He licked his lips, his gaze more serious. "I hope you don't mind." His voice softened.

She ran her finger over his wet mouth. "You know, I used to know someone who would run their tongue over their mouth when they found themselves in an uncomfortable situation. You nervous?"

"Yeah." A corner of his mouth rose. "There's this woman I know who loves me. I love her, too. I came to tell her I'm working on my problems. Wanted to know if we could work on our issues together." His eyes looked hopeful. "I'm scared as hell she'll say no."

"Hmmm. Sounds like teamwork to me."

"Yeah." He inched closer. "Teamwork. What do you think, Aurora? You game?"

She smiled. "Only if you kiss me."

He took her in his arms and held her close.

Then laid his hot mouth on hers.

Aurora relished the touch of him, and knew she'd never get enough.

"I hate to interrupt—" The instructor came up to them. He had already dropped and cleared his chute. The others were wrapping it up. "But good job, Aurora." He patted her on the back. "I'm glad you two found each other. We even now, Chief?"

"Yeah, Kenny." Tom's dimples showed. "We're more than even."

"Good, in that case, let's get you unwrapped."

"You know him?" Rorie asked.

Tom smirked. "I know the majority of the guys in the jump schools around here. Hell, I trained most of them."

"You did?" A jolt pulled their lower bodies together.

"Yeah." He held her closer and kissed her again, not letting her go when they were freed moments later.

Rorie noted that an experienced team helped a great deal in these situations. When Tom backed away, the others shook her hand and congratulated her then went off with the gear.

"Need a ride?" Tom stood up with her, sexy as hell in a black T-shirt, boots and jeans, and jerked his head toward his Harley.

"Don't know." She shrugged and shoved her hands in the back pockets of her jeans. "Never rode on a motorcycle before."

"Never?" He arched a brow then slipped next to her. "Well, come to think about it, I never had an adventuress ride on the back, either."

"An adventuress?" She slid her arms around his neck and teased a dimple with her thumb.

He held her flush against him. "I understand you recently came back from conquering the wilds of Panama. And just now you jumped into unchartered territory all by yourself."

She threw her head back and laughed. "Mmmm. So I did." She pressed her breasts against him.

He bit his lip. "Does taking this jump mean what I think it does?"

"Maybe." She fingered his mouth. "Does being with an adventuress make you nervous?"

"Yeah." He lowered his head to hers. "But I'm willing to take the chance."

"Her independence too much for you to take?"

"No." He swallowed. "Just the fact she doesn't need me."

"I do need you, Tom. More than you think."

"I love you, Aurora." He chewed on his bottom lip. "And it scares me."

"But you can do this," she said, bringing his lips close to hers.

"I can do this," he breathed against her mouth.

"You're brave."

"I'm brave."

"You're strong."

The corner of his mouth lifted. "I'm strong."

"I believe in you." She captured his lips.

"I believe in you, too," he uttered between breaths. "Aurora, you can do whatever you want, if you want to. And if I lose you, I'd rather it be from the 'death do us part' side of the equation than you leaving me because of my stupidity."

Tom would let her live her own life. He might not like some of it, but he would let her, Rorie thought.

She held his mouth to hers a moment then released him. "Take me home, Tom."

"Sure. Besides, I'd like to meet Vivian."

"How did you..."

Tom smiled. "She called me last night. How do you think I found you?"

Rorie grimaced. "I should have known."

He sidled up to her. "Aurora, your relationship with your mom will be all right, because we'll make it right."

After thinking on it, she nodded. They would make it right—make everything right for once.

"Your place then?" he said.

She chuckled and shook her head. "No. Yours. I know what I want now. You. And I'm willing to live with you to prove it—if you'll still have me."

He smiled and touched his forehead to hers. "Yeah, I'll still have you. I want you. Forever. But on one condition."

"What?" She studied his face, wondering—after all this—what could stop him now.

"Marry me, Aurora. Give me this one male ego-boosting pleasure of saying you're my woman. 'Cause I know I'll never be able to live another day without you."

She wouldn't cry. She promised herself. Instead she reached for his face and kissed his mouth, teasing his lips with the edge of her teeth.

He backed away a few inches. "Does that mean yes?" he said soberly and fingered her face.

Her head nodded like a bobble-head doll. "Yes. Tom, I don't ever want to lose you again. Besides…" She caressed his lips. "How could I refuse the man who saved me?"

"I did no more for you than what you've done for me. You've given me my life back." He embraced her, holding her in his arms and rocking her back and forth. He kissed her temple then held her away from him.

"Let's go home." Tom picked her up and carried her to the bike. Sitting her down, he handed her a helmet. "Here, princess."

Rorie took the hard covering. After tying it on, Tom smiled at her—his dimples deep, his eyes lighted with love—then jumped on the bike and took off.

"Home…" she murmured as they rode away and laughed. The sun glared on them. There was no sunset to ride into, but Rorie didn't care.

She imagined they would still have their issues from time to time, but working together, they would face their fears.

Filled with grace, Rorie had finally found her life—and her own brand of happily ever after.

Enjoy An Excerpt From:

INTIMATE DECEPTIONS

"Brodie, ease back, boy. She's on a job." Jake grabbed his arm.

If anything, Jake's words only inflamed him. This couldn't happen. Not to his beautiful Elena. Brodie broke away. Whether he ran or walked, he wasn't sure. Brodie only knew when he reached the bastard he jerked him up and off Elena. Slamming his fist in the cowboy's face, Brodie put the man flat on his back, sliding toward the broken bottles near the rest of the trash.

"Brodie!" Elena protested and grabbed for him. He blocked her arms and tossed her over his shoulder, turning to walk off—until he caught a glimpse of a two-by-four arcing toward him from somewhere behind. Brodie ducked just in time to avoid the strike and kicked his attacker in the gut. In seconds, Jake stood by him, unarming then grappling with the shadowed stranger who had come from nowhere.

The cowboy he'd thrown still lay on the pavement groaning.

"Put me down, you dumb jackass." Elena pounded on his back. "You're screwing everything up."

"I'm trying to. Hell if I'll have you getting screwed any ways else."

"Look, you arrogant prick. Don't even try to run my life." She squirmed in his grasp but Brodie had a death grip on her.

Jake and the attacker were about the same size and more evenly matched than Brodie would have expected. Jake, after all, had been a large man. Brodie wanted to put Elena down and help but he grew afraid she'd take off with her trick. Then he noticed a pair of handcuffs in her back pocket. Had she'd gotten into the kinky too? Without questioning her, Brodie grabbed the cuffs. Lowering Elena near the truck, he hooked a shackle around her wrist.

"Dammit, Brodie, what are you doing?" Elena pulled against him.

Brodie circled the chain a few times around the post to the driver's side mirror, tightening the length so she couldn't get loose, and cuffed her other hand. "This should hold you a minute."

"Damn you," she yelled and tugged against the chain.

Her john stood by the time Brodie finished. The eyes of her intended trick widened. The man took off before Brodie could stop him.

Thinking the jerk wouldn't be back, Brodie crossed his arms and leaned against the truck. Jake pressed the attacker into a grappling hold, though the man still struggled. "You need help?" Brodie asked.

Panting, Jake grinned. "Naw. Still got the touch. Feels good."

Brodie chuckled. "For an old man with a limp, you move pretty fast."

"Yuh never forget the training." Jake grunted as an elbow flew into his gut.

"Larry, stop." Elena ceased her struggles. "You're not helping."

"You know him?" Brodie asked.

"Yes, you stupid lummox." She tugged twice against the cuffs, the metal shackle clanging against the rod of the mirror.

"He your owner?"

"Owner?" She looked confused.

"Pimp, manager. Whatever you call the job these days." If he was, Brodie stood ready to murder the guy.

"Pimp?" She gave him that pissed-off look again, the one that said she would unleash her fury.

Thing was, he always thought she looked cute when she did that.

"*Oooooh, umph.*" She snapped her arms back, causing the links of the cuffs to tighten even more. "Get—the—key—out—of—my—pants—pocket."

"Sure thing, sugar." Brodie sauntered around back of her and let his hands slide from her ribs to her narrow waist and sensuous hips. "I didn't know you've been exploring the more perverse aspects of sex."

"Perverse? Errrr," she growled and let her head fall against his chest.

Brodie wrapped his arms around Elena and pulled her to him. "How much do you charge?" he whispered in her ear. "I'll pay for your time. We need to talk."

"Talk?" She glanced at him over her shoulder and arched a brow. "We needed to do that years ago but you wouldn't listen."

"I'm listening now." Brodie tried to ignore how warm, how right, she felt against him. His body didn't care what she'd been up to. He still wanted her.

"I charge two hundred and fifty an hour."

"Two fifty? Since when did streetwalkers start charging by the hour?"

She turned up her nose. Contempt riddled her voice. "I break the time up in ten-minute increments." She presented him a fake smile and batted her lashes. "Men don't last that long. The price is affordable and I can turn a lot of tricks."

Brodie held her tight to prevent himself from losing control. He wanted to cry, except men didn't do that. What had happened to cause Elena to lose her dreams? To become...

He couldn't think about her fall. He had to do something to bring her back. Fingering her pockets, he found the key and released the cuffs, letting them hang on the mirror.

She turned around and stepped away, massaging her wrists. "Brodie, you just cost me."

Pulling out his wallet, he shoved five hundred in her palm and closed her fingers around the money. "This will last us two hours, enough time to get me to a cash machine for more."

Her eyes narrowed. "I don't want your damn money."

He closed the gap between them and hovered over her. "I didn't think prostitutes were picky about who paid them as long as they got paid."

She dropped her arms. "Fine. But you're about to see how wrong you are. And for that you *will* pay." She took the cuffs off the mirror and shoved them into her back pocket, along with the money. "That man—" she pointed into the darkness where her squeeze had run, "was my score."

"Yeah," Brodie belted out. "Guess now you'll have to spend the night with me."

"I don't think so." She ignored him and walked toward Jake. "Let him go."

Jake eased his hold on the man but Brodie was too distracted to care.

"Why didn't you tell him?" Elena glared at Jake with her pissed-off look.

"I tried, but…" Jake shrugged.

"Yeah? Figures. He never did listen." She sauntered toward Brodie. "I'm going home. I suggest you do the same. Give that bastard father of yours my regards."

Brodie grabbed her arm. "You took my money, dammit. You'll provide a service for that."

Her partner jumped. Jake grabbed him back. "It's okay, Larry. They's old friends."

Irritated, Elena swerved on Brodie. "Look, you dumb idiot, you just cost me ten thousand. The five hundred will be compensation for that."

"What? How the hell did you think you'd make ten thousand on that john?" With growing irritation, Brodie listened to Jake chuckle and wondered what his friend thought so funny. None of this was a laughing matter.

"Because he wasn't a john." Elena tugged her arm free. Hands on hips, she stepped next to Brodie so their bodies touched. Livid, she looked up at him from his chest. "I was bringing him in. He's got a ten-thousand-dollar price on his head from the bank. I could've used that money."

Brodie felt the blood drain from his face. "You're a bounty hunter."

Why an electronic book?

We live in the Information Age—an exciting time in the history of human civilization, in which technology rules supreme and continues to progress in leaps and bounds every minute of every day. For a multitude of reasons, more and more avid literary fans are opting to purchase e-books instead of paper books. The question from those not yet initiated into the world of electronic reading is simply: *Why?*

1. ***Price.*** An electronic title at Ellora's Cave Publishing and Cerridwen Press runs anywhere from 40% to 75% less than the cover price of the exact same title in paperback format. Why? Basic mathematics and cost. It is less expensive to publish an e-book (no paper and printing, no warehousing and shipping) than it is to publish a paperback, so the savings are passed along to the consumer.

2. ***Space.*** Running out of room in your house for your books? That is one worry you will never have with electronic books. For a low one-time cost, you can purchase a handheld device specifically designed for e-reading. Many e-readers have large, convenient screens for viewing. Better yet, hundreds of titles can be stored within your new library—on a single microchip. There are a variety of e-readers from different manufacturers. You can also read e-books on your PC or laptop computer. (Please note that Ellora's

Cave does not endorse any specific brands. You can check our websites at www.ellorascave.com or www.cerridwenpress.com for information we make available to new consumers.)

3. *Mobility.* Because your new e-library consists of only a microchip within a small, easily transportable e-reader, your entire cache of books can be taken with you wherever you go.

4. *Personal Viewing Preferences.* Are the words you are currently reading too small? Too large? Too… ANNOYING? Paperback books cannot be modified according to personal preferences, but e-books can.

5. *Instant Gratification.* Is it the middle of the night and all the bookstores near you are closed? Are you tired of waiting days, sometimes weeks, for bookstores to ship the novels you bought? Ellora's Cave Publishing sells instantaneous downloads twenty-four hours a day, seven days a week, every day of the year. Our webstore is never closed. Our e-book delivery system is 100% automated, meaning your order is filled as soon as you pay for it.

Those are a few of the top reasons why electronic books are replacing paperbacks for many avid readers.

As always, Ellora's Cave and Cerridwen Press welcome your questions and comments. We invite you to email us at Comments@ellorascave.com or write to us directly at Ellora's Cave Publishing Inc., 1056 Home Avenue, Akron, OH 44310-3502.

CERRIDWEN PRESS

Cerridwen, the Celtic goddess of wisdom, was the muse who brought inspiration to storytellers and those in the creative arts.

Cerridwen Press encompasses the best and most innovative stories in all genres of today's fiction.

Visit our website and discover the newest titles by talented authors who still get inspired—much like the ancient storytellers did...

once upon a time.

www.cerridwenpress.com